DIRTY LYING SIRENS

THE ENCHANTED FATES SERIES

DIRTY LYING FAERIES

DIRTY LYING DRAGONS

DIRTY LYING WOLVES

DIRTY LYING SIRENS

DIRTY LYING SIRENS

SABRINA BLACKBURRY

 by wattpad books

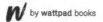 by wattpad books

An imprint of Wattpad WEBTOON Book Group

Content Warning: sex, language, violence, sensitive topic of the foster system, sensitive topic of unstable housing, kidnapping, and attempted assault.

Published in Canada by Wattpad WEBTOON Book Group, a division of Wattpad WEBTOON Studios, Inc.

36 Wellington Street E., Suite 200, Toronto, ON M5E 1C7 Canada

www.wattpad.com

First W by Wattpad Books edition: September 2025

ISBN 978-1-99834-132-0 (Trade Paper original)

ISBN 978-1-99834-133-7 (eBook edition)

Names, characters, places, and incidents featured in this publication are either the product of the author's imagination or are used fictitiously. Any resemblance to actual persons (living or dead), events, institutions, or locales, without satiric intent, is coincidental.

Library and Archives Canada Cataloguing in Publication information is available upon request.

Printed and bound in Canada

1 3 5 7 9 10 8 6 4 2

Cover design by Lesley Worrell
Images © Damsea via Shutterstock; © SuperStock
Typesetting by Delaney Anderson

To the girls who were told to be quiet.

CHAPTER ONE

MADELINE

I'd made it pretty far before the tears started spilling, but when the stupid strap popped out of my flip-flop yet again, that was the last straw. The waterworks began. I needed coffee, one little cup of hope or joy or whatever I thought that would be, which would let me sit down for ten minutes and stop my life from falling apart. Three other times in my life I'd needed a double-shot extra vanilla pump latte after nine at night—and tonight was the fourth.

The first time was senior year of high school, and I had an all-nighter of studying to pull off if I wanted to pass enough classes to graduate. Then, it was the night I drove from the middle of nowhere Michigan to get here to the Florida coast. Twenty hours of me and the highway, following the call of beach life and throwing away icy winters and dairy farms for good. The last time was the night I broke up with my boyfriend for being a gaslighting jerkoff and I had to pack everything I owned and leave while he was on his graveyard shift.

And now, after possibly the longest damn day of my life, when I'd found myself jobless, probably close to homeless, and with only a few nights to sort it out. Thus, the double-shot extra vanilla pump latte.

Wiping my face with my sleeve, I bent down to pop the stupid plastic strap back in place. Note to self: stop buying sandals from the dollar store. Except they were all I could afford.

The night air cooled my skin with a breeze that came in off the water. Since it was after sundown on a cloudless spring evening, the streetlights were lit, and the nightlife would be kicking up now. Tourist season was almost upon Iridian—if you didn't count the snowbirds who occupied the town in the offseason—and with that came an abundance of people. People emptying out the grocery stores on the weekends as they arrived at their vacation rentals, people taking up every parking spot and beach chair in sight, and people filing into my gym to keep up with their routines even on vacation.

My stomach churned. Not *my* gym anymore.

Screw tourist season. I didn't want more people to deal with; I'd rather keep to myself and to the smallest handful of familiar faces that I could. As I walked down the sidewalk, my sandals made soft slapping noises against the pavement leading to a coffee shop I knew would still be open.

To the right of the door was mostly brick, but the large window to the left showed a nearly empty shop—not too bad for a Tuesday right before spring break. If I was lucky, maybe they'd still have something to eat in the pastry cabinet that wasn't completely dried out. My fingers wrapped around the brass handle, and I swung the door open, stopping suddenly as I hit something.

"Caspian!" someone exclaimed from inside.

I dropped my grip on the door and my heart pounded in my ears as a pair of dangerously blue eyes met mine. They were framed by a stunned frown, which probably had something to do with the coffee-colored stain now dripping down his once-white button-up shirt. A half-empty paper cup with dark liquid dripping down the side of it was still held firmly in his hand.

I should apologize. I *needed* to apologize. But I was frozen. Old aversions about talking to strangers, especially men, crept up and kept my mouth firmly shut.

"Caspian, are you all right?" Another man, just a hair shorter and with a mildly lighter complexion, came to Caspian's side and spotted the spilled drink.

But Caspian wasn't looking at the problem or even at his friend; no, he was looking at me. A sharp, studying gaze that flowed from my eyes to the shape of my jaw to my mouth and back up again. Taking in my face while, admittedly, I took in his too. He finally tore his eyes away, breaking the tense air between us. When he looked down at his shirt, his frown deepened.

I bit my lower lip. Damn, he was attractive. But my heart whispered *get away, get away* as it beat.

"Shit," the other man hissed, pulling a fistful of paper napkins from the table by the door. "We have to meet them in twenty minutes."

"It's all right, Nikkos," Caspian said. "I've got a change of clothes on the ship. It was an accident, don't worry about it."

"I'm so sorry." I winced, moving to let the two men out the door.

He paused, turning back in my direction. "What are you doing away from the ocean?"

He had a strange accent. It wasn't heavy, but it was definitely there, and I liked it. A bit husky, one of those naturally low, seductive voices that should be illegal to use on poor, unsuspecting girls in need of double-pump vanilla lattes.

"The ocean?" I asked.

"We don't have time, Caspian," Nikkos hissed.

Caspian, not taking his eyes off me, raised his hand to silence his companion.

He stepped forward, close to me. "You don't know what I'm talking about, do you?" He murmured his question, not really looking for an answer. Those sharp eyes were now dark and calculating.

I shook my head, and the two men exchanged a look.

"Let it go for now, Caspian. Hold on, I'll get us a cab." Nikkos rushed to the street, his attention going back and forth between his phone and watching for a passing cab to flag down.

Caspian's eyes were still on me as Nikkos found them transportation. We seemed to be transfixed by each other. He had a small silver hoop high in his left ear and an expensive-looking watch on his wrist. His dark hair was swept back on his head, and my fingers itched to mess it up and see what the put-together man looked like just a little bit disheveled.

Keep it to your imagination, Mads. Men are more trouble than they're worth. Look what happened earlier today.

"What's your name?"

My tongue flicked out to wet my lips; his eyes followed the movement before crawling back up to mine. "Madeline."

He nodded at my response. "Where are you from, Madeline?"

I barely stopped myself from shivering. When he said my name with his accent, it felt intimate. It'd been a long time since someone had said my name quite like that.

Caspian was absolutely my type—dark hair and broad shoulders, a clear olive-toned complexion, and a hint of a toned figure under the shirt that clung to him thanks to the spilled coffee. It took me a second to realize what he had just asked me, and that I still needed to answer.

Short and sweet, Mads. Keep it short and sweet. No extra words.

"Michigan," I answered. "You?"

"An island in the Atlantic."

Made sense. He looked like a Greek god. Immediately, I pictured him on the beach with no shirt . . . which piqued my curiosity. I'm not a shy person; I'm really not. But I don't speak too much around people I don't know. In the past, talking has gotten me into a lot of trouble. My face was flushing as I looked at this guy, who was absolutely my type, and he probably thought I was a complete fool.

"Island?"

My expression seemed only to amuse him more, and his eyes crinkled as he held back a smile. Draining the rest of his coffee cup, he tossed it in the bin by the door next to us.

"It's small. You won't have seen it on any maps. So, Michigan—that's not near here, is it? Did you move with your family?"

I cringed, not wanting to get too deep into it with a complete stranger. "No family. Foster kid."

His brow furrowed and he looked as though he wanted to say something.

"Caspian!" Nikkos called, waving his companion over.

"I'll see you later, Madeline. Try not to spill any more coffee on unsuspecting people," he mused, which sent a delightful shiver down my back. And then he walked over to Nikkos, who was pointing to something on his phone.

Not wanting to know what Caspian's sudden interest in me was, and not wanting to deepen my interest in a man when I had bigger problems to fix first, I slipped into the shop with one last look their way.

The skin on my arms pebbled and the goose bumps continued up my neck. Must be the cool air of the shop. Yeah, it was warming up for spring outside, so it was the AC giving me chills. Definitely not the Adonis I'd just spilled coffee all over standing outside. *Fuck.*

I bit my lower lip and walked absently to the counter. Why did I always do this? Meet a guy and instinctually make it sexual. Especially when the rest of my life was a complete mess.

Priorities, dummy, I scolded myself.

"Hey, there." The girl behind the counter smiled warmly. "Don't feel too bad, I see that at least five times a day. No idea why they build the door to open inward, but half this building doesn't make much sense."

"I can't believe that happened," I admitted. Cassidy was my favorite barista, and being another girl I was somewhat familiar with made it easier for me to talk to her without making it weird. She had definitely earned more than one-word answers from me by now.

"Great way to meet guys, though," she said, checking Caspian out through the window. "And he's the hottest thing to walk in here today. God, I'm starved for eye-candy season. What brings you in this late—the usual?"

"The usual," I agreed. "Extra shot, extra pump."

She raised an eyebrow. "Pulling an all-nighter?"

"Yeah," I mumbled. "Something like that."

My eyes drifted down to the pastry case. *Empty.*

Cassidy turned away to make my drink, and I pulled out the exact change, sliding it toward the register while she worked. I let out a slow breath and scooted onto the stool at the end of the counter near the order pickup and waited.

Jobless. Shit. I'd never walked out on a job before, but today was the last straw. I buried my fingers in my hair, messing up my ponytail as I reflected on the afternoon. Giving up, I yanked it free and slid the hair tie onto my wrist.

I don't know what it is about me. My voice or my looks or what, but it seems like the moment I open my mouth, I invite the worst kind of trash to harass me. It definitely explained my dating history. And today, when that guy decided to be a pervert at work, I was beyond done with men.

Fucking pigs, all of them.

My shoulders slumped. That wasn't fair—just because I'd had bad luck up until now, it didn't mean I'd never meet anyone better. That was a bleak outlook for a twenty-six-year-old.

And then the recent memory of a low, smooth voice and sharp blue eyes pinning me in place crept forward.

I nearly looked toward the window, but stopped myself just in time.

Don't look, I urged myself. *Don't look, you idiot.*

But despite my better judgment, my eyes slid to the window where tall, dark, and coffee-stained stood on the sidewalk. At least he wasn't staring at me anymore. Instead, he was on the phone, absently rolling his sleeves up enough to show off his forearms, and distracting me completely until he hung up and pocketed the device. I watched as Nikkos waved him over to a rideshare that was just pulling up, and that was that—he was gone.

Thank goodness. The last thing I needed right now was a distraction. I met my ex while I was distracted, too, and look at how that ended.

"Order up." Cassidy smiled at me as she slid my coffee across the polished black counter. Next to the cup was a white paper bag, a tantalizing gray spot near the bottom promising buttery contents.

"What's this?" I asked.

"We were about to get rid of the old food, but I thought you could use a muffin at least." She shrugged. "I know a hard day when I see it."

7

"Thanks," I said earnestly, and pulled the bag toward me. Orange cranberry, my favorite, and the one they always seemed to run out of on the weekends. *Delicious.* Holding the cup in one hand, I let the chill from the AC melt away as I savored the muffin. How many more coffees and muffins could I afford with my savings? This one was a treat to make myself feel better but . . .

A sponge ran across the counter in front of me. "Wanna talk about it?" Cassidy asked, wiping down for the night. "It's just us in here, you can talk as much as you want. Or would you rather get your therapy across the street?"

The bar across the street already had a collection of smokers out front and a thrumming bass that could be heard from the coffee shop every time the door opened. At least her joke made me laugh a little. I took a sip of my coffee. "Quit my job."

"And I'm guessing you don't have a new one lined up?"

I shook my head. "My asshole boss is . . . he doesn't treat his female employees the same as the guys."

Cassidy's sponge paused. "Did he do something to you? Do you want me to call the cops?"

"No! No, nothing like that." Sputtering in my coffee, I put it down and wiped the foam off my upper lip with the back of my sleeve, eyeing the empty shop before I decided to let it all out. "A gym member tried to grab a handful of more than the kettlebells. I made a fuss, my boss told me the guy was just having some fun and if I didn't want the attention I shouldn't wear leggings at the gym. So I walked out."

"What the hell?" she asked. "What does he want you to wear, sweatpants?"

I shrugged.

"And you already have a hard time speaking up, don't you?" Sympathy crept onto Cassidy's face. "I'm sorry, Maddie."

"Appreciate the sympathy. But now I've got no job, and I'm not even sure my boss will give me my last check, or if I even want to go in to pick it up. And if I wait for him to mail it I won't make rent on the first. But I can't say I regret it."

"Hence the double shot. Got it. Can't blame you. A girl can only take so much of that nonsense." She turned her head to look out the window, an unreadable expression on her face melting into a shit-eating grin. "Hot as hell, wasn't he? I know you have that thing about strangers, but whatever you said was enough to have him checking you out. You interested?"

"I would be if it wasn't for the fact that my life is a mess. I'm in no position to date anyone when I can't even take care of myself right now."

"I hope you can turn things around." Cassidy shook her head. "I'd say work here, but we just hired someone yesterday."

"I'll figure it out. Thanks, though. And I should leave you to your closing up." Scooting off the stool, I took the rest of the muffin and the cup with me. "Thanks again for the food."

"No problem, good luck," Cassidy said. "Don't disappear entirely, or else what will I do at closing whenever we have leftover baked goods?"

With a short laugh, I looked at her from over my shoulder. "As soon as I have an income again, I'll be back, I'm sure."

Draining my coffee, I tossed the cup in the trash bin on my way out the door, which I opened very carefully this time. I checked the sidewalk and made sure Caspian and Nikkos were really gone. No sign of them.

Was I relieved or disappointed?

The door fell shut behind me and I took a breath of night air. The streetlights cast an orange glare down the road, which was still damp from a recent rain. Every breath tasted like the salt coming off the ocean. With a night of job searching and probably packing ahead of me, I embraced the caffeine rush. But first, a quick walk on the beach to clear my head.

What are you doing away from the ocean?

That was what he'd asked me.

I should get on my laptop and start making lists of places to call tomorrow but . . .

My flip-flops hit the sidewalk, and I decided to I take the long way home—the crashing waves at the end of the street were calling to me.

CHAPTER TWO

MADELINE

My pen scratched across the notebook paper as I struck a line through another place on my list.

"Thank you, anyway," I said into my phone. "Do you keep applications on file for future job openings or—"

Click.

"Fuck you, too, buddy," I snapped, tossing the phone onto the couch next to me.

Grunting, I flopped back into the cushions and grabbed a pillow to put over my face before releasing an aggravated scream. Tossing the pillow aside when I was done, I lifted my notepad above me to see how many places I had left to call.

Not many. Not enough.

"Dammit."

Getting up, I paced around my small living room, which was covered in boxes. The first of the month had come and gone, and so had the first warning from my landlord. We'd done this song and dance before, and I'd been told in no uncertain terms that it wasn't going to fly again. When I finally went in to get my last paycheck, I was told it was in the mail. Days with no luck finding work—and with no check—followed until all I could do was pack my things and hope that if I got evicted they'd all fit in my car. Apart from the thrift-store bed and the free sidewalk couch, I thought it all would. I hadn't brought much with me from Michigan, and I hadn't bought much when I got here.

"What a mess."

Footsteps echoed on the stairs outside my door, and I cringed. Three hard knocks on the metal door knocker. I rubbed my temples.

"Miss Lowe!" The shrill voice of my landlady pierced the thin walls. "Miss Lowe, I know you're in there!"

Plastering a fake smile across my face, I walked over and opened the door. "Hello, Mrs. Callahan."

She looked at me over her cat eye glasses, her bright-fuchsia lips pursed in perpetual judgment as she looked over my pajama shorts and tank top. She wore one of her usual tropical barf jump-suits with a matching scarf and bright, shiny white heels. A pair of bedazzled sunglasses perched in the crisp nest of yellow curls on her head, and the bug-eyed Chihuahua in her pink purse was looking at me with one eye and at the street with the other.

"Miss Lowe, I'm here to give you a last reminder that your rent was due three days ago."

"My paycheck is late, I'm so sorry."

My landlord's expression hardened, and I knew in my heart I'd done it again. *Shit.*

Her head pulled back and she crossed her arms over her chest. "You will *not* talk your way out of this one. Don't bother arguing if you only plan on trying to persuade me."

"I wasn't—"

"Miss Lowe, you have a history of late payments. I'm afraid we cannot continue to tolerate them. I shouldn't have to remind you of our rental policy, which only allows three strikes for late payments."

My mouth snapped shut. I had done it again. All I wanted to do was apologize, but I had opened my mouth and now she was giving me that look of disgust and suspicion. "I understand, Mrs. Callahan," I whispered.

"Good. Your lease renewal would have been signed for another six months on the fifteenth, but, considering your history, I'm afraid we will not be continuing to rent to you after this month."

Oh, no.

"But, Mrs. Callahan—"

"And if you cannot produce your rent by Friday, we will be evicting you sooner. Don't bother protesting, just nod if you understand."

My heart nearly stopped. Could she do that? I nodded.

"Have a good day, Miss Lowe," she said with the sincerity of an alligator, and turned on her heel to go right back down the stairs to her bubblegum-pink convertible, which probably cost more than the entire building.

"Fuck," I said. Even though I'd known it was coming, it still hit me like a truck.

I didn't think it was technically legal to shove me out so soon, but if I fought it, I'd still need a new place to stay in the meantime and money for legal fees.

What else can I try?

Working at a gym was the only job I'd ever held. Back in Michigan it had been my haven from the group home. Mr. Freeman gave me a place to be with a lot less stress and a chance to save up for when I aged out. He'd even yell at anyone who bothered me.

I always said the wrong things, or spoke with the wrong tone, or had an unpleasant voice. I'd speak, and then it was, *"Be quiet,"* or, *"You don't need to tell me, just do it,"* or just blatant, unsettled stares. Maybe it was because he needed hearing aids, or maybe it was because by the time I met him I'd already learned to keep my words short and direct, but Mr. Freeman didn't give me shit for existing around him. Keeping my sanity through high school was all thanks to his kindness. I thought it would be the same when I moved here, but there was no one in Florida quite like Mr. Freeman.

Still, a job was a job, and the gym was familiar. I guess I could try retail work, though most of those jobs had already staffed up for the upcoming spring-break season. Not my first choice, but certainly better than ending up starving and homeless.

Outside my window a pair of seagulls called. Probably looking for food to steal, the little bastards. Their cries made me think of the ocean, and in that split second, I was okay. I took a deep, calming breath. The ocean. It always evened out my mood. My own little magical place filled with peace.

Rummaging through the box I'd packed my clothes in, I grabbed the first swimsuit and pair of shorts I found and slipped them on. Taking my lanyard off the hook by the door and slipping on a pair of sandals, the strap freshly duct taped in place, I left the apartment to clear my head at the place that had drawn me all the way down here to begin with: the beach.

With every step that brought me closer to the sand, my heart lifted. The salt in my lungs, the boats on the horizon as they bobbed in and out of view, and the glistening waves beckoned me. If only I could just sail away from the shore and leave my problems behind. I couldn't afford to live right on the beach like I'd wanted, but being a mile away wasn't much of a sacrifice.

After a short walk, I found myself taking off my sandals and slipping my toes in the sand. Tourists were already here. Their travel coolers and colorful towels littered the clean sand. Even though it was busy, I was still able to find some empty space to stand in the ocean. Holding my sandals, I went straight to the waves that pushed and pulled against the beach. Once the cool saltwater hit my ankles, I sighed contentedly and closed my eyes.

Okay, this is as zen as I can get. So, what are my options?

If I had to live in my car, I could do that, but it would suck. Badly. How would I shower? What about a kitchen? I could eat out for every meal but that would get expensive fast. Maybe I could move to find work. Would Miami have more job prospects? Jacksonville? Tampa?

"Mads?"

My eyes flew open, and I turned to see the very *last* person I wanted to run into.

My ex—a little taller than me, blond hair perfectly sculpted back with gel, eyes doing that puppy-dog thing. His swim trunks hung low on his hips, and he had his surfboard under his arm, a cigarette in his other hand.

"Trent," I said.

He took a drag, finishing off his cig and flicking it to the ground by a trash can. "You're looking good."

The desire to clench my hands into fists was strong as I eyed the cigarette butt. When I met Trent's unbothered expression, he just nodded toward it as if I was still expected to clean up his messes. Maddie the doormat, Maddie the pushover. I could only meet his gaze for a heartbeat before reaching down to extinguish the cigarette and drop it in the can's attached receptacle.

"You're still wearing those shoes I bought you," he said, his smirk a battle flag. The beginning of his game. The look, the voice—he knew how to rile me up and shove me back down.

My grip tightened and I looked down at the sandals in my hands, wishing I'd brought the faulty dollar store ones instead. They were a birthday present from him a few months before we broke up. And here I was, too choked up to speak or else he'd claim I was leading him on again. My stupid words always betrayed me. Even after all these years I hadn't figured out how to speak clearly, because speaking only invited problems. Biting the inside of my cheek, I tried to pull my thoughts together through the distress of his presence. Still, I came up empty.

"You don't have to pay me back for them, or anything," Trent said. "It's good to see you using my present."

Frozen. I was absolutely frozen in his gaze. A deer in head-lights. Right back to where I was before I grew the balls to get out the last time.

I stiffened when he reached out a hand and put it on my arm. "Listen, Mads—"

Closing my eyes, I prepared myself to fight off whatever poison he was about to spew my way. To tell me what I should think. To touch my arm and possibly more if he felt like it because he was just being friendly, and there was nothing wrong with being friendly, right, Mads? I was so bad at talking that he should do the talking for the both of us. And make the decisions while he was at it.

I swallowed hard, the skin where he was touching me instantly numb and foreign.

"Madeline?"

That voice. I'd only heard it once before, but I knew who it was right away. Caspian. The sexy accented guy from the coffee shop. His presence pulled me from the frozen stupor that Trent had put me in, a life raft in the ocean of my past mistakes.

"Caspian."

Gone were his shirt and tie, and instead he wore some kind

of loose white pants. His beige linen shirt was open, as though he had thrown it on for the pretense of wearing clothes. It gave me an eyeful of what he'd been hiding before, and honestly, it was a damn crime against humanity that he hid that stomach under business attire. He was even barefoot, no shoes in sight. The cherry on top was that his neat hair was now disheveled, the wind toying with it and adding a boyish charm to a dangerously attractive man. And in his eyes was the one thing I never got from Trent: genuine concern.

Because the universe feels the need to taunt me in my darkest hours.

"What's going on here?" Caspian asked, his eyes locked on Trent's hand on my arm.

My eyes teared and I shook my head slightly. Just enough for Caspian to see. Trent frowned, taking a firmer hold on my arm and shaking me back to reality. "Babe, you know him?"

I yanked my arm from Trent's hand, the spell broken, and my thoughts were my own again as I backed up.

"I'm wondering the same thing," Caspian said. "It's your call here, Madeline. What do you want to happen?

What did *I want to happen?*

"I'm not your babe, Trent." My voice trembled as I took a step back. "And you need to leave me alone. We're over, we've *been* over, and you need to leave now."

Trent stepped toward me again, anger tinting his expression. But Caspian put his body in the way, and Trent paused.

"Whatever, Mads. See you around." Trent sneered at Caspian as he left, walking down the beach to put his board in the water.

I held my composure for a while, letting Trent get plenty far away before the shaky breath left me and my posture crumpled.

"What an unfortunate specimen," Caspian said. "Are you all right?"

I nodded vigorously. Not having to answer him out loud was a relief while I recovered myself.

"Good. I'm sorry if I overstepped—you looked uncomfortable, and I couldn't stop myself from making sure everything was okay." Caspian's eyes searched my face for something. Was he concerned, or did he just pity me? He'd found me in a shitty situation; two for two now. If Caspian was going to be aggressive with me, he would have done it when I spilled coffee on him, and he wouldn't have stepped in with Trent.

A few words at a time, I could handle that. Enough to see where it got me, enough to see if it changed how he acted around me.

"Thank you," I whispered.

His ocean-blue eyes were sharp, seeing the situation for what it was. I knew he could tell that whatever was left between me and Trent was toxic; anyone could have seen it by the end.

"I'm from a small island city," he said. Was this some kind of distraction? Something to take my mind off of what must have been an obvious moment of distress?

"We live on the water, with the water," he continued. "The island has the most beautiful beaches you've ever seen. Almost everything on the island is built from white stone."

Fair enough. He looked like the island type, standing there barefoot in the sand with his sun-kissed complexion. He paused, a glint of mischief in his eyes. "And the sea, we crave it. We live it, we breathe it. We wouldn't leave it if we didn't have to."

Sounded nice. Maybe it would be worth a few more words, just to keep the first pleasant conversation I'd had in days going.

"I can relate." And I could. Sometimes I felt awkward about how much I loved the water. I couldn't get enough of it back in Michigan, despite the abundance of shoreline available. There was something about the salt and the sea, though. I'd always craved it until one day I caved and moved down here. But Caspian had a community who accepted that. I wondered what other things we had in common. If I liked living on the Florida coast, how much different would it be to experience island life?

"It's definitely a sight you'll never forget," Caspian murmured.

"Sounds beautiful," I said. "Why'd you leave it?"

He shrugged. "My cousin Nikkos and I, you saw him with me the other night, we're here on business. It's been a hard couple of weeks and we're both ready to sail home. After our job is done, of course."

"Business?" I asked, slipping back into one-word answers with him out of habit.

"Looking for some solutions to a problem back home, but I won't bore you with all that."

The lingering traces of distress were fading. Caspian glanced over the water, almost willing his island to come to him from wherever it sat across the waves.

"Are you afraid of your voice?" he asked.

My heart stopped.

"You don't talk much, is all. You had a lot more to say to that Trent guy, but I get the short and sweet answers."

How do you tell someone, a stranger, that you think you are so bad at speaking that it makes people go crazy around you? "I don't like my voice. How I sound."

"That's a shame, no one should have to live with hating a part of themselves. I'm familiar with it," he said, "that kind of voice. There are many women on my island who have the sway."

Caspian put his hands in his pockets, silently watching. Waiting to see if I'd reply. There was no pressure to it, but the bait was dangled like a jewel in front of me. I'd struggled. Oh, I'd struggled.

19

I used to be a chatterbox, talking nonstop until I'd learned to keep my mouth shut. The adults made it very clear my voice made them uncomfortable. The kids didn't know what to make of me; I don't think they had the words to say I made them feel pressured to give me attention. I was a distraction, a nuisance. But Caspian, he just said he'd heard others like me before, and he even had a name for it. It took me a minute, but I wanted to know more despite the flare of panic over discussing my voice.

"Sway?" I asked.

"We call it magic, but you'd call it a trick of the voice. It elicits strong responses from people, doesn't it?"

Silence stretched between us; the space filled with the gentle crashing of waves on the beach. He knew, somehow. I could tell from the way he looked at me that he'd already figured out my life-long problem. Was this real? Could this actually be something other people have to deal with? I'd exhausted more than a few nights searching the internet for answers, not coming up with so much as a mention of it anywhere. I never thought I'd ever find out about my voice, let alone have someone to talk to about it, and it was paralyzing.

"If you ever want to talk, I'll be happy to explain more about the sway or my island." Caspian pulled a business card from his pocket and handed it to me. "We could have lunch sometime, maybe. Or message me, if that's more comfortable. I've been grabbing coffee at our café every night at the same time while I'm here."

Our café. I took the card from his hand, feeling the unspoken words hanging between us that he'd gone back to the coffee shop to see if I'd be there.

"Please take me up on my offer, Madeline," Caspian said. "If the allure of me does not sway you, the call of the sea might. We leave in six days, think about it."

The words weren't there for me yet, but my lips spread into a wide grin at his decisive phrasing. *Cocky bastard.*

He put his hands in his pockets and walked away. I watched him head for the wooden marina stairs on the other side of the beach. He boarded a pristine white sailing yacht and disappeared inside.

The card was a simple glossy white paper with his name and a number on it. I flipped it over a couple of times, finding no other information. Taking a few steps deeper into the water, I plopped down and let the ocean run over my legs up to my hips, not giving a damn that my shorts were getting soaked. I'd be lying if I said I wasn't attracted to Caspian. Maybe it was the way he spoke or the calm of his body language that enticed me. But I had talked to him twice now and he had listened. Even Cassidy had had a hard time following my words until she got used to me, but Caspian I'd just met. He didn't even react, not like Trent did. And Marshall, and Danny, and a slew of other impulse decisions that had started out feeling like I was being swept off my feet and ended feeling like I had somehow brought cruelty and abuse onto myself.

Sighing, I turned the card over in my fingers. Who exactly was Caspian, and why was I considering finding out?

CHAPTER THREE

CASPIAN

Madeline wasn't human.

There were suspicions when I first heard her voice. A voice that could move mountains and shake the seas, if only she knew how to use it properly. Now that I'd had a full-fledged conversation with her, I knew it for sure.

Madeline was a siren.

Fuck, she looked the part too. Every part of her was soft curves; those big doe eyes coupled with her unchecked power had undoubtedly been the downfall of more than a few unwitting partners. The way her lips parted when she was surprised was too enticing, and I had to keep my hands in my pockets so I wouldn't reach out to touch them. What would she look like if I slipped my thumb between those lips?

The image of her sucking on it, looking up at me through those soft, dark lashes was too dangerous to dwell on. A siren will do that to you—drive you mad with want, and I wasn't going to fall for that.

But I was going to get her back to Atlantis, where she deserved to be worshipped with her sisters.

The urge to hit that bastard on the beach had been strong, but the consequences of talking to the authorities would have raised too many questions. Maybe I should have done it anyway. It was a good thing that Madeline had told him off on her own before I did anything rash.

Back on the ship, my legs adjusted to accept the gentle rocking of the waves. It was nothing compared to being deep at sea, something I missed desperately every time we came to the States. I missed home. I missed Atlantis. And in one more week, we could leave and go back to the city-state in the Atlantic Ocean.

I went down the stairs and into the cabin area; Nikkos spotted me from the galley and put down his knife and whatever he had been chopping. The space was lined with cushioned benches except for the starboard side, which was interrupted by a fixed dining table and the galley. The navigation station was tucked away next to me on the port side. Sunlight came in from above and all around, providing enough light that we rarely turned the lights on during the day. My cousin came around the counter where he had been working.

"Where did you go just now?" he asked. "I'm making lunch."

Smelling the oils cooking, I suspected it would be the same meal we'd had for the last week, and shot Nikkos a tired look. "Is it eggs again?"

A blush crept onto his face, paired with an indignant frown. "Why don't you make lunch if you think you can do better?"

"Sorry, Nikkos. I'm just touchy today. I want to go home."

His eyes softened. "Me too. I don't like how these people live."

"When Dimitris says go make a deal with the mainlanders—"

"We do it." Nikkos sighed. "I know, I know. We're the aides, he's the senator. And you have the added joy of being related to him."

"Thank you for that, I'd nearly forgotten," I responded dryly. "I'm related to you, too, you know."

"Yes, but on the fun side of the family," he mused.

"Nikkos, your idea of fun is a bottle of wine on the beach with a book or five. Don't pretend to be any less stiff than Dimitris." Pinching the bridge of my nose, I moved on to work. "Have we heard back from the contact?"

"Partially," Nikkos answered, going back to the galley and resuming whatever he had been cutting. I followed, if only to better speak with him. "I called the witch again and she confirmed that she was able to set up the meeting. He's a pricey mercenary, but I hear he's one of the best."

"Dimitris has the money, that's not the problem. We just need this contact to meet with us in the first place," I said. "If this meeting goes well, this mercenary is supposed to be the one who can bring the artifact to fix Atlantis."

"If this amulet even exists," Nikkos added.

"It has to," I said. "It's detailed in more than one book back home, and there's no way the vampires would have let it out of their hands. They don't just let go of powerful treasures like that."

Nikkos paused, adding another tomato to his cutting board.

"Do you really imagine we can lift the city to join the rest of the world again?" Nikkos asked. "We've lived below the surface for so long, and most of the human world doesn't know about beings of a more *magical* nature around them. If this were to put the sirens in danger—"

"Never," I insisted. "My uncle is a curt, shrewd man, but he's careful and calculated in everything he does. The plan is to relieve the sirens of the burden of our survival, and then to slowly integrate with the world at large. It will begin with the supernatural community, or at least chosen parts of it. But first, we need that artifact."

Nikkos sighed, stopping his knife work and dumping a cutting board of diced tomatoes into the skillet. "I suppose we either come home the victor, or we leave hoping Horace and Nephele's plan worked out."

"That's not going to impress the Senate," I murmured. "I don't think dealing with the Circle of Warlocks is the best way to solve our sinking problem."

"Then let's hope our mercenary agrees to liaise for us."

"Or steal the artifact," I said. "One way or another, Dimitris will find a way to solve this problem, that's just who he is. Otherwise we, what, keep going as we have been? Basilli Ateio is content because the shrinkage of the bubble and the number of sirens being born going down is too small to affect his lifetime. His complacency is enough for the rest of the Senate to follow his lead and not worry about it, but by the time we have a new ruler in that seat, it will be an even bigger issue."

Nikkos didn't respond, but his expression darkened. Without the sirens, Atlantis would be washed away for good. If the siren population dwindled further, they wouldn't be enough to keep up the barrier that kept our people safe. Which was a vicious cycle, because while the sirens collectively raised their children, child-bearing would still remove a mother from duties for months of late pregnancy and early infancy. Enough didn't want to put that pressure on their sisters that it only turned the problem into a spiral as the younger generation of sirens who would take up the mantle grew smaller and smaller.

My mind wandered back to the beach earlier. Madeline. What would the Senate think about an Atlantean in North America? A siren, of all things. Surely every citizen is accounted for; how could a siren have ended up here?

The sirens were beloved by the people but also burdened by their task. However, they were one of our most important resources in the fight to both hide and protect Atlantis. Madeline didn't know what she was, but I would have to convince her to come with us. Somehow. And I had little time left to do that.

"Caspian?" Nikkos jarred me out of my drifting thoughts.

"Hm?"

"I asked you if you want onions in yours." Nikkos held up the half-diced onion.

"Sure," I murmured.

Nikkos shot me a concerned look but finished dicing the onion. "Is everything all right?"

"The siren is on the beach just outside," I said, sitting on the bench by the dining table and lying back on the cushions. "I spoke to her before coming back to the boat."

"Here?" Nikkos asked, looking in the direction of the beach, as though he could see through the galley. "What did she say? What did *you* say?"

"You knew when we saw her in the coffee shop that we would have to do something about her," I replied.

"Well, *yes*. Is she in control of her powers? Does she even understand them?"

"Not really," I replied. "Her sway was all over the place when I talked to her the first time, and again just now. She doesn't even know what she is. I'm sure of it."

"Truly?" he asked, tilting his head. "I wonder how one could have gotten all the way here to the mainland."

"I'm still trying to figure that out. She says she's been in the foster system, no parents." I sighed through my nose, crossing my arms over my chest. The pan sizzled under Nikkos's touch. He cracked a few eggs into it as the oil sputtered.

"She didn't form spontaneously on the mainland. How could we possibly have lost track of a *siren*?" he scoffed.

"I don't know, but she's standing right outside on the beach," I said.

"And you're sure she's one of ours?" Nikkos asked.

I looked at him pointedly.

"Right, of course." Nikkos sighed. "This will give credence to Basilli Ateio's argument that we have enough sirens. It's certainly not going to help our argument to use this artifact. Dimitris won't like this."

"Dimitris doesn't like anything," I answered, yawning. "We can't leave her here. It's been enough of a problem keeping their population up as it is, we can't let this one slip through our fingers. Besides, she doesn't seem to be doing well out here."

"Here, lunch." Nikkos poured half of the pan of eggs, cheese, onions, and tomatoes onto a plate and the rest onto another. Walking over with them, he sat on the bench opposite me and put our plates on the table between us.

"A siren on the mainland. Imagine the havoc she could wreak, if only she knew how. What do you propose we do?" Nikkos sounded weary.

"I need to convince her to come with us. Whatever difficulties she poses for Dimitris's plans, she's still a siren and needs to come home. Atlantis needs her as much as she needs Atlantis. Don't underestimate that. She's been without answers for what? At least twenty something years, if I had to guess?"

"So, we have to convince the siren to come with us to Atlantis. She needs training, and Atlantis needs the help. Good luck."

I laughed softly. "Leave Madeline to me. I have a plan."

My cabin on the ship was cramped, which was to be expected on a vessel of this size, so when the phone rang and I reached out to grab it, my hand smacked the wall, and my eyes snapped open.

"Shit," I grumbled, letting my eyes adjust to the dark and the illuminated phone screen.

Unknown number.

I checked the time. Nine in the morning. Annoying for me, as I was trying not to adjust to a different time zone before going back to my own, but really not an unreasonable time for someone to be calling. Putting the phone to my ear, I pinched the bridge of my nose as I carefully sat up in bed to answer. "This is Caspian."

"Hello. It's Maddie. Um, Madeline."

I dropped my free hand from my face, a smile spreading across my lips. "Hello, Madeline. Have you decided to take me up on my offer?"

Her breath caught. She seemed nervous. Frazzled.

I frowned. It hadn't been my intent to cause her distress when I'd hinted about her abilities. Her time out here with these non-Atlantean people who didn't understand her had closed her off. Her enjoyment of singing, or hell, even speaking, along with any desires she had for intimacy, and her warmth were probably tainted by the mainlanders.

"Hope this is a good time to call." The hesitation in her words was sobering. "I'd like to meet you for lunch. Sometime. When you're free. I have a few questions, if that's okay."

She must be desperate for answers, and the desire in her voice came through the phone. I straightened my back, my body reacting to her hopeful plea.

I wanted to give her all the answers, but I couldn't scare her away or make her distrust me. It was quite a story for someone who knew nothing about Atlantis. I would have to be careful if I was to guide an untrained siren home. A *siren*. What a gods-damned mess to fall into. She had no control over her sway at all. She desperately needed someone to show her how to master it, and the only ones who could do that were in Atlantis.

I cleared my throat, trying to remain aware of where my desires stopped and hers began. "I would love to answer your questions over lunch, Madeline."

Maybe not seeing her while that voice was all over the place would be better.

"Or," I offered, "I could answer some of them now on the phone, if you like."

A small sigh came from her end of the phone. Pleased. "That would be great. I wanted to talk about the water first. Specifically, what you said about loving the ocean."

"Did it strike a chord with you?" I asked. "Many of the women in my city have the same desire. It's a sacred place for all of us, but for some of us more than others."

Her breath caught. There was something soft about it. She wanted to open up more, press more. It was already a good sign that she had ditched her one-word answers, but anxiety held her back. Or assholes like Trent tangling up her past, more likely.

"You can say what you want to say around me," I promised. "The sway isn't as strong when you know about it."

"Is it only women who love the ocean? Not the men? Not you?" she asked.

"No more than anyone else who loves the sea that is such a part of their home," I said.

"But it's not the same as what you described to me yesterday, is it?"

Good, she was sharp. It would make it all the easier to gently lead her to a truth that would be upsetting for anyone to hear. It was always better to reach a conclusion on your own. Leaning back on my bed, I enjoyed the soothing calm that only a siren's voice could offer. A little piece of home all the way out here on the mainland.

"No," I answered. "It's not."

She was silent for a moment.

"But," I added, "it's perfectly normal where I'm from. The things you feel are nothing to be ashamed of."

"I never said I had those feelings about the water," she said.

"You didn't have to, you sound just like home to me."

"You can't know that," she argued weakly.

"My people practically live in the water. It's about two weeks of good sailing from here in my ship." I stretched my free arm behind my head. "And I know you are from there because I can hear it in your voice."

"I'm from Michigan," she protested.

"I would bet against that in a heartbeat."

"What about my voice?" she asked. "What is it that sounds so familiar to you?"

The tug again. She wanted it, and the magic of her voice was trying to make me give her what she wanted. Oh, it was subtle. Gentle. Such was the way of the sirens; you wouldn't know something was amiss until it was too late.

Resisting the urge to just tell her what she wanted, I instead gave her more to think about. "When was the last time your voice got you into trouble?"

30

"What do you mean?"

"The last time you opened your mouth and gained attention you didn't want?"

"The other day, in a coffee shop," she quipped.

I resisted the urge to laugh at her cheeky retort. Clever, and charming under all of that weight she lived under. A lethal combination. "We both know that's not what I'm talking about, but I'll bet it wasn't all bad either. How often did you get your way when you really shouldn't have? School, maybe. Or getting pulled over for a ticket and being let go. Maybe a past boyfriend who accused you of manipulating him. I could see that, in a society that doesn't know what you are."

Silence again. Gods, she was a quiet one. A siren who didn't use her voice; I never would have thought it possible. I was sure she had to be this way to navigate life here, but it was growing frustrating to think about what she'd been through.

"Madeline, we've barely met, but I suspect you're sharper than that. You understand what I'm talking about, and you fear finding out that all those strange occurrences might actually mean something."

More strained silence. I could picture her face, as conflicted as it was yesterday with the man harassing her on the beach. There was some history there, and I definitely didn't like him. Was he part of what had made Madeline so quiet? Alert? She had a playful nature under the surface when she let it slip out; the problem was that she kept herself so tightly sealed.

"Your voice has something my people call *the sway*." Partially true, but more commonly known as *siren sway*, which she wasn't ready to hear yet. "I'm more than happy to show you how it's used. Though, really, one of the women back home would be a better teacher."

"And where is home?" she asked again.

"Would you believe me if I told you Atlantis?"

She scoffed. "Very funny."

"Suit yourself. Do you have any more questions for me?"

"Can we meet for lunch later? If you're free. Or dinner, if that's better. I need to know more."

My heart jumped at the chance to see her again, and I faltered. This was my duty, entirely my duty to my country. And yet I genuinely liked Madeline, especially when she let those glimpses of herself shine though.

"Caspian?"

"I'm free if it's for you," I said. "What about tomorrow? Lunch will be perfect."

"Oh," she said, almost surprised at my easy answer. "Okay, yeah. I'll meet you by the coffee shop. Noonish?"

"I'll be there," I promised.

"Okay," she said breathily. "See you later, Caspian."

I shivered at the way she said my name. She had a long way to go to control herself.

"Later, Madeline," I replied, keeping my composure as best as I could.

And she hung up the phone.

I tossed my own device onto the side table and stared at the ceiling, my eyes having adjusted to the dim light. Madeline *had* to get this under control, which meant getting her to her sisters for guidance. Now, all I had to do was convince her of what she was and to return to Atlantis with me.

Simple.

CHAPTER FOUR

MADELINE

Sweat beaded on my neck as I stood in the midday sun outside the coffee shop. I was already itching to move my body just to make the anxiety go away. Would it be weird to do squats while I waited? It would be weird, right? Resisting the urge to pace, I kept eyeing the clock on the coffee shop wall. Ten minutes.

Why did I come so early? Not having a job was one reason. Walking a few applications to the few perspective new employers who still took paper applications on my way, another. When everyone else my age seemed to have a college education and still couldn't find a job, what chance did I have?

I glanced at the clock again. Nine minutes to go.

And I was nervous as hell. Caspian could be anybody. He could be a mobster? Not likely, but you couldn't rule these things out. A creep? A stalker? There was that guy I asked for directions outside the gas station who ended up following me until I pulled up by a police station and he left. The lady at the grocery store who wouldn't stop talking to me about my outfit, even as I was putting shopping bags in my car. Plenty of people have talked to me for less than five minutes and then made it creepy.

But Caspian knew about the water thing, my draw to it. He even called out the weirdness that came with my voice sometimes. Those weren't things I'd said out loud to *anyone*.

Could he read minds?

I looked at the clock. Eight minutes.

Or maybe he was genuinely who he seemed to be. A homesick businessman who sometimes went around in an open shirt on the beach. With a smooth voice and broad shoulders, and an easy presence that snapped me out of my trance so I could tell off Trent.

My tongue darted out to wet my dry lips.

Big dick energy.

Seven minutes.

But I wasn't stupid. That was why you took precautions like meeting at a coffee shop where the staff knows you. In the middle of the day it would be hard for him to cause a scene and get away with it. Right? Was I being as smart as I could about this situation?

"Hello, Madeline." Caspian was here. He called to me from the other direction, and I spun around to face him.

He was wearing another sharp suit, and I was a little disappointed he wasn't in the same kind of outfit from the beach. And here I was in a ratty high-school tank top and my duct-taped flip-flops. Attractive.

"Hey," I replied, my voice cracking, and I internally kicked myself.

It was one thing to want answers from him, but could my traitorous body just not be so easily horny for one second of my life?

His expression dazzled. "You look lovely today."

"Same," I whispered.

A dark chuckle from Caspian had me closing my eyes and my face heating up.

"Where would you like to eat? My treat, of course." Caspian smiled, putting his hands in his pockets.

I bit my lip. I had thought a lot about this, just in case. "Do you like fish?"

"Yes, you could say that," he said, smiling.

I blushed; he had dimples! How had I not noticed them before? *Focus, Maddie.*

"Right, you're from an island. Sorry." I stood awkwardly, one hand holding on to the opposite arm. "My favorite fish taco place is just around the corner from here. Hope that's not too casual for you."

"Not at all," Caspian said, tilting his head. "I've never had them before; it will be a new experience. Lead the way."

Our conversation gave me the confidence that didn't give off any creepy vibes. In fact, he looked like the kind of guy I'd hit on, maybe with a little more class. A definite upgrade from Trent. There was a bit of stubble on his strong jawline, like the first time I met him, and his eyes were so blue they were like a reflection of the ocean. Mine were basically the same shade, different enough that it was one more thing on the list of what made me stand uncomfortably out of place, but it wasn't like I could stare into my own eyes. Not the way I could stare at Caspian's. On him it looked good, normal, right.

"Madeline?"

My eyes widened. Had I just been staring at him this whole time?

"Right, this way." My blood burned as it rushed up my neck, and I turned on my heel, marching toward the taco place.

Idiot! This is how you're going to get kidnapped or murdered

or something one of these days. Keep it in your pants, Madeline.
He's not here for a date.

We walked in silence. Me not knowing what to say and Caspian seemingly comfortable with no conversation as he strolled along beside me.

Once we rounded the corner of the block past the coffee shop, the green and blue waves painted on the shaded food stall appeared. It was an old shipping container with a sunshade added to the front of it. It had an open window running along the front with a wooden bar and bar stools for customers to eat right there and watch the food being made. The far end was an order window where a small line was already forming with people wanting to grab lunch and go. It was the opposite direction from the beach, but that didn't stop the locals from buying tacos and walking down to the water.

And best of all, it was extremely visible. A good place to meet a somewhat stranger.

We stopped at the back of the line and Caspian read the chalkboard menu. "What do you recommend?"

"If you like spicy food, I recommend the volcano. If not, get the house tacos, they're the best."

Caspian nodded, looking down to me with a small smile. "What will you have, Madeline?"

"Two volcanoes," I said, looking up at the menu. "And a bottle of water, please?"

"You like it spicy?" he mused.

Goose bumps ran down my spine and landed right in the bottom of my stomach. Good god, who did he have to sell his soul to so he could talk like that? I looked away before I could feel my face heat up from his teasing.

"I guess I do," I said, focusing really, *really* hard on a tree across the street.

He chuckled, but didn't press further.

The line moved quickly enough, and we made light conversation about the menu and what exactly went into a fish taco. Once we got our food, Caspian led us to the bar stools, and we sat down next to each other.

He bit into his taco—he'd gotten one of each of my recommendations—and his eyes lit up.

"Good, right?" I asked.

He took a napkin and wiped his mouth before answering. "Yes, very."

I couldn't believe I was already having such easy conversations with Caspian. The amount of words spilling out of my mouth surprised me, but I wasn't bothered by it either. In a lot of ways, it was exciting to be this open and free with someone. When was the last time I had that outside of with a boyfriend? Did I even have that kind of freedom with a boyfriend? Maybe Mr. Freeman. Maybe one of the other girls at the group home, at least for a little while, considering the revolving door that place had been over the years. But now, in the moment, Caspian was making it easy.

"Did you think I was lying when I said they were the best?" I teased.

"No, but you forget I come from an island." He laughed. "It's hard to beat seafood fresh from your backyard."

"Yeah, I guess I compare it to getting fish back in Michigan. On our budget, that was most often frozen fish sticks, so you've got to imagine how impressed I was when I got here."

"I wanted to ask," he said. "Forgive me if it's a sensitive subject, but was your home in Michigan not pleasant for you?"

"It was okay, I guess. I've always had a hard time finding exactly what I want out of a place to live. I'm picky. But Florida is nice. The ocean helps."

37

"Do you miss anyone from your hometown?" he asked.

"Not much, I guess. My favorite person passed away after I moved down here. I regret that I didn't go back to visit at least once before he died. The group home, which is where I spent the longest time, was suffocating. Some girls made friends. I didn't. Plenty of us had struggles of other kinds, and there just wasn't enough support to help us all. The doors didn't lock, so there was a good chance you'd lose your stuff, and every hour of every day was structured. And the staff—I don't know what the job requirements were like, but the staff rotated a lot. Overall, it wasn't pleasant for me. School was . . . School was better. Michigan probably would have been fine to live in had I been there under different circumstances. Or at least, other kids from school seemed to be thriving in a way I couldn't."

Caspian was quiet; I was stunned.

"Sorry," I murmured. "I don't usually let it all spill out like that."

"Don't be sorry. Thank you for telling me," he said. "It sounds like things weren't ideal."

"Things sucked," I said. "But it's behind me now, and I like not thinking about it."

"Has it been better here?"

That earned him a laugh. "Oh, there've been struggles, but who doesn't have them after moving a thousand miles from home with no support system? But I've done well enough. I have a roof over my head and a pretty full job history. My first job back home was cleaning a gym. Mopping, cleaning shower stalls, sanitizing. That probably doesn't sound appealing, but it was the first place I found so much peace. I owe Mr. Freeman everything, may he rest in peace with all the nasty burnt coffee he could want."

Caspian chuckled, and it spurred me to keep going. This was more than I'd said to anyone in ages, and it felt good.

"He said it tasted better after it had time to age, as if it was wine or something." I smiled, picturing his coffee cup sitting on his desk by the radio. "That place held some kind of peace for him too. Now it feels so normal to move my body when I have worries. And when it's just me and the treadmill, or my headphones and the free weights? It drowns out all the other stuff. So, I kept doing it even after I moved here."

"Mr. Freeman was the person you missed," Caspian observed.

"Yeah."

"I'm glad you had a place that could bring you peace," he said.

Taking a long pause to drink from my water bottle, I screwed the top back on and changed subjects. "What about you? Where does Caspian, island boy and conductor of business, fit in?"

His laugh was genuine, pulling a smile onto my face to match. "Well," he began, "it starts with the 'island boy' part. You spend your days running around like the little pest you are. Playing a lot of games on the beach, running a lot of errands for your neighbor, who always forgot part of her shopping at the market, in exchange for one of the oranges from her yard, and growing up with your cousins."

"That sounds nice." A small pang of jealousy at the pretty picture he painted struck me, but only for a moment. "Lived with your cousins?"

"I did lose my parents young," he admitted. "Boating accident. My aunt took me in, and from there her brother, my uncle, brought me on as his aide—collecting information for his projects, putting them into reports, running related errands. I've worked for him and the Senate ever since."

"Like a secretary or an assistant?" I asked, and Caspian was already nodding. "So you've been on that path since you were younger, gotcha. Okay, and you grew up with Nikkos?"

"No, different cousin," he chuckled. "Nikkos is related to me, but not to my uncle, Dimitris. He's also not related to the aunt who finished raising me—other side of the family. But he is related. I'm probably making it sound more complicated than it is."

"I like hearing about it," I said. "It sounds like you have a big family."

"My fair share, I guess," he said. "No one pays attention to that back home. City's too small. If you're a kid, you're everyone's responsibility. If you pass too close to an elder, you may just get roped into taking down someone's laundry from the line."

I pulled my lips between my teeth to keep the laughter from bursting out of me.

"You laugh, but it's a real danger. Those streets aren't for the weakhearted," Caspian teased.

Playing with the cap of my water bottle, I let the silence between us fill with lunch-hour chatter and the distant sound of lapping waves from the beach for a moment before getting down to business. "So, what's with my voice?"

His eyebrows rose a bit in surprise. His eyes flicked around us, making sure no one was eavesdropping. "Getting right into it, are we?"

"My stupid voice has caused me more grief in my life than anything else," I admitted. "I never told anyone, in case they thought I was out of my mind or something. One time, I had a caseworker. My old one had retired, and I got handed off to this new lady. I didn't talk to her at first, but after I did, she became obsessed with checking in on me. At first it was to make sure I was doing okay at home and at school, but then it was constantly asking me about stupid stuff that wasn't her business. What kind of clothes and food I liked, what kind of movies or books I thought were cool. It was all the little things that you ask to fill out one of those adoption posters that get plastered on a website, so it wasn't too weird, but she kept going, you know?

"When she was bothering me every day about what kind of candy was best, I finally complained, and it stopped. How does a child reconcile the idea that when they open their mouth, people's whole attitudes might change in unpredictable ways? But the obsessed lady was better than the guy at school who got so friggin' mad at my existence. I don't know if it was him, or me, or what, but I'd just sit in the same class as him and get glares until the bell rang. God, that guy scared me. It was worse in the hallway because more than once I thought he was going to grab me or push me or something."

Trailing off with a sigh, I pulled myself back on track. Hell, I hadn't talked this much in ages, but it felt good. Like a dam finally bursting. "It's easier to stay quiet, right? Sometimes I speak and people want to just give me what I want. Other times, I speak and it grabs intense attention, and not in a good way. But you know about it. For the first time in my life someone said something that clicked. Actually, I kinda freaked out for the whole day before I decided to call you."

Caspian's features softened with every passing sentence. "I can only imagine what you've been through living among people who don't know how to handle the sway. None of that was your fault. Not one moment of it, all right?"

A flood of memories flew through my mind, but I pushed them aside for later. "What *is* the sway?"

He gave me a soft laugh before answering. "You already know what it is. You just never had a name for it before."

Taking another bite and chewing slowly, I let the volcano special burn my tongue as I thought about it. If there was a trick to making it work on purpose, I wanted to know about it. More importantly, I wanted to know how to turn it off.

"Can I get rid of it?"

"Madeline." His voice was so soft, so concerned, that I couldn't help but look at him. His expression matched his tone. "I don't know if there's a way to get rid of it. I've never met someone who wanted to."

The salty air and the screaming gulls filled our otherwise silent moment. The smell of fried food from the taco stand swept around us in the light afternoon breeze. Taking another bite, I pushed back the conversation again until I could work up the nerve to lighten my voice in a poor attempt to erase whatever seriousness I had caused just now.

I swallowed my bite before speaking again. "And it doesn't work on you?"

"It's easier to resist when you know about it, but, yes, it would work on me too. If you were able to try hard enough."

"So, you really won't tell me where you're from?" I pressed again. "Because Atlantis can't be real."

"You're not using nearly enough of the sway to make me tell you that." Caspian took another bite of his own lunch, unhurried and unbothered.

Now that he'd explained it to me, my life was starting to make sense. I had felt something work between us when I spoke before. The problem was, I couldn't do it on command, and I definitely couldn't stop my voice from doing it after it decided to start.

"Tell me," I insisted.

He just chuckled and took another bite.

Now I closed my eyes, concentrating on what it felt like those times my voice did that aggravating thing.

"Tell me, Caspian," I said, more demanding this time.

He just shook his head. "No. You don't want it bad enough."

My shoulders drooped as I gave up trying. "There's no On button for it?"

Caspian shook his head. "They say it has something to do with feeling in control. And something about your mood and your body. I can't explain it correctly, but if it helps, you were using the sway on the phone before."

That caught my attention. "I was?"

"Yes, can you remember how you were feeling when you asked me about your voice?" he asked.

Control, huh? Well, I might not have control over a lot of things in my life right now, but I did feel that way on the phone. I was the one who decided to reach out, I got to decide when and where to meet, and if I was being honest with myself, remembering how Caspian looked on the beach with his open shirt, well, that was something.

"Everything okay?" he asked. "Do you remember how you felt?"

I nodded. "Let me try again."

"Here, let me help you out," Caspian said, turning to face me. "A lot of them say they can feel it right . . . here."

He reached out, his fingertips lightly touching a spot just under the base of my neck.

"Does that make sense?" he asked.

My eyes widened. "I've tried so many times to make it work but I thought it was about the words I chose. I thought I was making it all up in my head."

"Try again," Caspian urged gently. "But this time, try it from there, in your chest."

Squaring my shoulders, sitting up confidently on the stool, and letting myself enjoy the view of Caspian in his sharp outfit, I took a breath.

You're the one in control here, Madeline. This is your town, your lunch spot, your meeting.

Looking up into Caspian's eyes, I asked the question again with a calm tone, a hand over the spot where my skin could still feel the soft brush of his fingertips. "Caspian, will you tell me where you come from?"

I felt it. Subtle, but there. That feeling that I sometimes got in my chest when my voice did whatever it did before people changed. It took me years to equate the feeling with the outcome, but now there were no doubts. It was sort of like a muscle, and I could flex it if I tried.

His lips parted, his eyes widening a fraction as he smiled.

"Atlantis," he said softly.

I frowned, smacking my hand on the counter. "Dammit, I thought I had it that time."

"Madeline." Caspian put his hand over mine, surprising me as I looked into his eyes again. "You did. I'm not lying when I say the name of my city is Atlantis."

"Really?" I asked.

He nodded. "It wasn't the strongest use of your voice, but I could tell you figured it out. Partly, at least."

"Huh." Atlantis. "The same name as that old legend. That's kind of cool."

His eyes crinkled with mirth. "It is, isn't it?"

"So, I really did do it?" I asked, cautiously excited.

He nodded. "It was light, but it was there."

My heart pounded. Could I really learn to control this? If I could make myself do it, could I make myself *not* do it? That would be the bigger accomplishment.

"Okay," I said. "How do I keep doing that? I want to get better."

Caspian hummed, tilting his head and looking at me thoughtfully. "Practice, Madeline." The taunting shape of his mouth was frustrating.

I drummed my fingers on the counter in annoyance, and he laughed.

"Okay," I said. "I think I understand. It's a confidence thing, right? Everyone loves confident people, that doesn't mean I have some kind of special voice."

"Try it again, then. Not on me, on someone you know isn't aware of it," Caspian said. "Try it on a stranger. Try it on . . ."

Caspian looked around us. The street was busy enough. The line for tacos had grown longer. People who worked in the neighborhood were out on their lunch breaks. There was a couple walking a dog, some kids playing, and other people just milling about or walking to the beach.

Caspian pointed to a man standing on a corner nearby, pulling a stick of gum from his pocket.

"Him. Go ask him for a stick of gum," Caspian said.

Frowning, I sat up straighter on the hard stool. "Does it have to be a guy?"

Caspian's sharp eyes were on me for a moment before he slid them back to the target. "No, it doesn't. If you don't feel ready to try—"

"No, no. It's not that." I licked my dry lips, my eyes roaming the sidewalks around us for a different stranger but coming up with no new ideas.

"Maybe we shouldn't push it," Caspian offered.

I wanted to believe Caspian. Years of life experience wouldn't let me trust him yet, but it meant a lot that he would offer. If I was going to test this out, I was going to do it on my own.

Shaking my head, I scooted off the stool. "No, I need to do something about this problem, and practice is the only way to get the hang of it. I'm going over there."

"You're sure?"

No. "Yeah."

"It won't be weird to him if you use the sway," Caspian insisted. "Go on, try it on him. Use that pressure on him, exactly like you did to me. Ease into it. As far as I've heard, too much can cause problems as well. Add a little of that pressure and ask for what you want."

I took a deep breath. "Fine. I'll try it."

"You can do it," Caspian said. "Be wary of his mood. I'm sure you know what happens when the sway goes awry. I'll be watching if you need help. You may instinctively try to pull back on your voice if you run into problems: resist that urge. Make different suggestions to get what you want or to make someone back off. You sure you're up to it?"

Nodding, I eyed my target briefly to make sure he was still there. I took one more bite of my lunch to stall and build myself up. I glanced at Caspian, but he just gestured at me to get on with it.

I swallowed. "Okay, fine."

I lifted my chin and squared my shoulders. Then, I walked. That kind of walk you do when you're in control of the situation. I wasn't sure if I really was in control of anything, but at least I could pretend, right?

The guy down the sidewalk was playing with his phone now, not really paying attention to his surroundings. He had a frat-boy air about him, and he was wearing sunglasses with a backward hat and basketball shorts. The glasses made me nervous since I couldn't see his expression, but it was too late to change my mind because I'd walked close enough that he looked up at me.

I took in a sharp breath, then forced the confident posture back into my body. "Hey, can I have a stick of gum?"

My heart pounded in my chest and blood drummed in my ears as I watched his reaction even as I felt nothing from that place in my throat. Panicking, I added another word with one firm push from my throat. "Please?"

He looked at me for a minute, moved his shades down to get a better view, then pulled the pack of gum from his pocket.

"Sure thing, gorgeous. Here you go." He handed me a stick, and I took it with a shocked smile.

It worked? Was controlling my voice really so fucking simple that I just needed to be told where the source of that sway thing came from? Or maybe I just needed someone to believe me, to confirm I wasn't making it all up in the first place.

But I wasn't quite convinced that the last attempt had actually added any sway. My shoulders sank. No, no need to get excited. It could just be a guy giving gum to a girl on the street.

"Are you from around here?" he asked. "Are you free right now?"

Whoops. Back up.

"I'm having lunch with a friend."

Looking back at the taco stand, I debated signaling for help. Caspian was watching intently, and his expression turned to concern. I shook my head slightly. Turning back to the gum guy, I took a nervous step backward. I wanted to try this on my own, no backup. Not just yet. Keeping that pressure in my voice steady, I tried to maintain the same level of confident demand as before.

"Maybe later, then?" he asked, his eyes roaming up and down as he enjoyed the view.

Oh. Oh no. Now I could see it crystal clear. This was exactly what happened before I got into stalker territory and the guy called me a bitch for leading him on.

Deep breath. I forced a firmness into my words.

"No, thank you. I have to go."

"You come around here much?" He pressed on, ignoring what I had said.

I knew it was too good to be true. I *knew* there wasn't some magic trick to make people listen to me. That would be impossible—the tallest tale to ever be told—and I'd fallen for it.

My heart slammed in my chest, my breath catching in my throat as the panic set in. I'd done whatever it was my voice always did, but I couldn't do the intentional thing that Caspian was trying to describe. If it even existed.

The guy took a step forward, holding out a hand. "I could grab your number for later?"

Panic shot up my throat, tightening it as my shoulders tensed. "No, please."

"Come on," he said. "I won't bite."

My eyes flew shut and my head turned down to the ground as I braced for. . . I didn't know what, but I was braced for it. Then I felt a heat at my back as someone came up right behind me.

"She said no." Caspian's voice was calm but firm.

Looking up at the scene, I could see the guy's attention was now over my head and eye to eye with Caspian. He backed off immediately, albeit with a frown on his face as he shook his head, as if snapping out of a daydream.

"Whatever." Gum guy turned to me with a confused look on his face, then spun and walked down the sidewalk.

My breath was shaky and my arms started to tremble.

"Madeline." Caspian tried to get my attention. "Madeline!" A tear pricked at my eye, and I wiped it away furiously with the heel of my hand.

"I'm sorry, I'm sorry, I thought I could do it."

"Shh, no." Caspian rubbed a big hand on my back. "You did everything right, but I'm not a S— I can't teach you as well as the ladies back home."

"Is it even real?" I demanded. "Are you just messing with me?

I thought I finally had an answer, or at least someone who knew what I was going through, but is this all bullshit?" Heat rushed at my face, but I stubbornly maintained eye contact with Caspian.

"Oh, Madeline." He looked about to reach for me but pulled back his hand. "It is real, I promise you that. I'm the one who's sorry—you're still so new to this I should have stuck closer. Come on, let's get you away from here. How about a coffee to settle your nerves?"

He seemed so convinced. Maybe that was why I hadn't questioned him before, but what he was describing with my voice wasn't real. That would be like magic, real-life magic, and I'd ditched those storybooks when I was a kid.

But, at this point, I believed that *he* believed this voice thing, so I went with it for now. I didn't have the words to press back, so I followed Caspian back to the taco stand. He cleaned up the trash from our lunch, and then we walked back to the coffee shop where we'd met. He settled me on a bench outside and got my order from me, returning a few minutes later with an iced latte in hand.

"Here, drink."

Taking a breath, I obliged.

"That was. . . . I had no idea it could be that bad," he murmured. "I really wish you could talk to one of the women back home; you need their help."

"I wish—" *I wish I could fully believe in this.* My face strained. "I wish I could talk to one of these women. I can't afford to travel abroad or anything. Maybe in a few years I can save up and . . ." The thought trailed off. And what? Get a fresh start again? I'd already done it once when I came down to Florida, but that hadn't gotten me much. Some sunshine and ocean, which made me happy, but I was struggling harder down here to keep a roof over my head than I ever had in Michigan.

"It doesn't have to be that complicated. I could take you there, you know," Caspian said softly.

"I'm not in any position right now to sail away with a man I met a few days ago. No offense."

"Absolutely none taken. I understand completely. I wish I could make this easier for you." Caspian sighed, taking a drink from his own cup before staring down the road to the thin line of blue ocean at the end of it. "Would you like to practice on someone less intimidating? Someone who couldn't hurt you if he tried, and who I could keep in line?"

My eyes shifted to Caspian with suspicion. "Who?"

"Nikkos. He's familiar with the sway, it won't drive him to do something stupid."

"It doesn't affect him?"

"Nikkos and I are used to it. We know what it is. The people from the mainland, they don't know what comes over them. I'm sure they can get a little wild from it."

I took another sip of my drink, trying not to dwell on past experiences.

"Would you like to practice some more under safer circumstances?" he asked.

His expression was so earnest. And it was help I desperately needed. There had to be a trick to my voice, there just had to be. Otherwise, every person who creeped on me after I talked to them made no sense. And that place, in my chest, it was really there and doing something. I could flex it, or move it, or I didn't know. I just wanted all the bad times to stop happening, and even if it did sound impossible, Caspian might have a way to help me do that.

This voice thing, it answered so many questions. Guys would claim I was a tease despite me not saying anything suggestive to them. Was it my voice? Then there were the asshole customers at the gym. An asshole boss or two as well. They all assumed I would be an easy lay and then got mad when I wasn't. Not that I have anything against sex. I really like sex. Sex is natural; sex is healthy. But not for the reasons they always thought. I never tried to seduce anyone, but maybe I was doing it by accident, and I hated the thought of that. What I needed was more control.

The gum was still in my hand, but I really didn't want it. Not yet. "Here, I want you to hold on to this until I can make you give it to me for real."

Caspian looked down at the gum, then back up at me with satisfaction. "Does this mean I can still try to help you?"

"Yeah. I don't want this back until I've earned it, if you'll help me."

Caspian took it with gentle hands. "Happily, Madeline."

And somehow this man's smile melted another layer of my shell. This was possibly the most reckless thing I'd ever let myself be talked into, but he reminded me of Mr. Freeman. Caspian was genuine about this, and I needed it to be true. Letting out a slow breath, I looked down the street to the line of deep blue water, then back to Caspian.

"Maddie," I said. "Please, call me Maddie."

CHAPTER FIVE

MADELINE

The first thing I really noticed about the sway was the feeling it put in my chest. Somewhere between my lungs and my throat sat a little pressure. Or maybe it vibrated. It did something when I was able to make the sway work, at any rate.

My time with Caspian was easier than it had been before. Honestly, I was waiting for the asshole in him to come out, because that was the only type of guy I seemed to be attracted to, and fuck, was I attracted to Caspian. Except so far, no asshole had shown himself.

He took the last swallow of his coffee and used a napkin to make sure he wasn't leaving anything behind. I handed off my own empty cup and he took our trash away, returning swiftly to sit next to me.

"If you think you have enough of the hang of it now, great," Caspian said. "If not, you might need to practice before we try it on Nikkos. Especially since he knows what it is."

"Oh, yeah? Who do you suggest I practice on?" I asked, feeling the light pressure in my chest that told me the sway was trying to push its way to the surface. It took me by surprise.

Shit. Why the hell would it do that right now?

Can't you keep it in your pants for five minutes, Mads? What is wrong with you?

Caspian let out a laugh, low and comfortable, as embarrassment burned up my neck.

"I didn't mean, I mean I was just— Fuck me." I sighed, covering my face with my hands.

Caspian leaned in, his breath tickling my ear as he whispered, "Not on the first date, darling."

I took in a sharp breath, and he chuckled at my reaction.

Fuck.

"But, if you feel like you need more practice, I could help you," Caspian offered. "I don't want you pressured into trying it with Nikkos if you don't feel ready."

"No, I want to try." I managed a small smile. "I need practice and talking it out with you has really made me understand this sway thing a little better."

"Good," Caspian said. "You took to it quickly. That's impressive."

"Now if only I could master it at the same pace." I stood, and we walked down the sidewalk. "I guess I just didn't have words to describe what was happening before. Honestly, I thought my *voice* was the problem for most of the years these incidents have been happening."

Caspian chuckled. "I believe you. Those Atlantean women really know how to work their voices."

He cleared his throat, turning his attention to fix the button on his sleeve cuff. The action distracted me a little, watching how his arms and chest strained against the fabric of his shirt when he moved.

"Anyway," Caspian continued, "I need to get back before Nikkos frets, he's good at that. I'll text you the plan in a bit, and we can accidentally bump into you on the beach later."

"Sounds good. Nice and accidental, all right." I laughed

He gave me a warm smile before his eyes went downward.

I frowned. "Hey, eyes up here, Caspian."

Not that my mind wasn't in roughly the same territory.

He looked up, a little startled for a moment. "Sorry, I was just thinking I wish I had something from back home for you to wear. These mainlander clothes are nice and all, but you'd be an absolute stunner in an Atlantean dress."

"Oh."

He raised both hands, palms out. "I didn't mean to make you uncomfortable. If it's any consolation, I'm a little worried that I'm putting all the power in your hands, unlocking the secrets of your voice."

I couldn't stop my face from turning sly. "Oh? I might like the sound of that."

His expression was delighted and surprised. Those dimples, his gorgeous smile. My heart hit my chest hard enough to make me aware of my increasing pulse. I bit back a groan.

Rein it in, Mads.

Why did I say that? Stuff like that was always coming out of my mouth. That was how I kept finding myself with jackasses like Trent. Though, admittedly, Caspian didn't act like Trent at all. He was smooth, but not fake.

"What kind of clothes do you wear in Atlantis?" I asked, reaching for something else, anything else, to focus on.

"Loose, a lot of whites, pale colors, or undyed fabric for casual wear. A lot of beads and embroidery. For more important things, bright, bold colors. A lot of bone and coral for details like buttons or jewelry."

"Oh!" I said. "Your clothes on the beach yesterday."

He smiled. "Yes, they were from back home. Good eye."

"I'll see what I have in my closet. No promises, though. I don't have that many nice things since my last move."

And this impending one. My expression faltered as I remembered half of my things were packed in boxes and the other half had about two days to be packed up as well before I was officially houseless.

"Everything okay?" Caspian asked.

"Yes. Text me the details and I'll see you tonight."

"I can do that."

His voice lowered and he leaned in, as if whispering a secret between us. "See you later, lovely siren."

My heart went wild, and I'd be lying if I said I wasn't a little disappointed that he wasn't doing what I thought he was about to do. His words caught up with me, and I almost laughed. "'siren,' huh? Do you expect me to lure you into the sea now?"

His eyes crinkled. "Maybe I'm the one luring you to my island, where we, my people, can treat you like a princess."

"Get out of here." I laughed. "I'll see you at the beach."

He nodded his acknowledgment, his mouth still curling at the corners, and we went our separate ways.

For now, at least.

The walk back to my apartment was spent in a daze. Caspian was hot as sin, and I was having a terrible time keeping my mind out of the gutter. It felt good to have an idea of where I was from, even if his claim to know just by my voice was a rather weak clue to go on.

Then again, he was spot-on about my issues with my voice and men. Or maybe I was grasping at straws.

When I reached my apartment, there was another yellow notice taped under the *B* on my metal door. Unlocking the door, I grabbed the notice, slipped inside, and then crumpled up the note.

"Let's take a look," I murmured as I opened a box of clothes. Tank tops. A few gym sweatshirts that, if I was being honest, I'd probably give to a thrift shop at some point. Shorts, swimsuits, nothing too interesting.

And then I found my white tunic shirt at the bottom of the box. My eyes flew to the pile of clothes I'd already removed, looking for things to pair with it.

I pulled the top out and smoothed out the wrinkles, pleased with what I had put together. It was cut lower than necessary, and it constantly fell off my shoulders. If I wore one of my lacy white bras with it, the whole look would come off as pretty sexy.

Do I want to be sexy in front of Caspian?

Yes.

I immediately went for another box that I knew had a pair of white cutoff shorts in it, and pulled the outfit together with a pair of wedges that made my ass pop.

"Perfect," I decided, getting changed and checking out the whole look in the mirror. I added a few gold bangles and a blue necklace; then it was down to the waiting game.

It gave me time to pack at least. I put most of my other clothes into boxes as well as the rest of my bathroom stuff. With a sigh, I shook my head at how few things I really owned. I never seemed to keep much each time I moved.

Or dumped an ex.

I chewed my lip, looking over my stuff. At least it would fit in my car. And then my phone buzzed.

Caspian: Let's see if we can push one of Nikkos's buttons tonight. If you can do it, I owe you a surprise

Chewing my bottom lip, I typed out a response.

Madeline: Deal!

Caspian: Have him ignore his phone. He can't stand not paying attention to it while we're on a business trip. I'll call him so it rings while we're together, and you can make him ignore it

"Sounds interesting."

A surprise, huh?

Caspian: Meet you in half an hour?

I looked at the time on my phone. More than enough time if I started walking now. No need to take my car if I didn't have to. Gas was money I didn't have to be spending.

Madeline: Yes

Time to see what I could really do. This was my chance to see if I could make my voice cooperate on command, and, even more importantly, if I could make it stop messing with people's heads. This experiment with Nikkos had better work, as I only had a few days of Caspian's guidance to master it before he went back home to his island.

My attention slid to my laptop. I had a few minutes before I had to leave, right? I could hustle there shortly. But first, some questions. I flipped it open and typed in my search: *Country of Atlantis.*

—

The evening air was pretty chilly for Florida. I noticed it more when I wasn't in the sun, which promised to disappear completely in a couple of hours. But soon enough I could hear the waves hitting the shore, and I picked up my pace to see the sun's glow shining on the water. The beach was almost empty. The locals would probably have their jackets on tonight, but I'd survived too many Michigan winters to be shivering in what the Floridians considered cold.

My nerves were on high alert. I'd decided to go all in and put my faith in this voice trick for now. This whole Nikkos thing felt like a test, like I had to succeed right now, or I wouldn't ever be able to control the effects of my voice. Which was silly—obviously I could continue to practice as much as I wanted, but I had limited time to practice with Caspian here to help me.

The beach breeze was relaxing as I watched the boats bob in the marina. For safety reasons it was separated from the beach by some distance of inaccessible rocky shore, but the sidewalk made an easy place to walk between the two.

Caspian and Nikkos finally appeared, coming down the wooden boards of the marina. Nikkos was typing something furiously on his phone, so he didn't see me, and I immediately turned like I was about to walk onto the beach. Standing where I could let the last rays of the sun coat my skin, I waited for their approach.

"Hello, siren." Caspian greeted with mischief in his voice.

When I opened my eyes, I pretended to be surprised to see them. "Hello, sailor," I teased back. "I was just here on my evening walk. Are you guys enjoying the beach?"

Nikkos looked skeptical and glanced at his cousin, but didn't say anything.

"Yes," Caspian said. "Mind if we join you?"

"Caspian," Nikkos hissed. "What are you doing?"

"We can tell her more about home," Caspian murmured.

Caspian turned his attention back to me and took in my outfit. I held in my satisfaction as his eyes followed the curve of my legs up to the breezy white top, not unlike his own shirt.

You like? I raised an eyebrow at him, earning myself a dimpled smile back.

Remembering what we'd come here for, I cleared my throat. "I was about to dip my feet in the water."

Bending forward, I took off my shoes a little slower than truly necessary, hoping Caspian was watching. Standing up with shoes in hand, I stepped onto the sand and tilted my head. "Do you want to come with?"

Maybe the flirting wasn't strictly necessary, but I loved doing it. I always had, even though my desire for things like sex and relationships had me jumping in too soon with partners I thought were going to be different and who soon enough proved me wrong. But Caspian, even if it was a tiny little thing, even if he was leaving soon, I still wanted to push, for a little bit of that flirtatious high that came with attraction to someone new.

Caspian looked amused, keeping his attention trained on me instead of answering the question. Nikkos thought for a moment before saying, "Sure, why not."

"What's the ocean like on your island?" I asked as they removed their shoes and joined me.

"It's the same ocean, Madeline," Caspian teased.

I turned to Nikkos. "You know how some beaches are rocky, some have white sand, some are murky, some are clear?"

"The eastern side of the island is white rock," Nikkos said. "Little sand and nowhere to walk into the water comfortably. The east end has sand as white as the rocks from the other side, and a coral reef around most of that. It grows around the ruins mostly."

"Ruins? That sounds so cool," I said. "What kind of ruins?"

Caspian coughed. "Just some things claimed by the sea. You know how it goes. Statues, other things."

We reached the water, and I happily sank my toes into the wet sand, waiting for the rush of cool waves to slam against me. The water hit my ankles, flooding the beach where I stood, and then pulled back as it dragged out again, removing sand from beneath me. Nikkos and Caspian did the same.

"That sounds amazing, actually," I said, even though I couldn't quite picture it in my mind.

"It is," Nikkos answered. "The unique geography and the slope of our underwater sections allows a plateau of resources that—"

"Nikkos," Caspian interrupted. "Too much."

Nikkos frowned, then his eyes widened as he turned to Caspian. "What, have you not told her yet?"

I frowned. "Told me what?"

The cousins looked at me, then at each other, then Caspian ran his fingers through his hair.

"I don't want him to bore you with details like that," Caspian answered. "And of course I told her where we're from, Nikkos."

"A place named after Atlantis, right?" I asked.

"'Named after—'" Nikkos blinked. "That is indeed the name of it, yes."

I lowered my eyebrows, now heavy with suspicion. Something about their reactions was off. My stomach twisted; when was Caspian going to call his cousin so I could do this? Or were we trying to get his guard down first?

" Maddie." Caspian got my attention. "What do you do for a living?"

"I'm between, uh, opportunities," I said, my face heating, worried they would judge me for being unemployed.

"What about your home, do you live with someone else paying the bills?" Nikkos asked.

I hesitated, then shook my head.

"Madeline . . ." Caspian started.

"It's fine," I insisted. "I'm putting my résumé out there, and then there's my savings."

Nikkos hummed. "Change of subject. What brought you to live here? Caspian tells me you're not from the area. Do you know where your parents were from?"

Okay, a little invasive, but maybe that's not a rude question where they're from.

"The call of the ocean brought me here, I guess. No idea about my parents, not one clue. My file is completely empty—they vanished without a trace when they left me with a thin white blanket and not so much as a note back in Michigan. And Caspian thinks maybe I'm from Atlantis, too, but how likely is that, really?"

Nikkos looked at me with concentration. Honestly assessing what he saw before him.

Taking a moment, I did the same. His eyes were as eerily blue as Caspian's, maybe slightly green as well. A bit startling, to say the least, but nothing terribly different from what I saw in a mirror. A tawny complexion, dark hair in loose curls, and a similar physique to his cousin. Nothing inherently stuck out beyond the eyes, but there was something about them. Something about all three of us that I couldn't quite figure out.

"If you were in Atlantis, you wouldn't be alone," Nikkos offered. "You shouldn't have to be so isolated."

My breath was a little rough. Isolated. Is that what this was? Maybe, because while I had a few people I would call friends from high school, we had completely lost touch when I moved. Had I made any friends here? Not really. The kind of friends you make out of co-workers, maybe, but they don't usually stick with you after you leave the job. There were sweet people, like Cassidy at the coffee shop, but it wasn't like we would hang out on the weekends. There were a few gym rats who would strike up conversations with me while using the same parts of the gym, but that chatter didn't amount to much either. *Isolated.* Yeah, I suppose so.

"Maybe you're right about where I'm from, and maybe you aren't," I murmured. "But why have I never heard of this place before? Is it that small?"

Caspian nodded. "You won't find it on many maps, that's for sure. It's barely a city-state of its own, let alone big enough to be considered a country."

"Interesting. Maybe I could visit someday."

It certainly beats the way things have been going for me here.

A ringing phone caused Nikkos to jump for his pocket.

Finally.

"Drat, who is it now?" Nikkos grumbled.

My eyes flicked to Caspian, whose hand was suspiciously in his pocket, and I took that as my cue to try out my control. I cleared my throat, reaching for that place that would make the pressure happen and praying that it would work this time.

"Nikkos, don't answer your phone," I insisted. Pushing, that feeling or vibration or whatever it was, hummed to life. I wanted him not to move his phone, needed him to not answer. Willing that phone to stay put, I stared at the device in his hand.

Nikkos's hand froze, holding his ringing phone as he was bringing it out of his pocket. I felt it when I told him not to answer, felt that place in my chest working. My pulse raced as my attention flicked between the phone and Nikkos, waiting.

"Shit," Nikkos hissed, glaring at the phone in his hand. His jaw ticked, then he shot me a pleading look. "Miss Madeline, if I could please just check this call . . ."

But he stood there, his hand not moving above his hip. A grin broke out across my face. Whatever this was, a trick of the mind, a manipulation of human reaction, it worked! This sway thing really worked like I wanted it to!

"Well?" Caspian asked, amused. "Go on, then."

Nikkos scowled at him, and I pumped my arms overhead and whooped in victory. Caspian gladly pulled the stick of gum out of his pocket and held it in front of me.

"Hand it over!" I stuck my hand out, and Caspian placed the prize in my open palm with a nod.

"Ahem," Nikkos interrupted.

"Sorry, Nikkos. Go ahead," I offered, pocketing the gum with a contented sigh.

His shoulders sagged and he smiled. "Thank you."

Nikkos looked at the caller ID, then scowled at Caspian, who burst out laughing.

"Very funny," Nikkos snapped.

My eyes stayed locked on Nikkos, staring at the point where the phone had stuck for him. With a moment to reflect, it really was strange. It was as if the device had been frozen, quite literally stuck in the air.

"Everything all right?" Caspian asked, shaking me from my thoughts.

"Yeah," I said, still staring at the empty space for a moment before dragging my gaze to the horizon. "This sway stuff is serious business. It almost works like magic or something."

But was it real, or were they toying with me? My gut told me they were being earnest, but the logical side of my brain refused to accept it. What had happened just now was way more than a cheap trick, something a magician could pull off. It was like magic, and that thought chilled me. How many nights had I stayed up wondering if I was cursed or haunted? On some level I'd questioned if there were paranormal factors at play, but this was too tangible. Too close, too real, too scary to think about.

When I turned my head back, the cousins were exchanging another look I couldn't read.

"Magic indeed," Nikkos said, and his cousin coughed.

"I wish we had more to show you back home," Caspian said, changing the subject. "Like one of Nikkos's books."

"If you're referring to my collection of the annotated history of the Senate, then you're trying to set her up for boredom. Those books require familiarity with legal jargon and a great deal of explanation," Nikkos scoffed. "The murals in Charmolipi Square would be a much better visual representation of Atlantis."

"What about a website?" I asked. "Like, a tourism site? Or local government?"

Caspian elbowed Nikkos. "Way to go."

"There's the matter of our language," Nikkos said. "You don't speak it, so I'm not sure what I could direct you to in English."

"True," I said.

"Do we have anything interesting on the ship?" Caspian wondered out loud. "Nikkos, did you bring anything?"

"Little other than work," Nikkos said. "But the whole ship is Atlantean make. Everything from the dishes to the doors to the limited furniture will look like a bit of home."

"Right you are," Caspian murmured, then turned to me. "Would you like to see it?"

I caught my bottom lip and worried it with my left front tooth. "I really want to say yes, but I'm not ready to get on a boat with two guys I don't know."

Caspian raised his hands in front of him. "Of course, that's fair. Maybe we could bring some things out to show you before we leave, or something."

"When do you leave?" I asked.

"Friday," Nikkos answered. "We're on a fairly tight schedule."

I nodded, stepping out of the water's reach with a sigh. "How does one get to Atlantis? If I ever wanted to visit. Fly there?"

"You won't find any flights to Atlantis," Caspian said. "You'd have to find someone with a boat who knows how to get there."

"It really is small, isn't it?" I asked.

"Something like that," Caspian answered, stepping out of the water behind me.

Stretching my arms behind my back, I threw Caspian a playful smile. "So, I did the phone thing. Do I get to know what my surprise is?"

Nikkos scoffed, heavy with indignation. "You're both scoundrels."

Caspian chuckled. "We did have a deal; I owe you now."

"You do," I prodded.

"If you two are quite done harassing me," Nikkos huffed, "I'll take my leave. Madeline, it was nice to meet you."

Nikkos nodded sharply and walked away, making his way to the sidewalk and the marina beyond.

"I hope he's not mad," I said.

Caspian couldn't stop himself from laughing as Nikkos disappeared. "He'll be fine, I promise. That was great. You're definitely getting the hang of it."

"Could he have stopped it if he really wanted to?" I asked.

Caspian's laughter died off as he sighed, still smiling and looking at where Nikkos had disappeared. "You did a wonderful job. You're getting the hang of the basics."

"I don't know, I think I was too comfortable here. It wasn't the same as with gum guy. That was almost . . ." *Scary.* I shivered.

"I still count this as a win, and so will Nikkos," he said, his voice falling soft at the end.

Caspian's guard was down. He looked happy. Relaxed. The air of peace was contagious, and it nearly made me forget the troubles I had to go home to.

"I want to treat you to dinner for all your hard work," he said.

"I'd like that."

"Maddie," Caspian said softly, not looking at me. "Come with us."

That caught me off guard, slowing me to a stop. My lips parted in surprise as my focus darted around his expression for a hint of amusement. There was none; he was serious.

"I can't," I answered, barely audible over the sounds of the waves behind us. "I have a life here," I whispered, beginning to ramble excuses. "And my car, and my apartment."

"Maddie," Caspian said, stopping me. "I understand. I don't like it, but I understand. But promise me something."

I wrapped my arms around myself, biting my lower lip. "What is it?"

"When the ocean calls to you a little too hard for you to resist, let me be the one to show you the way home."

My heart hit my chest hard. Home. Something I'd been looking for since I'd left Michigan. Maybe something I'd been looking for my whole life.

"Okay," I said softly. "I promise."

He stepped closer to me, reaching out and then stopping himself.

I reached out and took his hand. It was warm, and bigger than mine.

We leaned in at the same time and our lips met. A soft kiss. A parting kiss. He was so warm against the evening breeze. His cologne was light and earthy, and the brush of his soft, open shirt tickled my collarbone. His hand reached for the side of my neck as we kissed, his thumb brushing deliberately against my skin—a sensual touch that gave me goose bumps.

And almost as soon as it began, the moment was over, and we separated. This was going to drive me wild. How could Caspian and Nikkos not have gotten weird around me yet? Was it ever going to happen, or were the people from this Atlantis place just different?

"Good night, Madeline."

"Good night," I whispered.

And I watched him go.

Pulling my phone out of my pocket, I opened a new search window.

What is a siren?

CHAPTER SIX

CASPIAN

I shut the hatch the second I got back on the yacht and sat down with a *thud* on the bottom step.

Stupid.

It was stupid to kiss her.

But she was right there, and so close. And the raw, unrestricted allure of a siren is a great temptation to anyone. Especially when you're already attracted to her. I ran my fingers through my hair, the feeling of her lips on mine still lingering.

"What happened?" Nikkos was standing in the galley, and whipped around to face me.

Looking up, I met his concerned gaze.

I grunted. "Nothing."

"I've never seen you slam the hatch like that before," Nikkos argued. "That's not nothing."

"Leave it," I said.

"Caspian—"

"Leave it, Nikkos," I snapped.

I stalked past the galley to the short hallway that held the cabins and bathroom. Turning back to look at my cousin, I allowed my shoulders to sag.

"Sorry, Nikkos. Not now," I said, then changed my mind. "I kissed her."

"You did what?"

"She tastes like the sea," I said, quieter this time. Softer. "She *belongs* in Atlantis."

His eyes dropped all concern and moved to sympathy. We both wanted her home. A siren belongs at sea.

"That's not your decision to make," Nikkos murmured. "We've interfered enough, planted the seeds. We can ask the Senate what to do now, or Calliope. I'm sure the basilli will have his own opinions as well."

My eyes met his, my brow drawn low and tense. "Basilli Ateio unsettles me. I don't like how he looks at the sirens."

Adrion Ateio himself had famously fallen out of love with his wife not long into their marriage, which on its own was not a point to hold against anyone. But the way they acted together was just . . . odd. No one had a clear idea as to why they remained together, though power and image do a lot to keep the right couples bonded. Maybe it was the birth of their son, Calix, that made them stay together. The lady of the house, Helena, was withdrawn and secretive. The servants of the house were unusually silent and loyal to their masters, possibly out of love but just as likely out of fear. Word was that Helena had a sleeping problem and kept magical contraband—sleeping potions that she got from the gods knew where. But an Ateio would be able to contact the surface, I supposed. A handful of other extended family members were reputed to be constantly clamoring for part of Adrion's power.

"Everyone looks at the sirens like that," Nikkos argued.

"You don't," I shot back. "Dimitris doesn't. I don't." *Except for Maddie.*

Nikkos tightened his lips; nothing to say back to that.

"She isn't doing well here, you heard her say it herself. How long do you suppose she can last with no job? These mainlanders don't take care of their own like we do. She's putting on a front and you know it."

"But it's *her* decision," Nikkos argued. "We can't *make* a siren do anything. No one can."

"I know!" I pinched the bridge of my nose. "I get it, Nikkos."

"What do you want to do then?"

"We need to convince her," I said. "We can't leave her here."

"Oh, yes, let's just kidnap her, then! I'm sure the Senate would be thrilled. They'll throw a feast in our honor for so much as lifting a finger without their say-so. And against a siren at that!"

"Fuck the Senate," I snapped. "They spend months deliberating and bickering about what's best for Atlantis, but they fail spectacularly on time-sensitive matters. Some of them might want to take action, sure, but the rest would hold them back."

My cousin nodded slowly, and a grimace settled on his jaw. "Dimitris would demand to know why you didn't simply drag her back," Nikkos admitted.

"As you said, you can't make a siren do anything she doesn't want to do," I said, leaning against the front edge of the hallway.

He gave a dark laugh. "Dimitris wouldn't take that for an excuse, no matter how valid. Get it done and apologize later, right?"

"We have to convince her."

"And how do you propose we do that?" Nikkos asked, just as his phone went off.

"Oh for the love of—Caspian, are you calling me again?" Nikkos asked, pulling the device from his pocket. He frowned at the glowing screen.

"What is it?" I asked.

"Unknown number," Nikkos said, answering the phone. "Hello, this is Nikkos."

I watched my cousin's expression closely. It began as curiosity, then surprise.

"Yes, yes, that would work." He looked up at me, distress in his eyes. "Yes, we can do tonight if that's what has to happen."

"What is it?" I whispered, but Nikkos shook his head and focused on the call.

"Oh. Oh! Yes, we could do that. Yes. Yes. Thank you for telling me."

I stepped away from my cabin and back toward my cousin, trying to hear the other end of the call.

"Three hours? Of course. Thank you, I appreciate it." Nikkos ended the call, then shoved the phone back in his pocket.

"That was the mercenary, he finally got our message and is in town. He says he can do the job—get the relic from the vampires—but he wants to meet tonight to get the details," Nikkos said, now pacing in the small space the belly of the boat allowed us. "I think I'm going to be sick. It's finally time."

"Relax, Nikkos," I said. "We have his fee and then some, it's what we've been waiting for. Did he agree to the oath of silence?"

"Yes, yes." Nikkos waved me away, then turned sharply. "You don't understand. What if this doesn't lead us to the answer we want? What if he's a fraud? What if we go through the whole plan and it still fails? Atlantis is still sinking, Caspian. The sirens can't keep it together on their own anymore."

"We'll find a way," I insisted. "We've got to."

Nikkos resumed his pacing for a moment before stopping and spinning to face me with shock.

"What?" I asked.

"Three hours," he mumbled. "Caspian! We can enlist the siren's help. Madeline can come with us and make sure we're not being played."

"I don't want to use Madeline like that," I said. "She's barely gotten the basics of the sway down. Have a little more faith in yourself, Nikkos. You've been setting this up for months."

"Fine, yes, you're right. Meeting over drinks is part of him hearing us out, I've already planned as much. We can get this over with and finally go home."

Go home. This meeting would indeed bring our trip to an end, and with it my time with Madeline.

"Drinks—is it a restaurant or bar?"

"The Port and Mast," he answered.

"Reservations?" I asked.

"I've made them every night at different locations, knowing word may come last minute," he answered.

"I'll bring Madeline, if she's free. I owe her a nice dinner for our little trick out on the beach. It was something of a promise."

Nikkos made a face. "I'll make sure our reservation can accommodate dinner beforehand, you get Madeline and get her into a suitable dress. Formal wear is a must, it's that pompous place on the water. We can meet the mercenary after."

"We can try to explain more about home while we have her attention," I suggested.

"Yes, good," Nikkos said. "Maybe the wine will help our story go down a little easier."

"For you or for her?" I asked.

Nikkos shrugged, and I ran a hand down my face. "I'll call her."

"Good luck, cousin," Nikkos said. "You know what they say: to dance with a siren is to hand her the leash."

MADELINE

That *kiss*.

Touching my fingers to my lips, I grinned. My mouth was on fire from the heat, and the tenderness, and the salt of the water and air.

I stayed out on the beach a while longer, enjoying the temperature of the chilly water as it pushed and pulled the sand across my feet. Caspian was so warm, and under that no-nonsense mask he wore he was actually pretty playful and charming. And he was . . . he was . . .

He was leaving at the end of the week.

Every damn time I think something is going to go my way, and then it never fails to disappoint me. Every. Damn. Time.

And with Caspian I was already getting those too good to be true vibes. Too smooth, too handsome, too nice. That was how they all started off, and I fell for it every time.

Caspian was a beautiful, wonderful, glorious distraction. A dream, if only for a fleeting moment. But soon he'd leave, and any potential trouble would be gone with him. Then it would be right back to no job, and soon to be no apartment.

My phone vibrated in my pocket, and I contemplated ignoring it. With a groan I reached for it, and it lit up as I brought it in front of my face.

"Speak of the devil," I murmured.

Caspian.

"Hello?" I answered.

"Madeline." He seemed breathless, relieved. It sped my heart up just to hear him that way, and his accent just made it all the more attractive.

No, don't fall for it, Maddie.

My tongue darted out, wetting my lips and tasting the salt air.

"Caspian." I didn't know what else to say, only that I really wasn't ready to talk to him again like this. We had just kissed, and I had a lot to process after everything he and Nikkos had told me about their home. Possibly my home too.

"Madeline, we've just had a bit of a situation come up. Would you like to move our dinner up to tonight?"

"Tonight?" I asked, maybe a little too eager for the chance to spend more time with him. I could nearly smell his cologne, hear the way he laughed and the glint of mischief in his eyes, and try as I might, all my desires for him rushed back to the surface.

Fuck, Maddie, get it together! You're such a wet ho for dimples and a basic sense of respect.

"The contact we've come to the mainland to meet with is available tonight on short notice. That means our time here is cut short as well. Nikkos and I intend to wine and dine him, but I was thinking this might be the perfect opportunity to treat you as well, since our time is limited."

"Caspian, I, um, don't know anything about business. I don't even know what you do, actually."

Good point, Mads. What if he's in the Mafia?

He laughed, a soft sound that brushed against the phone. "Sorry, sorry. Let me start at the beginning. Nikkos and I have been charged by our boss, a senator, to secure a contract."

All right, not the Mafia, then.

"What kind of contract?" I asked.

"We are here working for Senator Dimitris, who is trying to secure an item that will assist in the . . . retention of the natural landscape of the island. This contact can get it for us. But I don't expect to bore you with that part, I'd just like to treat you to dinner. Nikkos and I would also like to tell you a little more about home."

Chewing on my bottom lip, I rolled the idea around my head.

"The business part makes me nervous. I don't want to mess things up for you by being there. What if I accidentally speak? And the sway comes out, and everything goes wrong?"

"Maddie." He said my name so softly, so gently over the phone that I nearly didn't hear it over the ocean breeze and distant birds. My throat tightened, ready for the demands. The conflict.

"I understand," Caspian said. "I won't force it on you."

I let out a strained breath.

What?

"You won't?" I asked.

"No, of course not. What kind of man would that make me?" he asked.

Trent. Kennedy. Alex. The whole list, actually.

"Oh," I breathed. Then it fully hit me all at once. Caspian was genuine. He wasn't Trent. He really was that serious mask with a playful guy under it. He was truly talking to me for the sake of it.

"How about this: I treat you to a nice dinner, and once our contact is there you're welcome to sit at the bar and open an obscene tab in my name for drinks and dessert."

At this point, he could ask for my sopping wet panties and I'd probably oblige.

"That's exactly the way to my heart," I answered. "You have a deal."

Caspian laughed, the low rumble of it traveling through the phone and plummeting straight into my chest, hot and comfortable. Goose bumps ran across my arms, and I found myself playing with my necklace, if only so my fingers had something to do.

"Thank you, Maddie. I'm glad to have the chance to treat you to another meal. But this place is also very upscale, do you have anything formal to wear?"

"No," I admitted. "I don't."

"Then it would be my pleasure to gift you something suitable."

"Are you serious?" I asked.

"Are you still on the beach?" Caspian asked, amusement ting-ing his voice with merriment. "We should have enough time to visit a shop before our reservation."

"You're serious," I said.

He laughed again. "Believe me when I say the pleasure is all mine. I'll be right there, stay where you are."

"All right, ack!" A fat drop of rain landed on my shoulder. "Great, it's sprinkling."

"We'll take a car. I'll be right there and we can get you inside somewhere before it really starts coming down. Just a minute, okay?"

"Okay, thank you," I answered, and he hung up.

Too good. Caspian was still too good to be true. And, hell, maybe he did have to leave and break my heart, but I could still return the dress and use the money to, you know, not be home-less. A silver lining to a short and tempting fling with a sexy island businessman.

I spotted him as he came down the steps to the sidewalk that would bring him back to me. I stared with no shame at the suit he had changed into, the picture of him taking off the outfit he had been wearing earlier while we were on the phone just now making me catch my lip between my teeth at the image.

Yeah, Caspian was too good to be true, and I was ready to indulge in the fantasy.

CHAPTER SEVEN

CASPIAN

Within an hour we were out of the rain and able to get a car to take us to a street lined with boutiques. Madeline had her pick of anything she wanted, but when the number of choices was too much to handle, we went with the first store that had a customer walking out of it with a shopping bag. It was clearly a good choice, because the selection of formal wear gave her several options, and when she stepped out of that dressing room in a blue dress that hugged and then draped in all the most flattering places, I thanked the gods for whatever luck had led us this way. And most importantly, she was happy.

We found ourselves outside in the humid evening air, the sidewalk freshly damp but the puddles already clearing up. The light from the shop at our backs cast long shadows across the sidewalk as the sun dipped below the horizon. Soon it would be gone completely, leaving us with the lights from the city and the few stars that shone through the city lights to accompany us into the night.

Madeline stood on the sidewalk, looking at me and letting her eyes linger where she pleased.

"Enjoying yourself?" I mused.

"Yes, actually."

I chuckled as we began to walk. I pulled out my phone again to check on our car. Nearly here, but not quite.

"So," she continued, "I should thank you for the dress. Sorry I didn't already have something nicer, but to be honest, I don't think I've ever worn anything like this before in my life."

"Everyone should be able to enjoy a night out like this at least once," I said.

More than once, for a siren.

She shrugged. "You're right. Too bad that's not the way the world works."

I tilted my head, looking her up and down again. Gods, she really was lovely. "What if I told you it's different in Atlantis?"

Her eyes darted up to meet mine, her full, flushed cheeks enticingly warm in the evening light. "Too good to be true. Everywhere has its problems."

"Nowhere is perfect. But Atlantis is small enough that we can care for all our people. Feeding and clothing and housing the population isn't an issue, we have enough to go around."

"What are your problems, then?" she asked.

I grimaced. "Let's say it's environmental."

"Like pollution?" she asked.

"No, no. It's complicated. Our shores are creeping closer and closer to our streets and homes," I answered.

"So it's sinking? Like Venice? Or Amsterdam?"

"Something like that, yes," I said, impressed. "Once we're in there with Nikkos, feel free to ask all the questions you want, and we'll try to answer them."

She smiled that sly mischievous smile that kept creeping up. I'd been catching more and more glimpses of it as we grew comfortable around each other.

"Are you trying to pitch me a time-share back home?" she asked.

I laughed, checking my phone again and seeing that the car was just around the corner.

"Hardly," I mused, stepping to the edge of the sidewalk and waiting for our ride. "But I have a few things to say about Atlantis that will seem impossible to believe. If I could convince you to come with us, I would love that. You, however, have the choice in your hands no matter what you decide to do. Let Nikkos and me spin you a fairy tale from back home and go on with your life with this night as a memory. Or . . ."

"Or?" she prodded.

"Or believe us, and come see it for yourself. The island would love to have you." The car showed up just in time, and I flagged it over.

Opening the door, I let a contemplative Madeline slide in first. "I hope you're hungry, this place has quite a reputation."

She was careful with the skirt of her dress as she tucked her legs into the car. "Where are we going?"

I closed her door and hurried to the other side, sitting next to her and closing my own door. The driver pulled into traffic and started toward the restaurant.

"It's called the Port and Mast," I answered.

Her eyes widened. "Oh my gosh, that building by the water with the giant pond out front?"

The car finally slowed to a stop, and the driver dropped us in front of the restaurant.

A large, well-sculpted pond lay between us and the front door of the Port and Mast. An elegantly curved bridge carried diners over the water and under an overhang where hanging lights offered a soft glow and a gate to the outdoor seating deck. A host's desk was ready and waiting with more than enough staff to seat each guest the moment they arrived. Just behind that, the stately windows gave a glimpse into the dining floor of the restaurant, where tables were spaced well apart and a violinist played soft music from his alcove stage.

"This is a lot fancier than I thought it was," Madeline observed.

I reached out and offered her my arm. "I'll be right here with you. It's just dinner. A nice dinner with me and Nikkos."

She slipped her arm through mine. "You're right."

"If at any time you become uncomfortable, let me know and I'll ensure you have a ride home. Don't just stay here on my account," I told her.

"No, it's not a problem. Besides, I'm glad to have met you, Caspian. Any more time I can spend with you before you leave is worth it."

My heart sank. Leaving. She still wasn't coming with us, and I had to keep reminding myself of that. A siren so far from Atlantis. But I couldn't make her decisions for her. Maybe next time I came to the mainland I could spend time with her again. Eventually convince her.

"Is everything okay?" Madeline asked.

"Of course. Let's go meet Nikkos, he's near the entrance. No one here is going to be able to keep their eyes off of you."

My arm was on fire from her touch as she leaned closer and whispered, "It's not just 'anyone' I'm hoping can't keep their eyes off of me."

This siren was going to be the death of me.

The worst part of it was that she fucking knew it as she edged the side of her breast into my arm as she held tight.

And we walked over the bridge and to the Port and Mast.

CHAPTER EIGHT

MADELINE

I'm a simple girl.

I like to dress up pretty. Check.

I like feeling sexy and being with men who *make* me feel sexy. Check.

I like music and dancing. Check.

And I really, *really* like food. Check.

The Port and Mast was gorgeous. This was no club, no dive bar, and no house party. The people were gorgeous, the decor was stunning, and the food wafting by on silver trays looked like art.

It was the perfect setting to ask an impossible question. I'd decided an hour ago that I either believed them or I didn't, but all thoughts took me down the same path: Was his Atlantis the one from the stories somehow? Because as much as that didn't seem possible, the things I could do with my voice shouldn't be either.

Caspian's arm was a comfortable place to be as we approached the front of the restaurant. Nikkos was dressed as sharply as his cousin. When we met up with him, he took one look at my appearance and then trained his gaze on the space on my forehead just above my eyebrows. "You look lovely, Madeline."

"Thank you." I stared at Nikkos a moment, unsure about his strange behavior until Caspian leaned into my ear.

"An old trick, to avoid being swayed by a . . . an Atlantean woman's beauty," he explained.

"Oh, okay," I replied. *But what was he going to say before he switched to* Atlantean woman, *I wonder.*

Nikkos went to check on our reservation, and in no time at all we were being seated. The inside of the Port and Mast was just as alluring as the outside as we walked through the interior to the open deck on the other side. The lighting was low and seductive, and the tall planter walls between each table added an air of privacy to an otherwise open space. We were taken to a corner table by the railing at the very edge of the deck. I had to hold in my excitement and remind myself not to stare at the water the whole night.

The curved wooden chairs were more comfortable to sit on than I thought they would be, and the table of thick cuts of dark wood was masculine against the light linen cloth that draped over it and fluttered in the breeze.

Caspian had pulled my chair out for me. He looked so serious. I guess playful Caspian was hidden when we were out in public.

The hostess nodded and stepped back once we were all in our seats. "Sean will be your server tonight, I'll send him right over."

The tables already had menus on them, as well as table settings, candles, and a fresh arrangement of white flowers. I picked up the leather menu folder in front of me and opened it. One page, no prices, and I only knew the dishes that had some kind of steak cut in the name. I quickly closed it again. Another, smaller menu was provided as well. I opened it but only found the wine list. Setting them both down, I looked up as our server approached the table with water and a chilled bottle of wine that Nikkos had requested.

"Good evening." He greeted us. "My name is Sean and I'll be serving your table tonight."

He placed a glass of water and an empty glass in front of each of us skillfully as he spoke.

"Would you like to hear the house specials, or do you have any questions about the menu?" Sean asked.

"Actually, can I see the label for this?" Nikkos said. "I may want to take a bottle home with us."

While Sean was distracting Nikkos with the wine, I nudged Caspian's knee with my own.

"Caspian, I don't know what half of this menu says," I whispered.

"Do you want me to order for you?" he offered.

"Please."

"Any allergies or things you don't like?" he murmured, leaning closer.

Fuck, he smells good.

Wait.

Focus, Maddie!

"Not really," I whispered. "No weird things like octopus or snails?"

He nodded. "I'll keep it safe."

The waiter listed off the evening specials and I listened half-heartedly as I took a drink of my water. He offered us something called a sommelier, which we apparently declined, and then Sean took our orders. Thankfully, I didn't really have to say anything, and Caspian ordered me something French, I think.

And then, finally, the commotion died down and the table drifted into casual conversation. A lot of it was Nikkos enthusing over the wine, but it was nice to just sit and listen as the quieter cousin had something to talk about that excited him. Caspian was content to lean back in his chair and enjoy the moment of peace as well.

At some point they brought bread, which was delicious. And then a salad, which was delicious. The soft violin being played inside could still be heard out here, and it almost put me to sleep.

"Madeline?" Nikkos brought me out of my contented haze.

"Hm?" I picked up my wine glass, taking another small mouthful and savoring it before letting it slide down my throat. Caspian checked that I wasn't getting drunk before offering to pour me another glass of the sweet red wine. I said yes, though I'd stop after this glass. I'd let him keep up some illusion that I was more refined than I really was; he didn't need to know I could kill a keg stand and that a glass of wine wouldn't get the better of me. Because tonight I could pretend all I wanted, and I chose to pretend I was a part of Caspian's easier world.

I liked these guys. Genuinely, I did. But it was probably time to throw my wild imagination out there and get this over with. Accusing two people you've just met of being from a fictional city was probably friendship-ending, right? Unless it turned out to be true—and if it *was* true, I had no idea what I was going to do with that information.

"All right." I leaned forward. "Thank you for the lovely dinner. I know we haven't made it through all the food yet, but I want to talk about Atlantis now."

"Of course," Nikkos said. "We promised you answers, what better time than the present?"

"You already know Atlantis is an island," Caspian began. "Our primary language is Atlantean, but many residents also speak second languages or more."

"Hold on." I paused him. "That's interesting and all, and I do want to ask about all that stuff. But first I have a specific question."

One that I hope doesn't sound too out there.

"Anything," Caspian said. "What is it?"

I licked my lips, taking a deep breath. "Are you talking about the real Atlantis and magic sirens?"

Nikkos spit out his wine.

"At this point, I think you just don't want me to write you off as making it all up. Or, I don't know, you believe it or it's all a hallucination or something. Right now, I'm going in with an open mind, okay? So all of this dancing around with your words can stop now, because I'm willing to hear you out, but only if you stop changing your sentences and eyeing each other like you have some big secret."

"She's not wrong," Caspian murmured.

"There's no precedent," Nikkos said. "How do we begin?"

I sat back, letting my words sink in. Nikkos and Caspian looked at each other, then glanced at me and said a few words in what I guessed was Atlantean. That was fine, let them deliberate. If anything, I was getting chills that they hadn't laughed in my face at the accusation. I mean, *Atlantis*. Sirens. Holy shit.

Finally, Caspian turned to me. "You're right. We owe you what we can tell you about the sirens."

"Now, Madeline," Nikkos started, "part of the slow nature of revealing things about our homeland is because we are very protective of it."

"But not to me," I said. "You can't tell me I'm part of it and then not let me in on the secret."

Nikkos pinched the bridge of his nose. "Yes, yes, you're right. But what I'm trying to say is that not everyone accepts the whole truth of it quickly. We had to divulge it in easy to swallow pieces."

"Madeline," Caspian said, his voice low and soft, "Atlantis is not named after the lost city."

"It *is* the lost city," Nikkos finished.

I went numb. It was like I expected it, but at the same time, I still didn't.

No, keep an open mind.

They'd just admitted they didn't want to scare me away. They were both sane and capable men, as far as I could tell. If they meant me harm, they would have done something to me by now. I could at least hear them out.

Caspian swept his fingers through his dark hair, closing his eyes and tipping his head back. "Do you remember when I told you the city was sinking? It happened a long time ago. Before any of us were born. And when you asked if it was like Venice, it's a little more serious than that."

I frowned. "How serious?"

"The city summit lies about thirty-seven meters below sea level," Nikkos answered.

I bit the inside of my cheek, trying not to have any weird out-bursts. Thinking before speaking wasn't always my strong suit, so I was doing my best to be careful.

"So, the island is gone?" I asked.

"No," Caspian said firmly. "A good portion of the city is still dry and populated. I never once lied to you when I said we had beaches, parks, houses, markets."

"Then how is that possible?" I asked.

"The sirens," Nikkos answered. "They—*you*—are capable of saving our civilization."

They were both anxiously watching for a reaction from me. I didn't blame them; what they were telling me was that they came from the lost city of Atlantis, and it was underwater.

Keep an open mind, Mads. You can do this.

I nodded slowly. "I'm still listening. How do the sirens do that, Nikkos?"

"Here we are." The server had returned, a dish in each hand and two servers following him with the rest.

My hand flew to my chest, and I closed my eyes. The server had startled the shit out of me, and just when I had asked my most bizarre question yet.

"Tagliatelle mare e monti with scampi all'aglio for the gentleman." Sean announced the dishes as he set a plate of what looked like black spaghetti in front of Nikkos.

My stomach sank. *Please,* please, *Caspian. Please have ordered me something normal.*

Sean took the dishes from the servers behind him. "The caramelized honey-ginger tenderloin in white truffle oil for the lady."

"No funny business," Caspian said as Sean placed my plate in front of me. He leaned back while the server put his own dish, a steak, in front of him.

Nikkos held a strained expression until the waitstaff was gone, then turned to me. "A moment, let's take a bite, and I'll answer when we're more secluded."

Sean had stopped nearby, answering questions for another table of guests. I nodded and turned to my plate.

Heaven. I could see why this place was so popular, but that was probably to be expected with the price tag. After the first bite, I was gone. I had to resist eating like the uncultured pig I wanted to be, but I was thoroughly distracted by the questions at hand. I set my fork down and looked at Nikkos.

He sighed, keeping his voice low as he eyed Sean retreating to the kitchens. "Just as you can use your voice to convince a person to do something, a siren can also learn to convince the ocean."

"Convince *the ocean*?" I repeated, just to make sure I understood.

Keep an open mind, Mads.

"Atlantis, or at least as much of the city as we could save after the catastrophe, is in a bubble. It was only thanks to the power of the sirens back then, and the continued power of the sirens today, that we survive."

"The sirens can sing to the ocean," Nikkos said, "and it sings to them in return."

My eyes widened. The ocean sings to the sirens. Calls them.

I whipped around to look over the railing and across the dark water. All those times I'd gotten the desire to go to the ocean. To swim out as far as I could or to dive down deep and just be in the water. I wasn't crazy; it was a siren thing.

Except that did sound crazy.

But what if it wasn't?

But what if it was?

"Maddie?" Caspian asked.

"I'm okay. I'm just taking it all in," I said. "So, these sirens keep the city safe how, exactly?"

"They hold the water at bay," Nikkos said. "A bubble of sorts, surrounding the city and holding back the tide."

"A magic bubble," I deadpanned. "Open mind, okay, bubble. Bubble it is. So, that's a big task, huh?"

Caspian frowned. "Their task is everything; without them, our people would be gone."

"To make matters worse," Nikkos added, "we've had a decline in numbers over the decades. Their work is a lot, and many choose not to remove themselves from the task to have children."

"Which is why we don't know how you could have possibly ended up out here," Caspian said. "No story to explain why you were in Michigan makes any sense. The sirens are loved and accounted for."

"Maybe you had a siren leave before and I'm a descendant?" I offered.

The pair shook their heads in unison as Nikkos spoke up. "The sirens don't leave. We don't have a case of that since before the sinking. Hundreds of years or more of recorded history, and not one missing siren."

Taking a bite of food, I chewed slowly and contemplated their story. So many unanswered questions, but so many things they'd said resonated with me. I took a deep breath, letting it out slowly. "Thank you for your honesty, both of you. I think I need time to absorb what you said."

"Of course," Caspian murmured. "Whenever you're ready for more, we'll be here to talk."

I ground my back teeth, curling my fingers into frustrated fists in my lap. "Except, you won't be. You're leaving after this meeting, right?"

"True, our responsibilities carry us back home," Nikkos said. "But we'll come back, and the Senate will very much want to know about you."

"Definitely come back," Caspian added. "We'll give you time to think all of this over."

"Okay." I sighed. "That makes sense. I can spend however long it takes you to come back around thinking about it, right?"

"Absolutely," Nikkos said.

"Because this is still a lot to swallow," I continued. "Atlantis? Sirens? I don't know if I believe it yet or if I think you're spinning the biggest story I've ever heard, and I'd be a fool to fall for it."

They didn't have anything to add to that, but one more question popped in my head. "Does this come with a tail?"

Nikkos frowned. "Tail?"

"Mermaids?" I asked, a tiny four-year-old part of me hopeful.

"No mermaid tails, I'm afraid." Caspian chuckled.

"Rip-off," I muttered. "All the trouble this voice has caused me, and I don't even get a magical tail."

Caspian covered his mouth with his fist, but I could still see the smile around it. At least Nikkos had the decency to hide his amusement with a napkin.

But in all seriousness, they were still telling me the wildest thing I'd ever heard.

A siren. *Those* sirens.

Atlantis. *That* Atlantis.

So help me, what was I really?

I just didn't know, and I didn't know that I was ready to.

We had dinner in relative silence after that. The food was good, but the distractions in my head were too consuming for me to also hold a conversation. I could only imagine it was the same for Caspian and Nikkos. We reached the pinnacle of the evening, and the air buzzed with tension.

It came on so suddenly I was startled. Sean had returned to clear our plates, but while he worked, Caspian and Nikkos were watching the door.

The hair on the back of my neck stood up at the sudden tension, and I reached for my wine glass. I wasn't entirely sure what was about to go down, but I was sure as hell I wanted alcohol with me when it did.

As Sean moved away with the last of our empty plates, Nikkos checked his phone. "He's here."

"Yeah, I sensed him," Caspian agreed, turning to me. "Are you still sure you want to wait for us? I don't think it will take long, but you never know."

"The business meeting, right." Goose bumps crawled across my arms. "What was this for again? Who is it you're meeting?"

Caspian's mouth was a thin line. Nikkos took a big drink of wine before answering. "It's about the sinking of Atlantis. We need him to negotiate for an item that might fix the problem."

"Like a lawyer or something?" I asked.

"No," they said in unison. Caspian sighed. "I'll tell you the whole story later, if it works out. For now, do you still want to wait for us at the bar or should I get you a ride?"

"I'll wait."

He slipped a large bill into my hand. "All right, go get yourself the most sugared-up desert you can order and another glass of wine."

"Good luck," I said as I walked away—and meant it. Making my way up to the bar, I shivered as a man passed by; I turned to watch him.

He was nearing middle age with a light brush of gray highlighting his temples in an otherwise ginger-colored head of hair. He carried himself like the most dangerous person in the room, and he probably was, though I didn't see a gun or anything on him. He wasn't dressed for this place at all, but despite his jeans and flannel shirt they let him in anyway. When he passed by me, his serious face dropped for long enough that I swear he shot me a wink and a grin, and then his mask of hardness slipped right back in place as he walked over to Caspian and Nikkos.

Maybe I was onto something with that Mafia idea.

Happy to turn my back on the intense man, I left them to their mysterious meeting and sat at the bar.

"Excuse me, what wine pairs with the most chocolate covered thing on your menu?" I asked.

The bartender made her way over and laughed. "For a cute

little thing like you? Let me see if the chef is feeling fancy and we'll whip you up a real treat."

"Thanks." I beamed.

I don't know if it was the sway or the wine or the dress I was wearing. but I was ready for a treat, and a few minutes later I was not disappointed with the plate and the wine that came to me.

And while I slid my tongue over a spoon that cut through a decadent slice of molten chocolate cake like butter, I let my imagination run wild with the intoxicating scent of Caspian that still hung around me.

Atlantis, huh? Maybe it wasn't such a stretch after all.

CHAPTER NINE

CASPIAN

Madeline was safely on her way to the bar while our contact approached. His shaggy orange hair and matching beard stood out against his green and black flannel shirt. His eyes looked as though they had seen a great number of years beyond what his physical appearance would convey, and he carried himself with an all-encompassing air of confidence. He strode through the Port and Mast without a care about anyone looking his way, heading straight for our table. He pulled out a chair with one booted foot and sat down.

"You lads are persistent, you know that?" he asked.

Nikkos exchanged a worried look with me, and I poured a glass of the wine, scooting it to the mercenary, while keeping my eyes on him. His accent was thick, starting from somewhere in Scotland, but with a hefty bit of other sounds mixed in over the years. He didn't stay in one place long, if his reputation was to be believed.

"If we came off as persistent, it's only because of how notable your skills are, Gavin," I offered. "When I heard you were in North America, I knew we had to meet."

Gavin eyed the wine for a moment before knocking it back in one go. Nikkos made a choking sound, probably internally screaming at the treatment of such an expensive vintage, but Gavin just set the empty glass aside and stared me down. "I was here visiting a friend. You're lucky the witching network could get a hold of me at all. I don't pay them much mind, as they aren't on good terms with someone I care about."

"Then it's fortunate for us the message got through," I said. "You have an impressive record of finishing difficult jobs, and what we ask might be *very* difficult."

He scratched his chin under his thick beard, eyes narrowing on me, clearly assessing both me and my cousin. "You've got me here now," Gavin said as he leaned forward. "I suggest ya get to the point."

I could feel Nikkos's foot bobbing up and down under the table, only his toes connected to the floor in a nervous tic of his. I couldn't blame him; this man radiated intent and skill. Gavin was dangerous.

"I'll get straight to it, then. My people are seeking an artifact, and I believe it's a vampire relic of power."

Gavin raised one thick eyebrow, crossing his arms as he leaned back in his chair. "I don't know what you've heard about me, but those cunts don' like me much. There'll be no waltzin' in and borrowing great-granny's teacups or whatever the fuck yer after."

"They don't like anyone, and your chances of locating such an item are much better than mine," I answered.

Gavin nodded slowly, a smile that was both eager and unsettling spreading across his face. "Aye, so they don't. Tell me one thing first. When you say your people need this item . . ." He trailed off, leaving me to fill in the blank.

Nikkos took a small box from his coat pocket and slid it across the table. Gavin opened it, revealing a small, unmarked bar of gold. The mercenary whistled, his eyes sharp and his smile spreading. "I s'pose I could hear you out."

"If you're willing to undergo a wordbinding, we can move forward with the discussion," I said. "As it stands, we've arranged for a witch from the area who is ready to perform the binding as early as tonight if you're ready."

Gavin chuckled, raising two fingers to his lips. "I'm no stranger to these things; I'd wondered as much from yer message. So I brought my own." He whistled, a loud, high sound that turned heads and visibly upset some of the staff. But a moment later, a woman in a black dress and combat boots was walking through the restaurant, straight toward our table.

Nikkos and I exchanged glances, and enough hushed words in Atlantean, to decide any witch would do, as long as they were of the Book of Sisters.

The woman—with dark hair, dark lipstick, dark every-thing—sat down next to Gavin. "Hello, there, I'm supposed to do a wordbinding?"

My cousin cleared his throat. "I'm Nikkos, a pleasure to—"

The witch held up a hand. "The less I know, the better. I'll do the binding according to the book, then I'm out of here." She looked at Gavin. "And I had to learn this stupid ritual just for you, ass."

Gavin pinched her cheek and gave it a little wiggle. "Aye, and I'm at yer eternal service for it."

She swatted his hand away and pulled out three silver coins. "Let's get this over with. Whoever wants to speak the secret, put one of these under your tongue. Gav, you too." Then she slipped one into her own mouth, securing her to the secret as well.

I pulled one toward me, eyeing the coin for long enough to

know there wasn't much that stood out about it, then slipped it under my tongue. The silver was unpleasant, but I knew it was something about purity or truths that made it a requirement.

The witch pulled a book from her bag and read from a marked page in a language I didn't understand, and then finished with the words that would start the binding. "Speak your secrets, keep them safe. No bond or blood can this binding break." When she was done, she pointed at me, and I took it as my signal to start.

Nikkos slid me the scrap of paper on which he had prepared our exact wording, the most inclusive detail we could manage. Reading from it, I did my best to speak clearly around the coin in my mouth.

"This task is for Atlantis," I began. Gavin's expression didn't move, but the witch's was filled with curiosity. "You will not speak of Atlantis, its people, or the task for which we wish to hire you. You will not reveal the location of the item we seek, or the location of Atlantis to others for any reason. You will not reveal what job is requested of you. You will not reveal the artifact we seek. You will not reveal myself or my cousin. You will not reveal the origin of the gold you have already received. You will not speak it, you will not show it, you will not reveal it."

"I will not speak it, I will not show it, I will not reveal it," Gavin said, then spit the coin from his mouth onto the table. "Bah, I need another drink."

"I will not speak it, I will not show it, I will not reveal it," the witch echoed, and removed her coin by hand to wipe it on a napkin. "It's done, I'm out."

She stood and walked away, just as abruptly as she'd come. Gavin scoffed. "Oy, I'm still ridin' back with ya, right?"

The witch disappeared into the restaurant without a word.

"Eh, I'll figure that one out in a bit." Gavin leaned forward. "So, you bastards really are still out there. I wondered as much," he murmured. "And what relic could you possibly want from the leeches?"

Nikkos pulled out a scrap of paper from his coat. It was a copy, as exact as we could make it, from an old tome in Atlantis—intel that our ancestors kept on other kingdoms in the lost worlds millennia ago. Possibly forgotten by all but us and the owners of the relic.

Nikkos slid the paper across to Gavin, and the mercenary studied the drawing of the three-jeweled amulet. The drawing itself depicted a structure built to house the artifact, and the description read out the purpose of magical amplification. Dimitris's hope, our hope, was that we could finally free Atlantis from the sea that fought tirelessly to swallow us whole. The gods our ancestors had angered long ago with our pride and arrogance hadn't been heard from in lifetimes, but their ancient curse still hungered for our watery grave.

"With the help of this relic, we hope to push back the sea once and for all," I said, as his eyes scrolled over every inch of the page.

"And what magic is it you possess that could perform that kind of feat? Even with this thing in your hands."

Shaking my head, I resisted the urge to glance over to Madeline. Above all else, any Atlantean would die before revealing our sirens.

"I'm afraid that will have to remain a secret."

Gavin grunted, his eyes falling back to the paper. "It won't be cheap. I'm not even sure where the damn thing is, if it still exists."

"But you know how to look," I pressed. "You have your ways, don't you?"

That smile crept back onto his face, an expression that had seen many dark and cruel twists of time, and that knew how to survive them. "I might know a dusty old bastard who can point me in a direction or two, though that bindin' will make it challenging. So, what's your offer?"

Nikkos was finally able to stop the shaking of his foot as the ghost of a smile lifted his expression. He was ready to answer this one. After all, much of the research and acquisition on this end had been his doing. "We are prepared to offer you two golden statues, each guaranteed to weigh more than your weight in pure Atlantean gold."

At that, Gavin's eyebrows shot up, his interest clearly piqued.

"And a boon from our superior and senator, Dimitris," I added, using terms for an unbreakable favor that anyone from the supernatural world would be accustomed to.

Gavin chuckled. "I'm no fae, Atlantean, but I'll take the boon all the same."

There was a lot of speculation as to what Gavin actually was, and we decided the boon would be temptation enough for most creatures, even non-fae.

"Do we have a deal?" Nikkos asked.

Gavin scratched his chin again, eyeing the page with the relic on it. "All right, you've got yourself a deal."

MADELINE

I stayed lost in my thoughts for the rest of our time in the Port and Mast. My head was spinning, and I kept glancing at Caspian and Nikkos and their mystery guests while I polished off my cake and wine. Who was that woman who had walked through here? She didn't even stay very long. And who was that scary guy? When he left, leaving the same way he had entered, goose bumps prickled down my back. But that also meant Caspian and Nikkos were done with their business, so I decided to get some fresh air before Caspian's presence could tempt me again. My thoughts were dangerous enough around him as it was.

My shoes clicked lightly as I walked away from the bar. Breathe in through the nose, out through the mouth. Moving across the deck and around to the front of the building, I walked over to the fencing by the pond and stared into the water.

Movement under the surface told me they stocked the pond with some kind of fish, though they also grew quite a few aquatic plants, so it was hard to see when patches of lily pads and tall reeds blocked the view through the water.

I sighed, laying my head in my arms on the rail, unsure how to feel about the evening. I loved it, and yet I couldn't stop thinking about their boat sailing away. But I had been able to spend time with Caspian and Nikkos, and that was pretty cool. I smiled at the thought. I'd never met anyone like them before, especially Caspian.

Atlantis, huh?

A ripple over the pond. A bug had landed on the water only to be gobbled up right away by a big goldfish. Or maybe a koi. I could probably have seen better in the daylight, but right now it was all a murky blur.

"Hey, are you all right?" The voice was low and warm, and I lifted my head to face Caspian.

"I was just getting some fresh air. But you look pleased after your meeting. Shouldn't you be in there celebrating?" I asked.

He breathed out a laugh. "It went well, but now I'm more worried about you."

I stood up straight and turned to face him. He had undone his tie and opened the top buttons of his shirt to show off a hint of golden chest underneath. His aftershave still clung lightly to him under the musk of wine and salt air.

"I'm fine. I guess I'm having mixed feelings on this sway thing," I admitted. "This siren thing too."

I need your touch.

We fell silent as we both looked out over the pond and to the ocean beyond it. The stars overhead were nearly visible. I hated how I couldn't see them properly out here. At least back in Michigan I had had a clear view from the middle-of-nowhere homes I'd grown up in. It was the one thing I really missed about that place. I thought back on the bonfires, waking up to cows from the farm down the road, muddy springs and frozen winters. It was a place worth being for some, but down here I felt a little closer to where I was supposed to be. I think.

I sighed, a crooked smile on my lips as I looked at him. "I'm jealous."

Caspian laughed, the bob of his throat distracting me. His loose tie moved as he tilted his head. "Of what?"

"You really love your island, huh?" I shrugged. "Michigan never felt like home. And I came here expecting life to get better, but I'm still struggling."

"And what would make somewhere exactly the place you'd want to be?" he asked.

I started slowly. "I would want a place where I could be active with friends. I thought the beach would offer a lot of swimming, running, surfing, dancing, things like that. One time I tried to join a volleyball league, but I chickened out on bonding, and by game three I don't think anyone even knew my name."

"You'd prefer to be active, and social," he murmured. "What else did you leave behind when you moved?"

How to explain the culture growing up in a small town. "I also wanted to find more community down here. I'll give that one to the Midwest, no one has dropped me off a bag of zucchini from the garden they overplanted since I've been down here, that's for sure."

"Too many of my neighbors are busybodies, but they mean well," Caspian said. "If Nonni down the corner catches me after a busy week, she pulls me into her kitchen and makes me eat or else she'll smack me with that wooden spoon she's always swinging about."

A laugh burst from me, picturing Caspian being scolded by an old lady. "Yes, that! That's exactly what I mean. It just feels like I can't fully be myself. Not comfortably. Something always goes wrong. I say the wrong things, call attention at the worst moments, or can't connect with new people in general. That's probably not a community problem, though; that's a me problem."

"I don't think that's true," Caspian said. "You've had a hard time, and you can't ignore the problems the sway has caused you, but you're too charming a person to say you should have a hard time making connections. Everyone deserves to feel loved, Maddie. I promise you that."

"Caspian, listen—"

"There you two are!" Nikkos came from behind us, loosening his own tie as he walked over.

"Maddie, what were you about to say?" Caspian asked, moving a hand to rest on my arm.

How ridiculous. I had enough problems as it was staying afloat in Florida. Why would I move to a new place where I really had no assets? At least here I could live in my car if I needed to. I knew what a food-pantry line was. I knew how to find a shelter if I had to. Asking for any more help leads to demands for repayment in one way or another. Besides, Caspian's offer scared me. Maybe they were right—maybe I was from there, but I didn't know anything about it. Moving to a whole new country was intimidating. And what was his plan anyway? Bring a strange girl back home with him, and then what—sleep with me and toss me out the door?

Except that didn't sound like Caspian. But I'd thought those things before, and it had never worked out. Not for me. Not for a kid who got passed from place to place because they wouldn't speak. The therapists didn't know what to do with me. The school didn't know what to do with me. My own parents didn't even leave me a name, just dropped me off in one of those fire station boxes. I don't know that I'd even want to know them if I was offered the chance. What I wanted now were the people who would choose me on their own.

Everything I desperately wanted could be summed up in five words: I wanted to be wanted.

"No, it's nothing. I just need to grab my bag from the coat check."

"I can take care of that," Nikkos offered. "Do you have your ticket?"

I pulled it from the top band of my dress and handed it over.

"I'll be right back." Nikkos took the ticket and went over by the host's desk to retrieve my things.

"Maddie." Caspian drew my attention again. His warm hand was still on my arm but I moved, and it fell away.

I took a slight step back. "I'm fine, really," I lied. "Just tired. I want to go home."

He studied my eyes for a moment. I wasn't using the sway on him. I *wouldn't* use the sway on him. No tricks, just backing off slowly and calmly until I had to watch him leave in a couple of days. Maybe I'd see him again in a few months. Long enough for me to figure out how I felt about all this Atlantis stuff. They did say they'd be back.

"Here you are," Nikkos announced, handing me my bag from the coat check. "Is that everything? I've ordered a ride, and it should be here any moment now."

"Maddie—"

"Yes, that's everything. Thank you for dinner, guys. I really appreciate it." I stepped away, not letting Caspian see my face as I walked over the bridge and to the parking lot.

CHAPTER TEN

MADELINE

The car ride was quiet.

Nikkos and Caspian were understandably pleased with the results of the night, whatever their meeting entailed, but even they must have been tired because they were both content to sit and relax. Their conversations were brief but celebratory as our driver took us down the road where I could watch the ocean on our way. I held my bag in my lap and wondered if I should have changed before riding in a crowded car all the way home.

The pull of the ocean. It was real. The sway was real too. It was all real.

I mean, of course I believed Caspian eventually, but the feel of the sway was becoming stronger, and now there was no denying it. Something was going on with my voice, and it kind of freaked me out. The stuff I'd found online about sirens was all so manipulative. Luring people in? Tricking them? Drowning them? I knew I wouldn't do that last part, but maybe the rest of it I'd already been doing by accident.

I lowered my head until I was practically leaning on the window. Fuck, what a disaster. If I'd known about this sway thing before, if I'd been in control of how to use it, or rather *not* use it, would I have ever ended up with Trent? Would I have still been called a slut throughout high school? What was wrong with me? What had I done to deserve this?

I never, *ever*, wanted to be with someone who didn't want to be with me of their own accord.

Sheepishly, I glanced over at Caspian. He was smiling, reading something on his phone while Nikkos was rambling in their native language.

Caspian, was our kiss even real?

My heart tightened in my chest, and I pressed a hand over it. Learning to control this was the best and possibly the worst thing to ever happen to me. Now I wouldn't be able to use it on people when I didn't want to, but now I would question every relationship I'd ever have going forward.

"Here's stop number one," the driver announced.

We slowed and pulled over on the street that ran in front of my apartment. It was just around a corner, facing an alley the taxi couldn't access, but as close as he could get to it.

I turned to face Caspian and Nikkos long enough to give them a smile. "Thank you again for dinner," I said.

"The pleasure was ours, Madeline," Nikkos answered. "I hope we can see you again before we go. We'll keep in touch either way, of course."

"Me too. Good night, guys." I turned to open the door and get out before either of them could see I was in my own head and about to lose it.

"Good night, Madeline," Caspian called after me. "I'll message you later."

"Okay." I answered without turning around, closing the door. The car pulled into the street again, rejoining traffic and carrying Nikkos and Caspian to the beach.

My bottom lip quivered, and I clutched my bag tight to my chest.

Get it together, Maddie. Sort it out tomorrow.

I let out a slow breath and began to walk.

The streetlights illuminated the area well. I had plenty of light to dig around in the bag and get my keys from my shorts pocket so I could get inside quickly and take off the dress. A dress I'd try to return or at least sell. Maybe a pawn shop? Or a secondhand clothing store? Whatever I could get for it would have to be enough for another month, so I could find more work, and I fucking hated that I was in this situation at all.

I wasn't paying a lot of attention to my surroundings while I was digging for my keys, so when a *bang* made me jump I looked up to see a dude in my doorway.

"Hey!" I shouted and stopped moving toward the building, making sure I was in the light and anyone who looked out after I yelled would see me. "What are you doing in my apartment?"

The door was open behind him, and when he turned and came out to face me he was holding one of my packed boxes, which he had just smacked against the doorway.

"Hey!" I screamed, hoping one of my neighbors would hear. "That's my stuff, thief!"

"Calm down, lady," the guy yelled back down to me from the second floor. "I'm putting it on the lawn and changing the lock. The landlord hired me, you're being evicted."

My heart stopped. "It's not Friday yet! I have until tomorrow!"

The guy looked down at his watch and I thought he was going to drop my box. "Friday is in half an hour. You got your rent?"

"Yes! I mean, not with me. Just give me a couple of hours, I'm sure I can find a pawnshop that's still open."

"Nah, sorry, lady. I've got another job after this one. Best of luck." The guy came out of the apartment and went down the stairs, where he set the box down on a big pile of stuff I hadn't seen in the dark.

"My stuff!" I yelled and ran over. "This isn't even legal, is it?"

By the time I made it to the spot, the guy was leaving, getting in a big black truck and starting the engine. He had left me behind with the exact thing I had been afraid of.

The little furniture I had was in a part of the yard that was always shaded and the grass had a hard time growing, meaning the rain from earlier in the day had made it a muddy mess seeping into my boxes and sofa.

I ran up to my apartment and tried the key. Just as the man had said, the locks had been changed. I took a moment to lean my forehead against the door, taking deep breaths. Then I headed back down to assess the damage.

I dropped my bag on the sofa and pulled off the nice shoes Caspian had bought me, then pulled open the random boxes. Clothes, the one picture album I had, shoes, random junk I didn't need like candles or old flower vases. Even my bed frame and mattress had been propped on their side against a corner of the building.

As I stood there in the nicest dress I'd ever owned, rummaging through my whole life's efforts in a dirty yard, the tears started, blurring my vision then running down my face and dripping off my chin in an endless trickle of sorrow and frustration.

I picked up one of the boxes to move it and the bottom of it fell open. Makeup, shower gel, hair accessories, and my box of cheap jewelry fell into the mud with a splash that scattered across my feet.

I reached out and held on to the arm of the sofa so I wouldn't just break down on my knees into the mud.

"Why?" I screamed and cried. I kicked. I threw the empty cardboard as far as it would go. The wind caught it, stopping it in its tracks and making it fall short with an unsatisfying smack on the grass. My shoulders shook, and my throat stung with grief and effort.

Why? Why me? Why was it always me? Why couldn't I pull myself out of this hellish spiral and onto solid ground for once? I sat there, curled up on my old sofa, sobbing my heart out. I cried so hard I nearly threw up. After a while, when I was finally out of tears and my stomach hurt from the emotional outburst that had just wrecked my body, I stood up.

"Fuck," I said, wiping my face with the back of my hand.

All right, okay, I could make it through this. Step one to any workout is to make a plan and warm up.

My eyes darted around the boxes. Make a plan. Okay. My plan for the immediate future should be somewhere to sleep, and some-where to keep my things. Right? Yes. So, if I put the essentials and anything that I really wanted to keep in my car, that would work for now. It wasn't ideal, but it was a dry place with locks.

Caspian surfaced in my thoughts for a moment, but I shut it down. I was a mess, way more of a mess than I'd told either of them. And I was still absorbing all that information from dinner; and they had to leave now that their business was done. There was no time for me to collect my life enough to move right now—I didn't have any rent money let alone however much it would cost to move to freaking Atlantis. No, I had to pull myself together, and when they came back to Florida I would be more prepared to go.

I walked over and began sorting. I didn't have a lot of stuff, but I still wasn't sure it would all fit. The furniture certainly wouldn't, but I wasn't attached to it anyway. But my bed had a quilt on it I'd gotten from some church donation one Christmas, and it was one of my favorite things, or at least something nice enough that I'd kept it with me since I was little-ish. There wasn't a lot of that to go around.

Pulling the quilt free of the mattress and grabbing a pillow while I was there, I walked around to the parking lot, where my car sat under a tree. Pillow, blanket, check. I could sleep and be warm.

Next, I pulled open another box, where I found my old backpack. It was my gym bag, but when I was going to see the inside of a gym again was beyond me. I emptied it of workout shirts and instead filled it with the things that had fallen from my bathroom box into the mud. Hygiene products, a towel, my makeup bag. Any remaining space was taken up by my laptop and charge cords. That went into the car too.

I eyed my jewelry box, but there wasn't much in there beyond trinkets from old boyfriends that I just didn't have the heart to care about anymore. Losing my apartment put a lot of things in perspective, and the reality was that I just didn't want as many of my possessions as much as I thought I did.

The rest of it was clothes and stupid decorations that I thought would make my life feel better. Cheap rugs, thrift-store art, and throw pillows. Things I had scavenged where I could find them. I sifted through my clothes for my favorite things and put them in the car. The rest could go to the next scavengers who needed them.

My coat, some clothes, and my photo album filled up my trunk while the back seat contained my new bedroom. Running my fingers over the glossy white cover of the photo album, I flipped it open. My favorite picture was front and center. Me and Mr. Freeman, and it was the most genuine smile I had in any picture I'd ever taken. There he was, sitting on his folding chair outside the gym. The door with chipped red paint, the hand-painted sign above us. He was even holding his coffee mug and a cigarette in the same hand. My bottom lip wobbled as if I was going to start bawling again, but I held it in. I closed the album. Mr. Freeman always said a tough place was just the time between two better places. I could do this. I could scrape myself together. Maybe even find work and save up enough to get an apartment in Atlantis, as bizarre as that thought was.

I took my old shower curtain, tossing the plastic layer and using the pink floral side to cover the things I owned so you couldn't look into my car and see my whole life laid out for the taking.

Once I had gone through everything, I looked at the mess that was left and flipped it off. Then I turned to my car. I refused to cry as I looked over what I'd done. It was a small car, for sure, but it didn't look half bad. I even thought I could get a good night's sleep in it. Just not here.

Still in my expensive dress, I got in the car and drove off. Somewhere. Anywhere. Something familiar that could give me whatever comfort I could take from my surroundings.

I drove down the coast. The ocean at night was stunning. If anything was going to comfort me tonight, it was going to be the stars over the dark water as it lapped at the sand.

Only a short distance from the apartment building was a favorite stop. I was familiar with it, and it had a gentle downhill view of the ocean and whatever we could see of the stars here in the city. The coffee shop was dark when I pulled up to the sidewalk across from it, but I knew in a few hours the early-bird baristas would be coming in to get ready to open.

That was a comfort. Comfort enough that I parked the car, pulled my front seats up all the way, and settled into the back seat. I even sucked it up and found an alley with hopefully no observers where I could pee behind a dumpster. It was probably the most humiliating thing I'd had to resort to so far, and I felt like I would have a lot worse ahead of me if I couldn't fix my situation soon.

I wiggled out of the dress. It wasn't easy and it took some time, but eventually I was able to lay it in the front seat and pull on an old gym shirt and a pair of shorts. With my quilt and pillow, I got somewhat comfortable in the seats so I could look out the back window and see a sliver of the sky.

Now, lying still in the back of an old beat-up car and pretending I was okay, the tears flowed.

Step one was out of the way, but what was step two? The car was only so safe to stay in, and without an address of my own, finding work just got ten times harder. I'd never been homeless before. I'd come close, but never quite landed there. Where did I start? What did I do? Where did I pee, or shower, or eat?

What good was my voice if it still landed me in this situation?

Asking myself the same questions over and over, I curled up tighter in my quilt. What now? How to fix it? The sounds of the nighttime traffic lulled me, but once again I was alone in the world. This time, I didn't even have hope.

CHAPTER ELEVEN

MADELINE

The snap of a ticket being placed under my windshield wipers startled me awake. The parking meters had started back up for the day and I hadn't put any money in mine. At least the ticket would act as enough of a decoy that I didn't have to put any coins in the meter now.

Paying for the ticket is a problem for later, Maddie.

I was wildly disoriented under my quilt, with a terrible pain in my neck and something hard poking my leg. And then it hit me that I was in my car. Because I was homeless. My stomach fell. What in the world was I supposed to do now? A homeless shelter?

Chin up, Mads. This isn't the first time you've had everything you own in your car. It's just the first time you were unsure of the destination at the other end.

My eyes slid down to my backpack. I could always do some research and find one. I was next to a café with free internet. Would they let me come in and just have water and use the Wi-Fi? But

I was hungry too. Café food wasn't exactly cheap, but it wasn't like I could go grocery shopping and make affordable home-cooked meals.

I pushed the quilt aside and sat up, rubbing the sleep out of my face and groaning. Where could I brush my teeth? The café? I eyed my backpack. It did have all my clean-up stuff in it, as well as my laptop. I might even change my clothes, and with a quick and dirty sink bath I could chill in the coffee shop and come up with a plan on how to get out of this mess.

With new determination, I pulled out my favorite T-shirt for good luck, and some other random clothes, and shoved them in my backpack. I got out of the car, trying to smooth out my hair and discreetly recover all my belongings with the shower curtain before locking the door.

I stood on the sidewalk, looking around, and my stomach growled.

The coffee shop was open, and being midmorning on a weekday maybe it wouldn't be too crowded.

When I entered the shop and the little bell announced my presence, one of the newer baristas welcomed me, but was paying more attention to their line of customers at the counter than the ones coming in.

Good. I probably looked like hell, and I didn't need anyone who knew me asking questions.

I went straight for the bathroom and locked the door behind me. Setting my bag down, I grimaced at the reflection in the mirror. My makeup from last night was a mess. At least I had face wipes in my bag, and maybe I'd save what makeup I had left for a job interview or something.

I cleaned up, making sure I looked as normal as possible, not only with a neat appearance but also covering up whatever stress

I was wearing on my face. I left the bathroom and headed for the counter.

I scanned the pastry case, hitting the prices before looking at the items themselves. Settling on something cheap enough, I made my way to the front of the line and placed my simple order of a toasted bagel with a cup of water.

Food in hand, I picked an out of the way table and set myself up to be there a while.

Deep breaths. They were becoming a habit.

"First things first, let's look at the situation," I murmured, opening my laptop.

Bank funds—low.

Job prospects—few.

Low-income housing—nothing open near me.

Homeless shelter—apparently the closest one to me was constantly at max capacity and I'd have to hope I could get a spot.

With a sigh, I closed my laptop and leaned back in the chair. I rubbed my temples where I felt the headache coming on.

Ugh.

Deep breaths.

"Okay, fine," I mumbled. "What's the one thing I can control?"

I leaned forward and grabbed my bagel, taking a bite out of it and watching out the window.

I'm not tied to this area. I could move down the coast. Or up the coast? I could find somewhere with more programs and opportunities for me.

Exiting the bathroom after a bio break, I decided the first order of business was making sure my old landlord would keep my paycheck.

No. No. No. Caspian and Nikkos were standing in line for coffee.

I closed the bathroom door again. I didn't think they'd seen me.

Calm down, Maddie, you haven't done anything wrong.

I just didn't want them to know about my new situation. Or did I? I hadn't shown them my rock bottom, and the shame of it was still gripping my chest. This was the last time I'd see them, at least for a while, maybe ever. They were supposed to be gone soon, and I didn't want to taint what Caspian and I had with my problems.

Besides, I had a few months to turn it all around before he came back, right? And who was to say I'd even see Caspian again, or that he'd want to see me.

Fuck, that kiss, though.

Okay, so they were out there, so what? They didn't know I'd lost my apartment. And it was only temporary anyway. I was a tough girl. I could make it work out somehow.

My heart sank as I stared myself in the eyes, knowing I didn't believe any of it. But I couldn't hide in a coffee shop bathroom forever.

I didn't look over at them as I sat back down in my unassuming corner. As long as I didn't draw attention to myself there shouldn't be any problems. But maybe I should tell them, maybe I could hitch a ride with them and pay them back later. The sirens had a job, right? Maybe I could do it, too, and give them the money I made. Maybe one of them had a spare room. Or maybe the whole train of thought was ludicrous, considering I'd known these men for literally days.

Taking another bite of what might be my last bagel, I noticed a big red tow truck slowing down across the street. Maybe they were here for a coffee?

The truck backed up toward the parked cars and stopped close to mine. The tow truck driver got out and walked around to the rope contraption on the back.

"Hey!" I said, as though he was going to hear me from across the street and inside a coffee shop. Wasting no time, I ran for the front door. I barely looked at the street as I ran across it, earning me an angry honk from a passing van.

"Hey!" I shouted at the tow truck while running down the sidewalk, but my car was already cranked up on the hook. "Stop!"

The driver shut his door, and the truck had already begun moving when I finally reached it. I ran alongside my car shouting.

"Wait! That's my car!" My voice was shrill with panic as I ran alongside, but the tow truck quickly picked up momentum. I reached for my car one more time, snagging a piece of paper in my fingers before the car slipped out of my grasp completely. I watched it disappear down the street and around the corner, vanishing from sight.

I was numb. I was cold. I dropped to my knees. Tears, hot and full, ran down my cheeks. I took in a quivering breath, then looked down at the paper I had grabbed.

This is private parking for the businesses here. Move your vehicle or I will have it towed.
—A concerned citizen

I stared at the paper for a long time. It was written on pink, floral stationary in an angry red pen but with deceptively neat hand-writing. I looked over my shoulder to the part of the street where I had parked. Sure enough, the space was the only one labeled for the alterations and embroidery shop while the others all had a city parking meter. But the kicker was how few other cars were even here. I get that I had parked in a space that wasn't for parking in, but it was so bitter, so petty. There were half a dozen other spots still open on the block, but they just had to have mine.

A tear fell onto the paper, smearing the *c* in citizen.

My eyes flew back to the shop. Somebody, probably from that shop, had just ruined what I had left to be thankful for. My throat tightened and I crumpled into a ball, right there. I wasn't quiet either. The tears came freely, and I vaguely wondered if I was going to go hoarse from screaming. My body shook with the tears; if I cried hard last night, it was nothing compared to this.

This was a complete loss. Everything I had was in that car, and there would be no way I had the cash to get it back.

"Madeline!" A voice was coming toward me, footsteps crossing the street in a hurry.

I flinched hard, on the defensive already, and wrapped my arms around myself as I turned to face the speaker.

Ocean-blue eyes. Cut jaw, dark hair, olive skin. Caspian. Still wearing his jacket and tie, he looked as frustratingly put together as always.

I started shaking. Taking a knee on the dirty street, Caspian rubbed his hand up and down my back the moment he reached me. His touch was warm and firm as he lifted my shame-filled face toward him with his free hand.

"Madeline, look at me," Caspian said. There was worry in his eyes, and my tears surfaced again, burning as they threatened to spill over anew. I relented, burying my face in Caspian's shoulder as he pulled me in tight for a hug.

I barely knew this man, but in that moment I needed someone. Anyone. Another person to hold me and just let me cry it out. Tell me it would work out, no matter how unlikely that really was.

Nikkos came more slowly. I didn't notice until he was standing over us, but while Caspian slowed running his hand up and down my back, I could feel the movement of him looking up at his cousin.

"Oh, Madeline," Nikkos said.

The tone of his voice caused me to look up. My face was probably a mess, but I blinked through the tears and saw what he was holding in his arms.

"I brought your things out for you," Nikkos said, holding up my backpack.

My heart stopped. "Did you see?"

Caspian pulled back. "See what?"

"I didn't mean to, but your tabs were all open. Madeline, did you lose your apartment?" Nikkos asked.

I barely managed to nod before the crying started back up.

"Shit, Madeline," Caspian said. His big arms pulled me into his chest as I cried.

"Your car just now . . ." Nikkos didn't finish his thought, but I knew what they were both thinking.

My face went numb with embarrassment. I nodded, Caspian's shoulder muffling my words as I spoke. "Everything I own was in my car or in that backpack."

Movement under me. My weight was shifted around, and I clutched blindly at Caspian's jacket until I felt him stand up. He got me to my feet, wrapping an arm around me to ensure I stayed upright.

"Do you have anywhere to go?" Caspian asked, his words soft and gentle in my ears.

"No." My voice cracked.

"Will you let me bring you to our ship until we sort this out?" he asked.

I nodded.

With no more conversation needed, Caspian walked me down the sidewalk like it was the most natural thing in the world. Nikkos walked behind us, and I just buried my face in my hands.

This man, these strangers, had shown me more compassion

than anyone had shown me in ages. My body was wrecked. Between the emotions of the last twelve hours and the physical exertion of crying, my body, which had finally gotten a chance to relax, was relaxing too hard.

Caspian didn't hesitate to stop walking and scoop me off my feet. From the emotional high of a mountain to the low relief of relative safety and human contact, I should have been ashamed to fall asleep in his arms as he walked the rest of the way down the hill to the beach.

But I couldn't. I had no shame left to give. All that was left now were the only hands that had reached out to me in the darkest hours of my adult life.

Caspian's.

CHAPTER TWELVE

MADELINE

The rocking of the bed was gentle. Up and down, swaying with the caress of water. I opened my eyes slowly. The room I was in was almost completely dark. Only a few narrow white lights illuminated the floor to prevent someone from tripping or running into the wall, but they didn't do more than that. Was it even called a wall? I knew almost nothing about ships except that everything had a new name.

I'd never fallen asleep over water like this before. I'd never had the chance.

Sitting up slowly, I assessed my physical state. My head hurt like hell; I probably needed water. My neck was less sore now that I had a proper bed, but it would still probably ache for a couple of days. I was starving, but half a bagel then an emotional breakdown would do that to anyone. I ran my fingers through my hair, pushing it out of my face and hopefully not looking like the mess I suspected I was.

"—going to be more complicated than you think."

I froze. Soft conversation seeped through the walls. Nikkos said, "The Senate will want to know why we didn't bring her back."

"Because she's her own person! You can't force someone to move their life and start anew in a foreign land."

Oh. That was definitely about me.

"It's not a foreign land, it's where she belongs. And she's clearly run out of options here!"

Okay, ouch.

"Now isn't the time," Caspian said. "She has too much on her shoulders as it is. Besides, you're the one who said it, Nikkos. You can't force a siren to do anything."

Siren. For some reason, the word made me uncomfortable, and I sat up rod straight in the bed.

Caspian and Nikkos were arguing about me. My stomach sank. I never wanted to be the cause of a fight between them. My presence was already becoming a burden, and I'd only been here long enough to sleep.

"I'm going to go check on her," Caspian said. "She should be a part of this conversation."

Yes, I absolutely should. The door opened slowly as he scanned the bed to see if I was still out.

"I was coming to see if you were still resting or if you needed anything." Caspian closed the door behind him and fiddled with a nob on the wall, turning some low lights on in the room allowing me to see everything much better.

Caspian adjusted the lights, illuminating the cabin. The bed took up most of the space, but there was definitely room to stand and get dressed. Cabinets lined the wall; I guess storage was important on a boat. There was a tiny window above the bed, but the cover was slid shut right now. Was it a still a porthole if it wasn't round?

"Are you hungry? We have some bread if you want a sandwich,

or Nikkos made hummus yesterday, if you'd like that." Caspian turned to face me, crossing his arms over his chest and looking at me with concern.

The pit of my stomach dropped as every embarrassing realization settled in. Caspian and Nikkos had definitely found me at my lowest, and then I fell asleep. "Food sounds great, but can we talk first? And do you know what time it is?"

Caspian gave me a twitch of a smile. "It's just after three. You must have been exhausted."

"Yeah." I groaned. "It all hit me at once, I guess."

"Let's get you something to eat, and if you're ready, we can talk about everything."

Everything. Did that entail the sirens as well? Or did he just mean my problems?

With a shaky breath, I swung my legs over the edge of the bed. I was still dressed in my clothing from that morning; my sandals were on the floor for me to slip on and my backpack was in the corner. "Okay."

Caspian nodded and offered a hand. I took it and stood up, the cramped cabin not letting me stand anywhere but right up against him.

"Let's sit up top so you can get some fresh air," he suggested. We stepped into a short hallway with other doors, which opened up to a space smaller than my apartment but somehow a hundred times more luxurious.

Nikkos was next to the kitchenette thing—a galley, I thought—and gave me a strained smile. "How are you feeling, Madeline?"

"Better, thank you."

"That's good to hear." He seemed relieved. Then he locked eyes with Caspian. They had some sort of wordless exchange wherein Nikkos raised his eyebrows and gestured to me and Caspian made a face I couldn't read. The whole thing ended when Nikkos rolled his eyes and went around the counter and deeper into the galley.

"Bring us out something to eat?" Caspian called after him.

"Something for her, yes," Nikkos answered. "You get your own, you great oaf."

"Come on, let's get up to the deck," Caspian said. I followed him up a short set of stairs, almost a nicer ladder, to where the hatch opened to the bright Florida sunshine.

The plush tan seats had water drops all over them. An afternoon shower must have swept through; this was more than just sea spray on a boat. But Caspian was already on top of it. He pulled a towel from a compartment under one of the seats and wiped down the surface.

"Take any seat you'd like," he said.

Forcing a smile, I sat on the nearest cushion. The place we came out of, the hatch, I guess, was near the middle of the boat in a raised part that made up the ceiling and windows to the main room we were just standing in down below. The back had two steering wheels from what I could see. Otherwise, the front of the deck was a wide-open space as long as you didn't run into the sails. There was one big semicircle of seating with a table bolted to the deck in front of it, and I was thankful for the big white shade angled over us as the sun beamed at us sharply.

The hatch door opened again and out came Nikkos with a big plate of hummus, bread pieces, and stuffed olives. Caspian and Nikkos sat toward the other end of the space, giving me plenty of room.

My stomach growled and I happily took a piece of bread, swiping it through the hummus. It hit my mouth and the savory, smooth taste of it instantly made me realize just how hungry I was.

"So, Madeline," Nikkos began with hesitation, "I'm sure you

hadn't intended for us to catch you in such an awkward moment. And I truly hope you can overlook the circumstances of that, but now that we know you're in trouble, we wish to help you."

"It seems your situation was more dire than you had let on," Caspian added.

Swallowing my bite, I opened my mouth and spoke at the same time as Caspian. "I want to come with you—"

"—come with us." Caspian said, then registered what I was also saying. "You will?"

"As much as I wanted to pull myself together and be ready for the next time you came to town, I can't be ashamed to ask for help anymore," I said.

"There is no shame in getting help," Nikkos offered, passing me a bottle of water.

The tears started again, and Caspian slid closer to hand me a napkin. "As soon as I have a job I'll start paying you for the trip. And if either of you have a spare room, I'll work for it. The moment I'm on my feet I'll get out of your way, I promise."

"Absolutely not!" Nikkos sounded offended. "You'll have your choice of places to live. There's no rent in Atlantis."

Of all the impossible things these two had told me, this one seemed the most outlandish. "You're messing with me."

"Afraid not," Caspian said, rubbing a hand on my back. "We have enough houses. We have extra houses, actually. I promise, no one in Atlantis goes unhoused."

I hiccupped, the waterworks starting up again. People don't catch a break like this one; *I* don't catch a break like this one. "I barely know you. You barely know *me*."

"It doesn't matter," Caspian said, leaning back so I could see the depth of his eyes. "Come with us."

"I want to—I'm worried about a few things, though. I don't

have a passport. I don't have any money. I don't speak your language."

"More of us speak English than you'd think, and as our guest, I insist we take care of you. You won't have anything to worry about," Caspian said soothingly.

"You're one of us, Madeline," Nikkos added. "We want you to come with us. You're not a burden, no matter what you've convinced yourself."

No one expects this much help for free; I was ready to earn my way. And now that they were giving me the help I'd asked for, no strings attached, my own stupid holdups from being my own support system for so long were getting in my way.

"But, why?" My voice cracked. "What do you get out of it?"

There was hurt in Nikkos's eyes, and I immediately regretted my words. Caspian's face closed off, hiding how he felt about my words, but I had a good guess. I needed to shut my damn mouth; they wanted to help. Why was it that the deeper the pile of shit, the less likely I was to ask for help climbing out of it?

"What we get out of it is you. A person's worth is not determined by the value of their assets, or what they can provide in return," Nikkos said. "I may not have known you long, but I know you wear your emotions on your sleeve, and you have a sense of guilt about spilling coffee on strange men."

Caspian snorted a laugh as my face heated up.

"You seem to be a happy-natured person, with a dazzling smile. It's just buried under a mountain of pressure right now. And, Madeline, we don't want to see that extinguished," Nikkos finished.

"You don't deserve what you've been through," Caspian added. "Come with us."

The tears were spilling again, but not for the reason they had been a moment ago. Nikkos and Caspian had nothing but raw honesty on their faces. They felt bad for me, but not out of pity. It wasn't often I met people who liked me for me. Hell, Nikkos had even listed the reasons he liked me.

"Thank you." My voice came out as a strained whisper. My knuckles were white as my fingers locked together to stop them from shaking. "Take me with you. Take me to Atlantis."

CHAPTER THIRTEEN

MADELINE

The first thing Nikkos did when I agreed to go with them was to practically force-feed me. He watched over me as I finished off the plate of food, muttering the whole time about malnourishment and a bigger dinner. Two minutes into his care and he was already a mother hen.

After eating, I washed my dish and acquainted myself with where things were on the ship. Nikkos called it a sailing yacht, and it had a very nice living space as well as two bedrooms.

I got my backpack out and laid my things on the seating under the window. I owned the outfit I was wearing and the outfit I had slept in last night, which was stuffed in my bag. A laptop, a phone, my bathroom bag with a towel and toothbrush and stuff, my headphones.

I sighed, looking at the spread. My biggest setback would be clothing. I could handle just about anything else when we arrived, but I wasn't looking forward to wearing the same two outfits for . . .

"Hey, Nikkos," I said, turning to spot him in the galley. "How long does it take to get to Atlantis?"

Nikkos was standing over the counter, cutting up things for dinner. "About two weeks, give or take. The weather has a lot to do with it."

"Thanks."

Turning back to my things spread across the seats I sighed. Two weeks and two outfits. Yay.

A sudden *thud* caused me to jump. Running for the steps, I popped my head of out the hatch to see what happened. The sound had come from where you step up on the boat from the dock; a cardboard box that hadn't been there a moment before was now sitting on the deck. Then another appeared on top of it.

Up and out, closing the hatch behind me, I went over to get a better look. Caspian was stepping onto the boat behind the boxes.

"Do you need some help?" I offered.

Caspian was still wearing his button-down shirt and business pants, but he had left his jacket and tie behind. With the top couple of buttons undone and his sleeves rolled up, I found myself appreciating the view.

"Sure, put them where you want them, and I'll go get the rest." Caspian hopped back onto the dock and walked away.

"Where I want them? How do I know where you want your stuff?" I peered down at the boxes. First things first, I needed to move them out of his way for when he came back. I pulled them toward the hatch, wondering how I was going to safely get them down the steps.

Nikkos was at the bottom when I opened the top, wiping his hands on a dishtowel. "What do we have here, food for the trip?"

"I'm not sure," I said, then took the lid off the first box.

My mouth popped open. This wasn't just any box, this was *my* box! I set the lid aside and pulled out a pair of sandals, my senior T-shirt, a pair of particularly scandalous shorts I had cut up. My favorite winter leggings were here, my sunglasses, the shirt from Freeman's Gym.

I pulled open the next box. More of the same. Another towel, some clothes, shoes.

"This is all my stuff!" I said, then looked down at Nikkos. "How did he get my stuff?"

Nikkos shrugged, reaching up to take the boxes from me and put them inside the yacht. "Caspian has his ways. When he's determined to do something, he usually succeeds."

I got the boxes out of the walkway before Caspian came back. This time, he carried a few loose things from the car, like my quilt and photo album. Nikkos walked over to take them from him, and Caspian left again.

I just sat by my things in stunned silence. I thought I was going to cry again, but after the last twenty-four hours, I was all out of tears. Nikkos walked past me, taking my things inside. It sparked me to move, and I added the new items to the boxes I'd already stacked in a corner.

Pushing everything against the window seats, I watched Caspian bring down one last armful of stuff. Feeling lightheaded, I let my weight fall back on the cushions.

"I left your winter coat, forgive me," Caspian said, sitting next to me. "You won't need a coat in Atlantis, it's quite warm."

I nodded, my eyes glued to the boxes.

"I can't believe you did that. How did you get everything out of my car?" I asked.

"I just paid the fine and brought the whole car," he said.

My eyes snapped to his. "You what?"

"It was the simplest way," he answered. "Do you have

everything now? We can also get you anything you need when we get there."

My eyes darted between my boxes, Nikkos, and Caspian. My breath caught. "No, this is more than anyone has ever done for me before. I don't know what to say."

I jumped to my feet and wrapped my arms around his neck. "Thank you." My voice wavered, but I kept myself from another emotional scene.

A heartbeat later I felt his arms wrap around my back, the warmth of him seeping into me as he returned my hug.

"Keep what you want, and we'll donate the rest," Nikkos said. "As for your vehicle, it won't fit on the yacht, obviously."

I pulled back from the hug with Caspian. "Guess I won't really have a use for a car in Florida if I go with you to Atlantis."

Caspian nodded. "I thought you might say that. I made a few calls to some local dealerships on the way back. I found one that would take it without a title, and a few that would take it with one. Do you still have the title?"

I nodded sheepishly. "Yeah, I keep it in the glove box."

Caspian laughed and looked away. Nikkos looked as though he was about to blow a gasket.

"You keep the title to your car . . . inside the car?" Nikkos asked.

"A few months ago I was leaving a bad situation, and I didn't have anywhere else to store it. I guess I never moved it." I shot them a strained smile that did nothing to ease the alarm on Nikkos's face.

He finally sighed, pinching the bridge of his nose. "I suppose it's better than not having it at all."

"I'll get it sold if you can sign the title over," Caspian said. "And I'll get you an account with the National Bank of Atlantis. They can exchange the local currency to ours."

My eyebrows shot up. "You can do that?"

He nodded. "I can, and I will. Let's get that taken care of, then we can buy groceries for the trip back."

"I'll do that," Nikkos offered. "Any special requests?"

Was there anything I would miss that I might not be able to get in another country? Some of my basics were a piece of fruit or bread. I might miss a few sugary cereals, but if I was being honest, I had wanted to kick that habit for a while now. The one thing I'd have a hard time leaving behind was the muffins from the coffee shop, but surely there was flour and sugar anywhere I went. I could learn to make them myself.

And then an idea hit me.

"Oh, I do have a request," I said. "I want to thank you guys. Let me make dinner. Can I text you a short list of things I'll need?"

Nikkos turned to Caspian. "My goodness, she's already more useful than you are, cousin."

Caspian shot him a dirty look, at which Nikkos and I both laughed.

"I'm going to make a call. Come out to the end of the dock when you're ready to sign," Caspian said to me as he stood from the window seat.

"I'll just be a minute. Thank you again," I said.

He looked back at me as he walked out the door, his expression softer. "Of course, Maddie."

I let out a slow breath, appreciating the sight of him as he left.

Careful there, Mads. A little freshly vulnerable to be checking out his ass, don't you think?

With a sigh, I stood from the window seat and faced Nikkos. Of course I wouldn't want to mess up the position we were all in. I had no business making things sexual between me and Caspian. We were three people sharing a tiny boat for the next two weeks or so.

And if I messed that up, it wasn't like any of us could go anywhere. No, I had to keep it to myself until I could stand on my own two feet. If I wanted Caspian, I'd have to work on myself first.

And, let's be honest, he was so fucking worth it.

Nikkos hummed, still amused by the earlier exchange, and pulled out his phone. "Here, I don't believe I've given you my number, though I only really use this thing on the mainland. We haven't managed phone reception in Atlantis yet."

"Will it not work at all?" I asked.

"We've figured out internet, so it'll work on the public Wi-Fi, but no calls as you know them," he answered, not looking up from copying his number into my contacts before handing my phone back.

"You're kidding."

"I'm afraid not," he said. "But if it makes you feel any better, you'll always be able to send emails. That's how we communicate with the people back home while we're out gathering supplies we can't make on the island."

Humming, I opened a fresh text to start my shopping list. "All right then, dinner. Are there any foods I should stay away from? Things you don't like or allergies?" I asked.

"No, no. We just appreciate the gesture," Nikkos said. "Don't be afraid to add peppers, they're good for Caspian, and he won't pick them out of a dish you made. Just send me your list and I'll pick up anything you need."

Biting back a smile at the image of Caspian picking out peppers, I began typing. "Thanks, Nikkos."

He reached out, putting a hand gently on my shoulder. "We're really glad to bring you back with us, Madeline. Welcome aboard."

"Thanks."

And as Nikkos went shopping, I went out to sign away the

title of my car. I couldn't bring it with me, and I sure as hell wasn't coming back for it.

I spent the next two hours sitting outside, watching the shore with a churning stomach. The paths I took for a morning jog, the places I stopped to grab tacos or coffee, and the gyms with all my favorite customers and past co-workers, whom I was actually friendly with. All gone. Maybe it had never been the community I'd wanted, but it was all I'd had for a while now. Mr. Freeman's gym closed two years ago, after he passed away. I'd lost touch with almost all of the others I'd been in the group homes with. Even my last caseworker had retired.

And this siren stuff. Yes, I knew there was something different about me. Yes, it was stupid to believe Caspian and Nikkos just on the basis of their story. And yet the fresh start felt like the last viable option I had.

I craved a home that wasn't really here and wasn't really in Michigan. I just had to hope I could pull together some of the pieces I actually liked and bring them with me to Atlantis.

CHAPTER FOURTEEN

CASPIAN

The sun was now brushing against the city, the rays breaking against the taller buildings and scattering across the water, where they rippled and shimmered like living glass.

That was one thing that never changed. No matter where Dimitris sent me, I would always have the familiarity of the water around me. I counted myself lucky to have a chance to walk along the sidewalk by the beach on my way back from the car dealership.

With Madeline's things taken care of, all that was left was to bring her back with us. I could have taken a rideshare back, but for whatever reason, I felt the need to collect myself with a walk instead.

Madeline. What a puzzle. How does a siren from Atlantis end up in landlocked Michigan? We kept a tight lock on where our people went, and no siren had wanted to leave before. Hell, no siren could stand being away from the water for so long.

My phone buzzed, and I pulled it from my pocket. If this was

Nikkos, he could wait. He knew how to buy for a trip; he didn't need me. Then again, it could also be from Madeline.

The screen lit up, not with a call but with an email. Dimitris.

How odd that he'd contacted me. Usually, I barely registered in his mind. Something must have happened to cause concern about our mission.

I brushed my thumb against the notification and my screen jumped to the full email. He couldn't call me, not here, but he could reach out like this.

Caspian,
Report your success and estimated arrival.
            —Dimitris

Short and to the point.

I started walking again. What could I tell him? It was true that we'd succeeded, but we'd ended up using Gavin's witch for the wordbinding. One of our few outside contacts, a coven that had dealt with our people previously for minor magics and potions, was what Dimitris expected. Not an unknown witch. Any deviation would annoy Dimitris, and I'd rather not deal with that while we were preparing to sail. And then there was the siren we'd found in a coffee shop in Florida, of all places.

I tapped the phone against my chin. Did I tell him about Madeline? He'd find out eventually. He might not like it.

My phone buzzed again.

I'm waiting.

He was in a foul mood, and I'd bet money that Basilli Ateio was getting on my uncle's nerves with his indifference to the problems of his office. Sighing, I quickly typed out a response that would satisfy him.

We secured our contact with Gavin. The wordbinding has been done and he has the information to seek the item, as well as how to contact us when he's ready to bring it. We will be leaving in the morning, projecting arrival in two weeks, weather cooperating.

—Caspian

I hit Send and watched for a reply, but I didn't particularly expect one. When I was confident there would be no more responses, I pocketed the phone again.

As I walked, I left those troubles for later. At least for now, I could enjoy a calm dinner with Nikkos and Madeline, then in the morning we could set out for home.

The red glow of sunset splashed against the white boats as they bobbed at the dock. I gave the sunset one last glance as I walked over the last few planks before stepping onto the deck of our ship, shaded from the sun's rays by the sail.

"Are you sure you don't need a hand?" That was Nikkos's voice.

"Nikkos, I'm fine. This is a thank you for everything, please go relax while I finish cooking," Madeline insisted.

Opening the door, I was ready to be amused from the sound of things.

Nikkos was just outside the galley, arms crossed in a classic Nikkos bout of anxiety. I could see Madeline behind the galley counter, frustrated by something. Probably Nikkos.

"What's going on here?" I asked.

The two of them turned to me as I closed the door behind me.

Madeline looked relieved, taking the opportunity to speak before Nikkos could.

"Nikkos needs to relax while I make dinner! It's my way of thanking you guys, so I *insist* he let me do it." Madeline leaned around my cousin and over the counter, causing Nikkos to back up a step.

"This isn't like a stationary kitchen," Nikkos fretted. "There are so many parts that move because of the water."

"And you showed them to me, didn't you?" Madeline said. "I'll call you if I have questions."

"Cousin." I reached out and put a hand on his shoulder. "Dimitris emailed me."

All of Nikkos's worries about dinner faded, and he turned a serious expression toward me. "What did he say?"

"He wanted an update," I said. "I sent him a brief report, but my guess is he'll ask us for the full details before we get back. Why don't you go work on it so it's ready when he asks?"

Nikkos mumbled his reply. "All right, I'm going to just go organize the summary for now. Thanks for the warning."

Nikkos went into his cabin long enough to grab his laptop before heading out to the deck where he could work in peace. As he shut the hatch door behind him, I could finally turn my attention to Madeline.

She sighed, her shoulders relaxing as she pulled her wavy brown ponytail tighter. She looked tired, but she also looked happier than I'd seen her since we'd met.

I put my hands in my pockets.

"Forgive Nikkos, he's a micromanager."

She huffed a laugh. "I couldn't tell."

Amusement twitched at the corners of my mouth, and I stepped into the galley doorway. "What's for dinner, chef?"

She had already picked up a wooden spoon, and brandished it at me like a sword. "Don't you start now, or I'll get you with my spoon like your neighbor. I just got rid of Nikkos. Go relax! I won't burn the ship down."

I leaned over the cooktop, chuckling. "I wasn't worried before, but now that you've said that . . ."

The smells hit me. Different from Atlantean food but still appetizing. She had multiple pans going at once and two bowls; we'd have plenty of dishes to wash later.

"It's nothing fancy, just spaghetti and meatballs. Store-bought noodles and sauce. But I did learn to make homemade meatballs back in Michigan, and I'm not too bad if I do say so myself. Although Mrs. Gracie would never admit that." Madeline beamed at me as she took the spoon and stirred the pot that had red sauce in it, adding salt and mixing it all together.

"Mrs. Gracie?" I asked.

"One of the people from the group home. Great cook, but kind of a grouch. Worth putting up with for mac and cheese night."

"She sounds charming," I mused.

"Almost done," she said, taking the lid off one of the pans to billow a savory steam up and out. "Do you have a colander or anything?"

I reached for a cabinet and pulled down a strainer for the pasta, setting it by the sink. She looked at me over her shoulder.

"Perfect." Madeline stopped stirring the sauce and tapped her spoon on the edge of the pot. "I think the noodles are nearly done, I can—*oof!*"

She turned to grab the strainer just as I stepped back, she must not have expected me to turn the way I did, but I was trying to get out of her way. She bumped into me, and my hands flew down on reflex to catch her shoulders.

"Are you all right?" I asked.

She tilted her face up at me. Her cheeks were flushed—either with embarrassment or heat from the kitchen. The slight part of her lips drew my eyes. The motion of her tongue darting out to wet her lips was enticing.

We both leaned in, a dangerous motion that needed a lot more reflection by both parties before we jumped into anything. Hot breath mixed together in the space between us, but Madeline pulled back first.

"Dinner is almost ready," she said, flustered.

"Maddie." A strand of hair fell from her ponytail, and I moved a hand to tuck it behind her ear.

"Sorry." She stepped back, fixing the piece of hair herself. "I'm growing out bangs from a bad decision last year and it just won't stay tied back quite the way I want it to yet. Sometimes you cut a guy out of your life, and you just want to take the scissors to your hair at two in the morning, you know? And I don't know why I just told you that. God, I'm a rambler."

She turned her eyes, not able to bring them to mine again as she busied herself with getting the strainer.

"Maddie," I started again.

"You don't have to stay, I can finish up and dinner will be in just a minute."

"Madeline," I said more firmly. "It's all right. The boat isn't that big, I expect we'll bump into each other again in the next couple of weeks. It happens."

She bit her bottom lip, nodding.

"Maddie, look at me," I said softly.

She blinked, then met my gaze. "Sorry."

"And stop with the apologizing."

"What are you going to do, spank me?" she asked, the instant teasing wiping away the remaining traces of whatever made her shy away a moment ago.

I just stared at her, stunned for a moment. Half a heartbeat later, she seemed to realize what she'd said, and her mouth popped open in shock.

Was she into that?

"Oh my god, I'm so sorry," she said, her voice higher than normal. "I didn't mean—it was a bad joke. I didn't mean to. Well, crap."

She covered her face with her hands and crouched down on the floor in one swift motion. "I swear I'm not usually this awkward." Her voice was muffled by her hands. "It was just the first stupid thing that popped into my head."

"You've done nothing wrong, and no amount of rambling is going to be worse than what I put up with when Nikkos gets stressed out."

That brought a meek smile to her face. I leaned down, taking her wrists gently and helping her to stand.

"Good. Now, no more apologies. Got it?" I asked.

"Got it," she said. "Should we talk about that? I mean, it's not that I don't want to. It's just, we're on this boat and I'm a mess, and you have a fancy Senate job and I'm . . . me."

It killed me that she thought so little of herself. It also killed me not to pull her in close again to connect that kiss we were clearly heading toward. But there was no escape on this small boat, and she had a lot everything ahead of her. I had no right to ask for more; she needed to get settled at home first. I had no claim to a siren.

"You're amazing," I insisted. "You're heading in all the right directions. Put all your focus on you for the moment, okay?"

"Okay," she agreed.

"That's better. I'll leave you to dinner since clearly, two is one too many cooks in this kitchen," I said.

"Yeah. Oh!" She spun, pulling the pot of noodles off the burner and rushing it to the sink. "My pasta!"

"I'll get Nikkos, and we'll set the table."

She was straining the noodles and turning off the other burners, clearly trying to manage everything at once. "Yup, 'kay."

Air, I needed air. Walking away took more from me than it should have, but I made myself climb out the hatch and take a deep breath before getting Nikkos inside so we wouldn't be alone again. The fresh air was a nice change from the steamy galley. Nikkos was sitting on the curved bench, his laptop on the table, and he was frowning as he concentrated on the screen.

"Dinner is almost ready," I said, grabbing his attention. "We're setting the table."

He looked up, sighing and stretching his back. "I think I can have some kind of a report soon. I might stay up tonight and finish. Start staggering our sleep schedules now."

"I'll take the night shifts."

He frowned, closing his laptop and putting it away. "You did the night shifts on our way here, it's my turn. Is everything okay?"

No, everything was not okay. If I spent all day alone with that gorgeous, charming, sunshine of a siren, I was going to slip up. "I insist. You're the better teacher for Madeline. She'll want to know more about Atlantis, probably some of the language."

Realization hit him. "Yes, of course. I'd be delighted to ease her entrance into Atlantis in any way I can. I should look through some of my books to see which might have relevant topics." He slung the laptop bag over his shoulder, then paused. "So, does it seem as though Madeline knows her way around a stovetop?"

"It smelled great," I said. "I'm surprised she could concentrate on it, considering how you must have harassed her in there."

Nikkos huffed, moving past me to go back inside. "I did no

such thing. It's just, to meet a siren who does her own cooking . . ."

"They can cook if they want to. I'm sure some of them do it for fun," I added.

I followed Nikkos inside and closed the hatch behind me. Nikkos set his laptop back in his room while I grabbed the plates and started setting everything up. By the time I finished, Madeline was wrangling the pots and cooking utensils into the sink.

"Are you guys ready?" she asked.

"Here, let me help you carry things," I offered.

"Nope, I've got it." She went into the galley again and returned a moment later with our biggest bowl filled to the brim with pasta, sauce, and meatballs.

"That actually does look delicious," Nikkos said, leaning in for a better look.

"You sound surprised," Madeline teased. "I told you I knew what I was doing."

Nikkos looked sheepish as he pulled a bottle from a cabinet and brought it to the table. "I brought some of our local wine to celebrate, *xino vasilias*."

"I'm excited to try it," Madeline said.

Once we were all seated, Nikkos pulled the cork from the bottle of the Atlantean wine and poured a glass for each of us while I dished out pasta onto all three plates.

Nikkos set the nearly empty bottle down after filling the glasses and took his in his hand to raise it over his plate. "*Chaara!*"

"Chaara," I echoed, lifting my own glass.

Madeline watched us, taking her own glass and doing the same. "H . . . haara!"

Nikkos and I both started laughing. I couldn't help it; her expression was just so cute.

She stuck out her tongue. "Ha-ha, at least I tried."

"Very good try," Nikkos said, taking a sip and setting his glass down. "It means *joy*, and it's like saying cheers. The long version translates to 'a glass of peaceful joy' but we don't usually say the whole thing."

"Chaara!" she said, her second attempt much better than the first.

We toasted. "Chaara!"

The golden drink from home was a little like a white wine but smelled mildly of apples. Madeline took a drink and held it in her mouth, then immediately made a face and swallowed. She coughed the moment her mouth was empty.

"That's why it's called the sour king," Nikkos said, handing me a napkin. "I should have warned you. Take a small sip at first until you get used to it."

She set her glass down, moving on to her plate. "It's good, but it definitely surprised me. Anything else I should watch out for in Atlantis?" Her tone was teasing, but it brought a darker question to the surface that Nikkos and I had been debating since we met her.

"We still don't know how you ended up here," Nikkos said. "I'm hoping the explanation is as simple as an unaccounted for siren, but . . ."

"The worst-case scenario is that someone removed a newborn siren from Atlantis," I finished the thought. "And unless we find out what happened for sure, we do need to be careful about who we trust."

"Good point," Madeline said, taking another, smaller, sip of her drink. "I'm glad I have you two to help me."

"Of course," Nikkos said. "We can start looking into it as soon as we're back home. The Senate offices have meticulous records. We can look for inconsistencies and start our search there."

"Thanks, guys," she said.

"Whatever you need, we're here," I offered. Moving to my plate, I took a bite, and my face lit up. "Gods, this is amazing."

Madeline perked up. "You doubted my skills?"

"This is outstanding," Nikkos said around a mouthful. One of the noodles on his fork fell into his lap and he let out a cry of indignation that was muffled by the food.

That was all it took to tip the serious topic into laughter. The rest of the meal we were able to keep lighthearted, avoiding the topic at hand. It was definitely a problem, but a problem we couldn't solve here.

When the sky darkened and the yawning set in, we sent Madeline off to my old cabin—which was now hers—and cleaned up the dishes. All that was left was to check the equipment and get ready to sail home.

One passenger fuller than when we'd come.

CHAPTER FIFTEEN

MADELINE

Throwing up the moment you wake is never pleasant.

But I was apparently not as okay with the rocking waves as I thought I was the night before. Not a heartbeat after I opened my eyes, I found myself running for the bathroom.

The one good thing about the location of my cabin was that I could escape to the bathroom and, unless someone was looking down the hallway next to the galley, they wouldn't be watching my mad dash to the toilet.

I was a mess. Fuck, I was a mess. I'd dreamed that I was with Caspian, singing along to a tune I didn't recognize and dancing on the bottom of the ocean floor. And how the hell would I know what the bottom of the ocean looked like? I was wearing the blue dress he'd bought me, and he was in a more formal looking version of the white linen clothes he wore.

I threw up in the bathroom, having a terrible time of it for several minutes until I was sure there was nothing left in my stomach to wretch up. Sweat beaded my forehead, and I was thankful that I had managed to keep my hair out of the way.

I cleaned up and sat back on the cool tile of the floor. It felt so good after everything I had just gone through, and I wasn't looking forward to getting myself back up to go back to bed. I looked up at the sink. My small bathroom bag was there. With my toothbrush. Yeah, after throwing up, I wanted to brush my teeth.

With a grunt, I hauled myself up to the sink and pulled out my toothbrush. After two good rounds of brushing, my mouth finally felt better, and so did the rest of me. I was just putting everything back in my bag when there was a knock at the door.

"Madeline? Are you all right?" It was Nikkos.

I zipped my bag and slid the door open. Giving him a sheepish look I answered. "Yeah."

"Seasick?" he asked.

"I knew we were going to start sailing with the tide but I thought I'd sleep through it."

"You did sleep through it, but the water is a little choppy right now," Nikkos said sympathetically. "Let me make you some broth. It should be easier on your stomach," he said, then turned and went into the galley.

"Thank you," I called after him, leaving the bathroom and heading back to my cabin to get changed.

I stepped into the doorway, then turned around suddenly. "Wait, you're awake? What time is it?"

Nikkos popped his head out of the galley. "About noon."

"Oh," I said weakly. "Okay."

Nikkos went back into the galley, and I closed the door to my cabin. I must have really slept, then. Maybe I shouldn't be surprised after the emotional day I'd had.

Clean outfit, hair pulled back, I left the cabin and closed the door quietly behind me. More than once I had to pause to hold on to anything bolted down while I made my way to see what Nikkos was putting together.

He stood over the stovetop, heating something up in a pot. Nikkos kept one hand on the pot's handle, lifting it off the burner completely if we hit a wave. He looked up with a warm smile when I walked into the room. "I hope you don't mind drinking it out of a mug. Liquids in bowls don't always stay still out here."

I returned the smile and pulled two mugs from the cabinet. They had plastic lids on them that only offered a small raised hole to drink from, effectively negating spillage. "Sounds perfect."

"Good, I was hoping we could share a bit of fresh air, and I could keep an eye on the ship at the same time," he said. "I've been at the control center all morning, things are fine enough that I can take a lunch break."

I frowned, setting the mugs on the counter next to the stovetop. "That sounds good to me. Where's Caspian?"

Nikkos stirred the savory-smelling broth, taking a look at it before turning the hot burner off and facing me. "When we're at sea we like to switch off day and night. That way someone is always paying attention. I'll be on day shift."

Pulling back from that almost kiss hadn't bothered Caspian, had it? Maybe my whole situation was too much of a turnoff. The last thing I wanted to do was make things so awkward he avoided me.

"But not to worry, I'll keep you company. I thought you might like to learn some of the basics of Atlantean."

That pulled at least a little bit of a smile out of me. "That sounds great."

"Wonderful," Nikkos said, grabbing the mugs and pouring the broth into each one. "Why don't we take these out to the deck ? I wish I had some simple texts with me so you could see the language as it's written. I have some fascinating books about our history back home if you'd like to borrow anything when we arrive. Of course, you'll have access to the Library of Atlantis as well. Far more delicate volumes than my own humble collection, but with your status, you'll have access to any of them for viewing."

He set the pot and wooden spoon in the sink before carrying our mugs out of the galley and to the door.

"My status?" I asked, following him out.

"Of course." Nikkos handed me the mugs for a moment while he opened the hatch. "As a siren there won't be much you won't have access to."

We stepped onto the deck and the sway of the waves suddenly made me question putting anything in my stomach again. But Nikkos directed us to the comfortable seats outside, the warm sun shielded by the open sail as it billowed in the wind and pushed the boat along.

Nikkos sat down and we each took a mug of broth. Admittedly, it smelled wonderful, but I decided to give it a bit before trying to keep it down. The waves were bigger than I'd expected on the open ocean, and I was having a hard enough time just keeping the liquid in my mug, despite the lid.

He seemed stiff at first glance, but once you got to know Nikkos, he was full of interesting facts, and was an endlessly patient teacher if you were truly interested in the subject. I asked him to help me speak his language, and he began teaching me the very basics. It was a lot like Greek from what I could tell, but Nikkos said they used some Latin and Arabic words too. But the root of it was still foreign enough that I could say with certainty that I hadn't heard anyone speak Atlantean before Caspian and Nikkos.

The afternoon faded into evening, and evening faded into night. I made dinner. Granted, it was just scrambled eggs with tomatoes, but it helped me feel like I was pulling some of my weight around the ship.

Nikkos made a passing comment when his cousin should have been up to share dinner with us, which was apparently normal for their sailing routine. But while I was cooking, Caspian slipped into the shower. After dinner, I was tired enough that I ended up going to my room to rest and reorganize my belongings, never having seen Caspian. The whole thing was starting to get in my head. Maybe he really was avoiding me; but if I was making it all up, I didn't want to sound silly.

Sleep was rough again, and despite keeping the light meals I'd eaten down, my stomach was still uneasy. Coupled with the fact that something was weird between me and Caspian, and I didn't know how to fix it, I wasn't getting much rest.

What had gone wrong? We had kissed twice now. Granted, the first kiss had the bittersweet taste of goodbye to it. And the last kiss had ended on a similar note. We almost had a third, but I was the one who stopped it before we started. Maybe I was misreading all the signals. Maybe there wasn't anything between us, and all the attraction was one-sided.

Maybe it was me, leading another man on. Trapping him.

I went numb, and pulled my blankets around me. No. I couldn't think like that. If I convinced myself of that, then Trent had won. Caspian would tell me if the sway was slipping out, wouldn't he?

When I finally went to sleep, my pillow was damp with tears.

That night, I dreamed the same dream again. Fits of restlessness, peppered with vivid images of the ocean floor. Dancing and singing. Caspian was there again, but this time we danced without touching each other. But the damn song persisted.

CHAPTER SIXTEEN

CASPIAN

Rain pattered against the windows as I sat inside the ship. Eight days I had tiptoed around Madeline. Kissing her felt right, but the rest of it didn't. She'd been with some pretty terrible people in the past, that much was clear. What made me any different? I didn't want to tread in unhealed waters. First things first, I needed to get my siren home where she could finally feel safe and loved.

Lightning flashed and thunder sounded in the distance, as if to add to my scolding.

As long as the storm didn't get too bad and we stayed on course, I wouldn't have to go out there. I made myself a sandwich, but barely ate half of it before setting it aside to gaze out the windows. I wondered briefly if I should stay up to help Nikkos with the storm, but if he needed the help he could always wake me up. Nikkos was no idiot, and both of us had too much respect for what the sea could do to a little ship like this one to not take precautions when needed.

The sun would be up in an hour or so, considering we were

charging headfirst into the eastern horizon. But for now, the common space was soft and quiet in the night, the only light coming from the tiny illuminated strips of white around the baseboards and the moonlight that graced the wooden floorboards.

I lay back on the seats, just watching the path of the raindrops sliding down the glass. After a long stretch of time to myself, I saw the clouds begin to lighten. The rain would probably stop soon, and the sun would dry off the deck.

A door slid open behind me; Nikkos coming out of the cabin we were now sharing.

"You're up early," I commented, still watching out the windows.

Nikkos walked over, stretching his shoulder. He was already neatly dressed in Atlantean clothing, loose linen pants under a longer-styled embroidered shirt. It would seem we were both done with the mainland clothing until our next trip out.

"I couldn't sleep, I guess," Nikkos said. "Any troubles during the night?"

"No. We're still making good time. If we don't run into anything big, we can probably expect to be home early," I said.

Nikkos nodded, going to the other end of the window seats as we heard the water in the shower turn on. "Looks like I'm not the only one the storm woke up."

I grimaced, counting down the minutes I had left before I'd need to get in the cabin I shared with Nikkos if I wanted to miss seeing her. Nikkos watched out the windows for a moment, then turned to me.

"Why are you avoiding her?" he asked.

I frowned. "We're on different sleep schedules," I said.

Nikkos sighed, sweeping his fingers through his hair and giving me a knowing frown. "You know what I mean."

I closed my eyes and leaned my head back on the seats. "It's complicated."

"Try me," he said.

"I just don't want her to get attached, okay?" I said. "In a week's time she's going to be put on a pedestal with the other sirens. She's important. Really important. And she doesn't know that yet, so it's not fair to engage in a flirtation when she has no idea she has the entire garden to pick from."

"And you're the sour tomato she would gladly skip over?" Nikkos said. "Is that your worry? Caspian, I'll be the first to caution you not to get emotionally involved with a siren, but it's clearly too late for that. For one thing, she's nothing like someone who was raised back home. Besides, you kissed her."

I frowned. "Did she tell you that?"

Nikkos shot me a puzzled look. "No, you told me that. Back on the mainland." Then his expression twisted into frustrated bewilderment. "Did you kiss her again?"

I turned away from him.

"You did, didn't you?" He threw his hands in the air. "Caspian, go after her or don't! Right now, I bet she's confused by why you're being an ass."

"I'm not!" I snapped. "At least, I'm not trying to be."

"Madeline is a genuinely sweet person," Nikkos said. "She won't say it, but you're hurting her."

"I know." I groaned.

"Then what are you *doing*?" Nikkos asked, exasperated. "It's been a week, Caspian. Are you trying to mess with her head?"

"No," I snapped. I stood, pacing the common space for a moment. When I took a deep breath, I turned back to Nikkos.

"Look, I don't want her to get tangled up with me. For one,

she'd be throwing aside all the benefits of her social status, which she doesn't grasp yet."

"I hope you have better reasons than that," Nikkos said, crossing his arms over his chest.

"I work directly for a senator who is trying to dismantle the sirens' place within Atlantis," I argued.

"Dimitris wants sirens to be free of their constant laboring to keep the bubble secured." He flung his arms, gesturing down the hallway. "She's been fantastic company, and a great student this week, but I've had enough of your moping about! You're going to fix this weird thing between you two."

My head jerked back. "Now?"

"Now!" He gestured down the hall again, only to be met with the sounds of the shower. "Fine, when she's done. But I'm going out that door to keep an eye on the sails, and you're going to fix this before I come back inside."

He stood from the seat, took his jacket off the hook by the door, and slid his arms in. "I mean it, Caspian."

"Okay, okay," I answered.

"Good." Nikkos gave me one last hard look, buttoned his outer layer, and through the hatch he went.

Sighing, I dropped back down. *Fantastic.* What was I supposed to say? My thoughts swam, heavy with what I wanted and the conflict of what I thought I was supposed to do. Did I care for her? Yes. Was I good enough for her? That was another question. Was I just putting her on this unattainable stage now that we were going home and she was going to be one of the city's beloved sirens? Maybe.

"Fuck, Caspian." I slid my hands down my face, groaning. And that was when the music started.

Dropping my hands, I looked down the hall. It was humming,

or possibly singing, though the words didn't come through the walls over the noise of the shower.

"Maddie?"

The humming grew louder, and in it slipped the sway. Letting out a slow breath, I didn't let it dig under my skin. The tune was unfamiliar, but what was familiar was the want in her voice. She wanted something. Love? Affection? The way my body was reacting, I wouldn't be surprised if it was something a little closer to the kiss we'd last shared. It made sense, but unfortunately it was burying that desire into the only victim around to hear it: me.

Dammit, Madeline.

My choices were to resist and block the sound or go address it so she could realize when her sway was slipping out and become more familiar with keeping it in check. With a grunt, I walked over to the door of the bathroom.

I closed my eyes, taking a deep breath through my nose and letting it out through my mouth.

"Madeline," I called through the door. "Are you okay in there?"

Immediately the humming stopped. The pull was gone, but the damage was done.

"Sorry, was I bothering you?" Madeline asked.

Were you bothering me? Yes! Fucking vixen that you are.

"Madeline." I chose my words carefully; it wasn't her fault she didn't know how to control it yet. "Were you humming in there?"

"Yeah," she answered sheepishly.

I closed my eyes, collecting myself. She was probably biting her bottom lip right now. If I was in there, she would be looking up at me through those long lashes, her cheeks pink.

Blood was already flowing south, and I clenched my jaw, trying to focus on something that wasn't as enticing as the naked siren in my shower.

"Your current . . . desires are leaking through the music," I explained. "Your voice, the sway, is having a stronger effect than you realize."

"Oh," she squeaked.

The water shut off immediately. Movement behind the door, then a moment later she slid the door open and peered up at me wearing nothing but her fucking towel.

Gods help me.

Her skin was still wet across her shoulders, beads of water clinging to her dark golden collarbone. Her dark hair was slick, pulled back from her face and flowing down her back.

"I'm so sorry!" Madeline looked up at me with regret. "I didn't know. It's just a stupid song that's been stuck in my head. I didn't know it would reach you, um, in that way."

"It's okay," I said. "No one expects you to master these skills overnight."

Her shoulders fell a bit. "I do wish that I understood more about them. Or how they work."

I let out a slow breath, trying my best to keep my eyes above towel level. "It's okay, I was just letting you know what was happening."

Before you lured me in and we did something we would both regret.

"I'll leave you to finish your shower." I drew back from the door, giving her ample space to close it again and resume what she was doing.

"Wait!" Madeline reached out a hand, gaining a small hold on the edge of my shirt and looking up at me with desperation. "Caspian, have I done something wrong?"

That knocked the wind out of me. I was gutted that she blamed herself for my behavior.

Of course she does, Caspian. You drew away with no explanation.

I took a breath, collecting myself before stepping closer to the door again. "No, Madeline. Nothing between us is your fault."

She let go of my shirt, her hand falling back to her side again. "Then, why?"

Why indeed.

"It's complicated," I said. "Look, you're about to be welcomed into a station in Atlantis that is well above me or Nikkos. I don't know what you've been through before, but my kindness isn't the last that you'll experience. I don't want you to disregard all the possibilities ahead of you to have whatever this would be between us, with me."

She frowned, brows knit together tight enough to form a crease between them. "Is that it?"

I was taken aback by her reaction. "Well, you don't know what's ahead of you. And, you don't know me that well yet. You haven't even seen Atlantis, or—"

"Are you kidding me?" she demanded. "I've been torturing myself over this bullshit? Are you attracted to me?"

How do you react to a question like that? By not lying, for starters.

"Yes," I admitted. "But—"

"I'm not finished," she snapped. "Would you be mad if I asked you out on a date?"

A siren. Asking someone on a date.

"No," I answered honestly.

"Caspian, I like you. And for maybe the first time in my life, I want something for myself that isn't a toxic mess. Can I kiss you?"

Recovering long enough to nod, I was pulled by my shirt to her level as her mouth met mine. The kiss was far different than the others we had shared. It was deep, hot, full of the desires that had caused her to sing me to her in the first place. Hungry, greedy kissing that didn't just stop at one.

Her hands found my back as she wrapped her arms around me. The only thing holding her towel up now was our bodies pressed together. My hands moved to her back. My lips moved from hers to explore her jaw, her neck, her shoulder. The sound of her breathing as it grew shallow and rapid was as enticing as anything else she had done to me.

When we finally pulled away from each other, her hands moved quickly to catch her towel. But not before a flash of her bare hip peeked out from behind it.

I gave her a mischievous smile. "Is that a tattoo?"

She blushed but threw me a knowing smirk. "Maybe you'll find out sometime."

I laughed and she adjusted her towel more securely. With a sigh, she tucked a bit of her still-damp hair behind her ear.

"Um, this has been great and all. I mean, resolving the weird-ness between us." She bit her lip, her eyes flicking to my mouth and then back up to meet my gaze. "But I want to finish my shower."

I smiled, stepping back out of the doorway. "Go ahead. We can talk more about this later."

She let out a slow breath, smiling. "Oh, we will. In fact, get Nikkos. I'll be in the galley in ten minutes, and while I grab break-fast you two can answer some of these damned questions before my head explodes."

"Yes, ma'am." I laughed.

"Good." She gave a curt nod. "Now, I'm going to finish my hair."

"Enjoy your shower," I told her, and she closed the door softly while I stepped away.

Whatever plans I thought I had upon returning home, Madeline had thoroughly taken them over.

So help me, I had left myself open to a siren.

CHAPTER SEVENTEEN

MADELINE

"Who is the governing body of Atlantis?" Nikkos quizzed me a few days later.

The weather had taken a rough turn again, and I had to anxiously occupy myself while the guys took care of the boat. But once it settled back down, Nikkos and I were shoving every bit of knowledge into my brain that we could. It was paying off—sort of.

I was learning things about Atlantis, but then Nikkos would dive into these tangents about things I wasn't sure were actually useful for my new life there. It was nice to know how they kept in touch with the outside world, or at least sent select individuals to keep up with the world at large and bring back new technologies. It was not as nice to get a two-hour lecture about the lady senator and her team who had spent a decade bringing the internet to Atlantis. Though it was probably revolutionary for the Atlanteans to keep up with the modern era.

"The governing body of Atlantis is the Senate," I answered.

"Led by . . . ?" Nikkos prodded.

"Senator Chrissa."

"Yes." Nikkos hummed. "But outside of the senators themselves is the . . ."

"Basilli!" I said. "The basilli, the king."

"Well, in English that may be the closest term. The basilli is the head of one of the five ancient houses between which the rulership of Atlantis rotates. One house rules for fifty years, then the burden is passed to the next house in line, and so on until the circle starts again. And the reason we rotate through the five ancient houses is so . . ."

"So they can avoid a certain amount of corruption. That's why the ancient houses can't be senators."

"Not quite," Nikkos said. "Each of the five ancient houses has a seat to fill on the Senate, but other representatives are sent for each of our societal concerns. A senator is elected by the people every five years to give a voice in the Senate for agriculture, technology, culture, health, things like that. And *those* cannot be held by the members of the five houses."

"But even the basilli doesn't have the final say in it all," I said.

"Somewhat true, though we can pick apart the details later." Nikkos stretched, leaning over to look at something or other on the horizon, and then up at the sails. "Let's stop here for now on the governing politics. Do you have another subject you want to cover?"

"Sorry, can I ask about sirens again? I think I came up with just one more question."

His smile was soft. "Of course. As many times as you need to."

"Thanks. I want to know how you become a siren. You have to be born one, right?" I asked.

"That's right," Nikkos answered. "The sway is genetic. Only a siren can give birth to a siren."

"And if the baby is a boy or something else?" I asked.

"We've never had a case of it, I'm afraid. I have no precedent to offer you."

"What? Not even one?"

"You have to remember, the siren population is quite small. If there had been a case of a genetically male child, or if a genetically female child had been born without the sway or to later identify elsewise, it would have happened before the sinking. We haven't seen it since, but I suppose it isn't impossible. Many records were lost at the time, but since then we've kept meticulous histories of the few remaining sirens."

"If you kept such good records, how did you lose track of me?" I asked.

Nikkos tapped his chin, a habit while he was thinking that I'd noticed. "That is an excellent question. And one we hope to find an answer to once we speak to the siren elders."

"Okay, that makes enough sense, I guess. Do the sirens have a seat on the Senate too?"

Nikkos looked taken back. "Sirens? No."

"Why not?" I asked. "Please don't tell me it's because they're all girls."

"No, nothing like that." Nikkos said. "The leader of our Senate is a woman, remember? Senator Chrissa. To be honest, I don't know why sirens were never offered a seat, but they are usually too pre-occupied with their duties keeping Atlantis from drowning to worry about the Senate."

"That sounds really important and intimidating."

"You won't be asked to do anything for a while, and certainly not until you're ready," he assured me. "The sirens are one of

Atlantis's most valuable resources. You won't be asked to do much you don't want to do."

Groaning, I pulled my legs onto the seat in front of me. "I'm nervous."

"Completely understandable," Nikkos said. "However, we'll be with you until you're comfortable. You aren't alone anymore."

Letting out a slow breath, I smiled. "Thanks, Nikkos. I don't know what I'd do without you guys."

"You'd be your charming self," he assured me. "And that's exactly why I know everyone will come to love you."

I shoved him lightly as he laughed and stood up.

"I'm going to go check on a thing or two, and then why don't we head in for *pliotov*?"

I froze at the word, then beamed. "Lunch!"

"You've got it!" Nikkos cheered. "It will all work out, Madeline. You're too clever to let it get you down now. I promise, we'll be home soon, and you'll see just how much you fit in."

Nikkos disappeared to check on whatever he was monitoring and left me to bask in the sun.

Fit in. I hoped so.

CHAPTER EIGHTEEN

MADELINE

I was going to explode if we didn't get off this damn boat. Thirteen days and my cabin fever had reached an all-time high. Not that I wasn't enjoying being on the water; it filled my heart with a satisfaction that I hadn't expected. Like scratching an itch I couldn't reach. But with little space to wander around and limited deck to sit on and watch the waves, some restlessness was to be expected.

However, when I woke up in the wee hours of the morning to Caspian's shouts of "We're here!" I didn't expect to spend the next hour sitting on the deck and waiting. Caspian and I had spent the last few days being friendly but not overly so. We shared glances when Nikkos wasn't with us, and even sometimes when he was but wasn't looking. But our limited interactions, which helped us keep cool heads until we reached Atlantis, were over, and all the tension that had built in me regarding setting foot in a new place had risen, tightening my throat as I sat on the deck and waited.

The moment Caspian shouted, Nikkos and I were on deck in a flash. The consuming darkness that usually met me when I stepped out at night was instead illuminated by a gentle blue that outlined a tower of white stone with a flat top. There was movement at the window in the top part of it, which also seemed to be the source of the blue glow. I'd had an hour to stare at it while Nikkos helped Caspian tie the boat off to one of the tower's jutting wooden posts. I still couldn't pry my eyes away. Why was it here? What was it sitting on? The water was too dark to see the supposed bubble underneath, though not for lack of me hanging over the edge and trying.

Then, Caspian disappeared. He climbed up a ladder that was rolled down from the windows, where a pair of slim hands seemed to help pull him inside.

And then we waited.

"What's up there?" I finally asked Nikkos when he was taking a break from boat things, or whatever he was doing to position us at this tower.

He looked over from where he was pulling out bags that would presumably come with us, including the things that I'd barely thrown in my backpack the night before. "Ah, you do need an explanation, don't you? I'm sorry, Madeline, I got caught up in sorting our things."

Nikkos set down a box with a grunt then came over to join me on the seats near the front of the boat. "This is a siren tower. It's the only way in or out of Atlantis."

My eyes were glued to the flashes of movement in the windows. "Then is there a siren up there?"

"Yes, there is," Nikkos said. "A few of them, I'd wager. Singing to the sea, keeping us hidden and keeping the protective shell around Atlantis in place."

My heart was beating hard, the choking sensation in my throat loosening as I wondered what it would be like to help. How they did what they did, and if I could really wrap my head around doing it too.

"There are other towers," Nikkos added. "Bigger ones, where other boats are anchored. We came to this one in the hopes that we could make your arrival as quiet as possible. Otherwise, we risk quite the spectacle as we descend. The last thing we want is for you to feel paraded across the city."

I grimaced. "Please don't do that."

Nikkos chuckled. "We won't. Though Caspian is meeting with a few of the sirens right now to let them know about you. As long as they agree, you can stay with Caspian for a few days as you meet everyone." He gestured to a ladder made with thick rope and wide wooden planks.

That brought a frown to my face and my eyes followed the ladder up to the window. "If they *let* him?"

"They do have more say than we do," Nikkos said. "I'm truly not worried that they won't allow it, Ashana is an incredibly wise person. She's the head keeper of the House of Sirens."

I nodded, somewhat understanding based on what I'd learned from Nikkos during the trip. A large house, and a room for every siren. People brought them many things they would need, like food and clothing, in exchange for the work they did to keep the bubble intact.

Turning back to the tower above, I watched as the rising sun illuminated the white stone, splashing the gentle blue glow with orange, pink, and yellow light from behind. "Why is the tower so tall?"

"The water can swell much higher than that," Nikkos said, standing to stretch before resuming moving the boxes and bags to the deck. I ran over to grab a teetering backpack from the pile to help. "Thank you, Madeline. And from the height of the towers, the sirens can keep the sea from swallowing them, of course, but placing the opening up high eliminates a certain amount of work on their part. They don't have to concern themselves with seawater unless it's truly a storm."

I slung the backpack over my shoulder and grabbed one of the boxes at the bottom of the hatch steps, bringing it up to add to the pile Nikkos had started.

"Come up!" Caspian called. "We're ready for you now."

"Finally," Nikkos grumbled. "I know we want to do this as calmly as possible, but I'm tired of sitting in the wind."

I took the first steps, but Nikkos stopped me with a gentle hand.

"Don't forget, we don't know why you went missing," he said. "I don't think the sirens would have had anything to do with it, but be careful who you trust. Tell us if anything feels off."

Swallowing the implication, I nodded. He was right; anyone older than me could have been around if something suspect did happen to me as a baby. I could hope this was all just an inherited genetics thing from a long-ago siren, but the truth was that we didn't know for sure.

"I'm not trying to scare you." Nikkos corrected himself. "Just, keep it in mind."

"You have a point, though. I'll stay aware."

Nikkos grabbed two bags of his own then began the climb. Thankfully, the ladder was solid, because I'd never felt quite comfortable with my weight on anything that creaked as I moved. The climb into the air wasn't helping, either, as I did my best to ignore the dark waves under me while looking up at Caspian's outstretched hand. Through the open window I could hear low singing, enchanting and full of promise.

My heart raced as I was pulled into the top of the tower and my hungry eyes searched for the promised sirens.

They were breathtaking. Three women sitting on floor cushions, eyes wide as they took me in with my cutoff shorts and an old gym tank top. The three of them were draped in white with luscious colored fringe, beads, and embroidery at every edge and seam. Their mouths were moving, making that enchanting sound that was like a song in that every note elicited a feeling from me like a song would, but there were no words. Magic. I'd call this magic, too, if I'd grown up around them. The thin walls between my disbelief about these supposed powers and what I was actually witnessing began to crumble. Whatever this was, it didn't need some label from me. I was mesmerized by them all the same.

The one on the left made a sign with her hands to the other sirens, and when they responded in kind she stopped her singing and stood. Shorter than me, with huge aqua eyes and black braids all the way down her back, she had no problem throwing herself at me in a hug. Caspian had to put a hand on my back to keep us from falling over.

"English, Amara."

"Yes, yes," the siren said in that same accent that Caspian and Nikkos had. She pulled back, taking a deep breath as she looked me up and down. "Welcome home, sister!"

Sister. The immediate proximity of the word and the promised community of Atlantis and the sirens was a tidal wave of numbness. My arms moved stiffly, returning the hug I was receiving so enthusiastically. And the more I wrapped my arms around Amara, this tiny stranger with the warm hug and enchanting voice, the more natural my hug became.

"I think the others are trying to get your attention," Caspian said.

And sure enough, the other two were making that motion with their hands again. A sort of rock paper scissors where they stuck different fingers out on one hand and smacked them into the open palm of the other. A type of sign language? Amara turned to me and gave me another quick hug before moving back to the cushions, taking up her place again and joining the song. The other two sirens took their turns greeting me just as Amara had, and I was on the verge of tears from it.

Once they were all back in place, they still watched me with interest even as they sang their song. The soft blue light I had seen before seemed to settle in the air around where the sirens sang, adding another puzzle for me to figure out later.

"Come on," Caspian said gently, his hand on my back steering me to a staircase I hadn't paid attention to due to the distraction of the sirens. "This way."

I finally looked around and realized the white tower was kind of barren. The floor cushions looked comfortable enough, there was some kind of game involving wooden pieces, which was likely some kind of entertainment, and a silver tray with crumbs on it sat to one side under a window. Otherwise, it was a blank slate cast in blue. I followed Caspian down the staircase, oil lanterns high on the wall illuminating the path.

Our footsteps echoed off the white stone stairs as Caspian spoke.

"There are six of these towers," he said. "The sirens take turns singing to the sea to keep us safe and hidden. The spires reach all the way down to where the salvaged part of Atlantis stands under their dome of protection."

"Are you telling me we're walking under the water?" I asked Nikkos.

"Thirty-seven meters from the highest point to the surface."

"And how many feet is that for the American in the room?"

Nikkos thought for a moment before answering. "Just a bit over one hundred and twenty feet."

That was a lot. Like, probably more than a person was supposed to go down a lot.

"Isn't that a dangerous amount?" I asked.

"Not for one of us," Nikkos said. "There is debate over the origins of our capabilities. Some scholars speculate it came with the curse that sank the city. Of course, the other side believes over time—"

"Not now, Nikkos." Caspian groaned, maneuvering until he could reach up and press a finger against a small bump behind my earlobe, on my neck. "Press here if you start to feel pressure. We all have those raised spots."

"I thought it was a birthmark," I said, my fingers finding their way up to my neck.

"In a way, I suppose they are," Nikkos said. "But, yes, my cousin is quite right. Press there if you feel discomfort, we will be to the bottom before you know it."

We continued walking, and I rubbed the spot behind my left ear absently. Something that was just a birthmark or something for the past two and a half decades now served a purpose.

Down, down, down we climbed, and I appreciated every leg day I'd ever had. As we climbed down the seemingly endless tower, Caspian broke the silence again.

"Calliope is waiting at the bottom for you," he said. "A keeper of the House of Sirens, Calliope is one of the elder sirens who will help us sort out what happened. Hopefully we can figure out why you were on the mainland at all."

"Are you still hosting Madeline at your home for now?" Nikkos asked.

"For now," Caspian confirmed.

It would have been nice to have time to decide how I felt about that, but any spare thought was wiped away when we finally made it to the landing.

At the bottom of the long, round staircase was another open room of white stone and cushions. Intricate glass sconces flickered, lighting the space. And standing in the middle was an ancient woman with two younger attendants by her side. She looked soft. Soft and kind, but also poised and regal. Her draped white dress had vivid red and orange fish embroidered at every hem, and gold fasteners at her shoulders and chest to keep it all in place. Her hair was twisted into small knots, little gray bumps with yet more gold ornaments hidden in them to match the rest of her outfit.

For a lack of other words, she was stunning.

"Calliope, this is Madeline." Caspian introduced me, then stepped aside. "Madeline, this is Siren Calliope. A keeper of the House of Sirens, and voice of the seas."

Caspian may have spoken in English, but one of the women at Calliope's side was translating into what I recognized now as Atlantean. My lessons with Nikkos hadn't prepared me enough to understand all the words, but I did catch one or two as she spoke. When she was done, the older woman smiled.

Calliope held her hands up, the wrinkles around her eyes creasing farther with the emotion in them as she grasped my hands in hers.

"Madeline," she said, her eyes not quite knowing where to stay on me, her thick accent barely pulling my name together on her tongue. But she managed it with such love that I could practically feel it. When Calliope began to speak again, the woman at her side translated for me.

"A thousand welcomes home. I wanted to see you for myself,"

she said, even as Calliope kept talking. "For now you will be with Caspian, but when you are settled we must gather at the House of Sirens to meet your sisters."

Calliope squeezed my hands in hers. I imagined this had to be what a grandma's affections were like.

"Our missing daughter," Caspian translated. "I don't know how we lost you, but we'll do everything we can to find out. Know now that you are wanted. You will be loved in this place. You belong here."

My throat tightened, and Calliope stepped back, pulling me with her. My eyes drifted to Caspian for guidance, but he was smiling as much as the sirens were, and I knew we were taking the right steps.

Calliope brought me to a large doorway at the far end of the room, and from there I had my first sight of Atlantis.

The tower was on the edge of a rocky white beach. A beach, under the water. Because just as I had been told, there was a huge pocket of air bubbled around a thriving city. The bubble was close enough to the surface to let quite a bit of the morning sunlight in, or maybe that was more of this siren magic. How we didn't see this giant place from above was beyond me, and I chalked it up to whatever other tricks were keeping the city in this state.

The buildings were all white or sandy brown, but decorated as vibrantly as the details on the sirens' dresses. Shutters, flowers, doors, windows, and artwork were bold colors and patterns. I wasn't close enough to see the finer details, but I could tell what the common architecture shapes were. Squares buildings with domed tops.

The streets held a lot of plant life as well. Despite the underwater location, I could see trees and shrubbery tucked in every available nook and cranny. I was also excited to see some kind of market waking up, with stalls and people rushing about.

The city was bright, alive, and wholly awe-inspiring.

"It's beautiful," I whispered.

"It is," Caspian agreed. "Maddie, welcome home."

CHAPTER NINETEEN

MADELINE

The tower was at the edge of the beach in a bubble. Enough water was allowed in from the bottom that it even afforded gentle waves, the morning light shining in shallow crescents as it moved onto the white sand. In the far distance I could even see the outlines of the other towers that rose to the surface, connecting Atlantis to the outside world.

The moment I hit the sand outside the tower's door, I had the urge to sink my bare feet into it. We were on a softer part, not quite where the jagged white rocks hugged the edge of the house-lined streets. When I looked down to admire the beach, I noticed Calliope and her company had no shoes on. It was all the encouragement I needed to ditch mine as well.

Everything in me wanted to jump out of my skin and explore as we walked. Even though it was early, people were awake. The market was waking up. Windows were popping open and airing out homes for the day. I was even thrilled to spot a small patch of field where a cluster of children were giggling about a game involving two balls in a circle drawn in the dirt. We followed a path of footprints through the sand until we reached a white stone staircase that led up to the street level.

"Ashana will meet you in the morning," Calliope's interpreter stated, catching my attention. "As will the other keepers of the House of Sirens."

"And Ashana is your leader?" I asked.

The woman nodded, her smile warm and open. "Indeed she is. As wise as she is skilled with the songs. She will know the most peaceful path to welcome you into our arms."

Peaceful sounded great. Considering I'd been agonizing over my unexpected reception in this unknown place, it was nice to hear they were at least trying to make it an easy transition.

"Basilli," Calliope said. That word I knew, and sure enough, ahead of us stood a man and a woman.

"Should I bow or anything?" I whispered to Nikkos.

"No, none of the sirens will," he answered.

Our group made our way to the two figures, the early sun casting the street in a cheerful pink glow. White petals from a nearby tree littered the street, and I was utterly charmed by the stone paths that veined the island. When Calliope stopped in front of the basilli, so did the rest of us.

"This must be the siren you found," the man said. He reached out to take my hand. "It's a pleasure to meet you. I am Basilli Ateio."

"I'm Madeline," I offered, and he brought the back of my hand to his lips in a light kiss.

This silver fox is a flirt. Not my favorite, but maybe that's charming here.

"This is my wife, Helena." He gestured to the woman at his side. For all the basilli was trying to charm, his wife was indifferent as a statue. She nodded, but didn't say anything more. If anything, her gaze turned cold looking between me and her husband, at where he'd kissed my hand.

Not my fault, lady.

He turned to his wife, speaking in Atlantean so fast that I didn't catch anything except my name. "We welcome you to Atlantis," the basilli said, turning back to me. "I know Calliope will see to your comfort,"—he winked at the older siren—"but please do not hesitate to ask my office for anything. You will find that the sirens are the treasure of Atlantis. Welcome to the island."

"Thank you," I said, not knowing how else to respond but finding myself stepping slightly closer to Caspian.

Satisfied, the basilli said a few things to Caspian and then to Calliope in their native language and then turned and took his cold wife down the street. Caspian's face darkened at whatever the basilli had said to him, and once the basilli was out of sight, I nudged Caspian's arm.

"What did he say?"

He shook his head. Okay, so not something to talk about here and now.

"How did he even find out we were here?" Nikkos wondered.

"He probably heard the commotion when a runner went to get Calliope," Caspian offered. "You know he likes to be where all the attention is."

Calliope talked to the sirens who walked beside her, nodding down the road in the same direction the basilli and his wife had left.

"We will walk with you some of the way to the home of Caspian," my translator said. "Today is a day for rest and to see whatever things you wish to see on our beautiful island. We have much to prepare for you, and tomorrow you are invited to share the morning meal in the House of Sirens."

That sounded all well and fine, but I gave Caspian a glance, and his nod reassured me.

"Thank you," I answered. "I look forward to it."

And so we walked, cool stone under my feet as we followed a twisty cobbled path up a gentle slope. Getting a close-up look at the houses was fascinating. Even more painted details were popping up for me to see now that I was next to them. Some of the domes were made of glass, and with the rising of the sun, I could easily spot which houses had glass and which were made of the same stuff as the base of the house. Tile doorsteps were vibrant with hand-painted ceramic squares. Baskets and pottery sat in gardens and windows, giving me more of an eyeful of the local beauty. It was all white where it could be, and decorated to the nines with saturated colors. Floral patterns, woven lines, and fish. I couldn't get enough of it. My eyes were hungry to see it, and it didn't go unnoticed how many Atlantean eyes were curiously watching our procession as well.

"What are they doing?" I whispered, seeing a pair of teenagers watching me from an upper balcony.

"They may have seen the basilli come this way," Caspian observed.

"That, or they want to know why Calliope is out and about," Nikkos said. "And if they noticed Calliope, they'll have noticed a new face. We don't get new faces, not here."

It made sense, but it also made me bashful. I stepped back and stopped being so obvious about my sightseeing. After all, now that I was here I had all the time in the world to learn about it.

The idea that anyone here could have something to do with my disappearance was hard to wrap my mind around. They were so happy I was here, as odd as that felt. Hell, some of them were probably younger than me anyway, so they couldn't be at fault for anything. I wouldn't ignore anything odd I saw, but for now I trusted the sirens.

Our path continued, and I realized that this was the main road of the island. It wound, it rose, it dipped, but it continued. The other paths that jutted off of it weren't as wide, and I could almost make out where the other end of this path crossed the island up to a large building at the summit, then down to the beach near another tower in the distance. We were halfway up the slope when Calliope stopped near a new road and spoke.

"There you can see the House of Sirens." Her translator pointed. Down the path they had stopped at was a lined road of red flowering bushes and a smattering of tall palms that reached high, as though they could brush the top of the impossibly tall bubble. At the end of the path was a mansion in the same sculpted white material as the other buildings we had seen. Its domed top was huge and glass, and I could see greenery peeking through even from this distance. Columns and statues gave it a more luxurious feel than the houses I'd seen so far.

"I will come to show you the way to breakfast tomorrow." The translator put a hand over her heart. "My name is Maya."

"Thank you, Maya," I said, and then Calliope pulled me into another unexpected hug. These sirens were all huggers, it would seem. Even the keepers of the House of Sirens weren't above it. Hugging her back, I met her warm smile with my own. There may be a language between us, but I remembered the greeting Nikkos had taught me, and I tried it out on Calliope. The letters were odd in my mouth, and I earned giggles at my attempt, but Calliope seemed to like it, and that was what mattered.

The ancient siren spent a moment speaking to Caspian and Nikkos in what I assumed was a scolding tone while the others present attempted to hide their amusement. With a nod, she turned, and I watched them stroll down their road to the grand House of Sirens.

"Why didn't Maya translate that?" I asked.

"Because we were being told under no uncertain terms to treat you like a treasure," Nikkos answered, trying to keep the smile off his face. "It wasn't for your ears."

"Are you sure you don't want to go with them?" Caspian asked. I could feel the heat from his body at my back as he came closer to me, and then I remembered what might be waiting for me at the end of this walk if I was staying in his house. We were off the boat now, so I could make a move, right?

"I've never been surer of anything in my life." Looking over my shoulder, I gave Caspian a coy smile, and he raised one eyebrow at me but didn't say anything more.

"I'll walk with you," Nikkos said, oblivious to our exchange. "It's mostly on the way to Dimitris anyway, and I have a report to give."

"All right, then, let's go." Caspian led the way, continuing up the same road as we passed several points of interest. There was a road that looked like it would take you to the market I'd seen from the beach; there was another one with an interesting pool of water at the end of it; and there was one more with larger buildings strung along a tree-lined path that I had no idea the purpose of, but wanted to find out someday.

As we intersected these paths, Caspian pointed out a set of colored tiles at the corners on the ground where two streets met. Each street had a different color pattern. The main streets were a solid color. We walked on a blue-blue-blue tile path, the House of Sirens was on a yellow-yellow-yellow one, and when we finally turned off the main road where Caspian walked with familiar ease, I was on a road patterned green-white-green.

"I'm a bit off the beaten path, I'm afraid," Caspian said, walking easily with his hands in his pockets and stealing a glance my way. "I can't offer you a house by the beach or an easy walk to the market."

"It's fine," I blurted a little too quickly. Caspian's eyes danced on my flourishing blush as I caught my bottom lip with my teeth. "I want to see it."

Nikkos, eyes narrowing as his gaze flitted between me and his cousin, pulled the bag from his shoulder and handed it to Caspian. "I'm going to go ahead to the Senate offices. I trust you'll get Madeline situated?"

"All tucked in tight," Caspian promised.

Nikkos shook his head, a mixture of amusement and exasperation surfacing as he turned to me. "I'll come back later today with more things from the ship. Get some rest on dry land, Madeline."

"Thanks, Nikkos." I smiled as he nodded to Caspian and walked away.

Being alone with Caspian made my heart race. This new place, the sirens—all of it was exciting, and everything I was ready to explore now that I was here. But Caspian? Caspian I had wanted to explore for longer than I had known about Atlantis.

"It's just this way," Caspian said, oblivious to the thoughts crossing my mind as I followed him. The houses here weren't huge but they looked well kept, with plenty of overflowing greenery to hide doors and windows, lending a degree of privacy that prompted a few absolutely filthy ideas to form in my head. When we stopped to go down a paved walkway, I knew we were at Caspian's house.

White, with two floors and a domed roof that wasn't glass, it was beautiful—half hidden in the shade of those towering palms, with tall flowering bushes and creeping vines making for a lush front lawn. A pool in the side yard held brightly colored fish, and every door, shutter, and window frame was painted in a serene blue that reminded me of the ocean back in Florida.

Caspian opened the front door, letting me inside first. I shrugged off my backpack and dropped it to the floor in the entryway. The tower where I had first seen the sirens was not the only place that had floor-level furniture. Cushions arranged like a sofa took up one wall under a row of windows in the main living space, looking like the most perfect lounging furniture I had ever seen. Tables, shelves of books and baubles, and a peek into the tiled kitchen showed me Caspian's house was as vibrant in detail as the rest of the city had been so far.

"I have a spare bedroom upstairs," Caspian offered, setting down his bag and the one Nikkos had handed him next to mine on the floor. "I'm sure you're hungry, we haven't had breakfast yet."

Fuck breakfast.

Firmly, but with gentle hands, I got Caspian's attention by urging him against the wall and kicking the front door shut.

"Rather than food, we have something between us to discuss." I pressed against him, the delicious heat of our bodies making every line and curve of us that touched burn in my awareness. "Don't you think?"

Caspian let out a low sound. Pleased, but still hesitant. "Maddie. . ."

"We're off the boat," I pointed out, but backed off because I wasn't about to be the person who didn't take no for an answer. "I thought we worked through all this back on the ship—oh!"

Caspian switched our positions with ease, now pressing me against the wall and claiming my mouth with his. His hands moved to feel my skin just under my tank top, his thumbs hooking in the waistband of my shorts.

We were breathing hard, and the kiss broke as Caspian groaned in my ear. "Nikkos is going to kill me for not feeding you first."

Heat was already rushing to my face, where he'd kissed me,

and my hips, where he was rubbing the pads of his thumbs in small, agonizing circles. "I'm not hungry."

"I am." He leaned down and nipped at my bottom lip, pulling a carnal sound from my throat.

"For breakfast?" I breathed.

I could feel the vibration of his laughter through his chest pressed against mine. "Something like that."

I squealed a laugh as Caspian moved his hands and sank his fingers into my plush thighs, lifting me off the floor as I wrapped my arms around his neck. We didn't go far before he set me down on the cushions in the living area.

"Am I going to finally see that tattoo?" he mused.

I had to swallow another laugh as I undid my shorts, sliding them off and leaving myself in a pair of pink lace panties, with the tattoo on my hip exposed. Caspian's gaze was hot on the apex of my thighs for a long moment before he moved his attention to the blue lines on my skin, rubbing them gently with the pad of his thumb.

"A compass rose," he murmured.

"Yeah, I don't know what you know about American teenagers, but every year I think some percentage of us get cringy wanderlust tattoos, and this one was mine," I said. "There, is your curiosity sated?"

My attention flew back to the tattoo when a pair of hot lips pressed into it. "It's cute," Caspian said. "But I'm not even close to done exploring you."

I started to smile at the sweet moment, until I felt the pressure of his fingers at my panties right over my entrance. My eyes flew to see for myself, making any sudden and heated feelings about the situation ten times worse. If we crossed this line, I was truly involved with Caspian.

Good.

"Be careful, Maddie," he said, his expression filled with mischief. "I hear a siren in bed can lose track of her sway if things get heated. Unless that's what you're going for?"

My breath caught even as he remained paused and waiting for my answer. A sly smile spread across my lips. "I would never do such a thing. You better tell me if I do."

"I will, cross my heart. Just know that I'm fine with it either way." His tone was so deep, from such a place of satisfaction and command of the situation that a delicious chill ran up my spine, even as he pushed me into the cushions.

Shorts gone, panties gone, Caspian's hands gripping my thighs and spreading them open like he was opening a present. The joy on his face, quickly followed by a dark smirk as he flicked his eyes up to mine right before settling between my thighs, sent my heart soaring.

Caspian dragged his tongue over my entrance, playful and exploratory at first but soon he was teasing my clit, and I was already squirming.

"You like that, do you?" he mused.

"My weak spot," I managed to get out. "Slightly higher, bigger cirCLE—"

Caspian barely needed the directions before he had me completely figured out. My breath quickly turned to needy panting, and at some point my hands moved down to thread my fingers through his lush, dark hair. It was as soft as I'd imagined.

Changing speed and rhythm, he had me at his mercy quickly. When I truly started to squirm for him, he seemed to sense the building climax winding me tight. He introduced a finger just inside my entrance, toying with me as his mouth focused on the bud of nerves that was driving me wild.

"Caspian—" I barely managed his name in warning when

he added a second finger, attacked my clit with new fervor, and unwound me entirely. I screamed, mostly figuring that out because I scared off a bird outside the window and its flapping wings registered in my ears. Caspian didn't stop until my orgasm had well and truly run out. With hazy vision, I moved my gaze to his.

"Fuck," I managed, drawing a satisfied sound from deep in his chest.

"That's the idea, Madeline." He slid his body up until he hovered over me. His hair was mussed from my fingers running through it and his mouth was wet and swollen from pleasuring me.

My eyes drifted down, where I had a good look of his hard chest through the top of his loose Atlantean shirt. Raising one leg gently, I made sure to brush it softly against the hardness I found in his pants. Good, if he was hard . . .

"My turn," I whispered, and his eyes darkened with a heated anticipation.

And then, the knock.

Three rapid knocks on the door had both of us frozen in place.

"Caspian!" Nikkos called at the most inopportune time imaginable, and Caspian let out a frustrated groan and raked his fingers through his hair, messing it up further. "I'm not coming in, I'm almost afraid of what I'll find in there, but Dimitris demands your presence immediately."

"Shit," Caspian said, rising off the cushions and helping me reach my discarded clothing.

"Do you have to go?" I asked.

He leveled his gaze on me, moving from my face to my hip to the job he had just done between my legs. "Unfortunately, he's not someone I can say no to."

I nodded; there wasn't much to say to that. I was the newcomer in this world, after all. "I understand."

He shot me a warm smile, and we were interrupted again by more of Nikkos's knocking. "Caspian?"

"I'm coming," he called back. Giving me one last look of disappointment, he straightened his appearance in a mirror near the door before slipping out with one last heated gaze my way.

My head flopped back onto the cushions. I should be sated with the amazing job Caspian just did on me, but I still found myself wanting more. I hadn't met this Dimitris yet, but he was currently number one on my shit list.

CHAPTER TWENTY

CASPIAN

Senator Dimitris Lykkosi was not a man to be taken lightly. Even as I left my house to join Nikkos on a brisk walk to the nearby Senate offices, I couldn't help but feel frustrated by my uncle's lack of patience. He secured himself a seat in the Senate representing the structural safety of Atlantis twelve years ago and hasn't even come close to being unseated. Normally, I could expect him to take his time, calculate the information Nikkos brought to him, and then act. But instead, he'd summoned me immediately, which could only mean he was angry about a certain piece of news that was likely now spreading through Atlantis like wildfire.

Madeline.

"What did he say when you told him about Madeline?" I asked, knowing my house was only a few minutes away, and we were growing closer by the second.

"He didn't say anything," Nikkos answered. "He made *the face*."

I grimaced. "The face," as we called Dimitris's expression of displeasure, was the last sign before Dimitris took measures against an obstacle. Madeline was a beacon of hope for the otherwise decreasing population of sirens who kept Atlantis from the watery death just outside of the ring of towers, but all of Dimitris's support for finding new ways to protect Atlantis hinged on the fact that the sirens were weakening, not growing in number.

We moved to the main road, then off to the summit of the city where most of the Senate offices had been built. The sandy brown building that held six of the offices, including the one Dimitris used, was a stately structure. Not only was it adorned with vibrant blue patterns around the doors and windows, but it also held carvings of the founders of the five ancient houses. The dome was one of the more expensive glass ones, made even more expensive by the stained-glass waves that patterned it.

Inside we entered a flowering atrium that basked in the blue and white light from the glass dome. It occupied the central area, and halls to each office radiated off it. The beauty of bringing the greenery inside was just another reminder of our limited space. A few familiar faces lingered in the common space, offering courteous nods but not interrupting our path to Dimitris. Nikkos shot me a look of concern before we turned to the leftmost hallway and knocked on the door.

"Enter," came Dimitris's cold acknowledgment.

Sighing, I let Nikkos and myself in through the heavy door and closed it behind us. The office was furnished simply and efficiently, much like everything my uncle did. There were no adornments aside from whatever embellishment came on the furnishings that had been here long before Dimitris took the office. He had a wall dedicated to shelves of books and files, a commanding desk near the room's large window, and a seating area, where he now occupied a heavy black chair across from the small sofa where he usually received guests.

His demeanor wasn't open or friendly, nor did I expect it to be, but today he looked tired, haggard, as though during the past few weeks that Nikkos and I were away he had been through something.

"Sit, boys," he said, gesturing to the sofa. We took our seats across from him, and his eyes settled on me.

"Tell me about this siren."

I closed my eyes. I had hoped this wasn't the reason he had called me here so urgently, but there was no avoiding it now.

"We found Madeline by chance on the mainland," I began. "The moment she spoke, we knew."

"We couldn't handle it just then," Nikkos added, "but we did run into her again. We didn't have to track her down as I'd feared we would."

Dimitris gave Nikkos a sharp look, silencing him. He wanted answers, but it was clear he wanted them from *me*. Turning his ire back to me, he folded his hands in front of him. "You were certain?"

"Yes," I said firmly. "She's had no training. She didn't even know what she was. Her unchecked abilities have given her more than a few hardships in her life."

"Unfortunate," Dimitris replied. I wasn't sure what part of it he felt was unfortunate: that Madeline had had a difficult life or that we had gone back to find her. "Am I to assume she is already in the care of the House of Sirens?"

Next to me, Nikkos stiffened. He hadn't included that in his report, apparently.

"She's staying with me for now, upon her request. She doesn't know anyone on the island yet, but she will be spending the morning with the other sirens tomorrow, and I expect she will be offered a place to stay with them after that."

Dimitris sighed and turned his attention to Nikkos. "You left the details of the mercenary on my desk?"

"Yes, everything is in the files provided," Nikkos answered.

"Good. One last thing. What did the basilli say when he met the siren?"

"He was pleased," I admitted. "He couldn't resist getting one last comment in before he left either."

Dimitris raised an eyebrow, waiting for me to continue.

"'With his aides bringing new sirens to Atlantis, Senator Dimitris is dismantling his own argument.'" I repeated what the basilli had said on the street.

He closed his eyes for a long moment. "He's not wrong. Nikkos, you're dismissed."

Nikkos gave me a stiff smile then left the room, closing the door behind him. My uncle watched him go, then stood from his chair. Just shorter than me but with a stockier build, his presence still took up more than his share of the space.

"She changes things," he said.

"One siren won't make a difference," I countered. "Not the difference we need. There are fewer and fewer sirens as the years pass. The ones we have are having to commit more time than ever to the towers."

"One siren makes enough of a difference," Dimitris said coldly. He moved to the big window of his office, looking out through the groomed garden in front of the building to the busy street. Throwing the curtain closed, he turned back my way. "One siren means hope, and hope will make more of the people want to hold out before trying a method that will endure without the sirens' abilities."

I ran a frustrated hand through my hair. "I understand the need for Atlantis to try new methods, but is it so bad that a siren has been found to help in the meantime? What I really want to know is why she was in the middle of the continent in the first place."

"That is a puzzle, but not one of my concerns. She's here now, so I trust you will handle it. A siren is still an Atlantean, and that means another tally in the book of people I am trying to save from this slow spiral into the sea," he spat. "Whether they grasp it or not."

My jaw tightened as I smoothed my tone. "And what if others were taken as well? Other children like Madeline, lost and unaware of their power? Not only does it attract the attention of the human population, but there are plenty in the supernatural community that we don't need to remind of the sirens' existence."

"Now, that *is* our concern. I'll bring it to the houses at the next Senate meeting," Dimitris said. "Let them handle the possibility, though I'm sure this will cause the unhurried fledglings to chitter in circles for days first. What I want to know is what you think of the mercenary. Will he fulfill his contract?"

Letting go of my annoyance, I switched gears to my business mask. "His reputation precedes him, and we did our research before settling on approaching Gavin. Nikkos and I spoke personally to what of his past clients we could find, and I was able to make a few calls through the witching networks. Apparently, he's had past dealings with the vampires. I believe he will see the job through."

"Good. Horace and Nephele are returning. Their attempt through that wolf pack in Norway didn't pan out, so let's hope yours doesn't disappoint."

I winced, not envious of Dimitris's ire at their failure. Dimitris moved from the window to his desk where he picked up the files Nikkos had brought him earlier, his eyes now roaming the pages and no longer piercing through me. "You are dismissed, I will see you in the morning to prepare for the next Senate gathering."

Standing, and more than a little relieved to be able to go back to Madeline after the way we'd left things, I saw myself out and closed the door behind me. Leaving the hall and stepping into the atrium, I found my cousin cornered by three other Senate aides.

"Is she pretty?" asked a short woman with an armful of folders.

"She's a siren," scoffed one I recognized as her co-worker; the pair worked for Chrissa, the senator of industry and the current leader of the Senate. "She might be pretty, but what does she sound like?"

"I'm really not at liberty—" Nikkos tried to interject as he backed into a palm tree in the cultivated center of the room.

"Will she be at the next veiled ball?" The speaker was one I knew, Calix. Son and aide to the leader of House Ateio, Adrion. The current basilli. Considering we were only a few years into Basilli Adrion's guidance, I was not looking forward to his retirement, when he would pass on the title to Calix.

My frown deepened as I moved toward the group, reaching a hand to Nikkos's shoulder, my gaze challenging Calix "There won't be any talk of a veiled ball, she's only just arrived. She had no idea what she even was a month ago. And—as if you needed more reason than that—the sirens would be the ones to make the call."

His easy smile hitched up at one side as he raised his hands in defeat. "At ease, Caspian. A man can hope for a ball, can't he? With a brand-new siren, no less. And if that siren would choose that man for her bed? Even better." Something about his grin disgusted me.

A veiled ball, an event the mainland would call a night of debauchery. But in Atlantis, it was a playground for the sirens. To thrill the crowd, to dance to their hearts' desires, and at the end of the night, to take whoever caught their eye to bed if they wanted to. Few sirens took partners for life, preferring to find their own ways to conceive while raising their children as a collective in the House

191

of Sirens. So it had been done for thousands of years, and the veiled balls provided our modern-day version of events. Of course a cur like Calix would hope for a veiled ball, no matter the reason it was being held.

"I hardly think they would hold a ball for a siren who hasn't learned her abilities yet," Nikkos quipped.

"Not at all?" the shorter girl asked.

"But how did she get to the mainland in the first place?" the other asked.

"Enough. Come on, Nikkos." I pulled my cousin free of the overbearing gossips and steered us to the door, much to the protest of the aides begging for scraps of information.

But before we quite left the building, Calix called after us: "Careful, Caspian. It almost sounds like you're laying a claim you have no right to."

Stopping, Nikkos shot me a concerned look. "Let it go, he just wants to rile you up."

I ignored him, turning back to Calix. "I have no claim over anyone, least of all a siren. But I did find her, and it's my job to protect her until I deliver her safely to the House of Sirens. And that, Calix, includes protection from your unwanted comments about a siren who hasn't been introduced to Atlantis yet."

Calix frowned, his lazy expression turning annoyed. Until the House of Sirens announced that Madeline was trained and willing to play her part as a siren for Atlantis, she was to be as protected from the comments and leers of others as a child would be. Even Adrian wouldn't be able to get his son out of trouble if it was decided that he spoke out of line about a siren who had not taken the commitment to Atlantis yet.

"Let's go," Nikkos urged. "She's likely waiting for you, and we should get her breakfast."

192

Dirty Lying Sirens

Nodding, I left with my cousin. The walk back gave me time to cool down.

"Don't let Calix get to you," Nikkos said. "We all know he's a walking dick with no other useful skills to offer."

I snorted. He did have a long list of escapades with the women of Atlantis, if the rumors were to be believed. And his performance as an aide to House Ateio had always left something to be desired.

We arrived at my front door, and I blocked the entrance with my body as I opened it, not knowing what state Madeline would be in when I returned. But there wasn't anything to worry about, and I let out a soft laugh and opened the door the rest of the way, letting Nikkos in with me.

Madeline had fallen asleep, curled up on the floor cushions.

Nikkos and I shared a look of amusement. "Come on," I whispered. "Let's make her a nice breakfast for when she wakes up."

CHAPTER TWENTY-ONE

MADELINE

Thankfully, I'd pulled my clothes back on before settling into the cushions, because when I woke up Nikkos and Caspian were in the kitchen. Then I felt the remnants of that slickness between my thighs and realized that my opportunity to pick back up where Caspian and I had left off had disappeared.

Groaning, I flopped backward on the cushions and threw an arm across my eyes.

"Good morning, Madeline." Nikkos came around the corner. "Did you sleep well?"

Sighing, because it wasn't Nikkos's fault, I rolled onto my side then sat up. "Yup, slept great. These cushions are really soft. Are they the standard furniture around here?"

Caspian came around the corner, wiping his hands on a towel. "Yes, you'll find lounging areas in every home and most public buildings. Always low to the ground."

"Lounging," I said aloud. "That sounds like a lost art."

Caspian chuckled. "Wait until your breakfast with the sirens tomorrow. *They* have it down to an art."

That sounded fabulous.

"Here we go," Nikkos said, bringing a large tray into the main space and setting it on the floor beside the cushions. My eyes went wide, roaming over everything as Nikkos and Caspian took their seats on either side of me. Nikkos with plenty of room between us, and Caspian with less.

"What is all this?" I asked.

"You fell asleep before we came back from the Senate offices," Caspian answered, "but we thought you might still like breakfast when you woke up. We all got up quite early, and it was an eventful walk to my house."

"You were only out an hour or so," Nikkos chimed in. "Just enough time for us to whip up a few Atlantean staples."

Caspian picked up the jug near the middle of the tray and poured a light-purple drink into three handleless ceramic cups. There was a spread of cut fruit, most of it recognizable, but some of it stumped me. There was a little plate of white cheese and crackers with seeds on them, and a bowl of what looked to be the fluffiest scrambled eggs I'd ever seen mixed with greens.

"Is this a typical breakfast?" I asked, picking up one of the crackers and taking an experimental bite. It was salty and crispy.

"That's all down to preference," Nikkos said. "But you're sure to see plenty of fruit. We call it the first sugars of the day, something to wake you up."

"And this is plum tea." Caspian set one of the cups in front of me. "Fruit teas for breakfast are another classic."

"How come we didn't eat this stuff on the boat?" Picking up the cup, I drank a cool, fruity mouthful of the tea. It was sweetened with honey, I thought.

0

"Fresh fruit doesn't keep well on a boat for weeks at a time," Nikkos said.

"And all Nikkos knows how to make are eggs," Caspian added, chuckling as his cousin scowled at him.

"Well, I appreciate everything anyway. Thank you both for breakfast, and for bringing me here." Reaching forward, I tried bits of everything. I watched Nikkos use two crackers to scoop up a sort of sandwich of the egg mixture and pop it into his mouth. I did the same, nearly choking before biting it in half; Caspian laughed at me, and I elbowed him for it. The fruit was delicious, the cheese was kind of salty but still tasty, and the eggs were hot and creamy. And when we were all stuffed, I lay back on the cushions with a contented sigh.

"That was amazing," I said.

"Do you want to walk off the meal?" Caspian asked.

"Ugh, I'm too full for a walk."

Caspian hummed as he piled the empty dishes together and moved them into the kitchen. "All right, you rest up."

"There are a few matters we need to begin dealing with," Nikkos said. "I know we went over this before, but have you thought of any clues at all as to who left you to be found as an infant?"

My smile fell, and I sat up. "None. My file has nothing, there wasn't even any camera footage. I was wrapped in a plain white blanket and had a cloth diaper. There was literally nothing else with me."

Nikkos sighed, tapping his chin. "Right, nothing at all."

"We'll have to begin the search from the other side," Caspian said, sitting back down. "If we can't find Maddie's parent through her side of things—"

"—we find the siren who was missing a child," Nikkos finished. "But there haven't been any such cases. No siren has been born outside of Atlantis. Ever."

The pause that filled the room was only broken by bird calls from outside. I should have been here. I should have been one of the kids playing games on the beach with Caspian. I should have been learning to control my voice with the other sirens my age. But I wasn't, and no one knew why. That childhood despair crept up on me, tendrils of doubt reminding me that my own parents had rather put me in a box at a fire station than keep me. At some point I'd told myself they couldn't keep me. That they knew I'd have a chance at a better life away from them.

But now I was a siren. A desirable member of this society. And I'd still been left in that box.

"The House of Sirens is expecting Maddie at breakfast tomorrow," Caspian said, breaking the solemn air. "That gives us this first day to ourselves. Why don't we get out of the house this morning? I'm already planning to begin inquiries first thing in the morning, once you're safely at the House of Sirens to meet the others."

"Okay," I managed to say. I don't know why it made me so depressed. It wasn't as though I had lost an answer. Just gained a few questions.

"We could show you to the nearest market," Nikkos added. "The one near the summit has the best clothing."

Nikkos wasn't even done speaking before I was climbing to my feet. "I absolutely need to get my hands on some of that."

Laughter followed me, but all I could focus on was grabbing my backpack and pulling out my wallet. This was exactly what I needed; I should be over the moon here. A new home, and already I'd received more smiles and hugs than I would have expected in a year back home. And then I froze, looking back at them with my wallet in hand. "I can't use any of my money here, can I?"

Not that I had a lot, but still.

"Remember when I said I'd set you up with the profits from

the sale of your car with Atlantean currency?" Caspian asked, and I nodded as the memory clicked. "I did it all over the phone before we got here. Do you want to go pull some of it out now?"

I threw my arms around his neck. "Yes! Holy cow, I have money!" Then I pulled back to look him in the eye. "How much money? What should I be saving? How much will clothes cost?"

"Slow down, Madeline." Nikkos piped up. "You have plenty for a trip to buy clothes. Let's sort out the details on the way."

"Deep breaths," Caspian murmured, his breath hot on my ear as he placed a commanding finger and thumb at the base of my neck. "In and out."

My insides thrummed at the command of his words, none of them harsh, but something in me wanted to do as he said. Nothing got my motor running quite like a confident man. Maybe that was what had drawn me to Caspian in the first place.

I took the deep breath, and Caspian's touch eased up and left my neck. "There we go, you're okay."

A slow breath left me, and I straightened out my clothes. Nikkos opened the front door with a creak, and the morning sun beamed in, as if calling us to come outside.

"Let's go then." Caspian followed his cousin out the door, pulling me out of the house.

In the sunshine of the greenery-lined street, I had to pay more attention to our surroundings than to the broad shape of Caspian's back, so I could focus on learning the ways of my new home.

I saw more white buildings with vibrant details. More people in those flowy clothes, made for the breezes that blew through the city. I asked why there was a breeze at all in a bubble underwater, but they said it was the flow of the sirens' magic between the towers, and I let it go at that. This was not the time to question the delectable salt air that brushed across my skin.

We went to a street that held several statues. Some gold, others marble, all of them acutely detailed. Between the statues and more lush greenery, the buildings seemed to have more business-oriented purpose than the houses I'd seen before. Nikkos and Caspian took me into one such place, where they helped me communicate with a banker and withdraw some coins that I had no idea the value of, but I trusted the guys I was with not to let me go into overdraft. But the moment I opened my mouth to ask questions, eyes fell on me and stayed there.

"They can tell you're a siren," Caspian whispered. "Don't mind them."

"They make it kind of hard to ignore," I muttered back. The rest of my questions were whispered to Nikkos or Caspian.

The amount of technology in the bank was in stark contrast to the ancient building and Atlantean style, but considering Caspian and Nikkos were well versed in laptops and cell phones, it made sense that technology from other parts of the world had trickled in. The banker used a computer, there were lights rigged up in the darker corners of the building, and more than one person behind the counter was looking at a screen of some kind or other. I hadn't really noticed dark corners inside Caspian's house, but the only things I'd paid much attention to so far were the food and Caspian.

With money in my pocket and shopping ahead of me, I left the bank behind and followed the guys a few streets down to the market. It was huge—a long and winding street that might have even been the one I'd seen in the distance from our entrance on the beach. Most of the stands were open-air tables, many with colorfully dyed shade cloths. There was everything available, from food to clothing to pottery and baskets and jewelry. A few more permanent structures had some things of interest. Tools, books, crafting supplies, and even what looked like a collection of generators, which Nikkos explained were developed locally as a solar-powered electrical source for homes and that adapted external technologies like my laptop.

But aside from the unexpected things I saw peering out of a few different stores, I managed to keep my sights set on clothing. And I was not disappointed.

We were walking along and Nikkos was explaining something about the origin of paint or something when I saw exactly what I was after. Hanging on high poles and strung wide for the whole market to admire, a stall of dresses displayed splayed-out skirts with dye and beads painting magical scenes along the bottom hem. Fields of flowers, turquoise waves, and flying birds dazzled me as I changed course to get a better look.

I reached out slowly to brush my fingers on a wooden bead that made up a blue bird's eye, and a man with wrinkles around his eyes and deep laugh lines by his silver beard came to my side. He said something in Atlantean, and the only word I caught was *beautiful*, but his tone was pleasant, so hopefully we were talking about the dress. I looked at him, baffled as he continued in his Atlantean speech, and noted his long beard, which had beads braided into it, and his light, open shirt with a pattern of dyed fish at the bottom, which looked very much like the art on the dresses of the shop.

"Oh, you're the shop owner!" I said, and his eyes went wide. He started speaking even faster, and I grimaced.

"I'm sorry, I don't speak well yet. Um, *parde . . . pardeci . . .* shit, what is the word for *a little bit*?"

"Hold on." Nikkos approached and then rattled off something in Atlantean to the man. Caspian came up to my side and put a hand on my shoulder. I sighed and leaned into him.

"You stepped away from us," he said. "It took us a moment to find you."

"Sorry, I was distracted by these."

Caspian looked up at the dresses in the stall. "Lovely. Are these what you'd like?"

"Would it be weird to wear them?" I asked. "I mean, they aren't for a specific thing, right? Would I look too dressed up?"

"No, not at all. Let's see." Caspian looked around the market. "There, do you see those dresses down the way? The ones that have more beading all over them, not just at the edges?"

Following where he pointed, it didn't take long to see them. "Yeah."

"That would be more formal. The ones you have here are for everyday use. You could find something with even less detail if you wanted, but these would be just fine."

"Okay, so those ones down the road are for fancy events?"

"Not exactly, just nicer than everyday clothes. For a truly grand event or for a holiday, the entire piece of clothing is dyed."

"Oh, wow," I whispered. "I'd love to see that."

"You will," Caspian said, and the emotion in his voice drew my eyes to his. They were warm, and something under the surface of his gaze tugged at my heartstrings.

"Can't wait," I managed to respond, and then Nikkos turned back to us again.

"All right." Nikkos clapped his hands. "I've got it all cleared up now. Were you wanting one of these dresses, Madeline?" The little old man in the booth looked on eagerly, waiting for my response beyond the language barrier.

My eyes roamed back to the dress with the birds on the bottom. "Can I afford this dress?" I asked.

Nikkos exchanged a few words with the man and laughed as he turned back to me. "Madeline, with what you have in your pocket you could afford a dozen of them."

My eyes lit up, and I turned back to the dresses hanging over the stand. "I want these six!" I pointed to the ones that had drawn my eye the most. "And I need to find some of those cute strappy sandals all the girls are wearing."

After some more translating by Nikkos, we had worked out a deal, and I gave up some of my coins to acquire the Atlantean clothing I'd had my heart set on. We left, and I practically floated behind Caspian as he took me to another place where I could get the sandals. According to Nikkos, both stands had given me a hefty discount because they could tell I was a siren. I tried to get the fair price, but there was no dissuading the old man at the dress shop or the fierce old lady who wove the sandals.

With the market done and my breakfast officially walked off, we headed back to Caspian's house for another round of tea.

Sinking into the cushions, I yawned. "I can't tell you the last time I got to shop to my heart's content."

Caspian snaked a warm hand onto my thigh, patting it and drawing heat to his touch, but he kept his words innocent. "Get used to it, there won't be any more worrying about your bed or your next meal. Not in Atlantis."

"Shoot," Nikkos said, looking through the big glass panes at the light. "We were out longer than expected. I need to get going, I have things to take care of."

Caspian nodded. "Take care, cousin."

"You too." Nikkos turned to me as he got up, flashing me a genuine smile. "And I hope you settle in well for the night. Try using a bed this time."

I threw one of the cushions in his direction while Caspian laughed.

"All right!" Nikkos put his hands up in defeat. "All right, I'm going. See you two later."

And Nikkos let himself out.

Immediately, my eyes turned to Caspian. "So what do we do now?" I asked, somewhat playful and somewhat heated, letting him pick the direction.

"Hmm, what to do with the siren in my house, lying on the cushions in front of me . . ."

Raising an eyebrow, I fluttered my lashes at him. "Nothing comes to mind?"

He laughed. "As much as I'd like to start something, I think I wouldn't be a very good host if I didn't offer you a bath in an authentic Atlantean soaking pond."

The sun here was warm, and I probably had a bit of sweat still clinging to me. Not to mention I was tired of the cramped shower from the boat. But an honest to goodness bath . . .

"Caspian," I purred, "if you don't show me this fancy bath right now, I'll never forgive you."

Caspian threw back his head and laughed. "Okay, okay. It's less of a bath and more of a place with hot water to relax. We shower first, then come out to soak. Let's get you a towel and a set of clothes to change into, and I'll show you the way."

"Perfect," I said, and I meant it. I did want the hot soak. Needed it, probably. And a part of me hoped this pond thing was big enough for two.

CHAPTER TWENTY-TWO

MADELINE

I hadn't explored much of Caspian's house. In fact, apart from the main living space and a very updated bathroom, I hadn't seen anything yet. The kitchen I had only seen from the doorway in the living room, and my bedroom I hadn't seen at all. But as Caspian helped me carry my new dresses and bags to a room upstairs, I was awed.

The mattress was on some kind of light, wood platform, low to the ground. Cream-colored bedding overflowed the bed, with green beads and tassels all around the edges. One wall had a window looking out to the side of the yard. There wasn't a lot to see that wasn't lush green plants, but I was still excited for it. Another wall held a wardrobe where Caspian hung my dresses, and the wall above the bed had a huge tapestry depicting a tree with a dozen colorful birds in it.

"It's gorgeous." I turned to Caspian as I dropped my bag on the floor. "Thank you for letting me stay tonight."

Caspian's eyes softened as he closed the wardrobe, finished hanging the dresses. "I'm happy to have you here."

Heat crept up my neck, and I changed the subject. "So, how does one use an Atlantean soaking pond? Do I need a bikini?"

Caspian chuckled, then his eyes turned sharp and hot. "Clothing optional."

The heat on my neck crept higher, but there was nothing but a smile on my face. "Oh? Is that normal, or is that a house rule?"

"It's not uncommon here," he said, shrugging off his shirt, and his scent mixed with the light sandalwood he burned in his house was intoxicating.

When bare-chested Caspian stood in front of me, it was easy to lean down and grab a towel from my bag. "No clothes, then."

Amusement crinkled at the edges of his face as he turned to leave the room. "I'll see you in the backyard, then. You know where the shower is, then the back door is just through the kitchen."

He left, carrying his shirt and closing my door behind him.

A delicious shiver ran down my back, and I practically skipped out the door and to the bathroom. I heard pipes in the walls before I even turned it on, so it would seem Caspian had his own bathroom as well.

After cleaning up quickly, I tied my hair up, unsure of how much actual soaking would happen in this little adventure we were about to have. I could always let my hair down later, but if we got frisky, and I sure as shit hoped we would, I didn't want sections of wet hair in my face to get in the way.

Wrapping my towel around me, I made my way through the house and into the kitchen. The room was warm and welcoming, with a small fireplace in one corner that looked quite old. But many things in Atlantis had been this way. A mix of old and new that reminded me of picturesque European villages. On the one hand, I loved the hand-painted and carved look of things here. On the other hand, showers and toilets from this decade were really nice to have. I knew they had been stuck in this bubble for centuries, but that hadn't stopped them from keeping up with modern luxuries.

My heart raced as I put my hand on the light-green painted door to the backyard. Caspian was already out there, right? His shower had stopped before mine had. What should I be expecting? The use of the word *pond* had me hesitating, but not for long, and I pushed open the door.

The evening light through the water high overhead cast an enchanting glow over the yard. A white wall bordered everything, but I almost couldn't see it through the ferns and flowering bushes. Even the neighbors' rooftops were barely visible, giving that element of privacy I'd been hoping for when we first walked down Caspian's street.

In the middle of the yard was a round pool of water, set in the ground and made of painted tiles. A matching hole with a short chimney hugged the far edge of it. Threads of smoke lifted, showing where Caspian had already put wood into it to make the water against that side warmer. The man himself was sitting with his back to me, his arms resting on the edge of the pool. He turned to see me, his expression filled with amusement. I couldn't tell if he was naked from this angle, but with my towel on, the same was true for him.

"It's beautiful," I murmured, my eyes following the ring of the pool. A reedy grass and floating flower pads edged a third of the pond, separated by more tile and situated away from the area with the fire. Movement in the water revealed tiny silver fish swimming, their scales reflecting off the evening light. Floating, glowing dots caught my eye as I followed the line of the yard.

"Fireflies?" I asked.

"Similar. Maybe a related breed. They're one of the best pollinators on the island. Them and the bees. They're to thank for all the flowers."

I smiled, stepping closer to one of the glowing insects, but it darted away too fast. Then my eyes landed on the pool again.

"So, do I just get right in? No stairs?" I asked.

Caspian nodded. "It's shallow, there's a bench around the whole wall for you to sit."

Getting closer, I could see the bench. Then an idea hit me, and I walked around the edge, away from Caspian. Looking back, I could see him watching me intently with a knowing look. He didn't make a move as I rounded to the opposite end. Now I had a full view of him under the water, and even in the fading light I could see his shape. I knew from all our previous interactions that Caspian was hard lines and broad shoulders, but all of him displayed in this relaxed position on the bench in the water . . . you could have told me he was a sculpture, and I would have believed you. My eyes shifted down, and he didn't make a move to cover himself. Whatever gods had given him this form were also generous with what he had below the water, and I moved my legs closer together as dirty thoughts began to heat me up.

"Clothing optional," I mused.

He smirked. "And what option did you choose, Maddie?"

My heart was racing, but I pulled open my towel and dropped it behind me. I liked feeling sexy; I always had. Maybe it was a siren thing, now that I thought about it. But in the first brief moment after I ditched my towel, every word I'd heard about my body was making its way to the surface of my thoughts. When bitter exes called out my thighs, my butt, my arms, for being bigger than they wanted. When I first found my love of working out at the gym and my history teacher made an offhand comment about adding more bulk to my frame. But all of the thoughts, daggers in my mind against my own body, were swept away by the look on Caspian's face.

My breath caught at the fire, the hunger, in his expression.

"Madeline," he whispered. "You're beautiful."

I could have melted at that, but I was too busy dipping my foot into the water to find the bench. The water was warm, matching the air from earlier when the sun was out, and Atlantis was in a fully-bloomed summer despite it being April. Finding my step, I sank into the water and walked slowly through it, making my way to Caspian. He moved to meet me, and we settled next to each other, our eyes locked.

"So," I murmured, "what now?"

Caspian leaned in. Just enough, teasing and tempting.

"I can tell you about the pond," he offered.

"No thanks, Nikkos." I laughed. "Try again."

"How about the plants I grow around it? There's a reason for them. Or maybe you want to learn about the fish?" The gravel in his voice deepened. "Or we could pick up where we left off this morning."

Oh, hell yeah. We have a winner. I don't think I had two clear thoughts to rub together in my head when I pressed forward, my bare chest hitting Caspian's as I kissed him.

The warmth of the water was nothing compared to the heat between us. The moment our lips met, he scooped me onto his lap to straddle him. One arm held on to his shoulder for support, the other had to reach up and cup his face, running fingers gently over his jaw and down his neck.

Caspian groaned, pulling back to lean his head against my shoulder. "I need to touch you."

Hungry, I kissed his temple. His neck. His ear. "Anywhere you want, Caspian."

A dark laugh from his chest bubbled between us, and I squeaked as he lifted me out of the water and sat me on the edge of the pool. The tiles were cool under my bare skin, but my feet were still in the water and the air was warm enough that I wasn't shivering. And all of those sensations fell away as Caspian knelt on the bench in the water, facing me. He nudged my knees apart and settled himself comfortably between them, distracting me further with another kiss.

My arms settled around his shoulders again before I started looking for places where he would enjoy my touch. His neck, his chest. Waiting for a sound or movement that told me I was on the right track. And then I felt his fingers brush the inside of my thigh. He ran a finger right up my opening, stopping over my clit. Even if it wasn't for the water, he would have found me sopping wet. Caspian made a very satisfying sound when I wriggled under his touch.

"Maddie." My name was a carnal moan. "I didn't want to leave you this morning, all you did was light a hotter fire in me."

I sucked in a breath. "This morning, I didn't get to reciprocate."

Caspian pulled back at that, his eyes searching mine. "You know I don't want you to reciprocate, right?"

Pausing, I tried to sift through his meaning.

A muscle in his jaw tightened. "Maddie, do you feel as though you need to do something for me? Because I'm doing something to bring you pleasure?"

Mixed feelings swirled through me for a moment. Maybe I felt a little called out, but he wasn't wrong. Caspian sighed, taking my hands in his and placing them on his shoulders as he spoke. "Madeline, whoever made you feel like sex was transactional was not worthy of the act. You shouldn't be doing anything that you feel obligated to do, it should be what you *want* to do."

My hands were firmly in place on his shoulders, and he looked me in the eyes. "Your hands are to stay right here, right where I put them. Okay?"

I nodded.

"Good girl."

My lips parted in surprise. I shivered, but my hands stayed on him.

"If those hands leave where I put them, I'm stopping. You don't want me to stop, do you, Madeline?"

My breath caught in my throat, and I shook my head. What the fuck was this man doing to me? He hadn't called me Madeline when it was just the two of us since I'd told him to use Maddie, but somehow he made it sound sensual. A secret between us. When his fingers found my thighs again, I sucked in a breath.

"That's it, hold on tight. No wandering hands. Just let me explore you and let go."

His words were a warm buzz in my head and on my skin as he sank one finger into my wet heat. Then another, then his thumb found my clit, and a whispered whine escaped my lips.

"That's it, Madeline." Caspian spoke soothingly. "And remember, you're a siren. One word from you and I stop. You have all the power here, all of it. But you won't need to use the sway, because I'm already at your beck and call. One word from your lips is all the command I need."

Caspian's hands were as skilled now as they had been in the morning, lifting me dangerously high up that cliff of tightly wound nerves before the plummet of release. His other hand took to exploring the rest of me. My ass, my breasts, cupping my face. His kisses were soft and sweet, but his words were fucking filthy.

"You feel amazing, Madeline. Hot and so very wet for me."

His low rumble in my ear was going to undo me completely. "Everything about you smells like sex. How many times on that boat did I want to bend you over the railing to fuck you in front of the sea?"

I started to move my hands, looking for something to do with them.

"Move your hands back where I fucking put them," Caspian murmured.

Immediately, I complied, digging my fingers in a little to make sure I wasn't moving them. He had made it clear I was to enjoy the ride and nothing else.

"Caspian." My voice was strained. I didn't know what I was even saying. A warning that I was close? A plea to finish me off? But whatever my meaning was, it didn't matter anymore as Caspian moved his mouth over mine, stimulating my clit with his thumb and hooking his fingers just inside of me at the perfect angle to make me explode.

And explode I did. He had me wound so high and so tight that my vision blurred as the orgasm hit me. And he didn't stop moving. Caspian had found the perfect buttons to push to make me come for him, and from the look in his eyes, he took deep satisfaction in it. He didn't let up until the last waves of pulsing muscles and screaming nerves left me a puddle in his arms. He even let my hands slip off of his shoulders without complaint.

"Thank you for showing me a little bit of heaven, Madeline," Caspian murmured, letting his fingers slip out of me as his other arm supported my back. "Do you want more?"

More? Hell fucking yes, I do.

"Shit," I breathed. "Yes, please." Absolute jelly, that was what I felt like in that afterglow. Caspian kissed me, taking his time as I recovered from the screaming sensitivity of what he had just done to me. And then he pulled back to see me better.

"If it's time to stop, you tell me to stop," Caspian said. The heat of his body moved away as I watched him reach for the towel I had discarded in the grass. Placing it behind me, he laid me on the soft surface. The grass underneath served as cushion, and the towel was a courtesy, a soft gesture at complete odds with his rough, commanding words.

"I'm going to pin your sexy body beneath me and fuck you right here in the grass until I hear my name on your lips again." His words were full of promise, but his eyes paused on me, giving me an opening. An out, if I wanted it.

I shook my head, smiling. After what he'd just done to me? He could do whatever he wanted. I had about two months left on my birth control shot, and anything after that was a problem for later.

Caspian's smile widened as he lifted himself out of the water. Making himself a space between my open legs, he took his cock in one hand, stroking it as he looked down at me. "Gorgeous."

I bit my lower lip, and my hands moved at my sides to grip the towel. Something, anything for my hands to do. Caspian's eyes flicked to the movement, and he stopped stroking himself to move over me.

"You know the rules, Madeline." He took my wrists and moved them above my head, gently caging a wrist on either side of my head with his hands. "No moving, no reciprocating. All you're allowed to do is lie there and enjoy, understand?"

I was way past words at this point, and I nodded vigorously while trying to catch my breath. Caspian smirked, freeing one of my wrists long enough to position himself at my entrance before trapping the wrist again.

And then he pushed. I could feel everything. How big he was, how wet he made me. Caspian pushed in until there was nowhere else to go. A perfect fit, making me feel so full and so hot.

His forehead came down to touch mine as he looked into my eyes. "You're perfect, Maddie."

My breath left me, and my whole body was on fire. I wriggled, trying to move that delicious friction inside me.

"Say it." Caspian pulled out and I whined at the loss, the emptiness I wanted him to fill again. "Repeat what I just said."

"Caspian . . ."

"Say it, Madeline," he growled. "Say how perfect you are."

Holy hell, this man. His gentlemanly act in front of other people was all a farce. Caspian was some kind of lust god, and I was only just finding that out now.

"I'm . . . perfect."

Caspian thrust in, hard and fast, bringing with him the pressure and friction my body craved.

"You deserve love." He pulled out again.

"I deserve love."

This time when he thrust, I couldn't help but loose another sound of wound-up pleasure.

"You are smart."

"I am smart."

"You are patient."

"I am patient."

"You are stunning."

"I am stunning."

On and on he went, his body and hands pinning me in place so thoroughly that there was little I could do but hold on for whatever ride Caspian wanted to take me on, repeating his affirmations and earning his cock in return. I had already come just minutes before, but already he had me back at the top of that cliff, ready to plunge off again.

"Caspian—" I moaned.

"Yes, Madeline," he said, planting a kiss on my lips. "I was waiting to hear my name on those sweet mouth of yours again. Now, come for me. Let me feel all of it."

And I did. I came so hard, completely pinned in place as the feeling of him hit me. I rode through his hard thrusts. I was barely coming down, not even finished clenching around Caspian when he groaned and his movements changed. I felt him spill into me, hot and wet when I was at my most sensitive, and I cried out again.

"Fuck, Caspian," I panted.

"That dirty mouth of yours." He kissed me, his face completely sated, though lust still sat heavy in his eyes.

I laughed. "You're one to talk."

He kissed me again, moving out of me and lying next to me on the grass. "You're perfect, Madeline," he murmured in my ear, and I shivered. "You're perfect, don't let anyone tell you otherwise ever again. And in time, I want you to take what you want."

Rolling over as Caspian pulled me into his arms, I vowed to follow that advice. No one would ever make me feel less again. Not even me.

CHAPTER TWENTY-THREE

MADELINE

Atlantis was a paradise, and I couldn't help but hold my breath and wait. Wait for the other shoe to drop, wait for a darker side to show itself. So far there wasn't one, but I hadn't survived this long by taking things at face value.

So when I walked through the streets, memorizing the color patterns so I could get back to Caspian's house on my own if need be, I wasn't surprised that my behavior was distressing to my guide.

"I'm not here to kidnap you," Maya said. "If you aren't ready to meet the sirens, I can go back and tell Calliope—"

"No! I'm okay, really." I flashed Maya a smile. "Maybe I'm nervous."

Nervous, because I was used to looking for an exit before I even arrived. It was due to being separated from Nikkos and Caspian. Still, it made me feel bad. I liked Calliope and Maya. A lot, actually, and I didn't want to go to this breakfast and mess things up.

Maya's face softened. "I'm sure you are. Would it help to know that some of the others are anxious to meet you too?"

"They are? Why?"

Maya laughed, a light and happy sound. "They think you'll be disappointed that we don't have everything the mainlands have to offer."

"No way, I already love it here."

"Good," Maya said. "Then I think you'll get along just fine."

We walked a few more minutes while the butterflies in my stomach settled down. "Hey, Maya?"

"Mm?"

"Are you a siren too?" I asked. I had assumed she was, since she'd arrived with Calliope yesterday, but it was never explicitly mentioned.

"No, I just wanted to volunteer to bring you, so you'd have a familiar face." Maya beamed at me. "I'm a translator by trade. With all the outside cultures, technology, and entertainment we have here on the island, it's important to have access to many languages."

"That's so cool. I've always wanted to learn another language, but I was garbage at it in school. How many do you speak?"

Maya laughed. "English, Arabic, Mandarin, Spanish, and of course Atlantean."

I whistled. "You're impressive, you know that?"

"I had to be, if I wanted a chance to see the surface. I haven't yet, but maybe someday," she answered.

"Wait, you've never been away from Atlantis?" I asked.

"Few have," she explained. "It's how we keep such a tight lock on our secrets. Plenty of Atlanteans would love to be able to see outside the bubble, but only select people with specific jobs ever get to go. Like the five houses, they can go. Or Caspian, if a senator sends him."

"But why?" I asked. I couldn't imagine not leaving my hometown. I mean, now that I was here, I could picture staying forever. It was paradise. But, still.

"We're in a very vulnerable state here. If enough of a powerful group, or if someone else who had magic like the sirens was to come here, it could be devastating."

"Others with magic?" I asked.

She shrugged. "I've heard the stories. Witches, people who cast magic. People who turn into wolves and things when the moon shines on them."

"Those are just stories," I said, but my words weren't very convincing.

Maya shook her head. "And I'm sure before you got here you thought the sirens were just stories too."

I didn't have a retort, because she was right.

We had arrived at the yellow road that would take us to the House of Sirens. Suddenly, my hands didn't know what to do. I wondered if my hair was out of place, if the dress I'd chosen with the waves dyed around the bottom would be out of place, if I'd say something weird.

The closer we came to the grand building, the more details I could see. If I thought Caspian's house was comfortable and accommodating, this place made that seem like sleeping in a cardboard box. Art. Everywhere. Sculptures, paintings, a stunning fountain in the side yard. Benches, cushions, and blankets strewn about, just asking passersby to take a nap on them. Flowers everywhere. It was gorgeous; it made me think of a palace fit for a princess. Which, in some ways, it was.

"She's here!"

Shorter than me, with huge aqua eyes and braids down to her butt, it took me a moment to recall the name of the first siren I'd met at the tower where we'd left the boat.

"Amara!" My chest warmed to have someone familiar here besides Maya. Especially since I didn't know if Maya would be staying, since she wasn't a siren.

Amara launched herself out of the now-open doors of the house, running barefoot with the lushest cream gown I'd seen yet billowing behind her and reminding me of fairy wings. Tiny pink beads and stitched silk ribbon settled around the edges in a braid of roses when Amara wrapped her arms around me in a fit of laughter.

"Easy, Amara," another woman called from the doorway, and I looked up to see a dozen pairs of eyes peering over shoulders to get a look at me. The one who spoke was tall and lean, holding herself regally and reminding me of a cat. Her hair was cropped short to her head, and she wore a long gown with deep-purple hyacinth decorations.

"*Agu'oh! Agu'oh matta!*" The tiniest old woman I've ever seen hobbled on a silver-capped cane to the elbow of the tall, queenly one, who moved out of her way. She was clearly speaking Atlantean, and I was thankful when Maya murmured next to my ear.

"Scoot, scoot over."

I slipped out of Amara's hug, and she took my hand firmly in hers to walk with me up the path to the house.

"That's Ashana," Amara told me. "She's the head keeper of the House of Sirens."

"What's a keeper?" I whispered.

"A siren whose voice has retired so that her mind can guide the sirens," Amara explained. It didn't completely answer my question, but I had a general idea.

Ashana, bless her, was barely bigger around than my thigh. But she commanded a space among the sirens crowding the doorway, and she looked at me with the most crystal-blue eyes.

Blue eyes. I suddenly felt very stupid looking into a dozen

blue-eyed faces. Some of them had tinges of green or darkness in their depths, but they were all some form of ocean. It clicked. I had them, Caspian and Nikkos had them, and so did every other person I'd met in Atlantis.

"Oh my god, everyone here has blue eyes," I said.

A small burst of laughter flitted through the crowd, followed by a translation and then a larger burst of giggles.

"Everyone in Atlantis," Maya clarified.

"Oh," I said, quieter. "That explains things."

My answer was met with more amusement. I saw Calliope in the back, smiling warmly. I smiled back, glad to have another familiar face. But by now we had reached the front door and Ashana. The old woman was in a billowy white blouse and wide-legged pants, but with more decoration on her than anyone else present, from gold-threaded embroidery to the bangles and rings she wore. She held her cane out for Amara to hold, then thrust her two wrinkled hands out and grabbed mine.

When she began rapidly speaking in Atlantean, I caught about three words of a greeting before I was totally lost. Thankfully, Maya took over.

"A thousand welcomes home. Our hearts overflow to know you. Please come feast at our table and let our hearth become your hearth—gah, sorry Madeline, she's speaking very formally and very fast."

Maya paused to listen to Ashana, her face scrunched in concentration so she could finish translating.

"Please join us in the back garden, we are bathing our feet and letting the ocean hear our hearts. We offer you a room with your sisters and the teachings of the keepers, so you may learn as one with us to sing to the water."

Okay. I sort of grasped the meanings there.

219

"Please tell me you'll be with me for this," I murmured to Maya, who laughed and then confirmed that she would.

After Ashana's greeting, I was crowded by a dozen women ranging in age from as old as Ashana and Calliope to a girl who was maybe twelve, all knees and elbows with her hair in two neat braids. With many exchanged greetings, both in English and Atlantean, I was ushered to the back where I was getting a . . . footbath? I wasn't sure from what Ashana said, to be honest, but it became clear when we walked around the House of Sirens, and I was greeted by a bathing pond.

Thankful that I knew what that was, I smiled, feeling the heat creep up my neck, remembering what Caspian and I had done in his just last night.

"This is a bathing pond," Maya explained. "The round pool is for us to use, and the crescent around it grows edible fish and plants. Most yards in Atlantis keep a bathing pond."

Keeping the knowledge of bathing ponds I'd recently gained— and how I got that knowledge—to myself, I joined the girls who all sat on the neat white tiles by the pool, dipping their feet in and clearing up the idea of a footbath. Maya and I had to take our sandals off, but everyone else was already barefoot.

"Next to me, Madeline," Amara all but demanded, as she tugged me down to sit with her.

Once we were all seated, even ancient Ashana dipped her feet in, though they barely reached the water. And with that, the feasting began. Food plates were brought over by two more women with big smiles on their faces. Their sarong-like skirts were dipped in vivid blues, giving their clothing an ombre effect, and they wore what I would call a halter top but with little shells sewn around the necklines. And fuck if they didn't look comfortable as hell.

"They care for the sirens," Maya whispered to me. "They are

paid handsomely, and it is a position of honor. They fought hard to be here."

Guessing this was something like being a butler for a rich family or an assistant to a celebrity, I hummed in acknowledgment. But they looked happy, they were paid, and I could roll with that. Especially after one of them came by to offer me some kind of fruit and honey pastry that melted in my mouth. Another soon joined, and I got a cup of that plum tea Caspian had given me yesterday.

It was the most pampered I'd ever felt. At first I was stiff, but these sirens made it too easy to get comfortable. My feet were soaking in a blissful pool of water, the sun was warm on my face, and the food was freely offered. I could really go for a vanilla latte, two shots, extra whip, but otherwise, this was perfection.

The morning slipped away easily. Amara could talk about a mile a minute, but her English was amazing, and I had no trouble catching what she said. Others pressed her or Maya to translate things for them, and even the shy little girl was giving me coy smiles, though she didn't try to communicate. I didn't blame her; there were a lot of mouths making noise already, and to be heard was a battle.

It all came to a baited hush when Ashana tapped the butt of her cane on the tiles next to her and the sirens stilled. It wasn't uncomfortable or anything, it was almost like they were expecting it. And then Ashana let out two notes, her tone clear, like she was singing a tune with no words, but it did something to me. Stirred inside me, sent chills down my arms.

The other sirens joined in. They all knew this tune, and again without words, they added their voices to Ashana's. Two simple notes, one low, the second high.

Heads turned to me, and Calliope said something.

"This is how they teach the young sirens," Maya translated. "And they want you to join them."

"Oh, boy," I whispered under my breath, but not softly enough to avoid giggles from a few English speakers who heard me.

I tried the two notes. A bit awkward at first, but then Ashana led us in another round and this time I joined when the others did. Soon, she added another pair of notes, going up higher again. Then another, then another, until it was time to bring the notes back down in a kind of stepping pattern.

It wasn't that the music was hard; I'd already picked up the repeating patterns of it. What lent it an eerie feeling was that I felt connected. My voice and those of the other sirens, all singing together. It had its own sort of vibration to it, like pieces of a puzzle that were meant to be together. I loved music, I loved singing, but this was something else entirely, and I knew in my heart I was supposed to be doing it.

This was heaven. This was flexing a muscle that had been itching to flex for twenty-six years. Several tears fell, and I couldn't have said if they were happy or sad or what. They just were, and so was this song.

When Ashana switched up the tune, we followed. This one felt different, because with this one everyone had their eyes on me. They raised their hands when the notes went high and brought them down when the notes went low. I sang with them, but what was about to happen that they all wanted to look at me?

Then I felt the buzz, the life dancing around the pond. Only it wasn't just the siren song I was feeling, it was something in between all of us.

The water lifted, higher and higher, as a wave formed in the middle of the pond. My eyes flew wide as I stared at it. Caspian and Nikkos could have told me the sirens commanded the sea and shaped the bubble until they were blue in the face, but it wasn't until this moment when it all hit home.

The sirens commanded the sea.

We didn't stop for a long time. My heart filled with their voices, the song spilled into my soul. Sometimes Ashana would switch it up, make it more complex or change the tempo, making the water in front of us roll or bounce or still. But always she started, and the rest of the sirens harmonized. I knew there was no way I could live without this again. Caspian had told me; I'd even told him I believed him. But here, sitting by the others and singing the song, I *knew* I was a siren.

I was home.

CHAPTER TWENTY-FOUR

CASPIAN

Madeline was with her sisters now, and I had tasks to focus on. Or so I kept telling myself while flipping through the driest text ever written on the census data from the years before Madeline would have been born. It was hard to know where to start. You'd think a siren with a missing baby from the last few decades would be a known thing, but so far no one had any answers. Was there the possibility that a siren had gotten out sooner, and that was Madeline's mother? There were too many ways in which something could have gone wrong, too many years to cover to find the missing link. Why would *anyone* want to remove a siren? Unless the reason to get rid of Madeline wasn't because of what she was. So what other reasons could there be?

Tapping my pen on my desk next to Dimitris's private office, I glanced out the window.

"You're going to wear a hole in your desk hammering it with your pen like that."

My eyes slid back into the office I shared with five other Senate assistants. The room was large, with space between desks and even private seating. But with just one small sofa and a table between me and Calix Ateio, it didn't feel big enough.

"Your dedication to the state of my furniture is commendable, Calix," I drawled. "Consider applying that same dedication to your own work."

Julian, another occupant of the shared space, snorted as he walked in with a stack of papers in his arms. Calix glared at the other man, who ignored him and sat down at his own desk.

And while I wasn't about to admit Calix was right about anything, I did put down my pen and lock away my work. This needed Nikkos's touch; I just needed to catch a few free moments with him to get me on track. I wasn't getting a damn thing done on my own today, that was for sure. I still had the taste of Madeline on my lips from last night, and I couldn't get her off my mind.

I had barely scooted my chair back to stand and leave when I spotted a familiar face through the doorway.

"Nephele?" I murmured, walking briskly toward her. My cousins, related on Dimitris's side, and not the side I shared with Nikkos, had returned from their own errand. Nephele was a scrawny girl who had gotten into her fair share of fights and broken her arm climbing trees on a near-annual basis, but had grown into a statuesque woman. Her hooked nose matched her brother's, her large eyes set under thick brows made for a strong face, but one she wore well. Horace, her twin, looked much the same. But some imbalance of power had happened in the womb, because while Nephele took all the spunk and confidence between them, Horace took all the softness and creativity.

"Nephele!" I called after her as I entered the atrium. The late-afternoon light shone down, adding a glow to the space. She turned, her short black hair swaying in thick waves against the warm umber of her skin. Her lips spread to a wide smile as she opened her arms to me.

"Caspian! Gods, it's good to be home."

We embraced, and I pulled away as Horace walked into the atrium from outside. "Horace, it's good to see you."

He smiled softly. "Thank you. It will be nice to sleep in my own bed tonight."

Nephele gave a low laugh. "You mean you can't wait to get back in the studio and away from my nagging."

"I didn't say that," Horace argued, but his eyes shifted away from his twin.

"You were gone longer than expected. Was there a problem?" I asked. Just as Nikkos and I were trying to implement our proposed plan for a solution to the problem, Nephele and Horace were out trying out their own.

They shared an uneasy look. Horace cleared his throat. "We haven't spoken to Dimitris yet, but . . ."

"It didn't go well," Nephele finished for her brother. "The pack we came across in our research seems to be in shambles. A shadow of their former power, they cannot do it."

I grimaced. This would lead to a displeased Dimitris, which none of us wanted to deal with.

"What of your attempts?" Horace prompted. "Did you find your mediator for the vampire relic?"

"Something like that," I offered. "When Nikkos and I found the texts about the relic that could be combined with the sirens' sway to reinforce the barrier, we tried to find someone the vampires would actually negotiate with. That was a failure, but we did manage to contact a noteworthy mercenary who was up for the work. Gavin has a reputation for getting things done."

The pair sighed in tandem.

"Good," Nephele said. "Maybe our news won't be as ill received."

"Good luck," I offered. "We should catch up soon. I won't keep you, though. You must be ready to report in and get home."

Nephele nodded, stepping toward the short hall that would carry them to Dimitris's office. But Horace paused, one big hand on my shoulder before I could step back.

"Come see us soon," he urged. "Mom misses you. She worries."

My expression softened. He and Nephele had been young when my parents had died in the boating accident. Their mother and mine were twins, a trait that seemed to run in our family. Their mother and mine were also the younger siblings of Dimitris, tying us all together. When I was parentless at seven, my aunt took me in. I stayed until I was sixteen and she had two preteens who kept her hands full, and that was when I moved into the house my parents had left me.

Aunt Karina was a saint to put up with me and a miracle worker to have raised Nephele without pulling out all of her hair.

"I'll visit soon," I promised.

Horace smiled, probably not fully believing me, and gave my shoulder a squeeze before dropping his hand and following his sister. I watched them disappear behind Dimitris's door.

There was little else for me to do now but go home. At one time I would have looked forward to the peace, but now my heart stilled, wondering if I'd find Madeline or if the sirens had stolen her away yet. Not that I'd blame them, and she did desperately need training. But at the same time, I'd miss her.

With a sigh, I left the building, then the street, putting the business and stress of the Senate behind me.

I followed the paths home, enjoying the peaceful way of Atlantis. Familiar faces on most streets. Waving to a neighbor playing with her children in the yard. Pausing when I saw old Dr. Hazim pluck an apricot from a tall branch, ensuring he made it safely down his ladder before I moved on. The sights, sounds, and smells welcomed me, bidding me to slow down and enjoy them while I walked.

Finally, down my street and at the bend where my front path wound to the familiar door, I made my way inside.

"Welcome home."

Somewhat startled, I found Madeline on the low cushions in the living space. She had managed to pull together a few random foods from the kitchen and had arranged everything on the tray Nikkos and I had used to show her a proper Atlantean breakfast. I mused at her random selection of things. It even looked like she'd bought a loaf of sweet bread from the market.

"You're staying here?" I asked, not daring to get my hopes up. She was a siren. She wasn't mine to keep, but all of Atlantis's to pamper.

"Yes, if that's okay."

"It's more than okay," I said. "But didn't the sirens want you to stay with them?"

She nodded. "And I will, every three days when I take lessons with the young sirens."

"But on your days away from lessons . . ."

"I want to spend them somewhere quiet with you, Caspian." Madeline smiled, and it was the brightest thing in the room.

"So . . . is this okay?" she asked.

I strode in, my knees barely falling to the cushions as I wrapped an arm around her and pulled her in for a heated kiss.

"Madeline," I said, pressing my forehead to hers, "it's perfect."

CHAPTER TWENTY-FIVE

MADELINE

My throat burned, and I drank deeply from the herbal tea that Jacinta, a young siren handed me. She was the shy girl who had been part of the group who had greeted me when I came to have breakfast. Some of the sirens I had come to recognize now, like Amara, were taking shifts in the towers that surrounded the bubble of island.

It had been a long morning of singing practice that had stretched my vocal cords in every direction as I tried to fill my mind with the nuances and repeating tones, and ways to make that pull in my chest, that sway, work when I wanted it to. It was only a handful of hours, since I was only able to work that hard for so long before my voice tired of being used. That was fine—it was just like working out my body after a long stretch out of the gym. I needed to build it up, and I was ready to try.

"Thanks." I sighed, passing the cup back to Jacinta. The shy girl gave me an amused smile, then tucked the cup and jug of tea away on a low table to the side of the large living room in the House of Sirens.

She didn't speak much, but it was just me, Jacinta, and the elder Ashana here for lessons. Luckily, there was little in the way of instructions for Jacinta to translate. For the most part, Ashana demonstrated and we mimicked, like baby birds.

Ashana was resting on one of the floor cushions, similar to the ones I'd come to love napping on in Caspian's house but made of finer threads and with more detailed embroidery on them. The older woman's eyes were closed, a smile on her lips as warm sun fell over her through the domed glass overhead.

Letting the air leave my lungs in a slow, tired hiss, I turned to my one classmate. "So, what's next?"

Jacinta shrugged, playing with the end of one of her twin braids as her eyes moved to the front door at the same time as mine. In danced four sirens: two I didn't recognize, but they could be big sisters or aunts to me; the other two I did know from my first meeting.

"Madeline." A slender, catlike siren with short, cropped hair brought the group's attention to me as they all came to settle in the living space around us. I didn't remember her name, but then I didn't remember many of the names from that first day. Thankfully, they hadn't seemed to expect me to absorb it all yet.

Two of the sirens sat on either side of Ashana, greeting her softly in Atlantean, and one kissing the old woman's cheek. The siren who'd said my name sat across from me and pointed to herself. "Larisa."

Memory lit my face. "Yes! Larisa, thank you."

She offered a smile that illuminated her face and danced in her eyes. Larisa was maybe in her midthirties, but already with a streak of silver forming just above each ear. "You will learn in time."

I'd already decided Ashana didn't wish me ill will, and Jacinta was too young. Larisa wouldn't have even been ten when I was a baby. I still hadn't met anyone who seemed off to me, and at this point I was all but sure it couldn't be a siren.

"Larisa, *daeiosalasa*—"

"Bah! English. We have a guest." Larisa chided another siren.

"Sorry." She shot me an apologetic look, then turned back to Larisa. "Do you want to go shopping for a new dress before the . . ." She screwed up her face, looking for the word.

"Ball?" Larisa supplied. "Dance?"

"Yes, that works. Do you want to go find new dresses together tomorrow?"

Larisa shrugged. "I sing in the north tower tomorrow." Then she turned to me. "Has anyone told you about our event yet?"

I shook my head, eyeing Ashana. As fruitful as my first lesson had been, the language barrier had been enough of a challenge that conversation hadn't strayed from absolute necessity. One of the older sirens was speaking to Ashana, and the old siren's face lit up. "*Vellieovasa!*" she exclaimed.

Larisa smacked a fist in the open palm of her other hand. "That's it: veiled ball. That's the translation."

I didn't know what a veiled ball was, but it sounded exciting, and I loved a good excuse to dance. "What's it like?" I was eager for more. More of Atlantis, more of the sirens.

"Oh, Madeline, it's amazing." Jacinta spoke up, more excited than I'd seen her either time I'd been with her. "The dresses are so bold and colorful, and we play music in all the big squares in the city under the stars. And there's dancing, and the sirens all wear veils, so no one knows who we are, and the rest of the dancers wear masks. And there's food and xino vasilias everywhere."

"Jacinta!" One of the older sirens was looking aghast at the girl. "What do you know of a veiled ball? You're not old enough for that!"

Jacinta's cheeks heated to a soft pink, and she stuck her chin out. "I'm old enough to watch!"

Larisa laughed, a full-bellied sound. "You most certainly are not. Who let you watch part of a ball? It was Amara, wasn't it?"

Jacinta's blush deepened against her fawn-colored complexion, her eyes shifting away.

"Jacinta." Ashana caught the younger girl's attention and uttered something quickly in Atlantean that had Jacinta nodding and standing from the cushions with a short reply that I recognized as agreement to whatever Ashana had said.

Larisa watched the young girl leave the room before turning to me again. "She had the start of it right. It's the end of the ball that she doesn't know about yet."

The look in Larisa's eyes made me catch my lip in my teeth with conspiratorial mischief. "Oh?"

Larisa nodded. "It's no secret that the sirens are free to be . . . promiscuous? Is that a good word for it? We like sex, and it isn't hard for us to find."

My eyes widened slightly. I certainly wasn't opposed; in fact, the idea sounded freeing. But now I really wanted to know what that had to do with these veiled balls.

"We end the night as we wish. Some sirens will go home, yes." Larisa shrugged one shoulder. "But some of us find a partner. It's dark and we're veiled and it's so . . ." She shivered.

"Deliciously mysterious," finished the other woman who had brought up the ball in the first place.

Larisa nodded her agreement. "It's a night of carnal fun, and if a siren is looking to have a baby, that's the night to do it."

That one took me back. "And if you're not trying to get knocked up?"

"Knocked . . . what?"

"Pregnant," I said quickly, wanting to hear more.

"Oh, yes. Like I said, it can just be a night of fun if that's all you want it to be. I suppose that sounds strange to you, doesn't it? Let me try to explain a little better. We're sirens, we only give birth to sirens, and we raise our children together."

I'd learned as much already from Caspian and Nikkos, but . . . "Wait. The fathers aren't involved *at all*?"

Larisa laughed. "No, we do it this way so the fathers can't be involved. It was done another way thousands of years ago, but this has worked out better for us."

"You don't have partners? Or get married?" I asked.

"Oh, some of us definitely keep partners," Larisa said. "Have you met Amara's Iris? What a lovely woman. How she puts up with Amara's endless energy, I'll never understand. Several of us have dedicated partners and live with them outside of this main house."

I blinked. So my pursuit of Caspian wasn't completely taboo. Good. "Okay, so when you want a baby you have one, and then it's raised here? With all of you?"

"Exactly," Larisa agreed. "Now you get it. That's my mother right there." Larisa pointed to the woman who had been speaking Atlantean to Ashana. The woman looked over and gave us a warm smile, not breaking her conversation with the elder siren.

"Oh," I said weakly. "Are the siren babies wanted? Like, are people happy they're born?"

Larisa reached out and placed a hand on my arm. "Yes, every one of them. We will find out what happened to you, this we swear. The senators are working on it, and as we sirens come and go from the towers we are catching up any who have not heard of you yet. The truth will be found."

It was so different. So unlike the foster system. My heart tightened. What would it have been like? To be raised here. Caspian said he was going to help me find out what happened to me and how I got to the mainland, but that was more of a hushed operation for now. The question seemed touchy for the most part, so it wasn't brought up with the sirens other than one short acknowledgment from Calliope that it was being investigated. But still, I could have been here the whole time, and it hurt that I wasn't.

Larisa patted my arm, bringing my head back into the present. "So, do you ever want a baby, or are you more of an auntie?"

"Me?" I took a moment to catch back up to the conversation. "I'm an auntie, for sure." After what I'd been through? I had no desire to be someone's mother. I'd be an anxious mess, not knowing what to do. Not having a mother figure to model myself after. But my heart was full with the idea that I could still help with the other kids, be around the children of the other sirens.

"Perfect," Larisa mused. "I'm going to take the fullest possible advantage of the next veiled ball if you know what I mean. You can help watch the baby so I can take a nap sometime."

I laughed, still not quite absorbing the concept but liking it more and more as I was hearing about it. "Deal."

"When is the next veiled ball?" Larisa asked, turning to her mother.

They exchanged a word or two in Atlantean that I didn't understand, then confirmed a two-week timeline.

"We can teach you some dances." Larisa ticked off each finger as she listed activities. "Get you a dress, find a veil, show you around the squares where we hold the festivities."

"I can join in?" I asked.

"Yes, why shouldn't you?" Larisa pulled my hands into hers. "You're a sister, of course you can come."

I beamed at her, the big cousin or young auntie I never knew I needed until now. Her voice was filled with enthusiasm. "Normally,

Dirty Lying Sirens

the rules are to keep your veil hidden before the ball, so no one knows who is who. But if you were to accidentally leave your veil out for someone to see, and if that someone were to be gifted a mask to wear the night of the ball, well . . ." She shrugged. "Sometimes it's okay to help fate along."

"Larisa!" The other woman who was talking with us about the ball smacked Larisa's knee as she cackled.

"What?" Larisa protested through a fit of giggles. "Like you haven't dropped *any* hints before a ball?"

"Hints about what?" Jacinta asked, coming into the room with a tray of cut fruit that she set in front of Ashana.

A few sirens laughed while Larisa's mother sighed, pulling Jacinta to her side and speaking in hushed Atlantan.

It certainly gave me things to think about. The pressure to have a baby was off, the pressure to get married was off, though I liked the idea of being together with Caspian as long as we both wanted it.

Yes, a picture of life in Atlantis was beginning to take shape the more I learned, and I was quickly finding that I liked it. I liked it very much.

235

CHAPTER TWENTY-SIX

MADELINE

I was never one to sleep in, and certainly not during the parts of my life that I was excited about. Now that my days were filled with lessons on the sway, the hand signs the sirens used to communicate in the towers while they had to keep up the songs that protected Atlantis, and the new culture I was assimilating into, I was definitely excited.

In the short time I'd been here, I'd formed a routine. Caspian left early, strained more with each passing day. Enough that I tried to offer to help, but it seemed the problem of how I became lost was taking its toll, so I stopped bringing it up and started sending him off with a kiss. Sometimes a lot more than that.

I put on my running shoes. Stretching on the front path of the house, I was greeted by more than one neighbor from their front yards or open windows. They let me stumble through my poor Atlantean small talk, and then I was off.

The salt in the air and the singing birds welcomed me as I

moved down the path. The view was glorious. I could almost forget that in the distance, past the expanse of water that was allowed in to make these gorgeous beaches, a dark wall of endless ocean was held back by magic. There was no other word for it—this was some kind of magic, and it gave me delighted goose bumps.

I kept a steady pace down the street, making the first turn and going down a mix of hill and stairs until I reached the fork that would take me to the beach market, as I called it. The bottom of a staircase opened to a rocky beach. Not so good for a swim, but the views were great and there were a few places where large slabs of rock made for solid ground above the water. Hitting the bottom stairs, I took a sharp right for breakfast. Four stalls at most, with the same collection of people sitting on cushions in the sand around them.

As I stood in line behind an older man, the stall owner spotted me and smiled, his moustache sweeping across his face. While he still spoke to the customer in front of me, his hands moved beneath the counter to make my smoothie.

Once my turn came, I set the coin on the counter that I had figured out was equal to one of these drinks. Frankly, I had no idea what was in it, but it was delicious, and my new favorite breakfast.

The stall owner spoke about as little English as I did Atlantean, but that was part of our morning exchange.

"Sing me, pretty siren," he said.

"Good morning, Mr. Smoothie Vendor," I answered in a sing-song voice. He nodded and slid me my drink with the biggest smile. "Thanks! *Houksha!*"

The cool drink hit my teeth with a shock, and I stood under a palm tree drinking it and watching the people make their way through lazy morning routines. Once I finished, I placed my cup on the table by the stand and made my way to one of the wide rock slabs.

A ball rolled into my path, and I kicked it to the kids who had lost control of it. They squealed and kicked it back to me. I gave them a few minutes of back and forth, and once they finally ran off in a fit of giggles, I went back to the rocks.

One of these days I'd bring a rug with me, or something that would make exercising on the rock more comfortable. But today, I stretched and went into lunges.

This place, with the smoothie vendor and the kids playing ball and the old ladies gossiping on the cushions by the stalls, where the warmth bathed my whole body and the breeze was so refreshing and the birds sang their songs. This place was heaven, and it felt so right.

Moving my body was great, but after my morning routine I hopped in the shower and then made my way to the House of Sirens. Lessons with Ashana and the few younger sirens weren't hard, but building up those muscles I'd had no control over for all these years was important. Maya didn't join us, but the little talking there was, Jacinta was able to translate.

After lessons came evenings with Caspian. Sometimes we made dinner with Nikkos, sometimes Caspian poured over books from work, still trying to figure out where I'd gotten lost along the way.

I was attempting to make a cheese-stuffed bread they sold at the markets from some dough our neighbor gave me to have with dinner, and it was just coming out of the oven in a billow of savory steam. The front door squeaked open as I finished pulling it out. I dusted my hands off with a towel, and my face fell when I saw Caspian.

"What's up?" I asked.

Caspian stepped into the house, Nikkos following him inside. "Actually, we have some news." Nikkos looked as serious as Caspian as they watched me.

My heartbeat sped up. "Do we . . . Should we sit down?"

Caspian's face relaxed a bit, his eyes softening. "Yeah, let's do that."

"I'm getting out your brandy," Nikkos said.

"Help yourself, it's been a long day."

The exchange was short, and only served to wind up my nerves.

We made our way to the cushions in the living room. I'd been watching a movie earlier, but now I scooted my laptop to the side and sat facing Caspian. I could tell from his mussed hair that he had run his fingers through it before coming home. When Nikkos came in with a full glass and sat on Caspian's other side, facing me, I couldn't take the silence anymore.

"What is it?" I asked.

I had been absolutely floating through my days, and before I knew it, a week had gone by as I settled into Atlantis. There was so much to learn, so much to see, that I had almost forgotten one very important matter that remained to be settled.

"It's about when you were found," Nikkos started. "You told us you were found with a thin white blanket. That stuck out to me enough and . . . would you take a look at this for me?"

Nikkos pulled a bundle of white cloth from his pocket and handed it over. My fingers brushed the rough surface, and while I hadn't had it in a long time, it brought back a flood of memories.

"What is this?" I whispered.

"This is the veil we cover our stillborn with," Caspian answered. "And, as you can imagine, we hold burials at sea here.

When a child is born sleeping, they're immediately wrapped, and the mother is given her last opportunity to hold them before taking them up the towers to be laid to rest."

"That's so sad," I said. "But what does that mean? That's like the blanket I was found in."

"That, I'm not sure," Caspian said. "The birth of a siren is a huge deal; many people would have been in the room. It's hard to know how you could have been mistaken as stillborn without trickery, but something obviously happened."

I was thought to be dead when I was born? "So, if someone said I was dead, and then wrapped me up. . . . I still don't know how that's possible."

"Neither do we," Nikkos murmured, "and yet, this is indeed the veil we use for that purpose and that purpose alone."

My heart tensed, and a flicker of thought struck me like a lightning bolt before Caspian spoke it into existence.

"Madeline," he said softly, "we may have found your mother."

My world tilted, and I steadied a hand against the wall beside me. I knew we'd try to find the reason I was left in Michigan as a baby, but I hadn't expected this. Somewhere in my brain over the last few days, I'd ditched the possibility of any of the sirens being directly related to me. Yes, in many ways all the sirens were somehow related to one another, but I thought I had met most of them already, and there had been no moment of recognition. No one who looked quite like me, or who even brought up the possibility of a lost daughter. There had to be a reason for what happened to me, but this wasn't how I expected to get to the bottom of it.

"Who?" I asked, my voice shaking.

"Her name is Tanis," Nikkos said simply.

Tanis. A name. My eyes fell to the middle distance, not taking in anything as my brain processed it.

"How sure are we?" I finally asked. "That she's my . . . that it's her."

Caspian reached out to take my hand, rubbing a thumb in small circles over my knuckles. "We're not positive, but it's the most likely scenario we've found so far."

I clenched and unclenched my fingers; they were going numb on me.

"Tanis is a special case among sirens," Caspian continued, still holding one hand. "Tanis doesn't speak."

I swallowed. "Is she okay?"

Nikkos cleared his throat. "She went through an illness near the end of her pregnancy that affected her throat. She still has her sway, but regular speech is very difficult for her. She mostly uses the signs that you've been learning."

I nodded. The sirens used them to communicate while they sang, and I was getting the hang of them. Faster than I was getting the hang of Atlantean, anyway.

"She was pregnant about the year you were born, but her baby didn't make it. Tanis had been ill during her pregnancy. It called for more concern, more people present at her delivery. And, from what I understand, she had so many complications that much of the attention that day was on her health, creating an opportunity for something to happen to the baby in the commotion. After that heartache, her voice all but failed her completely," Caspian said.

That gave me a moment of pause to process. "That doesn't necessarily mean she's my mother, though. This is a lot of 'what-if' talk."

"Yes, but Tanis was the only siren pregnant at the time. As I said, it's just a theory. But Calliope and the other keepers would like you two to meet."

"Callipe's been working with us on this," Nikkos added. "She

241

wants to know how a siren ended up on the mainland as much as we do."

With a nod, Caspian let my hand slip out of his while he moved closer to pull me into a loose hug. "Are you okay?"

Letting out a breath, I focused on his concerned face. "Yeah. Surprised, but okay. When do I meet this Tanis?"

"In two days, if you're up for it," Nikkos said, taking a long drink from his glass.

"That's right before the veiled ball." I counted the days in my head.

A flicker of surprise crossed the cousins' faces.

"You didn't know?" I asked.

"Not everyone attends," Nikkos said. "Not the one you'll be a part of, anyway."

"The night of dancing is held across the island," Caspian clarified. "But the sirens . . . you'll be in the largest three squares around the Fountain of Fortune. The ones in attendance there are selected by invitation from the House of Sirens."

"Oh," I murmured. Caspian looked disappointed for a split second, and then his calm mask slipped back into place, leaving only concern for me and my situation on display.

"The sirens will help you ready for the ball," Nikkos said, oblivious to the look on his cousin's face. "First, we can arrange your meeting with Tanis."

"Okay," I murmured, but my fingers reached out to clasp Caspian's.

"The reason you haven't seen Tanis before now is because she practically lives in the towers," Caspian said. "She has a small home on the beach closest to the largest tower, and she spends more of her time in the towers than the other sirens typically do."

"Because of her voice?" I asked.

Caspian nodded. "According to Calliope."

A charged silence filled the room. I wanted to ask more about Tanis, but it didn't feel right to talk so much about her when she wasn't here. And it wasn't like having that information would give us any answers anyway. I'd just have to wait until I could meet her. But then, one question did pop into my head that mattered.

"What will meeting Tanis do for us?" I asked. "How can that confirm anything?"

Nikkos drained his brandy, setting the empty glass down with a sigh. "The sirens say that your sway will sing to hers. Obviously, we don't know anything about the details of that."

Nodding, I absorbed the information. It didn't seem unbelievable. Not with the work I'd been doing with Ashana.

"Two days," I murmured. "Okay, I guess we'll see what happens."

"I'll finish getting dinner ready," Caspian said. "Nikkos, eat with us? It's been a long day."

"Thank you," Nikkos said, standing with his empty glass. "Let me give you a hand."

He paused to glance at me with a soft smile. "You sit back tonight, Madeline. And we're here if you need to talk."

I gave him a nod and a weak smile in return.

My mother. Maybe. It was a step. It was at least one step in the right direction to find out what had happened to me. I had almost decided to let it go, to not know what had happened or why I had ended up in Michigan. Atlantis was warm and welcoming. There hadn't been one sign so far that suggested that anyone wanted me gone. But I knew we had to know. Had to figure it out.

Then there was the ball. I'd have to find out how to get Caspian an invitation. A night of dancing and drinking was always fun, but I wasn't about to get down and dirty with anyone I didn't know.

Maybe that was how the sirens wanted to handle it, but that wasn't for me. Not with my past. It would be Caspian or no one.

But first, Tanis.

I sighed, sinking back onto the cushions. It was a lot to take in all at once. All I could do now was hope that meeting Tanis would lead to some answers. That was what we wanted, after all.

I think.

CHAPTER TWENTY-SEVEN

MADELINE

The sun was warm, even filtered through the layer of saltwater high above. The humidity was wreaking havoc on my hair as sweat dripped down my neck, and I wondered what a girl with chubby thighs was supposed to do without something like leggings to cut down on the friction problem. Maybe there was some kind of Atlantean athletic wear that would solve the problem, and I just didn't know it yet. For the time being, my morning workouts were performed in a pair of old cutoffs and a tank top from Freeman's Gym. Not very Atlantean of me, but as much as I loved the big colorful skirts, they didn't do my squat game any favors.

Either way, working out was a good distraction. A distraction from potentially meeting my mother. A distraction from the implication that someone wanted baby Madeline out of Atlantis bad enough that they were willing to drop me in the American Midwest. A distraction from the swell of dark ocean in the distance that, if I was being honest with myself, made me just a bit queasy to look at.

A distraction from my lessons, which were coming along well, but from which I needed a break. When I wasn't having voice lessons, I was learning language or history. A well-rounded citizen in the making—and who knew private tutoring would turn me from a straight C student to a quick study?

Yes, distraction. Distraction was good for an overthinker like me. Sometimes I needed a break from my own spiraling anxiety, which still couldn't accept that I was more than one bad paycheck from living in a car again.

Nope, that's spiraling. Not helping, Mads.

My thoughts drifted as I jogged along a new-to-me stretch of beach. A few eyes watched me from their backyards, not used to me in the same way as my regular morning people were. An old woman sitting and shelling some kind of nut waved and offered me a handful, making for a nice break in my workout. Another distraction while I asked her questions about the small grove of fruit and nut trees across the street from her house. Children were already playing in the grassy patches between houses, some of them boldly waving after me as I jogged along, yelling the Atlantean word for *singing* as they matched my pace. With a laugh, I belted out bits of an American pop song that I'd heard regularly on the radio before coming here. They had no clue what I was saying, but the exciting yelling it earned me brought a smile to my face as they went back to their games, and I continued on the beach. A little farther down, a goat bleated its disapproval at the teenager trying to wash it.

It was so peaceful, this place. This city, this island. The slow but playful life here, the dedication to crafts and community. Atlantis was quickly enchanting me in its own sort of siren's sway, lulling me into such a sense of security that I wasn't ready for the sight that met me when I turned to a new portion of the island I hadn't explored yet.

The beach took a sharp turn, and I had to wander around a large section of jagged rocks before finding a path again. The path was rocky and loose, and I had to slow down to make sure I wasn't going to fall. The beach that flowed into the distance was darker somehow. Rocky, but with angular shapes that didn't look natural. My eyes wanted to catch on the oddly smooth lines, the straight angles, but before I could grasp what I was looking at, I saw three familiar figures walking up the path from the direction of the nearest tower.

Two of the sirens I'd grown closest to, the slender, catlike Larisa and the bubbly Amara waved when they recognized me. The other, an older siren with a warm, motherly air, whom I'd seen a few times around the house but hadn't gotten to speak to, gave me a smile. Distracted from my previous curiosities on the beach, I made my way toward the three of them.

I met them down the path. They looked tired, which was understandable if they were just coming back from a turn in the towers. But after seeing who was coming my way, my eyes drifted around to the beach again as I walked. The closer I got to the strange rocky mass I had seen in the distance, the more my face fell. Amara noticed first, taking a few quick steps to reach me first and pull me into a hug. Her soft cloud of hair blocked the view as she squeezed me tight.

"It's good to see you exploring, Maddie. But I take it you haven't been to the low side before." Amara's words were kind, knowing, and tipped off the other two as to what was going on.

"No," I said. "What is this?"

Amara pulled back with a sigh, and Larisa took a place on the other side of me as we all turned to look down the rocky path to see where the beach turned into a graveyard.

The rocks I had thought were at odd angles to be natural were actually buildings. Or remnants of them. Corners too straight to be simple rocks. Domes too perfectly round to be shaped by the sea. Colors long faded and eaten away by the water as they sank down, down, down into the dark water. Coral had overtaken much of it. Fish of all kinds were happy to make their homes where once Atlanteans had thrived. My stomach turned as I stared down at the implications. How much of Atlantis had been lost?

"This is the low side of the island," Larisa explained after a minute. "The island we live on today was the highest point, the last part to sink. When the first magic was sung around the city, this was the cusp of what could not be saved. The rest of the nation was drowned, even as we managed to capture what you have seen so far in the bubble."

My eyes were trying to reconcile what I was seeing, and the sinking of my stomach told me as it was finally setting in. This was horrid, the swaths of streets that were destroyed. And I could only see so far, how much more had been lost? It was a miracle that there was any of Atlantis left, I knew that, but the catastrophe that stared back at me from the water . . . it was a wonder these people still had it in them to sing. Dance. Smile.

My throat tightened as my gaze moved back up the rocky coast to the tower in the distance. The one these three had just come from.

A warm hand snaked around my upper arm, gently turning me away from the sight of the long-ago disaster.

"Walk with us," Amara insisted, softly pulling me along. Larisa joined my other side after exchanging a few hand signs I was still learning with the third, older siren. She left, turning into the city proper, and Larisa matched her stride to mine.

Instead of moving back to the beach, we stepped up to the closest road that wound next to the rock and sand. The gentle swell of the water on the beach filled the silence.

Amara was the first one to speak. "It was a tragedy. Something that shapes our past, but it happened long before anyone here can remember."

"It's so sad." I choked on the words, feeling childish for having said it that way, but not feeling judged by either siren, at least. "What happened?"

"The old legends say we displeased a god," Larissa explained. "Our scientists believe it was more likely an unfortunate earthquake, a shifting of the tectonic plates, something like that. And we're still sinking to this day."

"That's why the sirens are so important," Amara added, breaking my train of thought. "There are fewer and fewer of us as the years pass. We're taking more and longer turns at the towers. It's a toll on us. Our voices, our bodies. It's hard work."

"But essential work," Larisa said firmly. "It's the only thing keeping Atlantis whole. If we weren't here, keeping the island alive . . ."

Our moods were somber after that. We meandered—to where, I didn't care. Maybe the House of Sirens. Maybe the market. All I knew was that I was glad to have them with me after the shocking realization.

"So, Larisa is going to have thirty babies and bounce the siren numbers back up," Amara said out of nowhere.

Larisa made an ugly noise, somewhere between disbelief and horror before it turned to giggles as she playfully shoved Amara.

"You and your girlfriend can be aunties, that's fine," Larisa quipped, "but don't you forget who's playing with the first twenty-nine while I'm making the thirtieth."

By now Amara was cackling, and the mood had lightened considerably. Even I cracked a smile as Amara stuck out her tongue and turned us to the market street.

"Come on, let's go shopping for the veiled ball. I want a new veil this year," Amara said.

"Why, so you have enough time to make sure Iris sees what it looks like?" Larisa teased.

Amara turned a wicked expression on the taller siren. "Maybe, or maybe Iris is in on it too. Maybe we've planned a wicked night with a third lovely partner and we want to look good for her."

I let loose a surprised laugh. "You sneaky thing!"

Amara giggled, and we went up the path to the largest market. And just like that, my surprise history lesson turned from somber to lighthearted. All thanks to my new sisters.

CHAPTER TWENTY-EIGHT

CASPIAN

The heat of the day had swelled to a level in the range of almost uncomfortable. Any number of things would be preferable to sitting in the stifling Senate hall. At the top of my mind was Madeline, and the conflicting emotions she'd been juggling since I broke the news about Tanis. I could be with her right now; today wasn't a day of lessons for her. But instead, here I sat, on the highest row of the circular bleacher-style seating with the other aides while the senators milled about on the lower rings and waited for the basilli to start.

Adrion Ateio. The words he said to me when he met Madeline that first morning still rang in my ears. There was no reason for the cutting remark, other than he knew it would get back to Dimitris and irk him. There had always been something about the way House Ateio held their cards close, revealing nothing of importance until it would leave the biggest impact.

Dimitris was in his seat, his posture relaxed for someone about to stand front and center to bring up the environmental crisis again.

His plan hadn't been revealed to the Senate yet, and he might get in trouble for acting without a vote, but all of this was in preparation before Gavin arrived with the relic.

"What did I miss?" Nikkos slid in beside me, an armload of files dropping onto the desk.

"Nothing yet," I said. "What are those?"

"Reference files," he explained, not taking his eyes off the Senate floor. "In case they're needed for today's argument."

"I don't think any more will happen today than it has all year when he takes the stage. Does Dimitris expect it?" I asked.

Nikkos shrugged. "No, but we do like to be ready, don't we?"

Muffled laughter made me look around Nikkos and down the same aisle we were on. A few seats down from me, Calix Ateio was murmuring sweet nothings into the ear of a blushing aide, completely distracting her from organizing the pile of notes in front of her. No doubt she was new, as I hadn't seen her face around before; Calix was always quick to jump on the new faces.

"It does little to enthuse me for the next seated basilli," Nikkos muttered.

"If you ask me, the apple doesn't fall far from the tree."

A brass ball was hammered against its matching plate a few times, drawing eyes down to the front and center table of the room, where Adrion's assistant was hushing the room while the man himself walked in. His clothes were crisp and commanding, his smile wide and lazy as he took his place at the head table reserved for the basilli. The room settled down, and I readied my things to take notes for Dimitris.

A short opening of the Senate, followed by the order of business, and then Adrion began the first item on the schedule. Dimitris's debate would come later, so there was still time before he needed us here.

"So, Madeline." A body moved to my left, settling itself onto the bench. "I finally got a good look at her yesterday."

Nikkos frowned but kept his eyes on the floor and his pen on his notepad.

"Mind your tongue and do your job, Ateio," I said. "Pay attention to the report, not gossip."

"She's got hips you could really sink your fingers into, doesn't she?" Calix leaned closer. "It must make her a really comfortable fuck."

He was trying to get a rise out of me. I knew it, he knew it, and the jagged line of pen that just jumped off my page and scratched the desk in front of me knew it. Calix, for whatever reason, had been particularly obnoxious since our confrontation that day when he was talking about a veiled ball with the other aides in the atrium. We had always been oil and water, but now he was provoking more than an argument, and he knew it.

Taking a breath, I tried to figure out why. Any other day I'd be happy to punch him in the face for what he said about someone else's body. But here in front of the entire Senate, Dimitris wouldn't tolerate it, not to mention the repercussions from the rest of the officials.

"What do you want, Calix?" I snapped.

His brows jumped in amusement. "Want? Not much. I'm just here making casual conversation with a colleague."

"Bullshit," I hissed. A few eyes darted our way, including those of my uncle, who leveled me a warning look.

"I wasn't aware the golden boy had a temper," Calix mused. "But this new development is absolutely delightful."

Ignore him.

"I've already been told all of House Ateio is on the list for the main square," Calix went on. "A brand-new siren shouldn't be left

253

to wander her very first ball away from the main square, don't you agree?"

Ignore him.

"Do you mind, Ateio?" Nikkos snapped. "Some of us take our work seriously."

Calix paid my cousin no attention. "I've already lined up a new black mask for the evening. Something that can easily stay on no matter the *activity*."

I stood up, the amusement on Calix's face only fueling my upset as I grabbed him by the collar and hauled him out of the room behind me.

"What are you doing?" Nikkos hissed, but didn't follow. No doubt several eyes were on us, including Dimitris, but it was better to handle this outside than in the active Senate.

Calix protested mildly, but since he found more entertainment in my annoyance than the Senate floor anyway, he came along to find out what I would do. As much as I wanted to slap some sense into him, I was above that. Barely.

I wasn't gentle when I pulled us through the busy atrium of the large building, collecting more curious stares as we moved outside and around to the shaded side of the building where I swung him around to smack his back against the wall.

"What the fuck is your problem?" I snarled. "You don't even know her, and now you want to do what, taunt me? What's your game?"

Calix sneered, brushing the front of his clothes. "I assure you, Caspian, my taunting of an obnoxious prick doesn't need some scheme behind it beyond the pleasure of your ruffled feathers. Was that all you wanted from this show? To pull me out here?"

I took a steadying breath before leveling my eyes on his. "Leave Madeline out of this."

A slow smirk spread across his face. "Gods, Caspian. I knew you were fond of the siren, but you've *truly* fallen for her."

Alarm shot through me. Not just at his recognition of it, but at my own. I didn't know if I'd fully fallen for Madeline yet, but I knew damn well that I was on my way.

"The stupidest thing you could do. I didn't take you for such a fool." Calix tilted his head, studying me. "Maybe you're less of a threat in the Senate than I thought."

"Threat?" I snorted. "Don't tell me you think you have any chance at a seat for yourself someday."

Calix sneered. "And if I do?"

"I'm no competition to you. The moment I'm freed of my familial duties I want nothing more than to wash my hands of the Senate and never look back."

Calix eyed me with suspicion. And I didn't blame him; a seat on the Senate would set you up nicely for as long as you served Atlantis. Of course, you'd have to actually do a good job, or the people would pounce to move someone else in. A small island community like this? I'd seen it happen plenty of times before. Calix may think it would be an easy job as an Ateio, but that would be for him to find out the hard way.

Instead, I gave him one last warning, my voice low and serious. "Leave Madeline alone. If I hear you've made unwanted advances, I'll do a lot more than warn you."

I pulled away from Calix, too hot to even look at him as I stuffed my anger down enough that I could go back inside. And I was angry. Angry at his behavior, but also angry that he was right and could see through me so easily. I didn't want to be this affected by Madeline, not when she was so new to Atlantis. But even if I was just a fling for her, I'd be damned if I let Calix anywhere near her. She deserved a hell of a lot more respect than that, and I didn't trust an Ateio to not be up to something, no matter what Calix said.

A few more deep breaths and I returned to the main room and to my seat. Nikkos, bless him, had taken the notes my uncle would be expecting later. Settling in during a report from the senator of education, I was surprised to have a note slipped to me from one of the other aides. Unfolding the paper, I saw it was from Dimitris.

My office. After the session.

My eyes darted to the front row where my uncle's head was turned, eyes on me.

I frowned but nodded. I was sure he would have a lecture on proper conduct waiting for me, adding to my already long day.

Still, taking notes would at least provide me with plenty of time to think. What was it I was doing with Madeline, and what would happen to the newest siren between now and the veiled ball? Tomorrow she would meet Tanis, and after that, the ball itself.

And there was little I could do for her but stay by her side. Gods help us.

CHAPTER TWENTY-NINE

MADELINE

Pacing had become my lifeline as the minutes slipped away before me; at the other end of this incessant wait would be Tanis.

Caspian, poor guy, was trying his best to keep my nerves from consuming me whole. I had already gotten up early and gone for a run on the sandy side of the island. When that didn't do it for me, I took a long bath and then resumed pacing. The living room. My room. Then the backyard when Caspian coaxed me outside with a drink and a fresh loaf of olive bread he'd bartered from his neighbor for some of the greens he was growing by the pool.

"You know, Maddie," Caspian said from his seat by the pool, "throwing up won't make a good first impression."

I paused, whirling to face him with horror on my face. "Why would you say that? Now I'm going to think that the whole time!"

Caspian sighed, rising to his feet to join me where I was pacing a rut in his grass. He placed a warm hand on each of my shoulders as if to pin me in place. "I'm sorry. I'm just trying to lighten the mood. You can't keep doing this to yourself, they'll be here soon."

"I know," I moaned. "And it's driving me wild."

The gentle creak of Caspian's front door froze me in place, my eyes wide like a deer caught in the headlights.

"Caspian?" Nikkos's familiar voice called from inside the house. "Madeline?"

Groaning, I rubbed my hands down my face.

Caspian patted my shoulder, calling toward the back door. "Outside!"

Nikkos joined us, a green bottle under one arm. "Good morning. Today is the big day, I thought you could use a stiff drink."

He barely finished his words when I had both hands in front of me expectantly. Nikkos chuckled and pulled the stopper out of the bottle. "Xino vasilias. Careful, it's a strong one."

I tipped it back, taking several good swallows before Caspian gently took it from my lips. "I don't think this is the way to go, either, Maddie."

Wiping my mouth with the back of my wrist, I eyed the bottle but didn't argue. I'd never had these kinds of nerves before, but Caspian was probably right.

"There is no pressure," Caspian said, "Even if Tanis does turn out to be your mother, there are no expectations. Calliope has already said that no relationships will be forced between you two, so take this slowly. Now, deep breath. In the nose, out the mouth. That's a good girl."

I did as I was told, breathing deeply and letting it out slowly to a pace that Caspian set. He had me do this a few more times before I calmed down, and that was when we heard the knock at the front door. Every bit of good the deep breaths had done was now swept away by a new wave of anxious anticipation.

"I'll get it," Nikkos said. "Should we do this inside or here?"

"Here," I choked. "Out here." I needed the space. I needed the air.

Nikkos disappeared into the house. Caspian pulled me into one last embrace, and I sank into his warmth. We stayed that way while we waited. Listening to the soft footsteps in the house, and finally the opening of the back door. My heart was hammering in my chest when Caspian let go of me, and I somehow found my feet when Calliope emerged. Behind her was the woman who had to be Tanis, and Nikkos followed after, closing the door.

Tanis. I had a lot of thoughts about Tanis.

Short. I had clearly gotten my height from my father, which was an entirely different bridge that I didn't want to think about. She may have been beautiful at one time, but the years had been hard on her. Not in a natural way, but in the way that can beat a person down. Caspian had said her pregnancy had left her voice damaged and her heart aching for a lost baby. Blue eyes, which was a given after having learned that all the Atlanteans had them, but they were rimmed with deep crow's feet. Her skin had signs of wear and tear that you get from staying in the sun for a long time over a period of years. Her hair, while gray at the temples, was a lot like mine. It was maybe the first thing I had noticed that we matched on. But on closer inspection, the shape of her mouth and chin looked not unlike a mirror image of mine. The shape of our eyes was different, and I had a stronger nose than her dainty one, but there was enough. Enough similarities to raise questions.

Calliope looked between us. Not unkindly, but with concentration. Caspian and Nikkos had stepped back, just watching it all unfold.

Tanis kept her eyes wide. There was caution in them, but the more we stared at each other, the more I could see the flicker of hope. Or maybe it was hope reflected back from my own eyes, because I couldn't stop myself from wanting it. Years of asking why I was abandoned flashed through me. A Mother's Day event that I sat out, crying in the bathroom at school instead. A crumpled letter that I'd written and rewritten a million times, just in case I ever found her. The nasty words I spit out about her as a teenager when under the bravado I wanted nothing more than to find her. Her, or another forever home where someone would hug me, ask about my day, nag me about a curfew. Care.

But what was Tanis to me? Could this really be my mother?

"How—" My voice croaked, and I swallowed despite my dry mouth. "How do we know for sure?"

Nikkos stepped forward to translate for Calliope and Tanis. Calliope murmured one word. "Sing."

Tanis gestured, the sign for agreement, and began to hum. Unlike the other sirens who always opened their mouth and sang to the skies, Tanis was more subdued, her tones low and deep, but still vibrantly the notes of a siren.

My own throat itched to join her. Not enough to get my hopes up when any of my teachers had done the same thing to me, but enough that I opened my mouth and joined her.

Everything clicked. Her notes and my notes, we even deviated from the song, and as Tanis hummed her melody, I felt compelled to sing around it, my tones dancing up and down and intertwining in a compliment to hers. It was a moment I'd never forget no matter how long I lived, the feeling of puzzle pieces sliding into place. I knew I was a siren; the evidence had stacked so high by now, and of course I was getting along well, fitting in with the others at the House of Sirens. But this, this sealed the deal. This was my one true link to this world and my heritage.

Tanis didn't take her eyes off of me, even when tears began to run down her face. What had she gone through? Thinking she'd lost her baby, the illness that took her health and her voice. Enough to make her want to live in a house away from everyone else and only do her work at the towers.

As our song faded to an end, we all stood there. Calliope was in absolute shock. Caspian and Nikkos stayed silent. Tanis stared, her eyes reflecting mine with welling tears threatening to spill over that might not end if they began.

But we couldn't quite move past this part, Tanis and me. My mother and me. I was ready to love her. I was ready to hate her. I was ready to scream at whatever circumstances brought me to this point. What I could have had, what I didn't have.

Shaking, Tanis reached out a hand. To touch me. Maybe hold my hand, maybe to lead to a hug. But it was too much for me, and I took a step back, spilling the first tears.

"Wait." My voice tremored, and my hands balled into fists, grabbing my dress at my sides. Everyone paused, not a soul ready to move. Tanis looked ready to break, like a glass sculpture tipping too far forward. I just needed a minute, but I owed this connection to the both of us.

"Okay," I breathed, opening my arms. Tanis didn't wait for a translation before flinging herself forward to wrap herself around me as tightly as she could. My hair, her hair, it was all the same color as our heads rested on one another's shoulder. My tears fell on her, hers fell on me, and we would both surely be a mess after this, but no one was going to say anything. Not to us, not for what we had both missed out on.

It felt like ages before I pulled away, and Tanis did the same. Caspian handed me a cloth to dry my face with, and someone passed Tanis one too.

"What now?" I asked.

Tanis spoke rapidly, Caspian trying to keep up as he translated. "She wants you to move in with her, or she will move to the House of Sirens. Whichever you prefer. She has—something, ah—many birthday gifts for you, she never stopped thinking about you."

It gutted me. Tanis was the mother I had wanted to know about for so long, and yet I had given up on her. She had every reason to think her baby was dead, and she had birthday gifts for me? Her grief ran so terribly deep I would probably never understand it. Or live up to it. What was expected of me now? She was here, finally. But she was still a stranger too.

"I—" My throat tightened. "I don't know what to say. Can we slow down? I'm so happy to have the answers now after all this time, but I want to know more about you. And me, you probably want to get used to me, too, right? I don't want to leave Caspian's house right now. It feels the most like . . ." *Home. It feels the most like home.*

Caspian stepped to me, translating and placing a warm hand on my back. It grounded me while he relayed my message. My head knew that nothing I had been through was Tanis's fault, but my heart was struggling to admit that. It was too much, too fast.

Tanis withdrew, a forced smile on her face as her hands moved in a flurry for Calliope to see. I caught a few words, but for the most part I was still very much a beginner and had to wait anxiously for Calliope to translate, and then Nikkos to translate her.

Calliope spoke, her eyes not leaving Tanis. Again, I only caught part of it, and Nikkos finally said it all in English.

"She understands. She would like to do whatever you want, as long as you will see her. Tanis is tired and would like to retire for the day with this new information," Nikkos said, a spear of guilt piercing my chest. "She is blessed by the gods to meet you, Madeline, and she hopes to see you on another day once you have both had time to reflect on everything."

Managing a nod, Calliope leaned forward and gave my shoulder a loving squeeze before turning to Tanis.

My mother, Tanis, took the few steps away as if she was going to give me space, but she stopped after a few feet. Her hands clenched and unclenched at her sides, and her mouth wobbled as though she was going to cry again, but with something of a smile that made me hope it wasn't all bad. Her hands moved slowly making three signs I had learned by now.

I, love, you.

She turned her head before any tears could start and made to leave. I watched them, the elder sirens, as they linked arms. Calliope only paused long enough to murmur something to Caspian, and then they were through the house and gone.

My chest was tight as Caspian pulled me inside to sit on the floor cushions while Nikkos poured glasses for all of us from the bottle he had brought. All I could do was sit and concentrate on breathing.

"Are you all right?" Caspian asked.

"What did she say to you?" I asked.

Caspian's mouth formed a hard line while he looked to his cousin, then back to me.

"There is no doubt that you are Tanis's lost daughter," Caspian said. "But now the question remains, how did you end up on the mainland? Our next steps are to find out who was present when Tanis was giving birth and figure out how they stole an entire infant."

I didn't know. I didn't know, and neither did anyone else here, and that was a problem. For all my heart was now invested in this place and its people, two facts remained that terrified me.

Who would cast me from Atlantis as a baby, and were they still around to try again?

CHAPTER THIRTY

MADELINE

Any news about the sirens, who were all admittedly some kind of celebrity, drew a lot of attention, so gossip about Tanis and Calliope's visit spread like wildfire through the island.

And I was stuck floating in a fog. I couldn't jog on the beach without stares, and I couldn't pick up my smoothie breakfast on my way through the market without a constant buzz of whispers. I couldn't even get through one Atlantean lesson with Nikkos without the neighbors peeking over the backyard greenery, because heaven forbid I have a lesson outside on a nice day.

And it was showing. It ran me ragged, and I had no time to even think about the implications of seeing my mother again. How did she feel? How did I feel? How was I supposed to feel? And why would someone want me halfway across the world instead of here in Atlantis?

Tanis had given me space, and I appreciated that. I wanted a relationship with her, but first I wanted to get through this ball thing. I don't know why I needed the extra time; I just did.

The whole parent thing was a long-dead dream. I'd given up on that years ago, instead choosing to focus on getting out of the group home and finding my way to a beach—I wasn't the daughter type; I only had myself to rely on. What made all of this worse was that Tanis was right there, clearly ready to make up for lost time. But she had no idea that the time she'd lost was what made me so uncomfortable with the idea of having her in my life. While Tanis did give me space, she'd sent me something every day since we met.

First, it was a baby's blanket. Probably meant to be mine. The next morning we found a basket of fruit and a hairpin in front of Caspian's door. I didn't know what would come next, but I was sure something would be waiting, allowing Tanis to let her love out in the only way she could right now.

And it made me feel fucking guilty. But I still needed a few days.

Shifting on the bed, I sat up. Moonlight fell through the window in a soft, silver blanket across the room. The bed was nice, but it was lonely, and I could have used company after so much vulnerability. Maybe Caspian would be here if I invited him, but the opportunity never came up. He'd been called away more than once to deal with this boss of his, Dimitris.

I was no honors student, and maybe there were better ways to handle stress, but I did know one surefire way to unwind, and it was best done in the dark of night anyway.

My eyes fell on the side table where a carefully wrapped present and an invitation in scrolling red lettering sat waiting. I had planned on giving them to Caspian the day he broke the news about Tanis to me, and they had been forgotten. But with the veiled ball quickly approaching, I knew there was only one person I wanted to be with that night, if I decided to take things that far.

I snatched the invitation and the mask I had bought him as a present and padded on bare feet across my room. I paused. It had been so humid at night that I'd been sleeping naked, and now I was frozen in front of the mirror, naked as the day I was born. Thick thighs, a bit of tummy, and arms with a mix of tone and softness. Even the stupid compass-rose tattoo sitting low on my hip. Caspian had already seen it all and had definitely accepted it.

Shrugging, I moved forward and out the door. Unless someone was going to interrupt us in the middle of the night, no one but Caspian was going to see me anyway.

Walking through the empty house gave me a thrill that covered my arms in goose bumps. Light came through the high windows of the main living space as I covered the distance with light foot-steps. I found myself moving down the hall that would bring me to Caspian's room. Listening at the door, I didn't hear any sounds coming from inside. Was he asleep? I wouldn't want to wake him, but if he was up I definitely wanted to see him.

My hand was firm on the cold wood of the door. I thought about making a small sound but decided against it, and let my hand fall with only the soft hush of my skin brushing against the wood. I stepped back, looking down at the gift and the invitation in my hand. Maybe this was stupid; I could easily give it to him in the morning.

Stepping away from the door, I had nearly turned around when a sound behind me drew my attention. The door opened, and there was an absolutely delicious-looking Caspian. Those loose white pants hanging low on his hips were all the clothes he wore, his hair was tousled perfectly, and his sleepy eyes landed on me, then widened.

"What's up?" he croaked, still groggy but a smile lighting up his face.

I turned back to him, not missing that his focus shifted below my face. "I didn't wake you, did I?"

"No, no." Caspian ran a hand through that tousled hair, the dark curls playing around his fingers until he let them go again. "I was asleep earlier, but I woke up, and now I can't fall asleep again. You too?"

"Yeah, you know. Too many thoughts running around." I shrugged. "I figured if you were up we could keep each other company."

He raised one eyebrow. "Company?"

My expression turned a little more wicked as I held out his gift. "Yeah, company. Here, I meant to give you this earlier."

Caspian reached out and took the gift, then stepped back into his room. He motioned for me to join him. His room was decorated in dark blues; a large bed with navy sheets took up one wall and simple, clean-edged furnishings took up the rest. A few bits and baubles sat on a shelf to one side—books, an interesting shell, some small paintings, a bowl of rocks, a brass sculpture. The kind of things you'd probably end up with after living here long enough.

While I was busy looking around the room, Caspian sat on his bed and read the invitation. It was in Atlantean, which I was barely beginning to speak and definitely couldn't read yet, but Amara assured me that it was a standard invitation to the party in the main square. Caspian read it, then met my gaze with amusement.

"And they told you what happens at these events?" he asked cautiously.

"They did. I was informed that any siren participation is completely optional." I smiled, and he made to reach for my waist, but I danced away from his hand, trying not to laugh.

His eyes shifted from playful to predator as I teased him. He set the invitation down.

"Open the other one," I insisted, making a big show of leaning over to watch, knowing just what kind of view he was getting.

Caspian laughed, a dark warm sound that crawled down my back, and I shivered. But he turned his focus to the gift, and opened it to reveal a golden mask that would match the pins for my veil. He ran his fingers over the gently curled edges that mimicked feathers at the tips of the decorations. Very fine glass beads sewn onto it gave it a textured look.

"So, are you going to be there?" I teased.

His mouth quirked up at the side as he set the mask and invitation on his side table. "I don't know, what do I get if I agree?"

I giggled as I let myself fall forward, his arms catching me as he allowed us fall onto the bed. Our lips met in a hungry kiss, and I could feel the tension that had built in me all day roll off my shoulders as his hands slid around my hips.

"Madeline, are you coming on to me?" Caspian purred.

Laughing, I gently shoved at his shoulders while he kissed down my neck. Rolling us over, Caspian pinned me beneath him on the bed, and my breath caught at the look in his eyes. Playtime was over, and serious Caspian was here.

"Maddie, do you want to do this tonight? You're not too tired?"

"I want to," I said eagerly. "Do you remember what you said to me that first night in the pond?"

"Yes," He moved a hand along my jaw, brushing his thumb across my bottom lip. "To take what you want? Of course I remember."

"What if what I want is for you to be in charge again? At least in the beginning. I like what you did when you told me to keep my hands in place."

"It's freeing, to not be in charge," he murmured. "Did me making the decisions help you relax before?"

"Yeah, I think it did," I admitted. "And I wouldn't mind something like that again. If you liked it, that is."

Caspian thought a moment. "If that's what my siren wants, I think I can make it happen. What do you say we take it a step further?"

A shiver struck me, but I liked the idea. I had liked being pinned in place last time, and I wanted to know what "further" looked like to a man like Caspian. "Tell me more."

His eyes crinkled. "I have some silk rope, easy on the skin. How about pinning you in place in a whole new way?"

I gave a nervous laugh. "Do I need a safe word for this?"

Caspian backed off a little, giving me air. "We don't have to do it at all if you don't want to."

"No! No. I want to."

Which was weird, because you'd think after everything I'd been through, I wouldn't want to give up an ounce of control over myself. But with Caspian, it was surprisingly okay. I trusted him, which wasn't something I did often. And if I wanted to flip the situation around halfway through, I could.

"As for a safe word, you can pick anything you want. But don't forget, Maddie, you're a siren. You can say anything at all, and I would stop."

That was right, the sway. After all the lessons I'd had, I was now in control of it. I'd had plenty of practice not using it, which gave me a devilish idea to practice with it on purpose.

"Let's settle on a word for both of us anyway," I said innocently. "How about . . ." I glanced at his shelf, spotting a painting. "Coral."

Caspian laughed. "*Coral?*"

"Shh, we can workshop it later," I said. "Just go with it."

His eyes darkened with anticipation, and he leaned over to give me a soft kiss. "As you wish."

I was heating up fast, and it had nothing to do with the warm night air. Caspian pulled out a length of shiny black rope from somewhere in his wardrobe, and I lay flat, trying to relax my excited muscles. Very much enjoying the view of Caspian's back as it flexed and checked the rope, I didn't see that it was more than one piece until he turned around and tossed them on the bed around me in three piles.

"What's this?" I sat up, but Caspian was already at the bed, a warm hand on my stomach urging me to lie back down.

"Let me show you what I've been thinking about ever since that first time."

Caspian moved to one of the bottom bedposts, tying the rope to one corner and then to my ankle with practiced ease.

"You've done this before," I said. "Let me guess, boats?"

Caspian laughed hard enough that it paused his progress on my other ankle. "These are definitely not boating knots."

I shrugged. What did I know about tying rope? Other than the fact that Caspian made it look easy. Soon enough, my ankles were both solidly held where he wanted them. The feeling was strange and thrilling, not being able to press my thighs together, and if Caspian didn't stop looking so damn delicious he was soon going to see how wet I was for him. But all thoughts drifted as he settled himself between my legs and reached for my hands.

"Now your wrists."

He described every move he made, pulling the rope around a bar in his headboard before tying each wrist. I had movement, but my hands rested comfortably just above my head without being able to go much lower. There would be no closing my legs, no reaching anywhere, and my heart was going wild in my chest.

Caspian backed off, still kneeling between my legs, but his torso was upright so he could look down at me. Strange as it was, I was completely at his mercy, but I was also hotter for sex than I could remember being before. What did I want again? Oh right, a distraction. This would certainly do it. But it was time to pull out my own trick.

"Caspian."

"Mm?" He looked so content in that moment, before my grin turned devilish.

"Lose the pants."

His eyes widened as the compulsion hit him. I put my sway into it, not enough that he wouldn't be able to fight it off, but firm enough that there was no way he didn't feel it. He tilted his head and looked down at me, even as he shifted his hands to his hips to slide his loose cotton pants off.

"Anything you want, and it's yours. Even if you are being a cheeky thing about it."

I laughed, then my attention focused as I watched him step off the bed long enough to drop his pants to the floor. That happened to be *all* he was wearing, and as he took his cock in his hand, slowly stroking it as he watched me suffering on his bed, I felt the need for something solid between my legs.

Watching him, watching his hand move up and down so deliciously slowly, was a blissful sort of torture. On instinct I tried to move my arms, and when that tug kept them above my head, a rush of excitement hit me. Whatever was about to happen, the only control I had here was my voice. I craved his hands, wanted to know exactly where on my body he would touch with unobstructed access. My thighs tried to move closer, but again that tug of the rope reminded me I didn't have full range.

Caspian leaned down, his hot breath fanning over my right nipple as it stiffened under his attention. Ever so gently, he nipped it between his lips and gave a gentle, tugging suck. "You're doing so good for me."

271

An unsightly noise came from me as I arched my back. Something between surprise and pleasure as he made his way across my exposed chest. A kiss here, a tug at my nipple, a taste of my skin. He made his way so agonizingly slowly down my chest and across my stomach that I was about ready to beg by the time he reached my hip. But when he got there, he planted a soft kiss on my stomach, and I felt his fingers at my entrance.

"Caspian." My voice was husky by now, caught between panting for air and sounding out every delicious sensation he gave me. My legs were almost shaking with how they wanted to close but couldn't.

Caspian continued with his mouth, making his way lazily down my side and over my thighs, while at the same time his fingers found my clit and made those slow, perfect circles I'd taught him that very first time in his living room. Fuck, he remembered every. Damn. Motion.

I was squirming for him by the time he had had his fill of my needy sounds, of my hands searching for anything to do, but he made sure to stay well away from them. There was well and truly nothing I could do from this position, and I loved it. The torture of what he was going to do next, the anticipation of his touch that I couldn't reach for, couldn't see.

He plunged in one finger . . . two, then his thumb found my clit again and he went back to kissing and sucking my skin. His hot mouth pressed against the tender skin on the underside of my breast. Caspian inhaled deeply, his fingers stroking that spot just inside me as he did so, and he moaned. "You're the most addicting high I've ever had, Maddie," he crooned, and I melted. "I could chase this for the rest of my life and never get enough of you."

"Caspian, I can't take much more of this," I begged. "Please, I need you in me *now*."

A little sway slipped into that last word. It was such a heated moment that I had no idea if I meant to or not, but Caspian's amused sound sent a shiver down my body as his fingers pulled away and his warm chest drew even with mine. Fuck, I wanted to wrap my arms around him, pull my legs around his back, but I *couldn't* and that made it all hotter. It was complete exposure, absolutely at his whim to give me the touch my body was demanding.

His eyes were so full of emotion, so warm when his face was close enough for me to see. I leaned up as best I could and kissed him just as I felt his cock at my entrance.

"Whatever you want, my siren," Caspian said softly.

And then he absolutely fucked me. I gasped when he pushed in with one hard motion. The feeling of being so full so suddenly when I was already so wet and teased and ready to go was a buzz of heaven in my head as all other thoughts were pushed away.

"You like this," he commented. Another thrust, a moan from me. "You're tighter than you've ever been for me, do you know that?" Another thrust, and all I could do was breathe out the tension that was building in a strained sound of agreement. Hot kisses and hard thrusts soon blurred as both of us chased whatever high of the night we were barreling toward with abandon.

I knew my muscles would ache tomorrow. The instinct to resist, to pull, to free myself from the ropes and their constant foreign sensation didn't fall away for a long while. Not being able to run my hands down Caspian's chest, to wrap my arms around his shoulders, hell, to hold on for dear life as he grabbed my hips and filled me.

"Fuck, Caspian." I couldn't catch my breath.

"Hold on a little longer for me, Madeline," Caspian growled in my ear, then grabbed one of my thighs, lifting it as much as the rope would allow to give himself a deeper reach into me.

Hold on, he'd said. I barely managed that; it felt more like I was along for the ride than anything else. Which was probably the ropes' doing, but it still made for one hell of a fuck, and I made mental notes to ask Caspian what else he'd been fantasizing about.

He slowed our motion just enough that I whined as he kissed me hard, my hands itching to reach for him, to feel what of him I could, but coming up empty.

"Come for me," Caspian commanded. And fuck if I didn't obey. He had me wound so wet, so hot, so tight, that the fall from that climax sent my head spinning. I know I called out some sound that could have been his name or just some scrambled word or other as he hit my inner walls in all the right places. Over and over he thrust, riding out my orgasm until he found his own. I did what I could to catch my breath when Caspian filled me with his heat.

He slid out of me, and I felt our combined climax dripping out of me. Caspian's fingers pressed it back in, and my whole body shivered. I still couldn't do a damn thing.

"The sight of you, tied in my bed and coming completely undone, is the most beautiful thing I've ever seen." Caspian kissed my temple, moving to inspect my wrists. Fuck, whatever he was doing, he could do it on his own for a minute while I floated through whatever clouds my head flew into after that climax.

"Are you okay?" Caspian asked.

"Mm. Mmmmm." My groans were definitely not fully formed thoughts let alone a response.

Caspian kissed my cheek. "Let me clean you up and help you out of the ropes." He left the bed while I collected myself, and when he came back he took care of me. He had a wet cloth to wipe me down, and he gently removed the ropes then rubbed an oil or something on my skin to bring the circulation back to my limbs. It smelled good. Earthy. It reminded me of him.

Caspian finished taking care of us, then filled me a glass of water from a pitcher he . . . did he already have it in the room, or did he bring it in after? Hell, who knew. Not Madeline. Madeline was currently floating on cloud nine and she wasn't coming down anytime soon.

I didn't realize how hard I was crashing until Caspian's warm body settled behind me while I curled up on my side. He pulled the sheets over me, draped a warm arm over my hip, and kissed my shoulder.

"Good night, Maddie," Caspian murmured.

"Night." And the sleep that had eluded me before found me. Warm and comfortable in Caspian's bed.

CHAPTER THIRTY-ONE

MADELINE

The House of Sirens was filled with music. The juxtaposition of the ancient building with a Bluetooth speaker still baffled me, but Atlantis had worked hard to incorporate what technology they did bring in while keeping it subtle. Any wires and infrastructure were kept so low-key that I almost never noticed them.

But there I was in the large communal room at the house, dancing with Jacinta under the supervision of Amara and her partner, Iris. It was good to finally put a face to the name, and the way Amara looked at the petite and bubbly Iris told me everything I needed to know about their love. It was cute, even if it did stir up some jealousy that I wasn't here dancing with Caspian.

"Watch your left foot," Amara called, somehow prying her eyes off of Iris for long enough to correct my dancing to match Jacinta's.

"Got it. Sorry, my mind is wandering."

"It's okay." Jacinta beamed. "I'm just excited that I get to go this time."

I smiled back at the young siren, who was putting her heart into the music and looking forward to the ball. It was true that Ashana had deemed her ready, albeit she would be taken back to the House of Sirens before the more adult activities began.

Dancing was a welcome reprieve from my worries, and loosening up my body after the feeling of the rope on my arms and legs last night was . . . I could feel the heat creep up my neck and across my face at the thought. I'd liked it, more than I thought I'd like the feeling of helplessness, considering the things I'd been through. But in the end I didn't feel helpless at all, I felt free. What did that say about me? I wasn't sure, but I wasn't about to question it either. For once in my life, I felt good, I had friends, and I was falling for a guy who wasn't an absolute pile of garbage. Quite the opposite. Caspian was a dream, and I was going to fuck his brains out at this ball.

"Okay, that's about enough for now," Amara said, sighing and slumping onto a nearby chaise-like pile of cushions, pulling a giggling Iris down with her.

"Yes!" Jacinta let go of my hands and ran to another set of cushions nearby, falling onto them with a grunt.

Finding my own cushioned surface to sink into, I propped my feet up on a pillow and laid my head back. "I'm already tired, I can't believe you expect me to do that all night."

"But it's so fun!" Amara beamed, throwing me the hand sign for *enjoyment* and *big* while Iris snuggled in next to her. "Oh, by the way, who did you give that invitation to?"

A smile crept over my face. "Caspian."

"Mmm, and he's such a good choice too," Amara said. "Did you happen to accidentally leave your veil out for him to see, or do I have a chance?"

Iris grabbed one of the pillows and smacked Amara with it, and the siren fell into a fit of laughter as she tried to defend herself.

"Joke! It was a joke!" Amara caught the pillow and took it from Iris before attacking her with kisses, and now it was Iris's turn to laugh. She recovered, wiping tears from her eyes. "Truly, though, if you're aiming for a specific partner you need to be *sure* it's them. It's going to be dark, and if you're anything like me, you'll be a little drunk, and the next day you don't want to be the gossip on everyone's tongues when you figure out midthrust you're smashing against the wrong body, and you scream."

"Amara!" Iris smacked her with the pillow again, evoking another fit of laughter.

"Yuck," Jacinta said, getting up. "I'm going to go make sure my new dress doesn't have any wrinkles."

The girl trotted off down a hall to her room. For a moment I pictured what that would be like to live in a big house with others who considered you family. Would it be like the group home? Maybe it was more relaxed, like Caspian's house . . .

My face felt flushed and I pressed a hand to my cheek. How long was I going to keep blushing every time I remembered what we'd done in his room? At some point, Amara or Larisa were going to catch on and tease me to no end.

"I should get going anyway." Amara yawned. "Time to take my sweet flower for our afternoon walk." She leaned over to kiss Iris on the cheek.

"Sounds good," I agreed. "I have things to do too."

Her face curled into mischief. "Are those things to do maybe Caspian?"

Grabbing the nearest cushion, I threw it at her face as she cackled.

Amara helped Ashana to her favorite afternoon sitting spot before wandering off with Iris, and I wasted no time in heading back to Caspian's house. The warmth of the afternoon offered a lazy walk through the market on my way back, allowing me to pick up a few oranges and enjoy the flowers before reaching the street that would take me to Caspian, who would probably be wandering home soon. A cozy house on a quiet street that was starting to feel just a little bit like home.

CHAPTER THIRTY-TWO

MADELINE

"If I don't get dicked down tonight, I'm going to be pissed," Larisa said demandingly, checking herself out in a mirror while Amara applied a rosy lip coloring to her.

"If you don't get dicked down tonight, I'll be pissed on your behalf," Amara answered half-heartedly. "Now, hold still or my beautiful work will be crooked."

I had been invited to sleep over at the House of Sirens. We stayed up late, drank wine, sang, and danced. Everyone assured me this was a typical night at the house for anyone who didn't feel like staying in their rooms. And the rooms were so comfortable. Small, but with beds that took up most of the space and that were covered in light, soft cotton dyed with beautiful patterns that rivaled the most intricate dresses at the market. I should know, I'd drooled over them more than once when Amara took me shopping for my veiled ball dress.

Since it was the eve of the vellieovasa, even the sirens who spent their nights at separate houses in the city had gathered to stay at the main house. Larisa and Amara shared a bed with me, and we fell asleep humming together. The morning was filled with activity—once everyone woke up, that was. More music, more singing and dancing, and plenty of helping each other get ready.

"Madeline," a thickly accented voice said from behind me.

I turned to one of the two older sirens who were taking great enjoyment in helping me get ready. I barely spoke Atlantean, and neither of them spoke English, but we had managed so far with hand signing.

"*Vaiya?*" I asked, something of an acknowledgment like *yeah, what* but more polite.

She signed something, and after some back and forth and pointing, I figured out she was asking about my hair. Then, the siren in front of me who had been doing my makeup joined in, making things more difficult for me to understand when they began to what I could only assume was bicker over how to style me, much to my amusement. We finally came to a consensus, or at least they did, and my hair was braided and pinned up.

It felt warm and tingly and strange to be fussed over like this, and I was keenly aware that they were old enough to be my mother. My mother, Tanis, was quietly getting ready in another room. I had half wondered if she would be out in one of the towers, but I was told she had insisted on joining this ball, and other sirens were sitting it out to maintain the songs at the towers tonight. Did she want to be here because of me? Was it simply time for her to show her face at a ball again? Was I in the wrong for keeping my distance?

Whatever the answer, it didn't come to me as I sat between the two women putting me together for the night. Eventually, my hair wound around the crown of my head and my veil was pinned in place with golden leaves. I wore a gorgeous red gown, unusually vibrant for Atlantis, but for celebrations like today colors would be bold and plentiful, not just dyed on edges and embroidered at hems. My lips and eyes had foreign-feeling makeup, but nothing heavy or unpleasant. Some jewelry was shoved in front of me, and when I mistakenly took just one piece of it, I was met with laughter and unceremoniously decorated with the lot of it, like a Christmas tree.

When the elder sirens Ashana and Calliope came into the room, dressed in their best with a spring in their step, the room fell into a hush of anticipation. Jacinta, practically bouncing off the walls in her seafoam dress and matching veil, pulled back a nearby curtain, and I could see the light starting to fade.

An announcement was made, and all the sirens stood to gather at the front door. Larisa hooked her arm through mine, and Amara joined her at my other arm right after.

"Ready?" Larisa asked.

"Ready as I'm going to be," I said. "Maybe a little nervous."

"What's there to be nervous about?" Amara asked. "You go, you eat, you dance, you sing, and you figure out where your Caspian is hiding in the crowd to end the night."

Amusement crept across my lips. "True, I am looking forward to that part."

Outside the door, the energy on the street was different. Decorations that must have been put up yesterday and today were strung everywhere, and thankfully my veil was fine enough to see them. Candles on windowsills, flowers in little pots along the road, and lots and lots of lanterns. The firefly things I'd seen in Caspian's yard were starting to come out, adding to the magic in the air. People were dressed in vibrant clothes, all of them wearing masks.

"Are the sirens the only ones with veils?" I asked. Amara nodded, and I went back to watching the streets around us.

The lanterns and flowers lined our path, and as we wound

through Atlantis, Calliope and Ashana at the lead, I heard the music. One by one, sirens split off as we passed intersections. Some would go to other chosen courtyards around Atlantis. Closer to their loved ones, spreading the songs of the festive night around the island. A handful would always volunteer to go to the high square in front of the Senate at the tallest point of Atlantis. A place for the most experienced sirens, and a training ground to navigate the vellieovasa for newer ones like me or Jacinta.

Amara said goodbye first, and I spotted Iris waiting on a corner to join her. Larisa stayed by my side until almost the end, kissing my cheek and removing her arm from mine.

"You'll do great," she whispered. "Good luck to us both tonight."

I gave her a brave smile, took a deep breath, then moved forward with the remaining sirens. Ashana and Calliope would be here, as well as several others I recognized, including the one who'd applied my makeup. Jacinta, excited but with a tinge of nerves creeping onto her expression, was soon surrounded by a few of the motherly sirens, in a sign of encouragement. It reminded me that the sirens raised their babies as a collective, and all of these women were likely a source of comfort for Jacinta. Something I was happy for my young friend, but that made me look away as an uncomfortable feeling settled in my stomach. Jealousy? Maybe. Uncomfortable with the foreignness of the love before me? Probably.

As I looked away, one set of eyes met my shifting gaze, and I was surprised to see Tanis. Beautiful in a dusty-rose dress with a long silver veil, something was settled in her expression, and I don't think either of us was ready to unpack that. Not tonight, not at the vellieovasa. We looked away at the same time, and thankfully, we had reached the summit.

Calliope made an announcement, and I caught several of the

words. Looking around the courtyard, I could see everything was decorated in vibrant colors. Tables laden with drinks and food were spaced around the square, so you were never far from one. Lights were everywhere—in glass lanterns that scattered a rainbow of dim lighting across the floor, the buildings, and the central fountain. And the people. I knew the ones here would be from the Senate and the basilli's family. A few other invited guests would be in the crowd too. Why this one was so exclusive I wasn't sure, but maybe it had something to do with the presence of the specific sirens in attendance.

Apart from the lanterns and food, there were also draped areas strung between buildings and in doorways. These were piled high with comfortable-looking cushions and a few tapestries on screens for what I assumed was privacy. The large columned front steps of the Senate building itself held many curtains as well, which created alcoves for what I imagined would be the end of the evening trysts. I shivered, delighted at the prospect.

Music filled the air, and all eyes were on the sirens. A tray was brought by and we were all offered wine except Jacinta, who had a cup of tea. As the glasses were handed out, Calliope was finishing her words, and I could feel the excitement building—building in me, in the other people around the square, and even the sirens themselves were growing restless. Some were even beginning to hum in a low tune with the music.

When Calliope raised her hand high, a glass of dark wine swirling above her, she called out to us all. "*Anan* vellieovasa. Chaara!"

"Chaara!" I was able to echo the cheers with the rest of the square around me, and the vellieovasa officially began.

CHAPTER THIRTY-THREE

CASPIAN

The excitement of the day was hard to ignore as the buzzing energy of people getting ready for the evening festivities surrounded me. My neighbors made food and lit their lanterns, and laughter came from the gathering families who would help one another get ready in their best clothes and adornments. It was too much, the anticipation of seeing Madeline at her first ball in the glow of the sirens. The chance to hold her, dance with her, do more if she was willing.

Packing up my work, I shut myself in the Senate office to do whatever I could to distract myself and make the time pass. Or at least, attempt to.

As the daylight dragged at a painstaking pace through the windows, I finished writing up my notes from the last Senate session and corresponded with several trivial contacts for Dimitris. The tint of the sky was just fading from its daytime blues when Nikkos walked in.

A mask tucked into his waistband and an already half-empty

bottle of wine under an arm, Nikkos looked more relaxed than I'd seen him in ages. His hair was still neatly combed back, but his stride was easy and comfortable, and he had a smile on his face.

"Good evening, cousin." Nikkos greeted as he sat down in the chair closest to my desk.

"What's got you in such a good mood?" I mused, pausing my work to stare at him.

Nikkos swirled the bottle, eyeing it as though he might make an attempt at the other half by himself right here and now but then decided against it. "It's a night to celebrate, isn't it? And I have some fantastic news."

"Oh? And what would that be?"

"Our contact from the mainland reached out! He wants to meet, he has news." Nikkos beamed.

After weeks of nothing, I had been starting to grow worried. But if Gavin had reached out with news, he must at least know where the relic was, if not already have it in his possession.

"Gavin did? When?" I stood from my desk while Nikkos pulled a paper from his pocket.

"Hold on, I took notes while we were on the phone. Let me see . . . He located the amulet," Nikkos said. "Something about a dead vampire, I didn't quite understand that part. But there is a small catch regarding the amulet."

"This better not complicate things, or Dimitris will be pissed." My uncle did not tolerate complications. "Did the vampire die because of Gavin? Or . . ."

"Unclear," Nikkos answered, still looking over his notes. "What's more interesting is the complications from the amulet. We have a new detail that the old texts didn't provide."

"Anything we can't handle?" I asked. "I don't like the sound of that."

"Hold on, it's not that bad. I think. Apparently, it requires a being of significant abilities to even hold the thing. He can't transport it without help, but he does have help."

"Are you telling me he invited someone here?"

"I know, Caspian, but we have few alternative options. Gavin and his associate would need to bring the amulet here in person."

"Fantastic. Another wordbinding?"

"That's the odd part," Nikkos said. "No wordbinding needed. Gavin insists they saw through the binding themselves. They already know about Atlantis."

We stood in silence, the implications sinking in. "We aren't going to have a choice, are we? We need that amulet here," I said.

"And we need a container of solid silver to house it once it arrives."

With a groan, I ran my fingers through my hair. "Dammit. All right, what manner of being is this other person?"

"A fae, of all things." Nikkos looked at his paper. "A fae with powers related to warding off the effects of the amulet or something like that. That's why they can help transport it."

"I know almost nothing about them."

Nikkos shrugged. "Neither do I. I suppose we have some reading up to do, then, if our old books even have much on the fae. But we're paying Gavin a very favorable amount for his work, and his reputation for getting the job done is impeccable."

"I know, I know." I waved off the concerns. "There's a lot riding on this. If that's truly the item and our research was correct, then we can potentially be done with the labors of the sirens. They would be free to live much different lives. Atlantis would be free to focus its efforts in much different ways."

It was everything Dimitris had promised the people who'd voted for him, and everything we had been working for. To ensure a safety for the island that didn't rely on the diminishing population of sirens. My mind went to Madeline, and the carefree life just out of reach for her. Without the responsibility of the sirens on her shoulders, what would she want to do with her days?

"He says he can be here in three days once we give him the coordinates," Nikkos said, disrupting my wandering thoughts.

"Three days?" I frowned. "It takes weeks to sail here, and there is nowhere for a plane to land. How does he plan on getting here?"

Nikkos shrugged. "I'm sure he has his ways."

Sighing, I looked out the window at the now properly fading light. "The ball will begin soon. Let's tell Dimitris in the morning."

"Not tonight?" Nikkos asked.

"I'm not sure we'll see him tonight," I said. "He doesn't show his face much at this kind of thing."

"True, true." Nikkos grunted as he stood up, wine in one hand, and stuffed the note back in his pocket. "Well, I have my own celebration to get to. My neighbor Iris invited me to join her in Palmway Square."

"Have fun." I clapped a hand on Nikkos's shoulder as he passed me. "Don't get too drunk."

He snorted. "I'd give you the same warning, but I rather like the idea of cutting loose a bit. Maybe you should as well."

The image of Madeline and the dark, unspoken promises we'd made for tonight flashed through my mind. "Oh, don't worry, cousin. I plan to enjoy the night to its fullest."

Nikkos chuckled as he walked through the office door, leaving me alone. I went back to my desk to grab the mask Madeline had given me and fixed it over my eyes. It left plenty of room to see but still covered enough of my face that it functioned as a mask. The ball should be starting any time now, and I locked up my work and hurried to step outside of the Senate building before I missed the sirens' arrival.

I slipped outside just in time. Music was already playing, people were already present, and the final touches were being placed on the buffet tables. It was beautifully decorated this year, and I eyed a few corners that were curtained off and filled with pillows. I smiled, picturing some things I could do with Madeline in those dark corners later.

After a while, a lull in the conversations snagged my attention. They were here. I watched the sirens coming up the path, dressed in their best with the added allure of the veils they wore. Carefully crafted adornments dripped from all of them, and the mystery the veils created in the rapidly dimming light only further enticed the audience.

The two keepers of the sirens, Calliope and Ashana, began the usual ceremonial words, but my eyes were searching for a different siren in the crowd. I reached up and brushed my fingers across my golden mask, remembering the shape of it and looking for the veil with pins to match it.

I spotted her quickly, the shape of her familiar as she squirmed in place with excitement. As Calliope was ending her words to the crowd and wineglasses were raised in cheers, I stepped down from the shadow of the Senate building. A hand fell on my shoulder.

"Caspian." My uncle's cool voice turned my head. He wore a simple mask for the occasion, but it was still easy to see who it was. "Any news?"

The same question he had asked me every time he had seen me for the last several days. Dimitris was growing impatient, and an impatient Dimitris made for an uncomfortable environment for all involved.

My shoulders sank slightly as I turned to face him. This would delay my first dance with Madeline, but maybe if I could get this over with quickly the evening could resume as planned.

"Yes. We just received word from our contact. I was going to find you in the morning if I didn't see you tonight."

"Where is Nikkos?"

"He is at one of the celebration squares, participating in the festivities." *Just like I should be.* But I kept any annoyance out of my voice. It wouldn't do anything but piss off Dimitris and delay my evening if he thought I was prioritizing anything over his goals, especially if that something was the romantic pursuit of a siren, the very thing he was trying to make obsolete to our survival.

His face was unreadable as he nodded. "Come, you can tell me everything you know in my office."

His words left no room for an argument of any kind, and he knew it. He turned without waiting for an answer from me and went back up the front steps of the Senate building.

I looked out at the group of sirens again. Madeline was already looking around the sizeable crowd, not having found me and the golden mask yet. My gut twisted to leave her, but I would make this quick and come right back as soon as I could.

Following Dimitris through the halls to his office, I filtered through all the details in my head that I could go over quickly the moment we were behind closed doors. I just hoped Madeline wouldn't be too upset with me for being a bit late.

CHAPTER THIRTY-FOUR

MADELINE

My skin felt electric. Like I could jump right out of it and dance all night long. I was so excited to be dancing, to be moving my body. In Atlantis, surrounded by the sirens, and searching for my man in a masked crowd with dim lighting felt like a sexy game of cat and mouse. It was thrilling, and I could get addicted to these veiled ball things.

We were cut loose after a toast that I only half understood, and that was fine by me. As soon as words were said and the wine was drunk, the sirens moved where they willed. Dancing was immediate, flirting even more so. If I didn't already feel a bit cocky in my bold red dress that hugged my favorite parts, the hungry eyes behind more than a few masks around the square would have sealed the deal. I could feel the power at play here, and the sirens absolutely held it in this crowd.

The energy of the night air was seductive and enticing. A night for passion, and there was only one person I wanted to share that with. For now, I was content to be swept away by the music as a buzzing song started to play, and my body wanted to move with it. I wanted to dance.

A woman, one who wasn't a siren, wearing a vibrant peacock mask, offered her hands to me with a playful sway of her hips. I laughed and obliged as the music kicked up. We danced, and she ran a hand down my arms in a move similar to one Amara had been teaching me just yesterday. I kept up well enough, but when the drinks started going to my head, my body moved to the music as it wanted, and no one seemed to care. When the woman and I were done dancing, not a word passed between us but she smiled as she reached for her next partner, and I turned to find one for myself.

This was everything I ever wanted. I was safe, there was no threat of hunger or homelessness, and my only worry in the world was who to dance with next. The night swept me away easily, but always in the back of my mind I was trying to spot that golden mask. The light faded, and I held so many hands. I danced with strangers, with sirens, and once I thought I danced with Maya, the woman who had been interpreting for me when I'd first arrived in Atlantis. Each song swept me away faster than the last, giving me small breaks to grab a bite or a drink from the festive tables around the square.

Watching the older sirens was a treat too. They really knew what they were doing, and some with obvious intent to the end of their night were humming along with the music or whispering in ears, drifting closer and closer to the nooks and crannies of curtains that had been set up for just this kind of thing. I saw one cheeky siren whose hands were snaking into the half-unbuttoned shirt of her dancing partner.

But when the tone of the night shifted, it shifted. No one in that square, no matter how many glasses of wine they had gone through, couldn't tell that something was in the air. The music paused, and the tables of food were consolidated down to three based off of what was left. The movement in the square chased off several people. Jacinta waved to me as she left with Calliope on one arm and Ashana on the other, the evening clearly done for the oldest sirens as well. One woman in a mask, clearly not a siren but someone who knew them, hovered near Ashana's elbow with the older woman's cane. I smiled to know they were being worried over on the walk back.

With a couple glasses of wine in my system and plenty of dancing already had, I was ready for something a little slower paced. It was time to find Caspian.

Draining a full glass of water to wake me up for the search, I popped a grape in my mouth and carried a handful away with me as I walked. Couples and more than a few larger groups were forming. You could tell by the way hands were touching and lips were whispering. But I didn't find a shape like Caspian's wearing a golden mask anywhere. Once my grapes were gone and I had already walked around the central fountain twice, I decided to opt for a different vantage point, and found the closest building with stairs. One large building stood out, and I headed for the top.

The steps were shallow and easy to climb, and at the top of them I found that I was several feet off the ground and could see most of the square better. The fact that night had officially fallen wasn't helping, but the scattered candles and lanterns did at least lend a romantic glow to the space. The music had turned slow with less urgency behind it. The buzz of energy the musicians were conveying before had now turned to murmurs of strings and wood-winds and drums. Sitting on the top step, I spent several minutes trying to pick out a masculine shape in the crowd. A body came up behind me.

An appreciative hum sent a delightful shiver down my back, and I turned to the darkened doorway to the building I had chosen. Dark clothing, broad shouldered, and the shadow of hair on his chin that he didn't usually let go that far. I recognized the golden mask that sprawled over a well-shaped face. Even in the dark with the few details I could pick out, I appreciated Caspian's look tonight.

"There you are," I scolded. "I was looking for you."

Not wasting any time, I slipped my arms around his waist and sighed as I laid my head on his chest. He had a spicy scent on him tonight, but underneath it all I could smell the sandalwood incense that was so heavily used on the island. He always smelled of it, and I'd grown to associate the smell with Caspian without really thinking about it.

He paused a moment before a pair of warm arms wrapped around my back. I hadn't noticed how cool the evening air had grown until there was someone warm against me.

"You feel so good right now." I sighed again, sinking into him. "I thought you weren't going to show up for a minute there, but you know I wanted to be alone with you tonight."

His answer was to stroke my back up and down with one big hand, humming softly to the music. I pulled away just enough to talk, my eyes roaming the square below. "Where can we go that's a little more private?"

A rumble of his chest in the form of a soft laugh, and he pulled my hand into his and took me into the building we had been standing in front of. A thrill went through my bones as we crossed the threshold into the Senate building. I'd seen it once before with Nikkos, but not inside alone and not at night.

Even this space was touched by the festivities, with candles in windows and lanterns in the large planters in the center of the main room where plants and trees were flowering in abundance. Caspian wound us around the planters and down one of the branching hall-ways to a room he had to unlock with a key.

The huge hall of the Senate building was a bowl of seating that ended at a central stage at the bottom, where all eyes could be on the speaker. A skylight let the moon and stars shine down on it, but we didn't go to the stage. Instead, we went to one of the wide benches at the very back of the room, obscured in skewed shadows.

I wasn't sure we were supposed to be here, and I didn't care. There was something about doing it in a place where we might get caught, where we shouldn't be doing this kind of thing to begin with.

The bench was surprisingly plush, covered in those cushions I had come to love about Atlantis, and was almost as wide as a twin bed with an excess of space. Enough to comfortably lie on, I realized.

I sat on the bench, Caspian beside me. He reached up to help me unpin my veil. Good, I was tired of it anyway. But when I reached up to help him remove his mask, his hand caught my wrist as he shook his head with a naughty smile.

My eyes crinkled as I laughed. "Okay, the mask stays, then."

He nudged me to turn around, and I obliged, happy to kick off my shoes and rest feet that ached from all the dancing on the soft bench. Strong hands dug into my shoulders, rubbing the tension out of them as he explored my neck and upper back.

A moan escaped me as he wandered lower, teasing the top of my dress as he slowly undid the ties that kept it on me. I giggled, probably still tipsy, as the air hit my bare skin and his warm hands wandered lower down my back.

His hand swept across my collarbone, and I was just moving to pull the front of my dress off my breasts when the sharp click of shoes echoed into the space. We both froze in the cover of the dark room and the expectation that this place would be empty. My heart slammed in my chest at the mix of thrill and dread that we would be caught.

Two people had entered, both wearing masks, one large shape and one dainty one that held herself in a way that tried to recall someone specific.

Arguing. Heated, bitter arguing came from a woman in Atlantean. I could only catch so many words of it, but my partner whispered in my ear. Barely audible and in a lighter tone than I'd heard from him before.

Where I heard words like *woman, fight*, and an Atlantean slang for *whore*, he translated.

"What does he think he's doing here with that woman?" Soft whispers unraveled the juicy argument unfolding at the bottom of the room. "Starting another fight with that—that whore."

Goose bumps covered me. There was something wrong with Caspian's voice, and I had the sudden urge to get away from all of this. But we were about to be caught in here when we probably shouldn't be, and a part of me felt the importance of the conversation we were eavesdropping on.

The larger shape put his hands on the woman's shoulders. "She has his lust, but you have his house. Everyone knows you rule Ateio, no matter who warms Adrion's bed. Don't work yourself up over it. Do you need one of your sleeping draughts, my love?"

The figure at my back stiffened at that last line, but he didn't stop translating for me.

"All those sirens are good for is spreading their legs!" The woman's sharp tones echoed off the walls in the otherwise empty room.

Siren? What siren was she talking about? The typical response of panic shot through me that I would be the one she was talking about, but I knew it wasn't me the moment I registered the name that was said just before this. Ateio. Adrion. Adrion Ateio, the basilli of Atlantis.

My heart stopped as I recognized Helena Ateio. She had been cold to me when we met. Maybe it wasn't just me she was being cold to, but a general distaste for sirens as a whole?

"What if he fucks her again and creates another Ateio bastard?" The woman huffed, and her companion wrapped his arms around her.

"Then you give me the order to take it away again. Tanis wouldn't survive another heartbreak like that."

"Fuck." That one was the whisper at my ear as a pair of hands drifted off my skin and away.

Cold. Everything went cold as the words sank in. Tanis was my mother, and if Tanis had a bastard child . . . a bastard child with Adrion Ateio. . . . My head hurt trying to piece the bits together. Adrion Ateio made a bastard baby with Tanis, and that caused Helena to, what, order this man to kidnap . . .

I was going to be sick. My mind was going numb, my body feeling suddenly detached. I didn't want to be in this place, hearing these things.

"I still wish you had killed that thing when you got rid of it. You're too soft, Eris," Helena chided. "Any bastards Adrion makes are a danger to my Calix. My son deserves his seat at the top."

"To kill a siren would anger the gods. My failures are my own, my love. They will never know what happened, don't worry. If I need to do it all over again for you, I will." The man, Eris, moved in to kiss her neck, drawing a moan from the otherwise cold Helena Ateio.

"Take me, Eris. I can't go back out there and watch him fuck that siren."

Eris moved swiftly to oblige, and I turned away.

I moved my head sharply to see where Caspian, or whoever I'd heard, was so we could get out of there, and bumped my forehead right into his cheek. We smacked each other audibly, and his mask slipped as he swore. It slipped right off his face, and I screamed.

Calix slapped his hand over my mouth at my shocked sound, shoving the mask back on his face, but it was too late. Helena and Eris were already turning our way, Eris charging up the stairs like a bull.

"Lock them in Adrion's office!" Helena shrieked, a finger pointing sharply in our direction. "Do what you must but get rid of them!"

It was no trouble for Eris to do it too. He was huge, and with ease he pulled Calix into a headlock with one arm.

This was it, though, this was the moment to put my sway to the test. I took in a sharp breath and started. "Hey—"

A fist was shoved into my stomach so hard that bile filled my mouth. The air was completely knocked out of me, and I was dragged along with a struggling Calix to a door at the back of the room. It would make sense that the basilli would have an office here, but the door was so seamless in the wall that I wouldn't have spotted it on my own. At least not now, in the dark. I was still choking and wheezing and pulling at the thick arm at my throat when I was thrown into the dark room. Eris said something in Atlantean, and the door slammed in our faces.

A *click* told me we were locked in, and the only one who knew where I was had just admitted she wanted me dead.

CHAPTER THIRTY-FIVE

CASPIAN

"Bring him."

Dimitris was never one to mince words, and the finite tone of his decision echoed off the walls of his office. I gritted my teeth. After a long stretch of inquisition in which Dimitris brought into question every detail he possibly could, he finally deemed it safe enough to bring Gavin and his escort to Atlantis.

The more practiced sirens like Calliope could weave the same kind of binding into their songs as the witch we'd contracted in Florida to swear Gavin to our deal, and we would do that with this escort of his. Gavin had the item, and finally, we could put our plan to the test.

A slow hiss of breath left me, my shoulders stiff. "It will be done, I'll send the coordinates tonight."

"Now." His answer was swift and unyielding. He leveled his gaze at me, even as he stood from his desk. "I've tolerated your relationship with the siren, but you will not let it distract you from securing Atlantis."

My jaw clenched. "Yes, Uncle."

"Good." Dimitris walked through his office, clapping my shoulder as he passed. "See that it doesn't."

Once he was gone, I gathered the bits of papers that I'd brought from my own desk just down the hall. Plugging my laptop into the secured internet connection, I sent Gavin what he would need to find and dock at the largest tower, as well as Dimitris's conditions for Gavin's escort.

With a sigh, I shut everything down and finally, *finally*, left the gods-forsaken Senate offices for the ball. My mask adjusted, my clothes brushed of any wrinkles, I was finally on my way.

The night had fully fallen, the glow of insects and lanterns the only light to see by. Draped silks and folding panels already hid the heady sounds of lust; the latter half of the festivities had begun. A grunt hit my chest with a rumble. I had missed the opportunity to dance with Madeline because of my uncle and the unfortunate timing of Gavin's correspondence. No matter, I would find her now and fulfill every dirty thought my little siren had.

The crowd was so thin and the heated pairings and groupings of bodies that had chosen to stay for the more carnal aspects of the night were most of what remained. With a grimace, I would have to wander near the darkened corners of the square if I hoped to catch Madeline. Then a thought stopped my heart for a beat. Was she participating in one of these trysts? Had she grown bored of waiting for me, or worse, was she angry that I hadn't shown up?

My footsteps were soft but hurried as I tried to spot the color of her delicious dress and ignore the other parts peeking from behind the flimsy cloth draping. A hand snagged at my bicep as I passed, and when I turned to see a veil-covered siren in a blue dress, the small hope I'd found in the instant was dashed.

"Are you looking for a bed to warm?" she purred. "Because I'm looking for someone to ease an itch."

Throaty and heated, her sway was creeping out to play for the evening. I dug my nails into my palm and shook my head. "Not tonight, beautiful siren. I'm looking for Madeline, her veil and pins match mine. Have you seen her?"

She let go of my arm and pouted for only a moment before she was lifted by the waist, her face going from surprise to a bubbling giggle.

"There you are! I told you I'd be back for another round, but you already snuck off, I see."

She was set down again by the masked man behind her, and she turned to kiss him, now completely occupied. My chance to ask about Madeline was gone, so I had little choice but to turn away and continue on.

Something wasn't right. Even if she was mad, I could beg forgiveness for that. But she wouldn't have just disappeared on me completely. I rounded the entire square with no luck, and there was no choice left but to slow my pace and pay more attention. A voice, a discarded garment, whatever I could see that had been allowed to slip outside the coverings. And then I saw the flash of a familiar head of hair as it was flung back in ecstasy, just outside a slip of silk drape before tucking back in.

My chest burned and my jaw ached from the grinding my molars had been doing in my search. Was that her? I supposed I could have been mistaken, but the familiarity of it, the wave to it, it was hard to explain. I made a straight line to the curtain in question.

Softening my steps, I stood outside the cove of fabric, not

knowing what to do. It was her right, of course, but some sick part of me still needed to know.

The slow, deep groan of a man in pleasure hit my ears. A man I recognized with horror.

"Fuck, your cunt is trying to swallow my cock whole, songbird."

Adrion Ateio. The basilli of Atlantis. And he was fucking someone in there who was definitely not his short-haired wife.

"Yes, that's right. Fuck yourself on me, take what you need, songbird. Take what you've missed all these years," Adrion crooned for his bedmate, and my stomach turned.

No, there was no way Madeline had chosen a man nearly twice her age in anger at me. Was there?

Suddenly the curtain was pushed aside as Adrion's hand moved it enough for him to get a good look at me from his position lying back on a pile of cushions. He wore a mask, but there was no mistaking him. "If you're looking for a bed to join, find another."

Dipping down from her seated, speared position, the siren with that familiar wave of hair leaned to kiss Adrion's neck, her breasts pressing into his chest and her veil pushed back to show her face. But it wasn't Madeline I caught sight of; it was Tanis.

"You're Dimitris's boy, aren't you?" Adrion asked, drawing my attention back to him. "Leave us."

"Yes, of course," I said. "Enjoy your night."

I took a quick step back, having no desire to see either my basilli or Madeline's mother in the throes of passion. But everything came to a halt when Adrion gave me that smile. That playful smile, one I could sculpt from memory. The perfect twitch up at the side, and the curve of the full bottom lip that rounded in the middle.

Spinning, I sprinted off as Adrion let the fabric fall back into place, obviously ready to continue his fun. But after what I'd just seen, what I needed to piece together . . .

In the darkened front steps of the main Senate building, I leaned against a pillar and slid down until I was sitting. Now that I had seen it, I couldn't unsee it. Adrion had Madeline's mouth. And, with a little more thought, he shared a lot more than that with her. The way one brow quirked up on one side more than the other, the curve of their noses. I vaguely knew that Adrion had a history with a siren outside of his marriage, but I had had no idea it was Tanis. Or if I did, I had forgotten until now, and the implications were horrific.

If Madeline was, in fact, the child of Tanis and Adrion Ateio, then she was a blood descendant to one of the ruling houses. Not just any house, either, but the one currently overseeing the Senate. The basilli's own child.

I ran a hand through my hair, looking around to ensure no one could see my panic. Madeline, if this was true, was an Ateio. That could change so, so much. It could explain any number of people wanting to get rid of her as an infant. One of the Senate, one of the other houses. Hell, I wouldn't put it past Calix, that bastard, except he wouldn't have been more than a toddler when Madeline was born.

Steps behind me had my back shooting straight, but I realized just in time that I would be out of sight if I stayed still. The last thing I wanted now was to see another person I knew fucking.

"Meet me at our usual place in an hour," a sharp voice murmured. "Get what I told you, and don't let anyone see you."

Odd words, but none of my business. Probably another affair, for all this night was prone to host them. But the man who walked down the Senate stairs, slinking to the side and to the back alleys, was Eris.

A heartbeat later, the practiced footfalls of thc lady of House Ateio descended the grand steps of the main Senate building, and my blood churned in my ears. Helena Ateio had been in the Senate building with Eris, and while her words from a moment ago could mean anything, something gripped my heart and would not let it go.

Who stood the most to lose if Adrion Ateio had had a bastard child with a siren? Who was cold enough, calculating enough, to dispose of an infant? One of Atlantis's precious sirens. The ancient houses were the most ruthless political powers I'd ever known, and the pinnacle of them was the power-hungry Ateios.

Helena Ateio.

I had to find Madeline, and I had to find her now.

CHAPTER THIRTY-SIX

MADELINE

I slammed my fists into the door hard enough that I was sure I'd crack my skin.

"Hey!" I shouted. "Heeey! Can anyone hear us?"

"It's no use," Calix said, standing behind me and pocketing his mask. "No one is going to hear you over the sound of the festival, even if it is winding down."

Whirling around to the bastard who'd tried to bed me not half an hour ago when he knew I thought he was Caspian, I ripped my veil from my hair and threw it to the floor then shoved him in the middle of his chest. Not hard enough to move him, but enough to let out some frustration and get my point across.

"That's your fucking mom out there, and she's going to have me killed! What would you have me do, try nothing?"

Calix's otherwise pretty face distorted into something unsure, anxious. "She wouldn't."

Rolling my eyes, I returned to the door. "If you're not going to help me, then stay out of my way."

I took a deep breath. "Hey!" I banged at the door again. "Hey!"

After minutes of trying until my throat hurt and my hands had truly started to crack and bleed, I slid down the door and lay back on the floor, worn out. "Fuck." A tear slipped from my eye, and I knew more would come if I dwelled on it. I had to think of a new plan.

"Hey," Calix said, his voice now a soft caress of some pretense of caring that made my stomach churn. I flinched as he leaned down and wiped away the tear sliding down my cheek.

Sitting up, I backed away until the door hit my back. "Get the fuck away from me."

His expression soured. "I'm trying to help."

"Like you were trying to help yourself to my body earlier?" I snapped. "I didn't fucking ask you for help."

Calix snarled. "I didn't hear you complaining."

"When I thought you were Caspian!" A hysterical laugh bubbled up from my chest. "You seriously don't see the problem? And now I find out that we're what, half-siblings? Ew!"

"I liked you better when you were just a piece of ass ready to spread her legs," Calix spat.

I stood up so fast that Calix did the same reflexively. Yanking back a fist, I threw the last ten years of deadlifts and cardio into it as I punched him right in the jaw, and it felt fan-fucking-tastic.

Calix stumbled back, clearly never having been hit like that before. His wide eyes fixed on me and his hands cupped his face where the blow had landed. "Crazy bitch!"

"Lowlife rapist," I snarled, stalking forward. "You . . ." But the thought trailed off as I spotted a narrow window at the back of the room. I hadn't seen it when we were first thrown in, but even in the dark the sheen of the moon glossed over the smooth glass surface.

"Hey!" I screamed, changing tactics and barging for the window. "Hey, is anyone out there?"

I didn't wait for an answer, and the window was so narrow there was no way my cushy ass was fitting through it, but with no sound barrier in the way maybe . . .

Rounding on the room, cursing the lack of chairs on this island, I looked for something else solid enough to use. Ignoring Calix, who watched me as though I was a wild animal, I settled on a heavy wooden tray near the door that was probably used for food services.

"What are you doing?" he asked.

I shot him a glare, satisfied when he flinched back, and lifted the tray overhead. It was heavy in my hands as I swung it down and smashed it against the window. The glass didn't budge, but it did make a loud-ass sound when the tray hit it.

"Hey!" I yelled again. "Is anyone there?" *Whack*, I smacked the window again. I lifted my arms again, already getting tired from the strain, and gave the window one more smash as finally the glass gave way and cracked into a thousand pieces of freedom.

"Hello!" I screamed over the shattering. "Over here!"

The angle of the window wasn't quite facing the square, but more to the side. If I stuck my face out I could just see a sliver of it with the draped fabrics and curtained hideaways dotting the edges anywhere a wall or a pillar or a statue allowed them to be hung. There was almost no one out there now, and even from here I could hear the sounds of sex.

Gripping my throat from behind, Calix caught me by surprise as he squeezed with surprising strength, pulling me away from the window.

"What?" I gasped through strained breath.

"I just realized what a bastard bitch like you would do to my position in the senate," Calix crooned in my ear. "We're barely into our reign, and I will be the next basilli that House Ateio puts on the high seat. You will *not* jeopardize that."

"I don't give a fuck about that!" Struggling, my hands went to my half-brother's wrists as I tried to claw free.

"My mother was right to get rid of you," Calix said. I struggled harder, my heart and neck both straining as I fought for my life.

"Once Mother realizes it's me in here with you, I have no doubts that I'll be fine," Calix went on. "She told Eris to come back with supplies, and I can only imagine what that means for you. He will probably drag you away somewhere, do whatever it is he's been ordered to do, and a search will unfold. Some of your siren bitch sisters will be sad for a while but don't worry, I'll be there to console them before the next ball. You'll be long gone, and things can go back to how they were meant to be."

He was delusional if he thought I'd go down without a fight, but it didn't stop my mind from racing. To Caspian, whom I was rushing dangerously close to love with. To Nikkos, who had become an honest to goodness friend, a rarity in my life. To the sirens, especially Amara and Jacinta, whom I'd spent the most time with. To Ashana, my teacher. Even to Tanis, who complicated things but was still just as lost in this relationship as I was. And now that I had the pieces of the puzzle that had torn us apart . . .

Calix chuckled as I strained. It was harder for him to maintain his hold on me than he would admit to, but I was still in his hold regardless. My breathing was strained and my head was spinning from the exertion.

A crash at the door drew our attention.

"Eris?" Calix called, uncertainty creeping into his voice.

Another crash, this one louder as a crack in the doorframe splintered. A push from the other side bowed in the door enough that the latch snapped and the door fell open, revealing a panting and disheveled Caspian.

He took one look at us, at me with Calix's hands around my throat, and lunged.

"Caspian," Calix tried to say, but the calm and collected Caspian, who would have minced words, was not here. Caspian threw himself into Calix, one arm pressing into the bastard's throat as we all tumbled down. Calix's grip on me was gone now, and as I landed I felt the hand that cushioned my head from slamming against the hard floor.

Thwack. Caspian's fist crashed into Calix's face. And then he did it again, and again.

"Caspian," I cried, relief flooding me. "Caspian, we have to go. Helena and Eris are the ones who sent me away as a baby."

Caspian threw one more punch in Calix's face, rendering him out cold. Hopefully not dead, which would make this situation worse, but still unmoving. Turning those soft eyes to me, Caspian got to his feet and helped me up.

"Go, get out of here," he said. "Run back to the house. We're not far. Get inside and lock the door until I get back."

"What are you going to do?" I asked, eyeing my half-brother.

"I'm going to drag this garbage out front, get a medical professional for him, and scream to the heavens for witnesses to this mess before the Ateios cover it up."

"You think they could do that?"

"I know they could," Caspian growled. He paused, pulling me in and giving me a deep kiss. I kissed him back, every part of me relieved to fit into him like a puzzle piece as the chills set in. Cold, always so cold when I got anxious, and now I worried I was going into shock.

"Not the house. Helena is going to look for me, and they'd find me there right away. I'll go to Mada's," I said, naming one of his sweet neighbors, who often traded us eggs for fruit from a tree in Caspian's yard.

"Good idea. Can you make it?" Caspian asked, drawing back.

"Yeah," I said. "I'll see you there."

He pulled me into another heated kiss, then moved away as quickly as he'd swooped in. "If anything happens, you scream bloody murder. You hear me?"

"Yes, I promise," I answered.

"Good." He nodded sharply, then turned his attention back to Calix. And he was right, I had to get away before Eris came back.

A shiver hit my spine as I ran through the audience room, where this whole nightmare had started. I tore out of there to the front door of the Senate, stopping only when I slammed into something hard.

"What are you doing here?" Eris growled, clearly caught by surprise.

Of course I'd take the same fucking path as Eris coming back to . . . to . . . whatever "get rid of them" means!

I opened my mouth to scream at the top of my lungs for someone, anyone, to hear me. To see me. We were so very close to people, a whole courtyard of people, and yet none of them would be able to hear me. To stop Eris as he closed a hand over my mouth. He pulled a bottle of something from his pocket with one hand, removed the cloth shoved into it, and stuffed it between his hand and my mouth.

My nightmare wasn't over, I realized, as the cloying smell of chemicals sank deep into my lungs and my vision faded. Just before the blackness took over, Eris hauled me over his giant shoulder. Caspian was only two rooms away, and it still wasn't close enough to save me a second time.

CHAPTER THIRTY-SEVEN

MADELINE

My head was pounding when I woke up. That was probably why it took me longer than it should have to remember how I'd gotten here, wherever "here" was.

I was in a completely dark room filled with stagnant air. A chill had set into my bones after Eris drugged me and hid me who knew where. Moving slowly, I crawled across the sloped floor. Even though I couldn't see what I was doing, I crawled forward anyway, pressing my hands out until I found a wall.

Cool clay was smooth to the touch and goose bumps crawled across my arms in a swirl of chill and fear. I'd never been drugged before, and the haze it put me in terrified me. My body might be here, but I didn't feel present in it. I'd always been a light sleeper, but to be out for so long while someone carried me . . .

My fingers hit a wall of the same clay the other buildings in Atlantis were made from. It gave nothing away, and a frustrated whine escaped my throat.

No, focus. Caspian would come looking for me, and he'd be quick enough to make a scene if it meant finding me. I had to do half of the work and figure out how to be found.

When I heard the sloshing of water, I knew I was close to the sea. Not that anywhere on Atlantis was particularly far, but I could hear that it was close. No, maybe more than that, I could almost feel it. I could definitely smell the salt in the air.

Still on my hands and knees, I followed the floor to another part of the room, shrieking when my hands hit a puddle. Cold and wet.

I backed up now, determined to find a door. My hands went to the walls again and I followed them in both directions until I knew where the water was, where one boarded-up window was, where there was a pile of moldy crates or something, but still no door. I pounded on the boarded-up window, but it was solid and unmoving. With all of the dry ground covered, I grimaced as I moved through the cool water; something that wouldn't bother me in the least when I could see was now another unknown element that brought on anxiety. My shoes were gone, and I was painfully aware that my dress was going to cling to me, probably make me ice cold if I had to sit in the open air after this. I found another window, just as tightly shut; then finally found a door, but it was just as immovable as the windows. There was no getting through it, even though I threw my body weight into my shoulder and tried to break it down.

Time passed. Not that I could tell how much, but a sliver of golden light worked through a hair-thin crack in the boarded-up window. If it was already daylight, then I'd been knocked out for at least half the night.

It was then that the reality set in, the horror of what Eris could be ordered to do to me. How, exactly, he could rid *her* of my presence. With every slasher movie I'd ever seen running on loop in the back of my mind, I decided my best course of action would be to save my energy for a fight.

Eris was big. Huge, really. A pile of muscles that would have been the envy of everyone at the gym. Outclassing him on strength wouldn't work; I'd have to use my sway. I spent my time humming, going through every melody I'd been taught. I flexed that part of me that knew when to turn on and off the sway, thought about what words to use firmly on Eris when he arrived.

And then I remembered one song. Most of what I knew about singing to the sea was to keep it at bay, but I knew one that would call the water to me. All around me. I'd played with it in the back-yard pond at the House of Sirens with Jacinta. I had gotten it to swell up around my legs as we splashed each other on one particularly humid day not too long ago.

And if I could move the water, maybe I could do more with it.

Humming, singing, calling, coaxing, I willed the water in this dark, dreary room to come to me. I had been sitting against the driest wall, but then I felt the shock of cold wet water reach my toes. I stopped singing in surprise and the water washed away again.

But if I'd done it once, I could do it again.

A thump against the door nearly gave me a heart attack. I stilled, holding my knees to my chest, as a second thump sounded and the door creaked open.

My eyes were shut tight against the harsh light after long hours with nothing, but with only a heartbeat to adjust, I could see the outline of Eris in the doorway.

"Stop!" I called. "Don't come any closer!"

I felt the sway, felt it push through me, through my words. The intent was strong and demanding. The others had praised me on a strong sway, and I was putting my everything into it. But to my horror, Eris didn't stop.

"Stop!" I screamed again. "Don't move!"

Eris leaned down and grabbed my arms, pulling a rope free from his belt. I kicked and screamed, raking my nails down his arms where I could, and then I saw them in his ears. Plugs, with tiny runes on them. If this was some kind of protection, some kind of trinket to protect himself from the sway or from hearing, I was screwed.

"Fuck off, you bastard!" I screeched as Eris finally caught both of my hands then bound them. It made it easy for him to throw me over his shoulder again, and the wind was knocked out of me as my stomach landed on the round of his shoulder.

He shoved something in my mouth, some kind of leaves or something. It was bitter and disgusting and pungent, and I spit it out immediately, but the damage was done and I was completely nauseated. My energy suddenly went into keeping myself from throwing up, my head spinning.

They had clearly thought this plan through.

Eris walked me right out of the building, and I finally got a look at what I was dealing with. No wonder the floor was slanted and the water covered half of it—we were on the broken part of the beach where no one went, the graveyard of half-drowned houses by the edge of the bubble where the ancient Atlanteans had died during the catastrophic sinking.

My head swam as I processed it. They had shoved me in what was considered a graveyard, a quiet place of the dead and drowned. I craned my neck to see where Eris could possibly be taking me, and I balked as our path appeared to be the closest tower. The tall spire would lead to a secluded room at the top, just like the one where I had first arrived and laid eyes on the sirens. Except this tower was different. This tower, the big tower as it was called, forked at the top to allow boats to anchor. Eris could bypass anyone seeing us, sirens included, and there was nothing I could do about it.

My panic spiked as we reached the entrance and slipped inside.

"Fuck you," I grunted as clearly as I could muster. "Fuck Adrion Ateio," I added for good measure. "And fuck Helena Ateio!"

I had kicked and struggled for so long that my energy was running out. As I sank all my dead weight onto Eris, the cloud of my thoughts finally pulled together. The water, I needed the water.

I hummed, which blessedly was easier than singing after whatever horrendous plant Eris had shoved into my mouth. And even that was wearing away as I gained strength.

Pull. Come. Embrace. I called to the water. I knew it was outside the tower, outside of the stone walls that spiraled us up to the sky. The water was what, three feet away? And yet untouchable. But still I called to it. I called, willed it, and finally, *felt it.*

The water wanted me—to hold me, to carry me away. The flow of it, the tides of it, just outside the tower. But I could feel it reaching, crawling upward. Up and up as Eris carried me, I could feel the matching water swirling just on the other side of the walls.

The tower, old as it must have been, started to creak. Eris paused, eyeing me for a moment, then continued our climb.

We were so high up now. My stomach turned as I saw the fork in the path. One set of stairs would take us to the sirens, the other to the boathouse, where most of Atlantis's ships were stored.

I hummed louder now, panic and fear urging me harder. I called, desperate to reach the water. What I would do when it came for me, I wasn't sure.

And then it happened. Eris had barely begun on the path to the ships when water rushed in from above. The bubble? The top of the tower? I didn't know. Swirling and leaping, trying to reach for me, and I for it. Eris swore and charged harder, higher. I had the water in sight now, but it was too late as Eris plowed through it, the last few steps to the top where a long-covered dock floated on the churning surface of the sea.

I was hauled, none too gently, to a boat not unlike Caspian's, but with older furnishings. Eris made quick work of the ropes and things as he maneuvered the boat away from the dock and slowly but surely out to sea.

A midday sun greeted us in a raw, blinding, windy expanse of sky. It was jarring after having been in the bubble of Atlantis for so long now. And I could see it, the bubble below that had become my home. Any minute now we would be free from it, and it would likely be the last time I ever laid eyes on it again.

Raw, nauseated, hungry, and shaking, I sang. I sang as loudly and desperately as I could. Eris was occupied with the boat, and while his attention was occupied, I sang.

My heart went into it, and the water listened. It rushed onto the boat. It crawled up the sides, across the deck, and over my legs where I sat, hands still bound. I sang until it crawled up my body, until it crawled up Eris too. He was yelling now, but I screamed out the melody all the same. Even as Eris struggled to reach me, the water held him back. The sea swirled around the boat in the beginnings of a whirlpool and the boat turned, no longer heading out to sea but now being pushed and pulled by the water itself until we were directly over the bubble.

I stared Eris in the eyes. He was cursing up a storm, but even if it cost me everything, I would make a mess that raised questions. The others needed to know. Tanis needed to know. A horrid crime was about to be repeated, and the people responsible needed to be held to account no matter what. I would not be a victim again, not without taking them down with me.

I sang loudly, and the water at the top of the bubble burst. Our boat would fall into Atlantis, and there was nothing Eris or Calix or Helena Ateio could do to stop it.

CHAPTER THIRTY-EIGHT

CASPIAN

I would go to hell for Madeline. I knew it the moment I hauled Calix up from the floor where I'd bloodied his face. I knew it when I hauled the prick over my shoulders and stepped out of the Senate building. And I knew the moment the first scream from a spectator rang through the square, that I'd hit an Ateio, the son of our basilli, that I would go through whatever hell this had earned me if it made them pay.

There was no going back now. Not when his hands had been on her throat.

Two men came up to me. I vaguely recognized them as faces of other Senate workers I'd seen around, but in the heat of my anger I couldn't picture who they worked for directly. All I knew when I shoved Calix into their arms was that I would tell them and any soul who would listen what he had done.

"I call for an investigation of the Senate into Calix Ateio for putting his hands on the throat of a siren!" My voice echoed in the square, and any lingering revelry died.

People pulled themselves back together, finding clothing and masks among the discarded piles and corners of the square. The crowd formed, curious, as I was questioned.

"What are you talking about?" one of the men asked as the other dragged Calix away.

"I'm talking about that bastard who had his hand around the neck of Madeline Lowe not twenty minutes ago." My reply was cold, firm, and loud. "The Ateio family needs to be investigated for harming a siren!"

I didn't know how the connection between Adrion Ateio and Madeline would affect this. Did they know? Did Ateio know? Did Tanis? Was I even right? No, I had to be onto something. Tanis was definitely Madeline's mother; there was no mistaking their resemblance. And while nights like this, the veiled balls, provided the sirens with the chance to take any willing participants and make children as they were able and wished to, there was no way Tanis wouldn't know a prominent figure like Adrion Ateio, even in a mask. She must have at least suspected, and my stomach sank to think how this was going to affect all involved.

"What is the meaning of this?" My uncle pushed through the crowd. Where he had been I didn't want to know; he wasn't one to participate but more likely to watch. Observe. But there he was, pushing through the crowd, fury on his face as he made a line straight for me.

"I found Calix Ateio with his hands around the throat of the Siren Madeline." I projected my voice, not wanting to keep the accusation quiet.

"And where is this siren now?" Dimitris spat.

"Hiding from her abusers," I snapped, challenging him. "I'll tell you where she is once an investigation begins and not one second before."

Dimitris's cold glare settled on me. No words were exchanged between us as hands pulled us apart.

"What is the meaning of this?" The basilli himself was now storming toward us, running a hand through his hair, his mask discarded but his clothes, thank the gods, were neatly in place. I wasn't ready to unpack Madeline's heritage yet, especially not without her consent. She needed to know first, and I wouldn't take that away from her if I could help it.

"Calix was choking Madeline Lowe." I threw an accusatory finger behind me to the Senate building. "There, in your own office."

The spectators were eating this up. Gossip was already spreading like wildfire, and the red fury on Adrion's face could either be directed at me or at his son, there was no telling. Maybe both. I steeled myself not to regret any outcome.

"Where is she?" A panicked, feminine lull parted the crowd. One of the sirens I recognized as important to the hierarchy, someone likely being groomed to join Ashana and Calliope when the time came. "Where is Madeline?"

The sway. I resisted with a grunt. Likely she was using it in panic, not quite a hold of herself. "I want to tell you, and I will the moment I hear confirmation the Senate will investigate."

"Yes, fine!" Adrion spat. "My people will investigate this."

"No." Dimitris's glacial expression was now turned on the basilli. "The Senate will investigate, and none of your people will be involved. The accused is your *son*, Adrion."

Through gritted teeth, the basilli agreed. "Fine, let it be done."

"There's a broken window." A woman from one of the other senator's offices, a buxom, muscled woman who worked for the senator of industry, I believed. She approached us with a chunk of glass in her hand. "The window in your office has been broken, along with a tray and visible damage to your door."

"Explain yourself," Dimitris commanded.

"The broken window and Madeline's cry for help is how I found them," I said, meeting eyes with several people in the crowd. I needed them to hear me and willed every one of them to take the seriousness of this to heart. "When I found them in the locked room, I heard sounds of a struggle and broke in. For that, I take full responsibility. There was a fight when I removed Calix's hands from her, and you can see how it ended."

I spotted Helena in the crowd, her face contorted in a pained expression. Someone approached her, pointed in the direction where they had taken Calix, and she ran off. My eyes moved back to Ateio.

"Now, an investigation is underway. Where is the siren?" Dimitris said, drawing my attention. The siren who had asked for Madeline's location was also standing impatiently, wringing her hands.

"With my neighbor Mada. I'll take you there." A great deal of the crowd scrambled to follow as I turned on my heel and walked, leading them to Madeline as I silently apologized for the storm that was about to overwhelm her. I would do everything I could to make this right for her, and hopefully my presence would be able to comfort her while it happened.

But Madeline had never made it to Mada's house or to mine.

With the basilli, my uncle, and a horde of curious and angry spectators at my back, I was suddenly faced with my side of the story, a beaten Calix, and a missing siren.

The search for Madeline was no small thing. Eyes were all over Atlantis for the rest of the night. Searches were underway through the twilight hours and into the sunrise. Calix woke up, stammered through his turn of events quickly, not really giving anyone a believable story in his defense. But of course, within minutes, Helena Ateio had her son in her custody and locked back in their home.

"Nothing on the south beach." Another negative report had come into the main hall of the Senate where Dimitris had taken up the podium along with several other senators with an interest in the investigation. By now, with my part done and the search started, I was forced to sit at the back of the hall answering redundant question after redundant question while a guard stood watch over me, as though I was the accused and not Calix.

Several sirens, including Calliope and Ashana, took up a row of benches as they restlessly awaited news. Tanis was there too.

"Send a fresh party for a second sweep, and move to the rocky beach." Dimitris looked up from an unfurled map for only a moment to give the order and then went straight back to it.

"Where exactly were you when you heard the window shatter?" The aged eyes of yet another investigator settled on me.

"Beside the third column out front." I sighed.

"And what were you doing there instead of participating in the festivities?" he asked, as though the only desire I should have had last night was to participate in the random, senseless fucking.

I threw a frustrated hand through my hair. "I was looking for Madeline! We were supposed to meet up."

He gave me a patronizing look. "The vellieovasa is held in anonymity. The intent is not to know who it is you meet that night."

I closed my eyes in frustration. It was no secret that more than a few people planned out their masks and veils for the express purpose of finding the right partners. "I understand that, but—"

A thunderous *boom* shook the Senate. Everything stilled for a moment as all eyes in the room looked for the source of it. And then the sound of rushing water, the sound of rain of all things, hit the roof. Rain, something Atlantis hadn't felt in centuries, as the shield of air around our island kept us from the elements. Our current infrastructure was not meant to handle it. Everything we had built included wells and ducts to carry any water we needed throughout the city, to water the land and fill the pools. Could our ancient rooftops even handle rain now?

A scramble to the doors, windows, anywhere we could see outside ensued. Even my guards, unsure what limits I really had beyond sitting in the Senate building, didn't drag me back as I ran for one of the front offices with a window.

Water poured in from the top of the bubble, spraying no more than the width of the main square outside and none of the rest of the island. I strained to see what had made the hole in the barrier, pushing away from the window a moment later as I changed course to the sirens.

Others were already helping to usher them outside, and I could hear the singing already. The building, and every other building near the square, which was both the center and the highest point of Atlantis, emptied to see. The sirens who were present were already joining voices, singing up the water as they tried to slow the spray of saltwater overhead.

"What is happening?" Dimitris's cold voice could be heard nearby on the front steps of the Senate. No one had an answer for him, until a long, dark shape above formed a shadow and fell.

High, impossibly high in the sky, was a ship. A class one or a class two, not much different from my own sailing yacht, was falling from the top of the barrier.

Whatever was happening, the sirens took charge. Singing, strongly singing, even more sirens rushed into the square from all sides to join their sisters. The water was slowing, barely, and was forming a cushion under the boat as it fell.

Down, down, the boat was carried, embraced by the sea as the sirens strengthened their numbers, strained their voices, and cushioned the boat onto the middle of the square even as they patched the barrier.

The moment the ship hit the square, I was one of the people rushing to it. My heart was pounding, and I dreaded what we would find. What did this mean? What could have made a hole in the barrier, and how much longer before it could happen again?

My feet hit the deck of the boat, tilted as it was against the central fountain, and my eyes landed on the source of all of the night's events.

Madeline.

CHAPTER THIRTY-NINE

MADELINE

Coughing up water, I lay on my side as best as I could. The slant of the deck had me wanting to slide down and roll onto the square, but I kept myself mostly in place despite my bound hands.

Eris had fared no better. He was more banged up than I was after our wild descent into Atlantis, and I could feel the other sways that had brought us down somewhat safely. It was a miracle that we had survived it at all.

"Madeline!"

Someone called to me, but it was fuzzy. Far away, like I was listening to them underwater even though I was in the open air again. My vision took a heartbeat to focus before it landed on Caspian. He wore his distress openly, taking a knee next to me while I willed the dizzying swirl of my head to steady.

"Hello, sailor."

The strained sound he let out was somewhere between a laugh and a cry of frustration, his hands wrapping around my shoulders and his forehead pressing gently against mine. "Hello, siren. You scared the shit out of me."

I sank my weight into him, and he scooped me up off the deck and climbed down to the stone square. Plenty of hands reached out to help him, some familiar and some not. A few more faces came into focus. Ashana, Jacinta, Amara. Tanis.

"He took me," I managed to say.

"Shh, it's okay." Caspian soothed me, even as his arms tensed at my accusation. "I'm here, it's going to be okay now."

Shouting in rapid Atlantean burst from the side of the crowd, and I missed almost all of what was said. The crowd parted against the commanding presence of Helena Ateio. I balked at the sight of her, and Caspian had to steady me. This woman wanted me dead. I knew it, and she had ordered Eris to do who knew what to get rid of me.

Caspian helped me stand, keeping an arm around me so I could stay upright. Ashana, bless the old siren and her cane, stood between us and Helena. Thankfully, Caspian murmured the rough translation to me as they argued.

"She is partly responsible for my son's injuries!" Helena snapped. "I demand she be shackled until a trial!"

"Absolutely not," Ashana replied. "She is a siren, will recover in the House of Sirens, and your kin will stay far away from her until we can sort this out."

"She must know what provoked my son!" Helena demanded. "He would not act that way if she hadn't coerced him somehow!"

More bickering erupted, but Caspian stopped translating. "This is nonsense and filth, you don't need to hear it. We need to talk though, now."

His face was hard, stone-like, as his eyes darted around the crowd, even as his hold on me was soft. I spotted a glimpse of Eris being bound at the wrists and taken up the stairs of the Senate building, and then an imposing man striding straight toward us.

He spoke to Caspian, and the two erupted in a flurry of heated words in rushed Atlantean. I barely caught any of them, getting me nowhere.

"Caspian," I demanded, putting my hand over the one he had around my ribs. "English."

"Madeline, this is my uncle, Senator Dimitris. Uncle, this is Madeline. Maddie, he is going to let us use his office to talk, but with the investigation underway, he's demanding witnesses and a clerk."

"Investigation?" I asked.

Caspian frowned. "Shit, that's right. You disappeared. We need your side of the story, but I've already started the process with Calix and what he did to you. Can you tell us what happened?"

I hardened my posture. "Yes, take me wherever. I'm happy to tell you everything."

"No!" Helena spat, lunging between Ashana and Caspian to throw a hand at me. Dimitris caught her wrist, glared at her, and hissed something in Atlantean that sounded a lot like a command to be silent.

I couldn't let it go on; they needed to know why she was attacking me. Heat rushed through my veins as I knew I was about to pull the spotlight and drop a bomb on this island, but they all had to know what was happening and why. Even if Helena succeeded in hurting me now somehow, the truth would be out there.

"Helena Ateio had me locked in the office and told Eris to get rid of me!" I yelled, hoping to be heard over the crowd. I was shaking in Caspian's hold, but he stood by me, supporting me and wrapping an arm around me in a tight hug.

Adrion Ateio, basilli of Atlantis, was now marching over and yelling something. The only word I caught was his wife's name. She snarled, not willing to take her attention off of me.

"You bitch!" Helena yelled, the only English I'd heard her use for my benefit. "Eris!"

At his lover's screech, Eris bull-rushed toward us. Toward me. My heart pounded as I saw him, just yards away and getting closer by the second. It was now or never to tell the story before he reached me. Bracing to dodge him or receive the impact, I screamed, "Adrion Ateio might be my father!"

And that was the source of it, right? The entire problem. The reason Helena would have Eris get rid of an infant in the first place.

But if my revelation shocked the crowd, it was only bolstered when Tanis shoved in front of Caspian and me at the last moment and sang.

This wasn't the hum of the broken woman I had met before. The siren who had lost her words, her voice, now stood between me and Eris with her arms outstretched in a shrieking lament of command. Both woven song and intent, with sway potent enough to choke the crowd. She may not have had her words, but she had her own power, and we all knew what she wanted.

Stop.

Eris stilled, his face contorted in pain even as his legs seemed to fumble. Tanis may have stopped him, but he was still close enough for the mountain of muscle with his hands tied together to fall into her, knocking us all back.

"Tanis!" My call for her was one of many as the other sirens rushed to our side. Arms pulled the tangle of bodies apart, some removing Eris, some removing Helena, and others helping Tanis, Caspian, and me to our feet.

The crowd, outraged, was silenced by Basilli Ateio. "Silence!"

He let the command ring out for a beat, then looked at me for the first time. Truly, actually looked at me. His eyes flicked to Tanis, then back to me. His scrutiny was uncomfortable, but it had to be done, even as I was shaking in Caspian's hold.

"We don't have to do this here," Caspian said.

"Quiet, boy," Dimitris snapped.

Adrion walked toward me, slowly and deliberately, as if he didn't want to scare a baby deer. It was Tanis who put an arm between us, barring Adrion's approach. His eyes slid to her, and he murmured something that even my understanding of Atlantean picked up.

"You knew."

Two simple words, which shook all who heard them. It was the sirens who recovered first. Ashana spoke quickly, and thank goodness Amara slid up to me, translating.

"The child of a siren is a siren, you have no power to hold her here."

Adrion's face hardened. "We've never had a known blood child born of the five houses who didn't claim their place in Atlantis."

"Her place is with us," Ashana said in return.

This was a lot. A lot, a lot. More than a guy grabbing my ass at the gym and being sacked by my slimy boss. More than sleeping in my car. This was too much.

"Stop," I said, my throat catching at first, so I had to repeat myself louder. "Stop."

Eyes turned my way. "Not here. Not now. We can . . . we can sort this out later. In case you forgot, I just rode a boat down a waterfall from the top of the bubble, and I'm pretty sure that trauma is going to hit me any second now."

It was true, my arms were already shaking, and goose bumps raced across my skin as I felt the freezing cold that was extreme stress coming on.

"I'm taking her home," Caspian announced. "Uncle, Ashana, you are welcome to come and ask your questions there."

He spoke for me to hear, so Amara had to translate for Ashana. I noticed how Caspian left out Adrion as he turned, scooped me up, and carried me in his arms down the path. I leaned my head on his shoulder, thankful for it. I really wasn't sure how much longer my feet would actually work, and that aforementioned shock was definitely starting to set in.

Caspian made the right move, it turned out, as I badly needed food, water, and all the blankets in his house. The walk there had been awkward, but once I was cocooned, fed, and watered, the questions began.

It was a blur. Ashana with Caspian's help was able to ask her questions first. How was I, how did I move the boat, how did I poke a hole in the bubble? Then Dimitris asked his questions. More calculated ones. What time did I think it was when I was abducted? Exactly what words were said in the Senate by both Helena and Eris?

More people came and went but Caspian never allowed more than two in at a time. More senators and clerks, more sirens. At one point, Nikkos showed up and cooked a feast of a dinner. Apparently, he had been among the search party at the far edges of the island, and had missed the whole ordeal. It still warmed my heart that he was searching for me.

It wasn't until late into the night that everyone seemed done with me. That or Caspian chased them all off so I could sleep. I still hadn't heard what had become of Eris, Helena, or Calix, despite my questions. Maybe nothing had happened yet. Maybe nothing would, though I wanted to think the fury of the sirens would come down on them in some way at the very least.

I didn't sleep alone that night. I couldn't. It took very little coaxing for Caspian to climb into bed with me, curling his body around me as I fell into an exhausted sleep at last.

Somehow alive, and home.

CHAPTER FORTY

CASPIAN

Madeline stirred in my arms, and I loosened my grip around her to allow whatever movement she needed. Sweat dotted her forehead, even as her eyes shut tighter before cracking open with a gasp.

"Shh, it's me," I murmured into her hair, kissing the top of her head. "You're safe."

Waking with a start, she sighed, her warm breath fanning against my chest. "What an ordeal that was."

I held her for a while, letting her heart rate settle until she wanted to talk about it. All she had done for a while now was talk. Answer questions, go silent, eat when fed, nap when told—though that was interrupted by nightmares each time. My little siren was exhausted.

"I keep feeling like I'm in that room," she whispered finally. "With no light, and a slanted floor, and water. I didn't know if I was going to die in there."

Holding her a little tighter, I pulled her closer. "It didn't happen. It won't happen again, I promise."

"I can't stop thinking about them. What happens if Eris and Helena don't get locked up? It happens, in other countries. Important people don't get punished."

Shifting on the mattress, I pulled our faces even with each other. I brushed a thumb over her cheek, and her tired eyes flicked between mine for understanding.

"They do here. I can't erase what was." Though gods knew I wish I could. "All I can do is ensure what will be. I want to be with you, Maddie. I want to hold you every night and listen to you sing. I want you to thrive, and go have your workouts, and feel safe. To feel at home. What can I do to make that happen for you?"

She smiled, a soft blush crossing the bridge of her nose. "Caspian, I don't know if I love you, but I'm well on my way. Please, just stay with me. I've lived in a lot of places, and I don't know that a building will ever feel like home to me, but you do. You feel like home."

I could have melted at that. Hell, maybe I did melt a little. Pulling her even tighter, I managed a whisper: "I'll say it first, then. Madeline. I do love you. When I thought I'd lost you, I was a mess. When I saw Calix's hands on you, I thought I might kill him. I wanted to."

"You didn't," she said.

Shaking my head. "I can't forgive any of them. The Ateios."

"I guess I'm one of them now." She flinched. "Aren't I?"

"Not if you don't want to be. Not by the rights of a siren. You don't have to claim any heritage you don't want to, and no one in Atlantis would make you."

"But the basilli."

"The basilli will be held to the same laws as the rest of us." That I could promise.

She relaxed at that. With a yawn, she curled up a little tighter in the blankets.

"You're tired, go back to sleep."

"Mmm. Will you be here when I wake up?"

"I'll try. I have an errand to run, but Nikkos is staying here for the time being. I would never leave you alone."

She nodded, satisfied, and it was only a few heartbeats before her breath evened back out in a deep sleep.

On light feet, I stepped out of Madeline's room and closed the door. Turning into the main living space, I found Nikkos sprawled in front of his laptop on the cushions, looking exhausted.

"Nikkos," I murmured, sitting beside him.

He stirred, having dozed off. "I'm up."

"Shh, don't wake her up, she finally got back to sleep."

"How is she?" he asked.

I grimaced. For the past day and a half, Madeline's sleep had been interrupted by nightmares. Not that anyone was surprised. I'd let a few visitors in since that first, terrifying day. Mostly a siren or two, and the sweet old man from the market where Madeline always bought a smoothie for breakfast on her morning run. Adrion had asked once, and I told him in no uncertain terms that he could wait for the Senate meeting that was going to be held tomorrow. Dimitris backed me up.

"She's doing as well as we can expect," I answered my cousin.

He looked over at his laptop and closed it. "Our contact will be here early next week with the item."

I nodded sharply. "Good. I think it's safe to say after this event with the barrier that we want the sirens to get all the help they can to reinforce the city's safety. Dimitris will be involved in that," I said dryly, then paused. "Dimitris . . ."

Nikkos frowned, sitting up straighter. "What are you thinking, cousin?"

Standing, I walked to the kitchen where I had been putting in bits of work and compiling Senate notes in the few minutes I could spare over the last two days. Shuffling papers, I found a small note I had made near the bottom of the pile and pulled it out.

"I was going to drop a few things off at my office, but I think I need to pay a visit to my uncle." I pocketed the note and then grabbed the file I was going to walk over anyway. "Nikkos, what was the founding declaration on the fountain in the Senate's square?"

His face scrunched, recalling the translation from an ancient version of Atlantean. "'The houses to raise the Senate, the Senate to raise Atlantis. The sirens to raise Atlantis, Atlantis to raise the world.'"

"Get me what you can on the intent behind that." I rushed to the door with my file, pulling on my shoes.

"Where are you going?" Nikkos asked.

"To the offices, just do it!" I left a sputtering Nikkos settling in by his laptop, already going to work on my request.

I took to the street with a long stride, papers tight under one arm as I made my way to my uncle's office. Shrewd as he was, demanding as he was, terrifying as he could be in the singular pursuit of his responsibilities to the city, he was a fair and just man when it came to Atlantis and the law.

I moved through the common space and arrived at his door. I knocked, hoping he was in.

"Open."

Bursting inside, I closed the door behind me and took a seat in front of Dimitris's desk. His unamused expression deepened as he templed his hands in front of him. "What is this?"

"Here are the notes from the last meeting." I slid the file across his desk, save for the scrawled note I had pulled out of my pile at home. "And here are your exact words from the day you gave Nikkos and me the go-ahead to try our plan."

I slid the paper across the polished wood, and Dimitris looked down at it for a long moment, unmoving. When he finally moved, he adjusted the note until the writing was correctly positioned for him to read it, and the ghost of a smile crossed his lips.

"Imagine what Atlantis could be if it had been left to thrive without fear and grow without a finite border. We're a shell of what we once were, and I will set us free of it."

"Those were your words, Uncle," I said. "What exactly did you mean by that last part?"

He slid the note back to me and crossed his arms over his chest. "I meant it as I said it. Atlantis was once a world power, a place of learning, technology, arts. I take my vow to ensure the safety and defense of it very seriously, but with that comes the desire to see it thrive. I would see the sirens unrequired of services and the care of Atlantis in the hands of the people."

"And what exactly does a free Atlantis look like to you? What do you mean about the sirens and the people?" My heart was hammering in my chest now, my mouth dry with anticipation of what I hoped was the correct interpretation of my uncle's wishes. His words had always been careful, deliberately chosen. And while I had always felt he had a vision in mind for the end of his legacy as a senator, I had never quite grasped what that might look like. Not until today.

He stood, moving to his window, where he looked out for a moment before drawing a curtain closed. He turned to me, fully facing me now as he leaned against the window frame. "Caspian, my nephew, I would relieve the sirens' burden and see Atlantis regain the ability to see the world, and the world to see it. Not right away, of course. With what we know, a certain amount of discretion would be needed. The sirens would be a marvel to modern science. Too many questions would be raised about our survival and sudden appearance. But our population is stagnant. Our people have been confined for far too long save for the ability of a fierce few who are willing and able to brave the seas to bring back supplies, technology, information."

"What you're saying is you want our people to have the ability to see the world?" I asked. "What of the rules set by the Senate?"

"Archaic." Dimitris waved a hand. "They need complete restructuring. Everything has been structured to a common vote, why do we still have an inherited leadership limited to the ancient houses and the basilli?"

A hundred years ago he would have been beheaded for his words. But now? Could it be possible? I knew why he hadn't spoken of it so plainly before; even now there was great risk in voicing these thoughts, especially in this building. Still . . .

Madeline had only been hurt because of what she was to Adrion Ateio, was only in the spotlight because of her siren gifts, and will be held down by responsibility for the rest of her life if she chose to stay here and join the rotation of ever-singing sirens that kept Atlantis from drowning. I could see that now. I had taken her from a terrible fate on the mainland, yes, but I had brought her to a different set of shackles. If I could free her, truly free her from any of it, how far could she fly? If anyone deserved a life of freedom and joy and kindness, it was my siren.

"Uncle, if that is what you want, I am at your command. I only ask for one thing in return, and you are the only one I believe who could do it."

Dimitris nodded, strolling back to his desk and sitting down. "What do you want, Caspian?"

Taking a deep breath, stress freeing from my body with every movement, I smiled. "Let the ones who wronged Madeline Lowe see justice, true justice. I know the five houses—I know what things

335

they've managed to sweep under the rug before, and I won't let this be one of them. Helena, of course, for her part. Eris, for what he did at her command. Calix, for what he was willing to do to keep his status, and whatever you want to be done to see the retirement of a system that allows a family like House Ateio to seek, keep, and strangle anyone around them for their power, I will help you see it through."

"It will be done, I assure you." Dimitris nodded. "The Senate meets tomorrow for trial, and the arrival of the item is scheduled for three days after. Wait for instructions, and I will show this city that we are capable of freeing ourselves from our own confines. Both physical, like the barrier, and political."

And he would do it too. If anyone could, it was Dimitris. It wouldn't be easy—it might even be bloody—and it certainly wouldn't be quick, but it would be done. And I would see to any task he handed me.

CHAPTER FORTY-ONE

MADELINE

I was numb, staring through the bars of Helena Ateio's gilded cage. She looked like shit, thankfully. What served as a prison here was just as beautiful as the rest of the city. She had been provided with furniture and a private bathroom, but it was still a cell with guards. Actually, it was nicer than a lot of apartments I'd lived in.

Helena sat on a plush cushion, her back against the far wall as she stared at me. An untouched plate of food sat on the table next to her. She even had a glass of wine. Her clothes were vastly downgraded from what a wife of the basilli would usually wear to the plain linens she wore now. But the sneer on her face was the same as it had been every time we'd met.

I stood outside of the bars that confined her. My dress was neat, clean, and trimmed in cute yellow birds made of beads and thread. Caspian stood a few feet away, giving me the space I wanted, and his uncle stood next to him. Dimitris was hard to read, but surprisingly, it was his authority that allowed me to stand here for whatever closure I wanted before the trial. Which, I was assured, was a formality at this point, considering the mountain of evidence against them.

But still, Helena Ateio had the audacity to glare at me.

"Why?" I asked. The sound of my voice was the only one in the chamber, and it bounced off the walls.

"Why?" Helena asked softly. "Why?"

She slammed her open palm on the side table, rattling the plate. Her long fingernails reminded me of claws. She pushed herself up, taking slow steps toward the bars.

"Why?" she asked again. "Do you know what it means to be in one of the five houses, bastard? It means the only breath of fresh air in this damned bubble! The chance to see the surface, the best luxury Atlantis has to offer, and power. The power to do whatever I want, whenever I want to. Being an Ateio means that not having the affection of my husband doesn't matter, because *my son* will be the next basilli. Adrion's reign has just begun, but his age works against him, and my Calix would be at the top before this circle for House Ateio is at its end!"

My face soured. "Calix can have it. I want nothing to do with any of you people or your stupid job."

"You don't know anything!" Helena screeched, reaching the bars and grabbing them with both hands. I jumped back, startled, and the guards moved closer, more alert now.

"I barely had Adrion's attention long enough to conceive Calix! My own husband would have cast me away for that whore if he ever knew you were his!" Helena screamed.

"Madeline is a siren," Caspian shouted. "She does not have to be caught up with House Ateio!"

"You know nothing of men in power," Helena hissed. "Their

promises mean nothing. The only love I can rely on is my own blood."

"How did you do it?" I asked, my voice cracking. "And why not just kill me?"

Helena glared at me, her fingers uncurling from the bars as she let her arms fall to her sides. "Who says I did it? I have nothing left to say to the likes of you."

She glided to her seat against the far wall, falling down until she was slumped against it, her former poise gone as she stared blankly at the nothing space between us.

Clenching my fists, I whirled to face Eris in the cell opposite Helena's.

He was dressed as plainly as she had been, but his expression wasn't angry like Helena's. His was one of love, and pain, as he looked past me and only at her.

"Why?" I asked him softly.

Caspian came up behind me, putting his hands on my arms and letting me lean into him. He translated to Eris for me.

Eris spoke back, and Caspian stilled.

"What is it?" I asked.

"He says it was all for his love," Caspian answered.

"How?" I asked.

Caspian spoke for me, and Eris's eyes never moved from Helena as he answered.

"Helena's sleeping draught," Caspian answered. "All Helena had to do was rub it on the baby's mouth as it came out. All Eris had to do was take a boat out to sea far enough from where we would send out the dead and intercept it."

I stared at him, this giant man who had committed such an offense against a baby. For what, love? A lot of good it was doing him now.

"Why not just kill me for real?" I asked, and Caspian spoke.

Eris paused before replying, his response being translated a moment later. "To kill a siren is to anger the gods."

What a bullshit answer. "How happy do you think your gods are with you now?"

Caspian translated.

Eris didn't answer.

And I walked out of the prison.

Thank goodness Atlantis wasn't like Florida. I'd had enough of the justice system in the States to last a lifetime. Tickets, evictions, other small nonsense like that. Don't get me started on state custody. After two days of questioning by every official under the sun, the collected testimonies were enough, and the trial could begin.

"It's okay, you can do this," Caspian murmured as he placed his hand on the flat of my back, leading me down the wide stairs and into the bowl of the Senate floor.

The room was crowded, the benches crammed full of senators and the people who worked for them. What space remained was filled with sirens and members of the old houses of Atlantis. My palms were sweaty. I'd been fidgeting all morning, and now it was my turn.

Near the open floor was a more comfortable seating arrangement where I spotted both Calliope and Ashana with a translator. On the floor itself was a slightly raised platform with cushions that I would have called a couch if it had a back to it. Caspian took me there, and I sat facing a table, on the other side of which were the three senators who were leading the trial. Dimitris was one of them.

Caspian stayed near me, ready to relay my words in Atlantean for the senators who did not know English, and English for me from the senators I couldn't understand.

"Madeline." The speaker was Senator Chrissa of industry, Caspian explained. "This Senate has heard from every party involved, save for your account. As a formality, would you please, in your words, tell us what happened the night of the vellieovasa?"

"I was with a man I believed to be Caspian. I even referred to him by name. It was Calix, knowingly deceiving me. We went into the Senate building at his suggestion." I grew quiet, the only sound now was Caspian catching up in Atlantean. His face was hard, but he kept his tone impartial. The expressions of two of the senators, Chrissa and Petrov, had darkened by the time Caspian finished. Dimitris remained stone-faced, but I had expected that.

It went on, a painfully slow process but one I was able to manage. Telling the Senate everything meant that the whole room heard my shame. What I had almost done with Calix still turned my stomach. I had always wondered if I had a sibling out there somewhere, but I never could have guessed they would be so terrible.

Once my story was done and I had answered more questions that were entirely redundant, I was finally allowed off the floor.

"Thank you, Madeline. The Senate has now heard from all parties and will resume after a brief break."

Once Caspian was done translating, he came and offered me an arm. The three senators stood from the table as I stood from my seat. Caspian took me up the stairs and off the main floor, and the senators went through the back door where the basilli's office was.

Caspian and I reached the top of the stairs, and when all the eyes that had followed us up were turned away, he stopped in the hallway just outside.

"You were amazing," he murmured, leaning in to meet my lips

for a deep kiss. I sank into him, my hands grabbing the front of his shirt. We parted and I sighed.

"I'm so ready for it to be over," I said.

He nodded. "I understand that, but something big is likely to happen after the break. Would you like me to see if I can find someplace out of sight to watch? No one would know we're here."

Mulling it over, I bit the inside of my cheek. "What's about to happen?"

"A decision will be made on the Ateios," he said, eyes wandering through the doorway to the main room. "But I believe my uncle is going to drop the news about what Nikkos and I were doing on the mainland in the first place as well."

My lips parted in surprise. "I almost forgot about that. The contact of yours? That was before I knew anything. What's going on?"

"Do you want to stay and hear about it, or do you want me to take you home and tell you later? Either way, I should be here for this."

Helena and Eris had wronged me in the worst possible way. "I want to watch as they're sentenced. I want to be able to look Helena in the eye."

Caspian rubbed my back, then took my hand as he brought us through the halls, into another room, and then out the back door so we were in an alcove. "This area is for my uncle's staff, but you'll get the full view, and it will be easy for Helena to see you when it's time."

"Good." Caspian leaned against the wall and I leaned on him. He kept an arm around me, his thumb circling my hip bone as we waited for the break to be over. It didn't take as long as I expected it to, and soon enough the senators were back at their table and the crowd hushed to hear what they would say. I noticed at one edge of the room, Adrion Ateio stood behind a railed portion of the topmost ring around the room, knuckles white and hard face focused on the floor.

I saw Helena when they brought her out. Wrists tied, she still kept her chin high. I could see the hate in her when she looked up at the balconies and locked eyes with me.

I didn't know if an Atlantean would even understand the gesture, but I flipped her off anyway.

The senators came back with a long speech. Since the details didn't matter to me anymore, not until I heard what would happen to the ones who had wronged me, I let the words gloss over me as background noise while I watched Dimitris's face. It was unreadable to me, who had, in all fairness, only seen him a handful of times. But his posture was perfectly straight, and somehow at ease all at once. He was comfortable with himself and overwhelmingly confident. I had felt it from him the few times we'd spoken, and I felt how starkly we differed in that aspect.

A smile tugged at my mouth as I thought about it. Oh, how far my confidence had risen. Maybe one day I'd catch up to the imposing and assured Dimitris. Minus the sour face.

"And so, from the precedented list of admissible punishments—"

"This is it," Caspian whispered.

"This Senate will hold Calix Ateio to six years of monitored laboring to maintain the tower song spaces and bring supplies to every tower daily with additional monetary repentance to the House of Sirens, and an equal amount to Madeline Lowe."

Caspian gasped, pausing to clear his throat as he told me the sum. It was a lot. A lot more than I ever thought I'd see in my lifetime.

Calix made an appalled sound that was quieted so quickly

from wherever in the room he was sitting that someone must have slapped a hand over his mouth or something. Good, let him be furious.

"The Senate will hold Eris Galatas and Helena Ateio to a choice between two punishments, their decisions to be given in twenty-four hours' time, or it will be chosen by the senate as a collective vote."

"Is that normal?" I whispered. "That they get to choose?"

Caspian's mouth was a tight line. "No, but let's see what they say."

"The charges are: conspiring to harm and remove an infant, successfully harming and removing an infant, conspiring to assault an Atlantean, assaulting an Atlantean, removing an Atlantean with the intent to harm, conspiring to assault a siren, assaulting a siren, removing a siren with the intent to harm, and disruption of the legal process of this state."

"That was a lot of words. What is the removing thing? Like kidnapping?" I asked.

Caspian nodded. "Legal terms, you know."

I shrugged. I didn't know, not really, but it was a long list of wrongs to atone for, and I was nearly bouncing on my heels, my fingers fidgeting with the folds of my dress as I awaited their fate.

"Our ancient laws were very precise in the choices left to you both," Senator Chrissa said solemnly. "The named parties may choose a right of trial by sea, or banishment without possession."

That caused a stir. The sounds of surprise and approval flooded the room, and the senators had a hard time quieting things.

"What is a trial by sea?" I asked.

Caspian grimaced. "It's an archaic tradition."

"Caspian."

He grunted. "To be stranded on an open rock in the sea for

twenty days and nights with nothing but the will of the sirens to keep you alive. It's within sight of the east tower, barely, and if you're alive at the end of it you'll be brought back to Atlantis for a communal punishment as the remainder of your sentence. Something like what Calix will be doing."

I winced. Twenty days at sea with nothing? No food, no shelter. I supposed if the sirens took pity they could shield you, send food to you. But after what they'd done . . .

"Has anyone ever come back?" I asked.

Caspian's grim expression said it all. Ah, so it was a chosen death. Probably some honor bullshit ending that didn't leave an execution in the hands of an Atlantean. We had essentially watched the fall of House Ateio in a matter of minutes. Adrion would be here, but his son's reputation was in tatters and his wife and a person in service to the house were now going to be gone for good. I didn't know how to feel about it. Adrion Ateio was my father, I guess, but he didn't mean anything to me. Not really.

"Hey, how long is the Ateio turn at being basilli?" I asked.

"About thirty more years, given the fifty-year cycle. I'd have to double check the exact dates."

He would either work well into his golden years, beyond what a taxing job like basilli probably entailed, or he would have to salvage Calix's reputation somehow to have him take up the mantle. It wouldn't be easy, but in that heartbeat, I knew beyond the shadow of a doubt that I wanted nothing to do with the Ateio name, or their miserable, archaic jobs.

Chrissa cleared her throat one last time, finally settling the crowd. "Helena Ateio and Eris Galatas, you will give us your answers through a Senate courier at any time in the next twenty-four hours. You are now excused from this room and will be taken to House Ateio under guarded watch."

Helena stood, a snarl on her face as she shoved her way to the floor in front of where Adrion Ateio stood way up at the top of the rings of seating. I stood up, and as if she knew that, Helena's head whipped around to look me in the eye. She stared at me and gave an answer in Atlantean.

Two large Senate aids quickly scooped her up, grabbing her by her bound wrists as Helena spat what must have been absolute venom up at the basilli, who remained stone faced and somber. Helena was quickly removed, screaming the entire way out.

"What did she say?" I asked Caspian. I was still standing, one hand on the railing with a white-knuckled grip.

He paused long enough, watching the scene she was causing, that I thought he wouldn't answer. "Nothing you should have to hear, but it involves his 'bastard child.' I don't want to go into the rest of it, please don't ask me to."

I shook my head; I wouldn't. I had enough of an imagination to picture what she could say about me by now. Clearly, even after everything she had done to me, she still didn't see that she was the one in the wrong. Whatever fate she chose for herself, I couldn't— wouldn't—feel sorry for her.

"She chose banishment," Caspian said. "She will be taken somewhere with nothing more than the clothes on her back."

"How do they pick where?" I asked.

"They don't," he answered. "The wronged party will choose."

The wronged party. "Me?"

"And Tanis," Caspian clarified.

Banishment. Where does it suck to live when you have nothing at all to your name? Even worse, the only language she seemed to speak wasn't spoken anywhere else in the world.

A slow grin spread across my face. "Maybe I'm being too merciful, but do you think my mother would let me have this one?"

"You'd have to ask her," Caspian said. "Why? Do you have a place in mind?"

"Yeah," I answered. "Florida."

Eris moved next, standing in front of the Senate and asking for trial by sea. I guess I sort of expected it from him, though part of me thought he would want to go wherever Helena was. Maybe the shame had caught up with him, maybe he had finally realized she was never going to love him the way he loved her. He and Calix were removed from the Senate floor much more peacefully than Helena, and as people began to stand and Chrissa called an end to the session, Dimitris finally stood up. Caspian squeezed my shoulder; this was the moment he wanted to watch.

Dimitris must have had quite the reputation, because his mere presence stilled the room. People sat back down, and his fellow senators eyed him curiously.

"Before we move to end the session and while we have witnesses present, I would like to alert the Senate to a move I will be making in preparation to improve the safety of Atlantis."

Chrissa balked. "What is this, Dimitris? What are you planning?"

"In a few days I'm having an item delivered that will help my means. I have every permit and notice that I've submitted to the Senate and had approved for the last four years. I would be happy to show you all of them." Dimitris's reply was calm, matter-of-fact.

"And what is it you plan on doing that you feel the need to announce it here?"

Dimitris waved over Nikkos, who I was surprised to see was carrying a rather old-looking piece of ceramic. It was broken from whatever original shape it had once been—an oval, maybe—and was painted with blues and oranges swirling into tiny patterns I couldn't make out from my position in the room.

"'The houses to raise the Senate, the Senate to raise Atlantis. The sirens to raise Atlantis, Atlantis to raise the world.' The founding decree at the shaping of this Senate and the formation of the rotating basilli." Dimitris's voice echoed as he spoke; not a soul in the room was making a sound. I wasn't sure anyone was moving, hell, maybe they weren't *breathing*. I knew I wasn't.

Dimitris swept out a hand in front of him, gesturing to the piece Nikkos carried. "Georgius Bausus, an ancestor to one of the five houses"—Dimitris paused to nod to an older woman sitting on one of the front benches near the floor—"said this to our people as a promise. Old Atlantean may be hard to decipher, but with enough digging, you can find the earliest writings on his famous speech."

"Where are you going with this?" Chrissa asked.

Dimitris waved at Nikkos, who walked the ceramic over to a table and set it down while Dimitris himself pulled a paper free from his pocket. "The houses *to be formed* to raise a Senate. And so, a Senate was formed. The second part as intended should be read in the modern tongue as the Senate to raise Atlantis *from the sea*."

Even Chrissa and the other senator were sitting now as Dimitris read from his notes. I wasn't following as well as someone born here, but I was starting to see a meaning forming.

"'The sirens to raise Atlantis,' that one is obviously the same intent as the previous line. But where the sirens are still doing their intended task to an extent, the Senate has long since stopped trying from our end."

"We have tried, Dimitris," Charissa said. "We've tried for centuries. Millennia."

"And it was a disservice to the island we serve that we stopped,"

Dimitris said dryly. "And then there's the last line, Atlantis to raise the world. Here is the other use of the word *raise* in the old tongue. To uplift, to enlighten. Atlantis was always intended to resume its place among the rest of the world."

That finally pulled hushed words from the audience.

"To show Atlantis to the whole world?" I choked, barely maintaining an urgent whisper.

"Get to the point, Dimitris." The voice of Adrion Ateio rang out, stamping out the rolling whispers as eyes finally turned to the basilli.

"The point, Adrion, was that we have lost the pursuit of our goal. A goal to remove these limitations to our land, our people, and our growth. There is a way to unshackle us from the confines of the barrier, and, as we speak, the item that we can use to do it is traveling this way. Why on earth do you think I took this *job*?"

"I've wondered that more than once, Uncle," Caspian murmured, eyes still on the floor.

Dimitris's eyes swept the other senators. "It cannot happen overnight, and we must use discretion, but there are peoples out there who would accept who we are and what we've been through without questions. Our people deserve the world, not just our corner of it, perfect as I believe it to be. I would put into motion the resolution of Georgius Bausus's promise to our people, and bring into the light the need to update our systems to meet the current needs of Atlantis."

And with that, the entire room erupted as Senator Dimitris Lykkosi shook Atlantis.

CHAPTER FORTY-TWO

MADELINE

The response to Dimitris's words was explosive. Not only had the Senate building dissolved into open upset and questions, but it spread to the streets and made it home before we did. Even our neighbors were sitting on their garden benches, waiting to ask Caspian what he knew.

And for two days Caspian and Nikkos spent long hours tirelessly sorting it all out. I was all but moved in with Amara at the House of Sirens for the time being while they worked. For one, it gave me the opportunity to hear some of the first gossip, as the sirens held such a place of importance and many people brought word to Calliope and Ashana. For the other, my nightmares were still very much present and likely wouldn't go away any time soon.

But what we were all really waiting on was these visitors. Dimitris had made a big promise, and he'd released flyers with his plan for the bubble. We got a little bit of information about this relic and what he hoped it could do for us. It could amplify our sway, perhaps enough to need far fewer sirens to maintain it or possibly even push Atlantis to the open air more permanently. We wouldn't really know until we tried it out, but the implications of freeing up the responsibilities of the sirens were immense. My heart swelled with pride to see Nikkos and Caspian's names credited as well.

And now, we waited. The sirens who stayed around the house tried to distract me from the trauma I'd experienced, and we all tried to distract each other from the wait we had to endure for Dimitris's plans to begin and this item to arrive. Jacinta tried to teach me a complicated game with painted wooden coins that was popular among the children of Atlantis, but I couldn't grasp the rules. I tried to get Amara and Iris to work out with me, but beyond the concept of going for a run neither of them were willing to stick it out with me for long. I tried to read, but with most available books being in Atlantean, I wasn't able to pick up more than a very basic children's story. In the end, the thing that helped me the most was learning how to cook a few Atlantean breads with the kind ladies in the kitchen.

"When you're done kneading it, shape it into a round and press the berries into the top." Jacinta stood at a counter in the kitchen, watching me attempt to follow the directions she was translating while simultaneously eating half the berries in the bowl next to me.

"And what berries am I supposed to press into the top if you're eating them all?" I teased.

Just to be cheeky, she smiled at me with mildly pink-stained teeth and popped another one in her mouth. I snorted and resumed my lumpy attempt at shaping the dough. It was so familial. I'd experienced so many things since coming to Atlantis that I'd longed to do as a kid. And maybe this wasn't quite making brownies with grandma or having a mother teach me to cook, but it was something, and it made my heart full. The sense of belonging was new and fresh and so, so warm.

Shouting in the streets stopped all of us. I turned my head in the direction of the front door, though there were walls in the way, and it wasn't as if I could see what was going on. I exchanged a look with Jacinta while wiping my hands on a towel at the counter, then we both ran to the door.

Several sirens were already there, a few on the front lawn, including Calliope, as two teenagers ran up the street shouting.

"What are they saying?" I asked Jacinta as we peeked out the front door around the other women standing there.

"Dimitris's guests are here!" Jacinta squealed. "Oh my gosh, what's going to happen now?"

"We'll find out soon enough," a siren next to us said. "They need the sirens to use this thing, right?"

The next few minutes were a flurry of gossip as we moved to the front lawn. Someone brought out a bench from the backyard to make a comfortable place under a large, shady tree for Calliope and Ashana to sit. I could have burst out of my skin, I was so curious as to what was happening, but I held it together. Mostly.

When the group of senators and their aides appeared at the crest of the hill, exclamations and excitement boiled over. I recognized one or two of the senators, but I didn't know their names. I saw several other people I knew worked for them, and then I saw Caspian.

My face broke into a delighted grin as he sped up, arriving just before the group to meet me and pull me to the side of the street, where he lifted me off the ground and spun me. I laughed, as did a few of the sirens nearby.

"I have never been happier to end a project than I am today," he said as he set me back on my feet, leaning in to kiss my cheek.

"Finally. But what happens now? Tell me everything!"

The others had already reached where Ashana and Calliope were sitting, and were talking to them in rushed Atlantean.

"We're going to bring them to the central square to meet the artifact." Caspian nodded at the older sirens. "And you, if you want to come with me, I'm going straight to the tower. Our guests will be arriving any minute now."

I gasped. "I can come to something that important?"

"Maddie, I came here specifically to get you. I thought you'd like to see this. When our contact, Gavin, told me this was how he was going to arrive, I didn't believe it at first."

"What does that mean?" I asked, but Caspian was already lacing my fingers with his and pulling me up the road.

"You'll see," he teased, and we ran.

People buzzed with gossip on our way. The sun, filtered through the water high above, beamed down in a warm and humid morning. Blood was rushing in my ears, and I was filled with adrenaline and excitement, and a little bit of fear of the unknown, which I knew was just my anxiety over things I couldn't control. But it was mostly exhilaration as we approached the tower.

"They're landing here?" I asked as we stepped into the stone archway at the bottom of the spiral steps.

"If they haven't already," he responded, and we climbed. Up, up, up the ancient tower. My legs were absolutely burning from the run followed by an immediate switch to the stairs, but I didn't care. Caspian and I were both winded by the time we neared the top, but when I heard voices, I was spurred on to finish the climb.

At the top of this tower, which I hadn't been in before, the room where the sirens sang was huge. Much larger than the small tower where we'd landed. But much like that first tower, three sirens lounged on cushions, and I waved at Larisa among them, who hand-signed a greeting back.

On the other side of this huge room was an open tunnel. Caspian walked us down it until we emerged onto a covered dock of sorts, built straight out of the side of the tower and with ramped docks floating with the water levels. I was sure the sirens and their sway were much of why this place could stay stable enough for a boat to dock out in the open sea away from shore. There were a few ships here, but plenty of room for whatever this party was arriving in.

Nikkos and Dimitris were having a conversation in Atlantean but paused as we entered, and switched to English for my benefit.

"Any sign yet?" Caspian asked.

"No, but Gavin was very specific regarding his expected arrival time. Any moment now," Nikkos answered.

"I trust the keepers of the sirens are being positioned?" Dimitris asked, one eyebrow raised.

"Yes, Uncle," Caspian answered. "As we speak, in the central square."

"Good. The first act we must take is to bind these guests from speaking of this location to others. Then, we can move forward with the artifact," Dimitris said.

I jumped as a huge *thud* hit the roof of the dock. The three men with me stopped talking, and all four pairs of eyes went to the ceiling.

"Could it be them?" Nikkos asked, slipping into Atlantean out of habit, though it was a simple enough sentence that I understood it.

But he received no answer as we all listened to the continuing thuds on the roof. They were smaller now, footsteps.

As they reached the end of the roof, we could hear the voices.

"Are you sure this is the right one?" A masculine voice called, "Oy, any fishies out here waitin' on us?"

Dimitris moved his unimpressed gaze to Nikkos, who forced a smile and a shrug.

"He comes highly recommended," he offered.

"This is the one." That voice was lighter, calmer, and self-assured.

And then something growled. Deep, terrible, terrifying. The hairs on the back of my neck stood straight up, and I looped my arm through Caspian's, stepping closer to him.

"Who tied your balls in a knot, you great whiny lizard? We're here now and I'm giving you a hell of a cut for it."

A figure jumped down from the roof to land on the end of the dock that wasn't covered. Wearing a black T-shirt, with a row of knives in some kind of holster slung across his chest and a pair of worn jeans was the man I'd caught a glimpse of all those months ago in the Port and Mast in Florida. I supposed I'd known that Caspian's contact from that night was the one coming here now, but it finally clicked into place.

Gavin scratched his orange beard while a smaller figure jumped down, landing on her feet like a cat, a package wrapped in red cloth tucked under one arm. She was . . . shimmery. Her orange pixie cut was cute, showing off long ears. I gasped when I noticed them.

"What is it?" Caspian murmured.

"Her ears," I hissed. "Don't you see them?"

The woman smoothed out her green sundress and turned to give me a better look. "Shall I show them, too, or would you be more comfortable if I tucked them away for you?"

The shimmer flared up, irritating my eyes. As I blinked the sight away, I looked at her again and the ears were short and round.

"How did you do that?" I asked.

She laughed, adjusting the item in her arms. "Am I your first fae? It's called a glamor. If I wanted to, I could unravel the whole thing and show you all my true form."

I didn't know what to say to that, so I kept silent. Caspian had warned me in passing that there were all manner of things in this world as mysterious as the sirens, but I hadn't taken him seriously until now.

"Gavin, welcome." Caspian stepped forward, offering a hand, which Gavin shook. "Thank you for coming all the way out here on your . . . I'm sorry, I'm not sure I read the message correctly."

"You did, he's just a grouch. Oy, Ryker! At least get down here in the shade. If I don't send you back in one piece Dani'll have my ass."

The roof creaked under the weight of something big, and a deep-green figure dropped onto the deck. It walked inside and fit itself just under the roof, barely.

"No way," I whispered. Two huge bat-like wings, green scales on a four-legged body, and a long tail. The huge head turned our way, huffed, then lay down. A dragon. An actual, breathing, enormous dragon.

"Don't mind him," Gavin said. "He's usually cranky when he's away from the missus. This is an old partner of mine."

Gavin patted the dragon on his side, and the creature snapped at him with a mouth full of sharp teeth.

"Do your own introduction, then! I'm sure we can find you some pants or something if you want."

This exchange was truly verging on the bizarre. I eyed the others. Caspian was keeping his cool well enough, Nikkos was pale, and Dimitris was as unchanged as he ever was.

"This's Caroline," Gavin went on. "She can hold this thing without shitting her britches."

The woman, Caroline, raised an eyebrow at Gavin. "Lovely."

"Caroline, it's nice to meet you." Caspian extended her a hand just as he'd done for Gavin. "You may call me Caspian."

Her eyes danced as she shook his hand. "Clever boy, you've done your homework. You may call me whatever you like, but Caroline will do best."

"Gavin, Caroline, this is Senator Dimitris Lykkosi. We're here to escort you to the container for the artifact, and as we explained before, we appreciate your cooperation in binding your words about Atlantis."

"We'll see if it sticks or not," Caroline said, seemingly to herself, before turning to Dimitris. "Hello, Senator. I've been looking forward to meeting you."

Dimitris frowned. "May I ask why one of your kind would have any interest in meeting a senator from Atlantis?"

"You may, and I may even answer." She beamed. "I've been seeing you for a while now, and I was wondering when it would happen in person."

Dimitris frowned deeper. "What, exactly, do you mean?"

Her eyes danced, clearly playing at something that brought her great amusement. "I see through things that want to stay hidden, you see. And I've seen Atlantis in my dreams for a while now. Mostly, I've seen that your people and my people can be great friends. I simply hope you are open to an offer to visit my homeland when your plan to open your borders comes to fruition."

Caspian and Nikkos exchanged a look before they both stared at their uncle.

I guessed that they were wondering how she knew about that, since they'd only just learned about it themselves.

"That is a conversation for later," Dimitris finally said. "Are you ready to affix the amulet in its new home?"

"Aye, you're payin' well enough." Gavin nodded to Dimitris. "Let's get this show on the road, then. I'm ready to be rid of it."

"Very good." Dimitris said. "Let's proceed to the Senate square."

CHAPTER FORTY-THREE

MADELINE

The procession from the tower was truly bizarre. The dragon opted to stay in the tower, which was probably a good thing considering the line of people who came out to watch. Dimitris strolled ahead, followed by Gavin and Caroline. The pair of them were not from Atlantis, and as such attracted a huge amount of attention. But it was the wrapped item in Caroline's arms that was the source of the most interest.

Caspian held my hand as we walked in the back near Nikkos, and I was happy not to have the attention on me. It felt like everyone was out to see what happened when Dimitris's mysterious artifact was put into place.

When we finally reached the square in front of the Senate, I saw the new addition to the fountain right away. The fountain had originally been built as the center point of the island, at the highest point. It was where the ancient sirens sang to begin the bubble that saved what of Atlantis it did, and it was in the very center between the towers where we sang now. And, on the top of the fountain, now sat a gilded cage of runes and wires.

"What is that?" I asked.

"To house the amulet, the relic," Caspian answered.

The procession reached the edge of the fountain where all the other senators, the basilli included, stood waiting. Ashana and Calliope were present, as were most of the other sirens, who stood in the crowd behind them. It was a matter of a few minutes for Gavin and Caroline to walk forward and do their wordbinding. It was a fascinating process to watch, as Calliope recited an oath with them in a singsong voice, and Ashana layered her sway heavily to a tune under their words. When the process was done, Caroline stood in the middle of the open space.

"And here it is, the artifact you requested," she said with a flourish, as she removed the cloth wrapping. I felt it, as did the others around us from what I could tell. It was . . . suffocating. It wanted to be out, to be used. There was no explanation for how I could know that, but the shared look I held with Caspian told me enough.

Besides the power it clearly held, it was proportionally huge. More like holding a frisbee than what I would have thought of as a necklace. It had a chain long enough that it might even go around the neck of something like the dragon they rode in on. It was round with three polished stones of different shades of green embedded in it.

"If you would put it in the structure, Caroline." Dimitris gestured to the cage-like contraption that now sat on the top of the fountain.

The fae nodded, stepping onto the fountain's edge then bracing a foot on the next level up as she leaned in and put the amulet in the cage itself, and the pressure emanating from the relic faded away. Almost, but not completely gone if you stood too close to the fountain. I had a feeling we would all be keeping a few feet back from it from now on.

Dimitris began speaking in Atlantean, and Caspian murmured the gist of it in my ear. The plan now was for the sirens to sing to the amulet, using the same sway we would to move the water out and away from Atlantis. If this amulet could hold our sway with little or even no maintenance, the sirens would be free to become more regular members of society. And Atlantis as a whole would finally be able to look outward, no longer hiding in the bubble completely.

There would be no joining the world's nations all at once, of course, but a secondary reason for inviting Gavin and now Caroline here was to set in motion the meeting of outsiders. We would be able to selectively invite communities of beings, supernaturals they were called, to the island. Fresh blood, fresh interaction, new people and customs and life. And Atlantis could slip out. Our goods could finally be traded, our people could explore other lands and return with new experiences. This would change everything for Atlantis, and it sent a thrill through my heart to hear the possibilities.

"Will this happen right away?" I asked excitedly.

Caspian chuckled. "No, it will take time. The Senate will fight about it, probably for months. That gives us time to vet the people we allow here first, but the fae are a heavy favorite to be first."

"Like Caroline?" I asked.

Caspian nodded, and Dimitris finished his speech.

Ashana and Calliope stepped forward, eyeing the amulet in its gilded cage. When they began to sing, it glowed.

Their sway was impressive. Precise, beautiful, and filled with their intent. Open, expand, protect. I could feel it, as could all the other sirens in the square. Hell, probably the ones in the towers too.

It took nothing for me to step forward with dozens of my sisters as we joined Ashana and Calliope.

The sway conjoined was like nothing I'd ever experienced. It had been magical enough when we sang together before, but this time, this purpose, it was so much more. Through me, around me, above me, we sang.

The amulet glowed, absorbing and projecting. Taking in the sway and making it so much more. I could see it in the barrier now. Where it was dark at the bottom with a backdrop of the deep ocean it was now pushing out, away. Where it was already thinner at the top with the light filtering through, it was growing lighter and lighter, warmer and warmer, until the *whoosh* of air as the top burst through the cresting waves high above.

Cheers, screams, and gasps flooded the air around us. The people watched on as the sirens continued to sing. It was strained now, slowing. We were at our limit. Calliope signed her hands for us, one more big push.

Looking around me, I saw sirens were locking hands with each other. On one side of me, Jacinta had slipped in, and her eyes danced as we laced fingers. And on my other side, I turned to find . . .

Tanis's eyes were warm. Sad, but warm, as our hands locked together. I wasn't sure how to feel about it. She had gone through an ordeal, and the revelation of the past week had brought it all back up to the surface for her. Now I knew it wasn't her fault. We might not get a normal mother-daughter relationship after this, but I was done fighting it. We had both been through enough, hadn't we?

We pushed as one now. Me, and Tanis, and Jacinta, and every other sister around us. One last big push as we strained ourselves, strained the amulet, and pushed out the barrier once more. The rushing water roared in protest around the island, like a thunderstorm, and then Ashana raised her cane in a significant swoop to drop off.

One by one but in the span of only a few heartbeats, we let our voices fall. I panted, raw and hoarse and buzzing from the sensation we had just undergone.

The bubble was so much bigger than before, now encompassing space well beyond the old confines and gaining us more land. It was bittersweet to know that land was going to be a graveyard of ruins, but it would be a start. It would be something

We sirens steadied ourselves, catching some much-needed breath and staring in awe at what that amulet had allowed us to do. I had no doubt in my mind that the power of the sway we had with just our numbers—far fewer now than they were centuries ago—wouldn't have been enough for us to do this on our own.

Ashana spoke to a few of the sirens near her, and six ran off in the directions of the towers.

"What . . . are they . . . doing?" I asked between breaths as Caspian pulled up beside me, rubbing the small of my back.

"She's stopping the singing at the towers to see if this holds. You all can catch the water if required since you're all still here."

I nodded, not able to hold a conversation beyond that.

Dimitris silenced the excited crowd with one word as it rang through the square. "Atlantis!"

All eyes, all ears, all attention was on him as he stepped forward from the line of senators. "Whether this holds or fails, what we have achieved today as a people is immensely significant. We have done something that we had stopped doing long ago. We tried. And without the sirens, this feat would not have been accomplished. For that, I thank you all."

Dimitris bowed. It was directed at Ashana and Calliope, but it was meant for all of us. Heat flooded my cheeks at whatever fraction of praise was directed my way, and right after Dimitris, others followed. The senators joined him, the people joined him, and when most of Atlantis was bowing their heads to the central point of the island, to the sirens, the applause began.

It roared through the square, echoing down the streets and turning into cheers and sounds and revelry. I didn't know where to look, and by the time my eyes stumbled all the way around us and back to where we started, I saw Caspian bowing, too, a smile on his face. My face reddened as I flipped him off, and he laughed.

The rest of the day was a blur. Celebration hit the square, and then all of Atlantis, rapidly. Music started, and people ran home for their instruments. Dancing began, and room was opened up enough for singing and rejoicing. The sirens were quickly met with bottles of water, juice, and wine—whatever we wanted to quench our throats after the feat we had achieved together.

Gavin and Caroline were swept up into the celebrations too. The scoundrel of a mercenary was pulled into dancing almost immediately by one of the older senators as she pulled his arms around her hips and moved to a song that had started up. Caroline was content to perch upon the steps of the Senate building, clapping and laughing as she watched it all happen.

Caspian was at the ready the moment the first beats of an upbeat song started near us, and he pulled my hands to him, shooting me a smoldering look as he claimed my mouth in a heated kiss. We danced, making up for the lost night of the veiled ball as he held me, spun me, moved with me as if we were the only two in the square.

Reports came in all through the evening as people reported just how far out the bubble went. The walls were holding with no sign of receding back in despite the fact that all sirens had stopped singing hours ago, even the ones in the towers.

It was a night to remember. More than the veiled ball, more than finding out I was a siren, or even about the sway. Almost more than running into, quite literally, a handsome stranger in a coffee shop doorway a million miles away on the coast of Florida. The last piece of a puzzle fell into place. I had safety, I had people who loved me, and purpose or not, Atlantis was my home. Never in all my time on this earth had I had more than one at a time.

I was nearly asleep on my feet by the time Caspian dragged me home; the party was far from over but we were both too exhausted to continue. We left Nikkos at Dimitris's side and came back to the quiet of the end of his street.

"I'm still in shock at how well it worked," Caspian said, kicking off his shoes and falling onto the cushions in the main living space.

I laughed, following suit as he pulled me into his arms. "I thought this was the plan you and Nikkos were working on, though."

"It was." Caspian paused, leaning forward to kiss the top of my head as he pulled me tighter to his chest. "Hey, Madeline . . ."

I pulled back to look at him, his tone having shifted lower and more serious. "What?"

"What would make you happy? The happiest woman in the world?" he asked.

I didn't know. A month ago I would have said I had it all, but now that I wasn't necessarily going to have to use my sway in the towers, I wasn't sure what my days would look like.

But my eyes moved to Caspian, then to the house around us, then back to his ocean-blue eyes. "I'd say I'm already there."

He gave me a crooked smile, then laid his head back against the cushions with a groan.

"What is it?" I asked, worried.

"I'm mad we didn't come back earlier," he said, his voice rolling over me in a playful caress. "I don't have the energy to fuck you like I want to."

My heart skipped as I gave him a devilish grin. "I just thought of one thing I want."

He raised an eyebrow, the smirk still on his lips. "Oh?"

"A vacation. Never in my whole life have I been able to travel for leisure, and especially not with someone I love. If the sirens are actually free to leave, I want you to take me on a trip, just the two of us."

I laid my head on his chest as he wrapped his arms around my back, rubbing a small circle with his thumb. "Anything you want, my siren. Anything at all."

CHAPTER FORTY-FOUR

CASPIAN

Lounging on the deck in a pleasantly overcast day, a glass of last year's first barrel in hand, I was content to watch my beloved siren's creased brow of concentration as she stared at my laptop. There was a lot less worry about navigating the open ocean when you had a siren on board, and we were already making incredible time. Winding our way overseas and across continents as we explored coastal towns and islands on our way around to the western coast of North America. Three weeks into the journey, and only a little more to go on our plans to visit a luxury resort in California, graciously arranged by Caroline and the Autumn Court. The catch? Having to bring Nikkos with us. Eventually we'd send him on ahead, and after our vacation was done we'd fly up to Seattle to meet him and enter talks with the fae to establish a point of contact for Atlanteans who wanted to visit other parts of the world. Not a bad deal, and after seven months of negotiations, legislation, and petty bickering, Atlantis was finally in a state of peace.

When Madeline sighed and her shoulders sagged, I sat up.

"Everything all right?"

She groaned, leaning into the seat and laying her head back on the half-round sofa on the deck of the ship. "My Atlantean sucks."

My lips tugged upward, and I hid the motion with another sip from my glass. "It does not."

"It does—look." She angled the laptop screen so I could see the latest in a long string of emails between Madeline and Tanis. The two hadn't grown particularly close in the months after the artifact stabilized Atlantis. It took Calliope coming up with the idea of them writing to each other, which began the development of a true bond between them. But since Tanis only spoke Atlantean, Madeline had more than a few moments like this where writing an email was challenging, frustrating, or both.

"I don't see the problem."

"Ugh! Right here." She jabbed a finger at the last words she had written. "I keep forgetting the right words, if I ever learned them in the first place, and I can't keep writing *saltwater chicken* instead of *seagull* and things like that."

I chuckled, leaning over to kiss her forehead. "*Sagassul.*"

She sighed, pulling the laptop back to her and began typing. "Thank you."

"You'll get there. Nikkos is impressed by your progress, and he's not easily impressed."

That delicious bottom lip caught in her teeth as a slight blush crawled across the bridge of her nose. "I'm almost done with my letter, and then I kinda want to grab something for lunch."

"Nikkos said there were leftovers from dinner still."

"That pasta? Hell, yeah, dibs." She furiously typed out the last few clicks of the keyboard. "And . . . Send."

She closed the laptop, then slid it into the protective bag and set it on the seat beside her. "What do you think Caroline wants from all this?"

367

It was a popular point of conversation for the three of us. When Caroline had first extended the offer of the trip for Madeline and myself, I had been wary. Gavin had had to provide more context for me, telling us a bit more about the odd fae and the court she called home. With some form of prophetic abilities, she apparently often made strange friendships and connections, but was mostly harmless, if confusing at times. Many times. After more back-and-forth and a lot of background checks, I agreed to the trip, and here we were.

"If there's a reason, she's not telling us. Though, from what Gavin said, that isn't anything unusual for her." I shrugged. "She did help us get the artifact to Atlantis, and we can't deny that she was cooperative with our wordbinding and precautions."

"True. If she really does have those kinds of powers, I wish she could tell us how the tangle of the Senate is going to work itself out."

I barked a laugh. "If only it was that easy. I'm sure it will take years if not decades to rebuild the Senate system. Dimitris still thinks he can see the dismantlement of the hereditary roles within his lifetime."

Madeline snorted. "Could you imagine if I hadn't tossed out the Ateio name? I'd be a senator in so many years. You'd be calling me Senator Maddie."

"I can say with certainty that I've seen plenty of politicians do a far worse job than you would have," I mused. "It's not too late—after our trip we can still go back and you can ask Adrion for a name, a title, and the keys to his office."

Madeline scowled playfully and threw a pillow at me. I had to move my glass out of the way, nearly spilling the last of my wine.

Her scowl turned to a soft smile as she moved the laptop bag from between us on the seat and leaned over until she slid down, laying her head on my lap. "No more politicians, let's talk about our friends. Do you think Seattle could really be a place for Atlanteans to visit?"

I hummed a noncommittal tune. "Perhaps. I want to meet the rest of these courts first, and of course Nikkos will be going ahead of us to test the waters."

"If this works and we have a safe place for someone like a siren to set foot on the mainland, I want to bring Jacinta to an amusement park." She smiled, her eyes drifting into the middle distance as she daydreamed. "And I want to go shopping with Amara and Iris, and I want to show Larissa a nightclub." Her expression turned wicked. "Oh my god, a nightclub. I haven't been to one in ages and now that I can control the sway . . ."

I pulled her up from my lap and she lost herself in a fit of giggles as I positioned her to straddle me, sliding my hand up to cup her jaw and force eye contact. "And what exactly is my little siren going to do with her sway in a nightclub?" The menacing tone in my voice was all bark and no bite, and my minx knew it as she brazenly wiggled her eyebrows.

Heat graced her cheeks even as the hungry gleam in her eyes promised dancing of a different kind later. "Oh, you know. A little of this, a little of that. Sample a bit of what the Seattle nightlife has to offer."

I smacked my palm on the round of her ass, making her gasp. She flung her arms around my neck with a chuckle. "Mercy! I'm only kidding. You're the only one I want to sample."

I leaned in to kiss her neck. She pulled back far enough so I could find her mouth with mine. The kiss was soft but deep. Slow, sultry, with a hint of the wine we'd been drinking all morning, as her tongue slid to meet mine. The taste of her lips was heaven as I moved in and out for more. To kiss that plump bottom lip of hers, the corners of her upturned mouth, to pepper her jaw with a few more kisses before finding her lips again.

Her hand moved to the top buttons of my shirt, which I

hadn't bothered to close since we'd left Atlantis and the bulk of my responsibilities behind. Sliding those fingers inside, she played at the topmost buttoned barrier and worked it open, even as we continued our kissing.

My hands moved to her hips, already playing with the most sensitive places I knew could draw a sharp breath from those pretty lips. Sliding up to brush the underside of her breasts and around back to find the knot of the bikini top she liked to wear around the ship. It would be so easy to tug that string, to free her in the open breeze and take one of those nipples that I was sure would be hard and waiting for me into my mouth.

"Caspian," she whispered my name, a secret on her lips meant only for me, as if she knew what I was thinking. One of her hands found its way up to run fingers though the hair at my temple, the other working on the next button.

"Lunch, you two!" Nikkos called.

I groaned, leaning my head forward to land on Madeline's shoulder as she snapped her head toward the open door.

"You have really bad fucking timing, Nikkos!" she yelled.

"I made a chocolate mousse!" he retorted.

Madeline paused, then answered. "I forgive you, this time."

I pulled my head off her shoulder, laughing at the expression on her face, which was somewhere between distress and anticipation.

"Come on." I lifted her from my lap and helped her onto her feet. "Food first. We have all the time in the world to finish what we started later."

Her expression softened as she turned to me, then laced her fingers in mine as she pulled us toward the door. "Yeah, we do."

And we stepped into the galley, another perfect day on our trip across the ocean. My siren was finally set free.

ACKNOWLEDGMENTS

I love the acknowledgment section. I don't think a lot of people read this bit, but it's fun to think back on all the people who helped me get here. And, oh boy, was this book a struggle for me.

To the lovely folks at Wattpad WEBTOON Book Group, specifically W by Wattpad Books. Thank you so much for bringing *Dirty Lying Sirens* to life. Deanna, thank you again for putting up with me. This one was more of a struggle to knock into shape, but I'm so glad you stuck with me through it. To everyone who copy edited, formatted, worked on the cover, and all the other important bits and pieces: thank you!

To the corners of the internet filled with people willing to offer their perspectives on topics I am not versed in, thank you. I met so many kind and interesting people, and the internet never ceases to amaze me.

My agent, Ali, you always impress me. I'm so glad to have you in my corner. I promise I'm working on more things to send your way, because I would do this a hundred times over with your help.

My husband, my support system, thank you for helping me so much. You kept the home life balanced enough that I could work and also spend time with you and our son. I love you. Thank you for being my biggest supporter.

And for the readers who have sent me messages, letters, and emails this past year. You don't know it, but you are what kept me pressing forward through my most difficult edit yet. I love all of you so much, I wish I could come to all the corners of the world to meet you guys in person.

And finally, to Expo brand dry-erase markers. That bump in sales you saw last year was me getting a giant whiteboard in my office and letting my thoughts spill out with your markers until I understood whatever problem I was currently working through. I've entered my dry-erase era and it's doing good things for my writing process.

Thank you to everyone who has played a part in my life this past year, however big or small. I appreciate all of you, and I can't wait to see where I go from here! Happy reading.

ABOUT THE AUTHOR

Sabrina Blackburry writes romantasy escapes with passionate women finding their places in the world, witty side characters, and love with a touch of magic. From Wattpad to bookshelves, Sabrina's debut novel, *Dirty Lying Faeries*, kicked off her career in 2022. She remains a staunch believer that anyone can become a writer if they have the heart to make it happen.

From central Missouri, Sabrina lived with her grandparents throughout her childhood where her love of reading and taste for fairytales took root. Her hobbies include gardening, walking nature trails, and getting involved with the local renaissance festival, but none of these take priority over a cat, a coffee, and a good book.

Want more from Sabrina Blackburry?

Keep reading for a excerpt of

Half
Wylde

Coming soon from W by Wattpad Books!

One

I had always thought drowning would be a terrible way to die. Surely something quick would be better. A beheading, maybe, or poison, if it were the right sort. But floating under the burning surface of the lake, it was hard to argue with the dark and comfortable sleep that beckoned.

My eyes closed, heavy and tired. How much time had passed? My chest—which had seared with the strain to contain what air I could—was now numbed, my lungs ready to let go. The fire overhead promised no escape, a dancing watercolor of oranges and reds obscured by the rippling surface of the lake. Maybe wherever you go after death wouldn't care that I was half monster. My lips parted, the water flooding in so hard that I couldn't change my mind now even if I wanted to. I could feel myself fading. Leaving.

That is, until something splashed above me.

I tried to pry my eyelids open but they wouldn't budge. The sway of the water around me pushed through my foggy consciousness as something took hold of my body. The hard angles of an arm wrapped around me, fingers digging into my ribs as it pulled. Up I went. The water grew hot from the fire that floated on it, like burning oil ready to boil me alive if I was dragged too close. The heat on my face grew stronger as I got closer. A pause, a motion that moved me wildly around as the water rushed in every direction, and for a moment, the fire was gone. We broke the surface, and I blacked out.

~

I woke with a start, expelling all the water I had swallowed. Violently. The retching roared in my ears along with the blood trying to circulate once again after my cold encounter with the lake.

Still heaving, I listened and felt for everything around me while I tried to lessen the swirling in my head, not yet able to sit upright. Clearly I wasn't in the lake anymore, so where was I? A warm crackle at my back soothed my frozen bones. A fire. I listened, but the clanking metal of the raiders no longer rang through the village. Screams were replaced by cries of pain and loss. My head finally calm, or at least no longer threatening more sickness on me, I wiped my mouth with the back of my hand and sat up.

All around me, bodies huddled for warmth. Moans of the injured and dying murmured under the crackling of the fire. Why was I here? Why were they allowing me to sit so close? My only guess was the shared horrors of being caught in a raid prevented anyone from bothering with me. I judged less than a quarter of the village sat here: the elders, the injured, and some women and children. But none of them were Bryn. The last thing I remember was walking by the lake when the raiders came, and he threw me into the water.

"Who has seen the woodcutter?" I asked. My voice crackled like the fire, my throat still raw.

Some of the people looked at me for a heartbeat, but I wasn't surprised to find that none of them met my gaze. Few of them spoke to me on a good day, and right now was certainly less than good. We might as well have been a pile of dogs crowding the hearth.

With no answer, I'd have to make a bolder move and find out for myself. Unsettled dread seeped into my heart. Standing slowly, a bit of a shake in my legs, I looked around and demanded an answer.

"Where is Bryn, the woodcutter?"

Some watched me from the corner of their eyes with shock and suspicion. I doubt any of them had heard me speak up before. Others just stared ahead, gray-faced and motionless, watching with hollow eyes as their world burned. And it did burn. I looked over my shoulder to see what remained of the settlements by the lake, and my heart sank. A once thriving fishing village was now blackened with ash in a stark contrast to the light snow around it.

"Everember oil, they called it," Shanna, a fisherman's daughter, whispered nearby. She had my full attention if she knew anything about what had happened. "It's on everything." Her body and voice both shook, stubbornness barely holding her in one piece. She glanced at me with those sharp eyes, and then, as if she had just realized who she was talking to, she turned up her nose and staed ahead. She was clearly haunted by the sights before her, but the sight of me must have snapped her out of it. No one wants to talk to the half-monster. Especially not proud Shanna.

An old woman—Gerdie, I think her name was—fell in a heap from where she was sitting on a sack of grain. The sound startled me, as well as most of the survivors of the attack. Almost immediately, I smelled the piss. The woman next to her leaned over to confirm what I suspected; her body was limp with death. They rolled her out of the way, and two more took her place by the warm fire without so much as a word. I said a silent prayer to the Mother. Gerdie hadn't been nice to me, but at least she hadn't been cruel either.

I reached up, lightly touching my arm. I would have a bruise where Bryn grabbed me and threw me into the water, but I was otherwise unharmed. There was nothing left for me at the fire but comfort from the snow and little in the way of answers. I walked away, and my place was quickly taken by other frozen bodies. So be it. I didn't need to sit by the fire; I needed to find Bryn.

Pieces of the puzzle fell into place as I walked the village. The blacksmith and his boys were pulling people from the lake who had tried to escape the flames. Most had jumped in. I was thrown in right before that putrid oil coated the surface and set it ablaze. That couldn't have been that long ago; my clothes were still damp. So where were the raiders? Where was Bryn? My heart started to hurt as I walked.

My eyes drifted to a slow motion by the edge of the water. An old woman hunched over the lake, the villagers giving her a wide berth. An ancient raven perched on her shoulder, one clear eye turned towards me. Mila the Witch. She rarely came to the village, but I was glad to have a friendly face here. One that would actually talk to me. I quickened my pace.

The smells assaulted me as I walked towards the water. A fiendish aroma of cooking meat seared my nose and watered my eyes. Tears fell, loosening the caked-on soot down my face. I tried not to look around me as I kept walking, not letting myself imagine what meat could be cooking right now. I just focused on the watchful raven sitting on the old woman's back.

The witch shuffled a few feet and dipped back to the water as I drew near. Feathers and bones adorning her neck, her hands rustled in the breeze over the lake. Her black dress billowed to her side as the wind tugged at it. The air around her was heavy with old magic.

"Wren, I see you survived." She didn't even turn to me as she collected a sample of the oil floating on the water. "Good. The Mother blesses you."

"Where is Bryn?" I asked, a tremor to my voice.

She turned to me now and looked me in the eye, her face soft. Wrinkled fingers reached for my hands, and she rubbed them gently. "You're chilled to the bone, child. You should have stayed by the fire."

My hands went numb. My heart tightened in my chest. "Where is Bryn?"

"I know he was as a father to you," Mila's words were slow, deliberate.

"*No,*" I choked. My stomach dropped.

"He is gone, Wren," she said.

I fell to my knees, my legs suddenly losing whatever strength they had left. Tears welled and fell, distorting my vision as I scrambled to see where he had fallen. She couldn't be so sure of it, not in the chaos that overtook the village. Somewhere along the bank, near the dock but past the baker's house. That's where he'd pushed me in. Maybe he was still alive. Mila could be wrong. Maybe he needed help, or . . . or . . .

"Danger is still in the wind, and we need to prepare ourselves. Live now to mourn later."

"No! He . . . he can't be. He can't be dead." My throat tightened. My stubbornness held as the last dam of defense against the spilling of my grief. The admission of my loss. Keeping me in one piece, if only for a moment. Bryn was my only family, and without him, I had absolutely nothing.

A fool. I was a fool not to admit it when I didn't wake up to his smiling face. He wouldn't have left me alone by choice and certainly not during a raid. Bryn was gone, and I could swear I heard the sound of my heart breaking as the first sob escaped me.

"Caution, child. Your danger has not yet ended," Mila warned, her voice stern but her warm hand rubbing my back.

I tried to swallow the lump in my throat unsuccessfully. "What does it matter? My only family is dead."

"And Bryn would have you to die as well?" Mila asked, more harshly.

I was numb. Empty. A coldness had settled over me that I wasn't trying to fight off.

"No," I whispered.

"Then get up." She grunted as she stood and dipped an empty bottle a few steps down the lake.

"I don't know what to do. Where is Bryn's . . . body?" I sniffed. *Body*. The word was disgusting to even think about—that it could be used to describe what was left of him.

"He will burn with the rest of the lost villagers," Mila said. "You do not need to see what remains of him. He would not want it."

I shivered. Her words promised a terrible end. "Still—"

"No. Not like this. Leave him a stone on his burning pyre, but do not seek him out in this moment." Mila studied one of the vials in her hand then looked down at where I sat on the hard ground. "Get up, child. To your feet. You should be moving soon."

"Why must I move? Why do you rush?" I asked.

Her aged face stilled, those eyes boring through me with deep sorrow and patience. Mila's words were never long, but she did attempt kindness in the moments when she remembered me as the child she had taught how to read and write and decipher plants of the mountains. "This is a village of humans, Wren, and as much as you or I appear to be the same, they will remember our differences the moment they find their anger through their grief. Both of us must prepare to move on."

Our differences.

Still feeling numb, I stood up as Mila bent to scoop a new vial of oil. Lost for any actions that weren't handed to me and ready to obey Mila's advice until I could regain myself. I wiped my face with my sleeve, eyeing the smoldering buildings behind me.

"Where are the raiders? How did any of us survive?" I asked.

Mila sighed, looking her raven in its blind eye for a moment.

"Something from the Wyldes came down from the mountains

and slaughtered the raiders." Mila stood, brushing her knees. "It has been an age since I last laid eyes on a fae."

The numbness in my body subsided briefly, just enough to let in a jolt of fear.

"A *fae*?" My heart sputtered. "Here?"

"Do not bring fear of the fae into your heart, child." Mila came up to me and stroked the hair hanging over what remained of my left ear. "He killed only the raiders. If he wanted to do the same to the village, he would have done it, not pulled you from the lake."

My body froze, but my eyes darted wildly. I looked at the lake, then the path to the small fire for the injured. I looked to the remaining buildings, and to the men scrambling to save what they could. The blacksmith still stirred the waters for more people.

"A creature from the Wyldes carried me to the fire?" I asked.

Mila nodded.

"A *thing* from the north pulled me from the burning lake, but not one of the villagers?"

"They would not save you. The fae saw this and pulled you free himself." Mila rubbed her bad wrist. "They may have saved you last, but only after their own had been rescued. Is this a surprise to you?"

"No," I murmured. Numbness, emptiness, grief, all replaced by a burning hate in my chest. Clenching my fists, I took a calming breath. It didn't work. I turned and watched the people at work.

"Bryn would have saved anyone!" My voice cracked as I spat my words at the village. At anyone who would listen, though none were close enough to hear me.

"I know, child." Mila reached to pat my arm. A tear trickled down my face. I ignored it and steeled myself away from it.

"What am I to do now?" I cried, furiously wiping my face on

my sleeve. "My . . . I can't hold him. I can't . . . I can't even see him."

"Bryn is gone, child. But the one who saved you is yet here, the fae. The villagers do not dare approach him." Mila scanned my face. "There is fear in the hearts of men of what is unfamiliar to them. *You* have no reason to fear him, and at the very least, you owe him your gratitude."

I looked to where she pointed. South of the village, a dark figure moved among the dead. He walked slowly between the pile of horses and plainsmen, bending down on occasion, looking for something.

My eyes darted again to the village. Some threw worried glances behind them. They were staying well out of his way. Bumps coated my arms, and my breath came fast. The people of the mountains might not trust the fae, but they didn't trust me either.

"I thought you told me not to thank them," I said.

"Do not thank one needlessly, Wren," Mila said. "But I would say this is one instance in which it is a requirement. There are consequences to owing a debt to a fae, this is true. But to not thank one who saved your life would be far worse."

My hurting heart sank. I was trapped without a choice. I blinked away the freshest tears in my eyes, my throat tightening again as my body trembled to release my grief.

"Mila," I whispered.

"You are more than the fear of the humans in this mountain, child. Show him respect and then go home. The shock of this day will wear off eventually, and I would have you warm in your bed when it does. Prepare your things. I will find you and send you on your way."

Mila gave me a rare smile. She wouldn't lead me astray. So be it.

I took a quivering breath, and I turned to approach the figure to the south. The pine needles crunched underfoot in rhythm with my beating heart. I drew the dotted circle of protection over my heart when I was only steps away from the creature.

"Hello, sir. Can you understand me?" He looked down at me, and my eyes widened as I finally looked at him closely.

He was huge. His skin was blue as midnight. His shaggy hair, barely long enough to tie in a ponytail, was just a shade darker— almost black. Blood speckled him like stars, and beneath the blood a collection of scars told a long tale of violence. His silver eyes were as sharp as his teeth and both looked about to pierce me straight through.

My eyes flicked up to the telltale pointed ears of the fae, then back to his face. He stared at me for a moment, then he gave me a slow nod. "I understand you."

I shivered at his voice, low and soft. Something about it warned me to be cautious around him. The numbness of Bryn's loss was replaced by the panic I had before this fae, if only while I was in his presence. I trembled like a rabbit before the fox.

"Thank you," I managed to whisper. "For saving me."

He narrowed his eyes at me and looked me up and down. "I accept your thanks."

Swallowing the lump in my throat, I waited for his next move. Some kind of trick or a sinister laugh of triumph that he had fooled me. But instead, he turned his attention away from me and back to what he had been doing.

The fae studied each body and only occasionally stooped down to pull something free. I watched as he ripped a dagger from the belly of a horse, throwing it onto a pile of bloody weapons. The blade had pierced the animal's intestines; I could almost taste it in the air. It was lucky that my stomach was already empty or my last meal would be on the ground right now. I resisted covering my nose. Something feral about the fae told me not to show any signs of weakness.

I watched as he worked, fascinated at his speed and precision but more fascinated by his struggle. Something in this task was burdensome to him; I just hadn't figured out what that was yet. Should I assist in this task, or would I be underfoot if I tried? With my thanks given, I had nothing left to offer here, so I turned from him to see if I could find Bryn's body, despite Mila's warnings.

A hand shot out and grabbed my shoulder. I turned, my heart thumping. The fae's arm had stopped me where I stood, and I nearly fainted.

"Wait."

The look on his face was not a pleasant one, and he turned his nose to me like a wolf scenting his prey. He brought his other hand up, still gripping my shoulder, and delicately brushed the braided hair from the side of my face. He exposed my ear. My shame.

The tips of both ears had been cut off in horrible, jagged lines. Ugly and scarred—a glaring reminder that I was only half a human. The reason I was abandoned. The reason the village hated me.

Tears and hatred burned my eyes. Before they spilled over, I pushed at his chest, as deep an insult as I could muster. I hated him in that moment. Hated that he could tell I wasn't one of the people of the village. Tearing from his grip I ran for the woods, praying to anyone who was listening that he wouldn't follow. From what I could tell, he didn't, and while my prayers were working, I also asked never to lay eyes on another fae.